Praise for
Welcome to Temptation

"Bright, funny, sexy, and wise."

—*Kirkus Reviews*

"Crusie charms with her brisk, edgy style. . . . A romantic comedy that adds luster to the genre, this effervescent tale will please readers."

—*Publishers Weekly* (starred review)

"Crusie blends a combination of likable characters, gossipy small-town life, and a plot spiced with some steamy sexual situations into a highly entertaining read."

—*Library Journal*

"Funny and inventive, this is sure to please Crusie's enthusiastic fans and attract new converts."

—*Booklist*

"A book you'll want to read again and again and recommend to your friends . . . a masterpiece of sensationally wicked humor and spicy sex . . . one bite and you're hooked. If you only buy one [book], let it be this one. It's phenomenal!"

—*The Belles and Beaux of Romance*

Welcome to Temptation

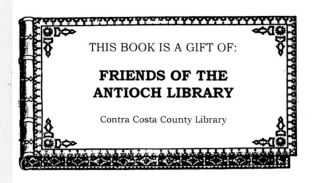

Welcome
to Temptation

Jennifer Crusie

St. Martin's Griffin
New York

WELCOME TO TEMPTATION. Copyright © 2000 by Jennifer Crusie Smith. All rights reserved. Printed in the United States of America. For information, address St. Martin's Press, 175 Fifth Avenue, New York, N.Y. 10010.

www.stmartins.com

The Library of Congress has cataloged the hardcover edition as follows:

Crusie, Jennifer.
    Welcome to Temptation / Jennifer Crusie.—1st ed.
        p. cm.
    ISBN 978-0-312-25294-6
    1. Documentary films—Production and direction—Fiction.
2. Women motion picture producers and directors—Fiction. 3. Motion picture actors and actresses—Fiction. 4. Sisters—fiction. 5. Ohio—Fiction. I. Title.
    PS3553.R7858 W45 2000
    813'.6—dc21

                                                                        99055739

ISBN 978-0-312-64137-5 (trade paperback)

First St. Martin's Griffin Edition: September 2010

10 9 8 7 6 5 4 3 2 1

For
Meg Ruley,
the world's greatest agent,
who believed in this book
when it was called Hot Fleshy Thighs;

and for
Jennifer Enderlin,
the world's greatest editor,
who said, "Why don't we get another title?"
and then waited with the patience
of a thousand saints
until it was done.

Acknowledgments

I must thank Valerie Taylor, who has read in manuscript every book I've written since 1993 and who has made them all immeasurably better with her critiques; and Chene Heady, who read all of my MFA work and then still managed to write the magnificent "Salvation in Thirty Seconds or Less."

My thanks also go to Tom Stillman, who taught me how to play pool; Jeff MacGregor, who taught me how to make pornography; Monica McLean, who told me how to hide money offshore; Laurie Grant, who told me how to almost kill people; Jack Smith, who taught me how to electrocute people; and John Finocharo, who told me how to get away with killing people. Without the help of these fine people, this would have been a book about lemonade, ice cream, and wallpaper.

I wrote the story myself. It's about a girl who lost her reputation and never missed it.

— *Mae West*

Welcome
to Temptation

Chapter One

Sophie Dempsey didn't like Temptation even before the Garveys smashed into her '86 Civic, broke her sister's sunglasses, and confirmed all her worst suspicions about people from small towns who drove beige Cadillacs.

Half an hour earlier, Sophie's sister Amy had been happily driving too fast down Highway 32, her bright hair ruffling in the wind as she sang "In the Middle of Nowhere" with Dusty Springfield on the tape deck. Maple trees had waved cheerfully in the warm breeze, cotton clouds had bounced across the blue, blue sky, and the late-August sun had blasted everything in sight.

And Sophie had felt a chill, courtesy, she was sure, of the sixth sense that had kept generations of Dempseys out of jail most of the time.

"Slow down," she told Amy. "There's no need to rush." She stared out the window as she twisted the rings on her middle fingers. More riotously happy, southern Ohio landscape. That couldn't be good.

"Oh, relax." Amy peered at Sophie over the top of her cat's-eye sunglasses. "It's a video shoot, not a bank heist. What could go wrong?"

"Don't *say* that." Sophie sank lower in her seat. "Anytime anybody in a movie says, 'What could go wrong?' something goes wrong."

A green sign that read *Temptation ¼ Mile* loomed ahead, and Sophie reviewed her situation for the eleventh time that hour. She was going to a small town to make an unscripted video for a washed-up actress she didn't trust. There were going to be problems. They'd show up at any minute, like bats, dive-bombing them from out of nowhere. A strand of her dark curly hair blew across her eyes, and she jammed it back into the knot on top of her head with one finger. "Bats," she said out loud, and Amy said, "What?"

Sophie let her head fall back against the seat. "'We can't stop here. This is bat country.'"

"Johnny Depp," Amy said. "*Fear and Loathing in Las Vegas.* Stop quoting. There's nothing to be nervous about, you're just overreacting." She turned off the highway and onto the old road that led into Temptation. The exit was marked by a shiny new gas station and a less shiny but still-plastic Larry's Motel.

"Colorful," Amy said.

"Trouble," Sophie said.

"Oh, for heaven's sake," Amy said. "It's not the Bates Motel."

"You have no idea how dangerous small towns are." Sophie scowled out the window. "You were only ten when we moved to the city. You can't remember what hell all those little places we lived in were."

"Sophie."

"And it's not as if we have a plan." Sophie stared with deep suspicion as they passed a blackened, log-built bar that sported a rusting neon sign: *Temptation Tavern. Beer. Music.* "It's all very well for Clea to say, 'We'll improvise,' but even if this is just an audition video, I need more of a script than 'Clea goes back to her creepy hometown and meets her long-lost love, Fred.'"

"Frank." Amy shook her head. "I don't believe you. We're finally filming something besides a wedding, and all you can say is, 'Trouble ahead,' and, 'Why can't we stay in Cincinnati?' and, 'I don't trust Clea.' Face it, the only reason you don't like Clea is because she dumped Davy to marry a TV anchorman. That's very sisterly of you, but it's time to get over it."

"That's not it," Sophie said. "I don't know what it is, it's just—"

"Come on, Sophie. This is good for you. It gets you away from Brandon."

Oh, yeah, sure this is good for me, Sophie thought, but Amy couldn't help it. It was in her blood to turn everything into a con.

"Why you're dating your therapist is beyond me," Amy was saying. "Your health insurance covered his fees."

"My *ex*-therapist." Sophie squinted at the deserted tree-lined road before them. Ominous. "It saved a lot of time. You don't know what a relief it was not to have to explain the family to him."

"You know, sometimes I think it's just our destiny to be bad." Amy took her eyes off the road to smile at Sophie. "What do you say we quit making wedding videos and fall like the rest of the Dempseys?"

"No," Sophie said. "The fall will kill us."

She waited for an argument, but Amy was already distracted.

"Oh, wow." She leaned forward and slowed the car. "*Gotta* love these road signs."

Sophie read the battered white-and-black signs: *Temptation Rotary Club, First Lutheran Church of Temptation, Temptation Ladies' Club, Temptation Nighttime Theater.* The last one was a corroded green-and-cream metal sign that said, *Welcome to Temptation.* Under it a smaller sign in the same rusted antique green said, *Phineas T. Tucker, Mayor.* And under that, a newer but still battered sign said, *We Believe in Family Values.*

"Get me out of here," Sophie said.

"Can you imagine how old Phineas T. must be if the sign is that rusted?" Amy said. "Older than God. Hasn't had sex since the Bicentennial. Do you think the Church of Temptation is like the Church of Baseball?"

"Not if it's Lutheran," Sophie said.

Then they crested the hill and there was Temptation.

"Pleasantville," Amy said, taking off her sunglasses.

"Amityville," Sophie said.

The town proper was on the other side of a muddy river that streamed sullenly under a gunmetal bridge at the bottom of the hill. Beyond the bridge, the land rose up green and lush behind smug little brick-and-frame houses, and as the hills rose, the houses got bigger, much bigger. Sophie knew the kind of people who lived in houses like that. Not Her Kind. "'It's quiet,'" she told Amy as they started down the hill. "'Too quiet.'" But Amy was gaping at something in the distance.

"Oh my God!" Amy pulled off the road. "Look at that water tower!"

"What?" Sophie leaned forward to look.

The flesh-colored, bullet-shaped tower thrust through the trees at the top of the hill, so aggressively phallic that Sophie forgot to fidget with her rings as she stared at it. "Hello. Do you suppose they did that on purpose? I mean, you couldn't *accidentally* paint it to look like that, could you?"

"Maybe Phineas T. is compensating. I don't care. *I love this town.*" Amy handed Sophie her sunglasses, yanked her orange tube top into place, and reached between the seats for her camera. "My God, the visual opportunities. Change places with me."

"Why?" Sophie said, but she climbed over the stick shift and into the driver's seat as Amy got out of the car. "Okay, the water tower is cute, but 'I bet the Chinese food here is terrible.'" When Amy gave her a dirty look, she said, "I'm not whining, it's a line. *My Cousin Vinny.*" Sophie squinted out at the road. "I *will* bet they don't have a decent pool table. Probably out-lawed them. Where are we going now?"

"Back to the beginning." Amy got in the passenger-side door. "I have to get all of this. The Church of Temptation, Phineas T. Tucker, and that big hard-on of a water tower. This is our opening-credits crawl."

"Can we film in public without a permit?" Sophie put on Amy's sunglasses with only a brief thought as to how pink plastic and rhinestones would look with her plain white blouse and khaki shorts. She double-checked the road and then pulled out and made a U-turn. "Because breaking the law is out."

"They'll never know," Amy said, sounding way too much like their father. She braced the camera on the window and added, "I'll keep watch this way and you keep an eye on the rearview in case somebody comes up behind us. Go about five miles an hour. I want to get all of this."

Sophie drove back to where the signs began and turned around, keeping an eye on the rearview mirror as Amy filmed. All they needed was to get rear-ended by some irate Citizen of Temptation—

Then, as they reached the crest of the hill, the beige Caddy zoomed out of a side road that Sophie hadn't even seen and smashed into their front fender.

Sophie hit the brakes as she felt the impact, and the sound of crunching metal tore through her head at the same time Amy's sunglasses flew off her nose and hit the dashboard. She tasted blood as she bit her lip, gagged once as the seatbelt cut into her stomach, and then it was over, and they were sitting in the wrong lane with Dusty singing "I'll Try Anything" as if nothing had happened. There was no one coming the other way, so Sophie breathed deep, licked her bleeding lip, let go of the steering wheel, and turned to deal with the situation.

Amy was bent over, her head at a funny angle under the dashboard.

"Amy!"

Amy straightened, holding the video camera. "It's okay. I dropped it but it's fine." She scowled at the dash and picked up her glasses, and the broken lenses fell out. "But my sunglasses are history, damn it."

Sophie swallowed her panic and tried to stop shaking. "Oh. Good. Good. The camera's okay. Good. Sorry about the glasses." She turned Dusty off in the middle of "Playing it safe is just for fools," and said, "How are you?"

"Me?" Amy scowled out the window. "I'm pissed as hell at the asshole who hit us."

Sophie peered through the window at the asshole. A bulky, white-haired, fifty-something Pillar of the Community stalked around their right front fender, thick with righteousness. "Oh, no, I hate these guys. He's going to try to make this our fault." She fumbled in her purse for her insurance card, thanking God it wasn't their fault since Amy's previous disregard for the laws of the road had already hiked their premium. "You keep quiet. I'll get us out of here, and the insurance people can handle everyth—"

"Well, actually, it is our fault." Amy dropped her sunglasses back on the dash. "We sort of ran a stop sign."

Sophie froze, clutching her insurance card. "We did *what*?"

"If I'd told you, you would have stopped," Amy said reasonably. "I was *panning*."

"Terrific." Sophie took a deep breath as the Pillar showed up at her window. She got out, making him step back as she did so.

"That was extremely reckless driving, young lady." The Pillar drew himself up to his full, blue-suited, stern-jawed height, which, since Sophie met him eye-to-eye, was about five-seven. "You were speeding. Do you have insurance?" His hands were shaking, Sophie noticed, but before she could ask if he was all right, Amy stuck her head out Sophie's window.

"No way in hell were we speeding. We weren't going any faster than five miles an hour, tops. This is your fault, Grandpa."

"Shut up, Amy," Sophie said, thrusting the insurance card at her. "Copy that information down and do *not* say anything else." Then she turned back to the Pillar, determined to escape without giving him anything. "I'm so sorry," she said to him, flashing her family's stock-in-trade gotta-love-me-give-me-what-I-want smile.

The Pillar stopped glaring at Amy and turned back to Sophie. Amy said, "Hey—" but shut up when Sophie held up one finger behind her back. *One: Make the mark smile.*

"Someday my sister's brain will catch up with her mouth," Sophie said, "but until then I apologize for her." She deepened her smile and looked at the Pillar through her lashes.

"Well, I don't know," the Pillar said, and his scowl faded a little.

Sophie held up two fingers behind her back. *Two: Get the*

mark to agree with you. "We're new here so we don't know the roads," Sophie went on. "You know how confusing it can be driving in a new place."

"Well, yes," the Pillar said. "But that doesn't—"

Three: Make the mark feel superior. "Of course, you're probably never confused." Sophie smiled up at him, no mean trick since they were the same height. She widened her eyes. "I bet you always know where you're going."

"Well, of course," the Pillar said, relaxing now. "However—"

"And now we've stopped you in the middle of all this heat," Sophie went on, apology thick in her voice. She nodded to the Pillar's trembling hands. "And we've upset you." *Four: Give the mark something.* "We really should let you go on. Standing here waiting for the police isn't going to do any of us any good." She smiled again at the Pillar, who began to smile back, looking a little confused.

"Well, that's true," he said. "It could be hours before Wes or Duane comes by."

Great. He knew the cops by their first names. Sophie kept her smile in place. *Five: Get what you want and get out.* "Amy, do you have the insurance information?"

The Pillar looked past her to Amy, and his face darkened. "What is that?"

Sophie turned around to see Amy checking the camera.

"That's a video camera," the Pillar said, sputtering. "What are you doing?"

"Making a movie, obviously." Amy looked at him with patent scorn. "And I'm telling you, you better have insurance because this is a classic car and it's not gonna be cheap to restore."

The Pillar flushed in fury, and Sophie thought, *Oh, thanks, Ame.* She moved to block Amy and sidetrack any debate over the classic status of an '86 Civic. "So we'll just—"

"This is outrageous." The Pillar expanded as he blustered.

"You ran a stop sign. My wife is very upset. What kind of movie are you making? You can't do that here."

"Your wife?" Sophie abandoned the con for the time being and looked past him to see a faded-blonde woman leaning against the back fender of the other car, her chubby face a pasty white. "What are you doing over here if she looks like that?" Sophie turned her back on him and pointed her finger at Amy. "Do not talk to this man. Hand him the information, roll up that window, get the car off the road, and wait for me."

"Your lip's bleeding," Amy said, and handed her a Kleenex.

Sophie took it and blotted her lip as she walked around the still-protesting Pillar and crossed the road. The poor woman had made her way to the Caddy's passenger door, and Sophie bent to look in her eyes. "Are you hurt?"

"Oh." The woman seemed dazed, her pale blue eyes blinking up at Sophie in the sun as she plucked at the collar of her Pepto-Bismol pink suit, but her pupils looked all right. And there wasn't a hair on her head out of place, although that might have been the hairspray.

Sophie took her arm anyway. "You'd better sit down." She opened the passenger door, and the woman got in obediently. "Put your head between your knees." Sophie blotted her lip again. "Take some deep breaths."

The woman put her forehead on her plump knees, which she kept clamped together, and began to gasp.

"Not that deep," Sophie said, before she hyperventilated. "If you spread your knees apart, you can get your head lower."

"Virginia, what are you *doing*?"

Virginia straightened with a jerk, and Sophie turned on the Pillar in exasperation. "She's trying to get some blood back to her head." *If I was married to you, I'd keep my knees together, too.* "Did my sister give you the insurance information?" she asked, and then saw the paper trembling in his hand. "Fine. I understand that you want to get your wife home, and that's no problem for us." He started to protest, and she added, "We'll be at the Whipple farm until Sunday. After that we'll be back in Cincinnati."

"Your insurance agent—" the Pillar began, but this time his wife interrupted him.

"Are you friends of Clea Whipple's?" Virginia said from the front seat, her color returning. "Is she home again? Oh, Stephen, did you hear that? We haven't seen Clea for over twenty years. Except in the movies, of course."

Movie, Sophie wanted to say, since Clea had only made one, but the last thing she wanted was more conversation with the Pillars. She began to back away. "She's home, but only until Sunday. Now, please, don't let me keep you."

"Well, that's so exciting." Virginia trilled. "Is she still married to that handsome Zane Black? We watch him every night on the news." Sophie turned to make her escape, and Virginia raised her voice to compensate. "You tell her Virginia Garvey said hi!"

"They've got movie equipment," Stephen bellowed. "And they're filming on public land which is *clearly illegal*."

"A movie?" Virginia's face lit up and her voice rose to a shout. "Oh, wait, tell me—"

Sophie reached the other side of the road, pretending not to hear. Ahead of her, a torn and faded campaign poster fluttered on a tree: *Tucker for Mayor: More of the Same.*

"Dear God, I hope not," she said under her breath. She got in the car and maneuvered it back on the road while Stephen Garvey glared at her and Virginia fluttered her hand. The front fender scraped against the tire as she searched for the lane to the farm, touching her lip with the Kleenex to see if the bleeding had stopped.

"What a butthead that guy was," Amy said. "Are you all right?"

"No." Sophie looked for the Whipple mailbox. "I've got a smashed car, a moving violation, a sister who screws up my getaway, and a dead white male telling the whole damn town we're making a movie." She slowed as the bridge loomed ahead, and scowled over the steering wheel. "And we must have missed the turnoff for the farm because we're almost in town now."

"No, there's the mailbox." Amy pointed with her broken sunglasses. "Turn left."

Sophie turned down the farm lane Clea had promised them was a good half-mile long. "This place gives me the creeps. . . ." Her voice trailed off as the dusty yard of a dilapidated farm-house came into view. "Didn't Clea say the farmhouse was a long way off the road?"

"Maybe they moved the road," Amy said as they pulled up in front of the house. "It's been twenty-four years since she's been back." She peered through the windshield at the farm-house. "Understandably."

Sophie tried to be fair as she turned off the ignition. The paint was peeling in dingy white strips from the side of the clapboards, and the gutter hung loose across the front of the peaked roof, but the house wasn't a complete loss. There was a wide front porch across the entire front with a swing. And there was . . .

Sophie looked around the dusty, barren yard. Nope, the porch was about it. "Great place to film. Yeah, we can trust Clea. I smell trouble."

Amy sniffed the air. "That's dead fish. Must be the river."

She opened her car door as the screen door banged, and Clea Whipple came out onto her porch, her lush body strain-ing at her bright blue sundress, her white-blonde hair almost incandescent in the sun. She shaded her cameo-perfect face with her hand and called, "You're late."

"And hello to you, too," Sophie said, and got out of the car to unload their supplies, starting with their cooler. It was full of Dempsey life essentials—lemonade and Dove Bars—and she was in need of immediate essential comfort.

Amy went toward the house with the camera. "Isn't this going to be wonderful?"

Sophie looked at Clea, the most self-absorbed woman in the universe, staring blankly back at her from the derelict front porch. "Oh, yeah," she said as she hauled the cooler out of the car.

Nothing but good times ahead.

Eight miles up the road, in Temptation's marble-and-sandstone courthouse, Mayor Phineas T. Tucker wondered not for the first time why he was cursed with a council made up of a blow-hard, a doormat, a high-school English teacher, the town coroner, an amateur actor, and his mother. The combination was depressing to contemplate even with the blowhard and the doormat missing, so while Hildy Mallow waxed poetic over the aesthetic benefits of reproduction vintage streetlights, Phin leaned back from the oak table to distract himself with his council secretary's legs.

Rachel Garvey had excellent legs. Of course, with only twenty years on them, they were too young for him no matter what his mother and hers thought, but they were still fine to look at.

". . . and since their beauty would discourage vandalism, the extra cost will pay for itself over time," Hildy finished, confusing Phin until he remembered that Hildy was talking about streetlights and not Rachel's legs.

"That may be a little optimistic." Liz Tucker's voice was as cool as her champagne-tinted hair. "Of course, our alternative is those horrible modern lights that would clash with the nineteenth-century architecture."

Phin winced. The only nineteenth-century architecture in Temptation was in the wealthy part of town. Grateful that only a few citizens were sitting in the front row listening to his mother forget the little people once again, Phin sat up to head her off before she could offer them cake.

"Yeah, but the good streetlights would go everywhere, right?" Frank Lutz said before Phin could intervene.

"Right," Phin said.

"Okay." Frank sat back and ran his hand over his matinee-idol hair, clearly relieved that the new development he'd built on the west side of town would have class lighting, too. "I'm for it. Let's vote."

"Can we do that without Stephen and Virginia?" Liz said, and Hildy straightened her cardigan and said, "Certainly. If we all agree, we'll have a majority no matter how they voted. And we all agree, right?"

She stared pointedly at the fourth member of the council, Dr. Ed Yarnell, who gazed back, unfazed, armored with thirty years of council experience. If Phin thought about Ed too much, it depressed him, knowing that thirty years down the line he could *be* Ed: bald, sixty-something, and still staring at the same WPA mural of *Justice Meeting Mercy*. It was not how he wanted to spend his sixties. Hell, it wasn't how he wanted to spend his thirties. He glanced guiltily at the sepia-toned photos of three of the four previous mayors—Phineas T. Tucker, his father; Phineas T. Tucker, his grandfather; and Phineas T. Tucker, his great-grandfather—all staring down their high-bridged noses, with cold eyes, at their latest and laziest incarnation.

"Then we'll vote," Hildy said.

"Call the roll, Rachel," Phin said, and Rachel called Lutz, Mallow, Tucker, and Yarnell and got four yeses. "Motion passed. What's next?"

"The water tower," Liz said, and Hildy said, "I don't see why—" and then the double doors from the marble hall opened and the Garveys came in.

"There was an accident." Virginia plopped herself down in her chair, looking like a wad of bubblegum with big hair. "Hello, baby," she said to Rachel, reaching across to pat her daughter's hand. "This car came out of nowhere and *didn't stop.* Two women, a snippy little redhead, Stephen says, and a nice brunette who was sweet to me. Curly hair. Low-class. They're staying at the Whipple farm. And they're making a *movie. . . .*"

Phin watched Liz draw back, probably because "low-class" was such a low-class thing to say. "I'll never understand why Stephen married one of his counter clerks," he'd heard her tell his father once. "His mother must be revolving in her grave."

"Enough," Stephen said now. "We've held up this meeting by coming late, let's not waste more time with gossip."

"Are you all right?" Liz asked, and Virginia nodded.

"Wait a minute, they're making a movie?" Hildy said, and Virginia transferred her nod to her.

"The water tower is on the table," Phin said, deep-sixing his own interest in the news so he could get the meeting over with. If somebody really was making a movie, the whole town would have the details by nightfall anyway. "Stephen, you put it on the agenda."

"I certainly did." Stephen collected himself. "That water tower is a disgrace."

"Well, white looks so drab a few weeks after we paint it—" Hildy began.

"I have an appointment at four-thirty at the Whipple farm, and a rehearsal at six," Frank told Phin under his breath as Hildy elaborated on the "drab" problem. *"Carousel.* I'm the lead." Phin nodded as he spoke, trying not to picture forty-two-year-old Frank walking through a storm with his head held high.

"—and so I thought it would look better in peach," Hildy finished.

Stephen said, "Hell, Hildy, it's not your laundry. It's a water tower, it's supposed to be white—all water towers are white."

Hildy sniffed. "The water tower in Groveport is blue."

"Well, my God, *Groveport.*" Keeping one eye on the four constituents in the front row, Stephen turned back to Phin. "A competent, *concerned* mayor would do his *civic duty* here. We have *family values* to protect."

Here we go again, Phin thought. There had been a time when Stephen's blatant pandering had enraged him, but after nine mind-numbing years as mayor, nothing made him lose his temper anymore. He let Stephen wind down, and then he said, "Hildy, I agree that only people with dirty minds would think it looks like anything but a water tower, but there appear to be a lot of people with dirty minds. We're going to have an accident any day now, what with all the people pulling off the highway with their Polaroids. It's a safety issue." Phin tried to look sympathetically into Hildy's eyes.

Hildy looked at him as if he were a Republican.

"This is a disgrace," Stephen said, playing to the front row again. "You call this leadership?"

"I've got an appointment and then rehearsal," Frank announced. "I'm playing Billy Bigelow. *Carousel.* I can't be late."

For this I spent six years in college, Phin thought. "Let's vote."

"You gotta have a motion," Rachel said, still bent over her pad.

"I move we repaint the water tower back to the old red-and-white we always had," Stephen said. "School colors. That's what it should have been all—"

Phin sighed. "Just move we repaint the water tower, Stephen."

"I move we repaint the water tower red and white," Stephen said.

"I second," Virginia said from beside him, pleased with herself.

The vote went three to three, with Stephen, Virginia, and Liz voting for the new paint job, and Hildy, Ed, and Frank—"I'm putting a sign out there for the theater, good advertising"—voting to keep the peach.

"Did you ever think about being anything but a yes-woman?" Hildy snapped at Virginia, who straightened and fussed with her jacket.

"Virginia votes her conscience, Hildy," Stephen said.

"The motion is tied," Rachel said over Hildy's snort. "The vote goes to the mayor. Tucker."

"Yes," Phin said. "Sorry, Hildy."

"Motion passes, four to three," Rachel said, and Hildy smacked her notebook down on the table, and said, "So now I have to do this all over again."

"Just tell the Coreys to charge the new paint at Stephen's," Phin told her. "They know what to do."

"Funny how Garvey's Hardware is getting twice as much business because of this." Hildy sat back and crossed her arms. "Clear conflict of interest, if you ask me. He shouldn't have been voting."

"That's a good point," Frank said, visibly struck by the argument. Whenever Frank had a thought, it was visible.

"Why didn't you refuse to sell her the peach paint?" he asked Stephen.

"I sold Hildy the paint," Rachel said as her father began to sputter with indignation. "It was, like, all my fault."

Five different council members fell all over themselves telling Rachel it certainly wasn't her fault, while Ed sat silent and smiling at her, and Phin marveled at the way big blue eyes and taffy-blonde hair could snow the hell out of people.

"Well, it doesn't matter now anyway," Rachel said. "I got the vote recorded."

"If there's no new business—" Phin began, but Stephen said, "Wait. We need to talk about this movie."

"Well, Stephen, I *tried* to talk about it—" Virginia began, and Stephen spoke over her.

"Not gossip. We need to consider the impact on the town. The pitfalls." He looked slyly at Phin from the corner of his eyes, and Phin thought, *What are you up to now?* "The *dangers*," Stephen went on. "We're a town that believes in *family values*, and after all, you remember Clea."

Phin definitely remembered Clea. The last time he'd seen her in the flesh, he'd been twelve and she'd leaned over to give him the money on his paper route. He'd looked down her blouse and fallen off his bike and ended up with nine stitches in his chin, but it had been worth it. He was fairly sure she'd jump-started his puberty.

"I don't see any dangers." Frank stood up to go. "And I have to leave. I'm late."

"Sit down," Stephen said. "Some of us think of other things besides *acting*." He sent a dismissive glance at Phin. "Or playing pool."

"Yeah, like painting the water tower twice to double your profit," Frank said.

"There is that," Hildy said.

"Could you forget that so we can speak to the *issues*?" Stephen said.

"I think that making double your profit at the expense of the taxpayers is an issue," Frank said.

"Oh, for heaven's sake, I'll *give* you the damn paint!" Stephen said, and Phin said, "Thank you, Stephen, we accept. Now if there's nothing else—"

"This *movie*." Stephen put his hands on the table. "Clea made that one movie, remember? We don't want that kind of movie made here."

"*Always Tomorrow*." Virginia nodded. "But I really think the nudity in that was for artistic purposes, and it wasn't very much. And she died in the end so she was punished."

Phin spared a brief thought as to what it must be like to be married to Virginia if she thought nudity was punishable by death, but then Stephen caught his attention again.

"No, not *Always Tomorrow*," Stephen was saying, and Frank said, "Oh," and sat down again.

Virginia looked mystified; Rachel looked intrigued; Liz and Hildy looked at the ceiling; and Phin remembered *Coming Clean*, a plotless, straight-to-video movie set in a car wash that Clea undoubtedly did not have on her résumé since she'd been billed as "Candy Suds." He didn't know how Stephen had gotten hold of it; Phin had only seen it because Ed had it in his extensive pornography collection.

"Stephen, I doubt she's shooting porn here," Phin said, and Rachel said, "Clea Whipple made a dirty movie? Fabulous."

Stephen nodded. "There. See? That's what I'm talking about. Family values. We let Clea make this kind of movie here, and our children will think it's all right because we approved of it. And those women with the camera looked loose."

Excellent, Phin thought. At last, some *good* news.

His mother shot him a sharp look.

"We should have a policy on this," Stephen went on. "We won't give a filming permit to anyone unless they sign a no-nudity clause."

"How many movies do you think Temptation is going to get?" Phin said, but Frank said, "Hey, it could happen. Although, with a no-nudity clause—" He shook his head. "That's too strict, Stephen. We don't want to stifle the film industry here."

Stephen zeroed in on Phin. "Responsible leadership demands responsible legislation. It's our civic duty—"

The problem, Phin thought—not for the first time, as Stephen ranted on—wasn't that Stephen was a fathead and Virginia was a gossip, it was that Stephen was a driven fathead with a large conservative following, and Virginia talked to everybody. Phin could hear her now: "Well, of course Phin's a lovely boy, but he was actually for pornography, can you imagine?" Yeah, that would get out the votes in November.

On the other hand, there were some things that Phin was willing to fight for. "I'm against censorship, Stephen," he said, interrupting the older man in mid-tirade. "It comes with owning a bookstore. No banned books."

"How about a pornography clause?" Virginia said. "That's not nudity, and it's not censorship because pornography is bad. We have to protect our children." She gave Rachel her usual obsessively loving smile, including Phin in it, too, as her future son-in-law. *Such a nice couple*, her smile said. *What lovely grandchildren they'll give me. And they'll live right next door.*

Phin's answering smile said, *Not a chance in hell*, while Rachel gazed at Justice and Mercy, pretending she'd never heard of pornography or sex, or Phin, for that matter.

Phin said, "And how would we define 'pornography'?"

"Everybody knows pornography when they see it," Stephen said.

"There's some difference of opinion on that," Phin said. "I don't think we should make law on 'Everybody knows.'"

"Stephen may be right," Liz said, and Phin thought, *Oh, hell, Mom, shut up.* "We have an obligation to the citizens of Temptation." She cast a calculating look at the four citizens in the audience, undoubtedly sizing up the situation in terms of getting her son reelected in November. "We could pass a no-pornography ordinance, and stipulate that 'pornography' is to be defined by the council."

"I think that's unconstitutional," Phin said. "You can't make a law that gets defined later. People have to know what they're breaking."

"It's not a law," Stephen said. "It's an ordinance. I move that Temptation adopt an antipornography ordinance."

"No," Phin said. "I'm not going to have you going through the bookstore and throwing out *Lady Chatterley*."

"I move that Temptation adopt an antipornographic *movie* ordinance," Virginia said, and Stephen said, "I second it."

Phin looked at his council and thought, *Why do I put up with this?* It was a stupid ordinance, and probably unconstitutional, and definitely a waste of time. On the other hand, talking the council out of it would take another hour which would cut into the semiregular late-afternoon pool game he played with Temptation's police chief. And, since it was highly unlikely that anybody but Clea Whipple would ever want to make a movie in Temptation, and, in fact, highly unlikely that Clea Whipple *did* want to make a movie in Temptation, he'd be fighting for a principle that was never going to be tested. "Call the roll, Rachel."

The vote went four in favor of establishing the ordinance, to two against, with Frank voting no to defend the infant Temptation film industry and Ed dissenting without comment. Hildy should have voted against it as an anticensorship

English teacher, but the look she shot Phin as she voted made it clear that this was payback time.

Stephen said, "I'll draft the ordinance tonight and we'll call a special meeting to pass it."

"No, we won't," Phin said. "We'll vote on it next Wednesday, same time, same place. And now, if there are no objections, I move we close this meeting."

"Second." Frank stood up to go. "And by the way, Stephen, we voted to buy the fancy streetlights while you were gone."

"You *what*?" Stephen's roar was outraged.

"You're late for your appointment, Frank." Phin stood up. "This meeting is dismissed." When Stephen drew breath to protest, he added, "Everybody *leave*."

Rachel snickered and closed her notebook.

"We shouldn't wait on the ordinance," Stephen said, as the others left, and Phin said, "Sure we should. Legislate in haste, repent at leisure. Next week is fine."

"Well, then, we're going to reconsider those streetlights next week, too." Stephen shook his head, clearly disgusted with the state of politics in Temptation.

Phin smiled at Rachel as he headed for the door. "Thank you, Rachel, for taking the blame for the paint. That was very noble."

Rachel grinned at him, and Phin saw his mother waiting for him by the door, relaxing into a half-smile as she watched the future daughter-in-law of her choice. *Fat chance*, he wanted to tell her, but that was another argument he didn't want to have. He'd already told his mother that it was out of the question—Rachel said "like" a lot, she didn't read, and she played lousy pool—but Liz Tucker hadn't gotten to be First Lady of Temptation by taking "no" for an answer.

"Wait a moment," she said to her son now as he went past her, and he shook his head.

"Can't stay. I'll talk to you at dinner." He escaped into the marble hall only to find himself waylaid by Ed Yarnell, who looked at him with naked contempt.

"Interesting council meeting you missed just now, Phineas," Ed said. "You just sit there staring into space with your thumb up your butt while Stephen rams through a censorship law."

"Thanks, Ed," Phin said, trying to move away. "Can't stay—"

"You're getting to be too much like your old man, rolling over for Stephen."

Phin felt his temper rise and repressed it from long practice. "Dad never rolled over, he was just careful. This is politics, Ed."

"This is crap," Ed said. "I thought it was a good thing you'd cooled your jets some over the years, considering what a reckless dumbass you used to be, but now I don't know. It's been a good long time since I've seen you break a sweat over anything."

Phin clapped him on the shoulder. "Well, thanks for the advice, Ed. Have a nice evening."

Ed shook his head as Phin escaped again, this time through the wide-arched door of the little courthouse. An architectural gem, a tourist had once told him. "Well, we like it," Phin had said, but it was hard to be impartial since he'd grown up in the place. Generations of Tucker mayors had run the courthouse and Temptation, except for those two dark Garvey years when Stephen's father had wrested the office from Phin's father over the New Bridge controversy.

That was what Stephen was looking for now, Phin knew as he went down the marble steps to the old-fashioned storefronts of Temptation's Main Street. Some controversy that he could exploit the same way his father had exploited the New Bridge. The water tower had been small potatoes, and

Stephen wasn't getting anywhere on his anti–new streetlight campaign, but the way he'd jumped on the porn thing, he might be thinking that was his ticket. Which only went to show how desperate Stephen was.

Of course, having your Cadillac hit by loose, low-class women could rattle a man.

Phin reached the pale green Victorian that housed Tucker Books, climbed the wide wooden steps to the porch, and flipped over the sign that said *Back at 4:30* in childishly skewed, crayoned printing. Then he sat down in one of the cushioned porch chairs and thought of the upcoming election with fatalistic distaste. He didn't care if he won; it was losing that would make him crazy. Tuckers didn't lose. Especially since losing would carry with it the extra burden of watching Stephen Garvey run Temptation into the ground with his nutso family values. God forbid there should be another Garvey Reign of Error. Phin was still sitting there half an hour later, lost in thoughts of streetlights, water towers, and porn permits, when Temptation's police chief pulled up in front.

"Stephen stopped by the station," Wes Mazur said as he got out of the patrol car.

"Don't tell me, let me guess," Phin said. "He wants me arrested for un-mayorlike conduct. Dereliction of civic duty."

"Close." Wes came up the steps looking as unconcerned as ever behind his heavy black glasses. "He wants me to go out to the Whipple farm and investigate some women that ran into him."

Phin nodded. "He mentioned them. They're loose women. And possible pornographers."

"Really?" Wes looked encouraged as he sat down. "And we know this how? No, wait, I've got it. The Whipple farm. Clea Whipple. *Coming Clean.*"

"There you go." Phin put his feet on the porch rail and leaned back in his chair. "The keen mind of the law at work."

"So Clea's coming here to make a movie." Wes looked almost enthusiastic. Then reality set in. "Why?"

"Excellent question. If only Stephen would ask it occasionally."

"He can't. It would slow down the leaps he makes to get to his conclusions." Wes frowned out at the street. "You know, I was considering just letting the insurance agents handle the accident, but now I think I better go out there, make sure everything's okay."

"Check out Clea in the flesh."

"My civic duty."

"Not to mention the loose women."

"That, too." Wes stood up, checking his watch. "It's five. You want to close up and come with me?"

"Oh, yeah," Phin said. "My civic duty, too. We can play pool later."

"We live to serve," Wes said.

"I just want another look at Clea," Phin said.

Sophie unpacked their supplies and organized the dingy kitchen while ignoring the truly ugly cherry wallpaper on one wall, and Clea talked to her the entire time, not helping at all. "Frank's going to be here any minute," she kept saying, sounding almost excited, which was unlike her; she'd been beautifully bored for the five years Sophie had known her.

After half an hour, Sophie had heard enough about Frank the football star; Frank the high-school-theater leading man; Frank the wealthy developer; Frank, the generally magnificent. "Interesting wallpaper," she said, trying to change the conversation.

Clea looked at the wall and shrugged. "My mom put it up. She got that one wall done and my father saw it and made her take the rest of the wallpaper back. He was a tight old bastard."

Sophie looked at the huge ugly bluish cherries. "Maybe he just had good taste."

"No." Clea turned her back on the cherries. "He was just a bastard. He was lousy at taking care of us, but he was a real pro at saying no." She seemed bored by the change of subject and drifted out the door, leaving Sophie to scrub the sink.

When Sophie finished the kitchen, she put her suitcase in a sweltering bedroom that included a hideous blue china dolphin lamp, and then she cleaned the bathroom, although she couldn't manage to unclog the showerhead or find a replacement for the pink-and-blue-fish-covered, mildew-encrusted shower curtain. Finally she went back to the kitchen, put *Dusty in Memphis* on their CD player, and made ham-and-cheese sandwiches to "Just a Little Lovin'."

"The plumbing works, sort of," Sophie told Amy when she came in. She rinsed out a glass in the kitchen sink and then watched the water seep down the drain. "Although showers will be a problem. I haven't checked the electricity—the basement looks like the pit of hell—but the refrigerator is on again and we're leaving Sunday. We can stand anything for five days."

"You haven't met our leading man." Amy picked up a ham sandwich and bit into it. "A charter member in Buttheads Anonymous."

"This would be Frank?"

"This would be Frank. He got here half an hour ago, and already I want him dead." Amy dropped into one of the dingy white wooden kitchen chairs in front of the mutant-berry wallpaper. "He looks like Kurt Russell did in *Used Cars*, I mean, he's wearing a *green suit*, for heaven's sake, and he's drooling into Clea's cleavage."

"The police and the mayor are here," Clea said from the archway, making Amy choke on her sandwich. "Frank says he'll handle it."

"Oh, no he won't," Sophie said.

When she went out on the porch, tensed for battle, a guy in a green suit was talking with a cop in uniform, but they looked manageable. It was the third man, leaning bored against the passenger side of the squad car, who sent every instinct she had into overdrive.

He had broad shoulders, mirrored sunglasses, and no smile, and Sophie could hear ominous music on the soundtrack in her head as her heart started to pound. His fair hair shone in the late-afternoon sun, his profile was classic and beautiful, the sleeves of his tailored white shirt were rolled precisely to his elbows, and his khaki slacks were immaculate and pressed. He looked like every glossy frat boy in every nerd movie ever made, like every popular town boy who'd ever looked right through her in high school, like every rotten rich kid who'd ever belonged where she hadn't.

My mama warned me about guys like you.

He turned to her as if he'd heard her and took off his sunglasses, and she went down the steps to meet him, wiping her sweaty palms on her dust-smeared khaki shorts. "Hi, I'm Sophie Dempsey," she said, flashing the Dempsey gotta-love-me grin as she held out her hot, grimy hand, and after a moment he took it.

His hand was clean and cool and dry, and her heart pounded harder as she looked into his remote, gray eyes.

"Hello, Sophie Dempsey," her worst nightmare said. "Welcome to Temptation."

Chapter Two

Sophie's nightmare had a good six inches on her, and it was hard to smile looking that far up into cool eyes while her heart tried to pound its way out of her rib cage. "Oh. Thank you."

He nodded down at her, his eyes never leaving her face as he favored her with a politician's practiced smile. "I'm Phin Tucker, the mayor, and this is Wes Mazur, our police chief."

The cop had come to stand next to them, shorter than the mayor and pale in his white shirt and black pants. Under his brown crewcut, he peered out of serious, heavy black-rimmed glasses.

"We came about the accident. . . ." the cop began, and then his voice trailed off and Sophie turned to see Clea floating down the steps, looking as blonde and lush as ever.

"Did I hear you say you're Phin Tucker?" Clea drifted past Sophie to take the mayor's arm. "I can't believe it. The last time I saw you, you fell off your bike." She let her eyes slide up to his.

"I'm having the same feeling now. Hello, Clea. Welcome home." The mayor looked down into Clea's blue eyes, but he didn't sound off-balance in the slightest. He was probably never off-balance. Sophie felt annoyed with him for that.

"And who's this?" Clea gazed past his shoulder at the police chief.

"Police chief," a deep voice said from behind Wes. "They want to know about some accident."

Sophie turned. Medium, dark, and smug, the green suit had too much hair mousse and a slight paunch, and he'd slung his suit jacket over one shoulder in a misbegotten attempt to look cool. His shirt had green and white stripes, and his tie was bright yellow.

"You must be Frank," Sophie said.

"That's me. Now don't you worry about a thing." Frank winked at Sophie. "I can handle this for you. I'm on the council."

"Nothing to handle," the cop said mildly, and Sophie shot Clea a look that said, *Do something with this guy.*

Clea took Frank's arm. "Why don't we go up on the porch and discuss your scenes for tomorrow?"

Frank looked stunned, as if he couldn't believe she was touching him, and let her tow him off.

One confirmed jackass out of the way. Two possible wolves to go.

"Well, that's the car," she told the cop, and the mayor looked at her one last time and then left them to walk over to it, evidently having seen all he needed. "It's registered to my sister and me." She turned back to the dilapidated porch where Amy was now leaning against the post, chewing her ham-and-cheese sandwich and looking exotic in her orange tube top and purple capris, her red hair flaming in the sun. "That's my sister."

"Oh," the cop said, looking at Amy.

The mayor called the cop over, and he went as Amy put her sandwich on the porch rail and came down the steps.

"I told you so," Sophie said to Amy under her breath. "The Pillars reported us to 'some outback nazi law-enforcement agency and now they've run us down like dogs—' "

"*Fear and Loathing* again. You're getting boring." She studied the two men. "So that's Phineas T. Tucker. We were wrong. He's having sex. And he can have more with me."

"Concentrate," Sophie said. "The cop's name is Wes Mazur. Get over there and give him anything he wants so he'll go away and we can get to work."

"I'd rather give it to the mayor." Amy sighed. "Unfortunately, he appears to want it from you."

"What?" Sophie said. "Amy, *concentrate*."

"I was standing in the doorway when he said hi," Amy said. "And from the look on his face, what he has for you is not the key to the city."

"There was no look on his face," Sophie said. The mayor was now gazing at the car with the same lack of expression he'd been sporting since he'd arrived. Clearly a product of too much inbreeding. "I don't think he has anything for anybody. Go get rid of them."

Fifteen minutes later, after the cop had gone back to the patrol car, gotten a crowbar, and pried the fender off the tire, Amy came back to the porch with the two men behind her. "Wes has a few questions."

Wes? "Questions?" Sophie clasped her hands together to keep from fidgeting and then began to twist her rings instead.

The cop gestured to the swing, and she sat down. When

he started to sit on the porch rail, Sophie said, "No!" and lunged for the rail, grabbing Amy's sandwich before he sat on it. "Sorry," she told him, handing the sandwich to Amy.

"Thank you." He sat on the rail while the mayor leaned on the post behind him, looking amused, which did nothing to endear him to Sophie. He was starring in *The Philadelphia Story*; she looked like an extra from *The Grapes of Wrath*. Life was so unfair.

"Just tell me what happened," the cop said.

Sophie turned her back on the mayor and told the nice policeman everything, and when she was finished, she said, "I just wasn't looking and missed the sign. We didn't break the law on purpose."

The mayor stirred a little. "Actually, you did." He sounded as if he didn't care. "You left the scene of an accident."

"Understandable under the circumstances," the cop said before Sophie could speak. "Amy says we can have the tape of the accident if we bring it back tomorrow, so we'll bring the accident report for you to sign then."

"Amy asked you to come back." Sophie bit her lip, wondering why her mother had insisted on having three children.

"She also mentioned something about the electricity and plumbing," the cop said, smiling at Amy.

"A good reason to call an electrician and a plumber," Sophie said brightly. *Not the police and the government, Amy.* "Really, there's no need—"

"Not a problem," the cop said. "My pleasure."

"—certainly not for both of you—" Sophie began again, hoping at least to avoid the mayor. But when she looked at him, he was staring at her mouth, and she blushed and then felt her temper rise.

"Did you get hurt in the accident?" he said, and Sophie blinked. "Your lip. It's bleeding."

"Oh." Sophie licked her bottom lip and tasted salt. "I bit it when he hit us. It'll be all right."

His eyes lingered on her mouth for another moment, and then he nodded.

It was time to get rid of the mayor.

One. "But thank you for asking," Sophie said, smiling the Dempsey smile.

The mayor looked startled for an instant, and then his lips quirked a little.

Two. "But I think my mouth will recover, don't you?" Sophie said, flirting up at him.

"Oh, yes," he said, meeting her eyes.

Three. "I'd forgotten all about it," Sophie said, truthfully. "You must be very observant."

"I try," the mayor said, openly appraising her now.

Four. Sophie stood up, including the cop in her smile. "You've been wonderfully kind, and we really can't ask you for anything else; certainly not another trip out here. So I'll come in tomorrow and sign the accident report and—"

"I can ask them," Amy said from behind her. "I want plumbing that works and electricity that won't kill me."

Sophie tried to keep the exasperation off her face but the mayor must have seen it anyway because he grinned at her, a real smile this time, and she thought, *Of course you'd be gorgeous.*

"We'll be back tomorrow," he said, straightening away from the porch post, and all Sophie could say was, "Thank you."

When they were gone, Sophie turned to Amy. "Let's review the plan. It's going to be just the three of us and *we're not going to attract attention.*"

"You know there's such a thing as being too cautious," Amy said. "We need the plumbing and electricity fixed and they'll do it for free."

"The hell they will," Sophie said, thinking of the mayor. "We'll pay one way or another."

"And I don't care what you say," Amy went on. "The mayor is hot."

"I didn't say he wasn't hot." Sophie stood up and let the swing bounce behind her. "I said we were going to stay away from him. He's trouble, it's in his eyes. He's a hard mark."

"I bet he is," Amy said.

"Will you concentrate? We stay away from the mayor."

"Yes, but will the mayor stay away from us?" Amy said.

"God, I hope so," Sophie said, licking her lip as it started to bleed again, pretty sure she meant it.

Phin sat in the passenger seat of the squad car and considered running the Dempsey sisters out of town on a rail. He had no legal grounds, of course, but it was his job to ensure the peace, and he had a feeling that getting rid of the Dempseys would be a good start, even if it was only for *his* peace. There was something wrong there.

Besides the brunette's lush, red, swollen lip.

He shook his head to get rid of the image and Wes said, "What?"

"The brunette. She bothers me. Why is she so tense?"

"That's not why she bothers you."

Phin ignored him. "The way she twisted her rings, I thought her fingers were going to fall off. And then she turned on the charm. She'd have had me, too, if she hadn't been so abrupt about it."

"She had you anyway," Wes said. "Her name's Sophie. I like her, but it is hard to believe she's Amy's sister."

"Amy's a hot little number." *Sophie hadn't been hot*, he thought, concentrating on the older sister's shortcomings so he could forget about her mouth. She'd had the potential to be as attractive as Amy—all that dark curly hair knotted on the top of her head, and a good-enough ivory-pale face with those big brown eyes—but the tension had radiated off her so hard that it had been exhausting just standing next to her. "Sophie's wound so tight she doesn't even breathe," he told Wes. "That cut on her lip had to hurt like hell, and she never mentioned it, never even touched it." He shook his head. "She's trying too hard to pretend everything's all right. Which means she's up to something, and it has to be about that movie." He didn't like women who were up to something. Not that they all weren't. "Which reminds me, you're going to have a new ordinance to enforce next week. Antiporn. So if they're shooting sex, you get to arrest Amy and her tube top."

Wes closed his eyes. "Oh, fuck, why didn't you kill it?"

"Because the majority of the council wanted it, and we're not likely to see a lot of movie companies coming in here, so—" Phin shrugged.

"I don't think Clea Whipple should be discouraged from making pornography," Wes said. "That's just wrong."

"Yeah, well, you run for mayor and fight the good fight." The vague uneasiness Phin had felt about the porn ordinance returned and made him cranky. "I thought I handled it pretty well, considering."

"Nobody died." Wes drove across the New Bridge and surveyed the town as it spread out before them with satisfaction. "That's pretty much my bottom line. No blood, no death, no sweat."

"It's an elemental life, law enforcement," Phin said.

"Beats mayor."

"Right now, yes."

Wes was quiet for a moment, and then he said, "That Amy is something."

"Go for it," Phin said. "You've got until Sunday." That was a cheering thought, that the Dempseys would be gone that soon. "Maybe once they're gone, Stephen will give up on this porn thing."

"I wouldn't underestimate him," Wes said. "The election's coming up." He slowed and made a U-turn to park in front of the bookstore.

"In two months," Phin said in monotone. "As I keep telling my mother. Plenty of time."

Wes shook his head. "Stephen's determined not to lose this time. It's been twenty years since his father won and made a mess of everything. People forget. He could win if you just sit on the porch and watch the world go by, and I don't even want to think about what could happen then."

Phin felt a real stirring of alarm. "Are you saying I should be campaigning? Okay, we'll put the posters up early."

"I'm saying," Wes said carefully, "that Stephen is standing on years of Garvey defeats. Losing over and over again like that wears on a man's soul. He's obsessed, Phin. I think he'll do damn near anything to win this time, and if he does he'll spend the next two years trying to drag us back to the Stone Age."

Phin got out of the car. "There's irony for you. I've had enough mayor to last me a lifetime, and Stephen wants it bad, and we're both stuck."

"That makes it worse," Wes said. "You don't even want what he craves. And you won't give it to him, either. At least, I hope you won't."

Phin looked down the street to the sandstone-and-marble courthouse. Tuckers did not lose. "Okay, we're watching that movie company, then, since that's where Stephen seems to be going with his latest dumbass legislation. Especially we're watching what's-her-name. Sophie. A woman that tense and devious is going to be trouble for anybody who gets involved with her." Phin thought about her mouth again, and the smile she'd hit him with when she'd decided to snow him. If she ever relaxed, she'd be the kind of woman his father had warned him about, the devil's candy, a woman who'd ruin you as soon as look at you. Phin had been enthusiastic about the idea until he'd run afoul of one.

"You're safe, then," Wes was saying as they went up the steps to the bookstore. "Seeing as you're not getting involved."

Phin nodded as he unlocked the door. "Yeah, but I'm going back with you tomorrow to find out what she's up to with this movie."

"That's what you're going back for, huh?"

"That and to see if Georgia Lutz strangles Clea Whipple when she finds out what Frank's up to." Phin held the door open for Wes.

"Don't even joke about it," Wes said. "We haven't had a murder here for forty years, and I don't want the next one on my watch." He glanced up the street, which was as empty as usual for the dinner hour. "Do you have to get home to Dillie or do you have time for a game?"

"I always have time for a game." Phin motioned him inside. "It's my reason for living."

"I thought that was politics," Wes said as he went in.

"No, that's my mother's reason for living. I live for pool."

"Loose women would be good, too."

Phin thought of Sophie, wound so tight she vibrated. "Yeah, well, if you find any, let me know. In the meantime, we play pool."

Before dinner that night, when the sun had gone down and the air had cooled off a little, Amy made them go out on the porch to talk. She'd grouped what looked like a thousand candles on the porch rails and the upper windowsill near the swing, and Clea reclined on the end that had the candlelight, which was fine by Sophie. She sat in the relative dimness at the other end, listening to the crickets and the soft wash of the river, calming down in the twilight as she swung them back and forth with the tip of her foot. Even the creak of the swing was nice. Maybe all her premonitions had been just funk after all, since the police chief had turned out to be a human being. She tried not to think about the mayor at all. She heard "I Only Want to Be with You" start in the kitchen, which meant Amy had put on *The Very Best of Dusty*. That felt right, too.

"Don't you guys ever play anything else?" Clea said.

Sophie shook her head. "Dusty is comfort music," she told Clea. "My mom used to sing along with Dusty every night." She let her head fall back against the swing, sang along softly, and thought of Davy and Amy when they'd all been together, and the last of her tension slipped away.

"Sorry," Clea said. "I didn't mean to sound bitchy. Zane called while you were out in the yard. Doesn't mean I should take it out on you."

Sophie stopped swinging. "Something wrong?"

"I left him. So now he wants to come down here and talk to me about it." Clea rolled her eyes, and Sophie thought, *This is not good.*

Amy came out on the porch with a pitcher of cider and three tall glasses, and smiled at her. "Cider and peach brandy."

"Ooooh," Clea said after her first sip.

"So is Zane coming?" Sophie said as she clutched her glass. "Because we don't need any more people here." Especially angry, semifamous people. Virginia Garvey would be out like a shot to see her favorite news anchor.

"Who?" Amy said, and Sophie filled her in.

"I told him not to," Clea said. "I already filed for divorce. What he's upset about is the money."

Sophie's tension doubled. "Money?"

"I'm selling the farm," Clea said. "There's a big chunk of land on this side of the highway and this house." She frowned as she looked around. "It doesn't look like much, but Frank says it should bring close to three-quarters of a million."

Sophie sat up. "For this house?"

"No, for the land." Clea pushed the swing, and Sophie slumped against the back so she wouldn't fall off. "My dad sold the biggest part of the farm right after I married Zane five years ago. I inherited almost two million dollars from my dad, and it's gone now." Clea took a deep breath and added, "Zane did something with it in the past six months, spent it, I don't know. We had a big fight about it and that's when I filed. My lawyer says he's going to have to explain in court where that money went. And that's not going to do his career any good at all." She set her jaw. "I want that money back."

"Well, Amy always said—" Sophie looked around for her sister. "Amy?"

Amy had faded off into the darkness of the yard, and Sophie could see her moving in the bushes beside the porch. "What are you doing?"

"Just checking to make sure we put the equipment away." Amy came back on the porch, picked up her drink, and she and Clea began to talk about the video.

"I want the tape to send to L.A.," Clea said. "To a producer I know out there, Leo Kingsley."

"That sounds familiar," Amy said to Sophie.

Sophie nodded. "Davy used to work for him. That's how he met Clea." *And then he brought her home to meet the family and she dumped him for Zane.* Sophie took another sip of cider and brandy. She should get over that since Zane had turned out to be enough punishment all by himself. She let her head fall back and listened to Dusty and looked out into the lush green darkness of the trees that separated the house from the river.

"So what about this Frank?" Amy said.

"Frank." Clea didn't sound nearly as excited about Frank as she had earlier in the day. "He called about a month ago, and it made me . . . nostalgic. He said, 'Why don't you come home, we'll talk about the deal here, it'll be just like old times,' and I thought, what a great idea to film for an audition tape—going home, meeting my old high-school flame, sort of a love story/documentary, you know?"

Amy nodded. "How long did you and Frank go together?"

"One night." Clea emptied her glass and reached for the pitcher to pour another. "I, of course, thought it was going to be forever."

"One night?" Sophie thought of Frank: pudgy, badly dressed, and annoying as hell. One night would be plenty.

"I was in love." Clea made it sound like, *I had the plague.* "And he *acted* like he was. And he was so good-looking—"

"Frank was good-looking?" Sophie said.

"It was twenty-four years ago," Amy said. "Shut up and let her talk."

"—and we were doing *Taming of the Shrew* for the senior play," Clea was saying. "And you know how it is when you rehearse and rehearse and pretend you're in love. Except I really was. He was just everything back then."

If Temptation was a place where Frank was just everything, Sophie was leaving town. Somebody smart, good-looking, and successful, somebody like the damn mayor, that made sense. But Frank?

"He'd been dating Georgia Funk forever," Clea said. "But on Saturday night, after the cast party, Frank took me out to the Tavern for a Coke, which, let me tell you, was big stuff. And he parked in the back which is pretty much Temptation's lovers' lane, and he made his move, and that's when I lost my virginity." Clea drained her second glass.

"Ouch," Sophie said.

"He promised me he was through with Georgia," Clea said. "But when I got to school on Monday, she was wearing this tiny chip of an engagement ring."

"Maybe we could film a murder mystery," Amy said.

"He said she was pregnant," Clea said, "and they got married fast enough. And then eleven months later, sure enough, she had a baby." Clea reached for the pitcher again, and Sophie held out her glass.

"So she lied or he lied," Amy said.

"She lied," Clea said, as she poured Sophie's cider. "Their wedding picture was in the paper. You've never seen a more miserable-looking groom." She took a sip from her glass and then topped it up from the pitcher. "And that's how I lost my virginity and went to Hollywood to become a movie star." She laughed, but she looked grim, even in the candlelight.

"Does anybody ever have a good losing-my-virginity story?" Amy said. "I lost mine to Darrin Sunderland after the homecoming game my junior year, and it was lousy." She sipped her cider and brightened. "Fortunately, sex got better."

"It was pretty good with Frank," Clea said. "I mean, the sex wasn't wonderful, but he was nice to me. And really grateful."

"Darrin was too drunk to be grateful," Amy said. "Which taught me my first lesson about sex: They have to be sober. It's one of the 'Classic Blunders,' right up there with 'never get involved in a land war in Asia.' "

"My first lesson was not to believe anything a guy tells you when he wants it," Clea said. "The best guy I was ever with was a crook, so that tells you about my taste in men."

"You didn't know Zane was a crook," Sophie said.

"No, Zane's a mistake," Clea said. "*Davy's* a crook." When Sophie sat up fast and rocked the swing, she added, "And you know it, so don't even try to defend him. I know you love him, but he's as crooked as everybody else in your family tree."

"Excuse me?" Sophie said, ice in her voice.

"Except for you and Amy," Clea said. "And sometimes I have my doubts about Amy."

"Everybody does," Amy said cheerfully.

"But I have no doubts about you, Sophie," Clea went on. "You'll never do anything wrong. I've never met anybody as straight as you. I bet you even lost your virginity well. Elegantly, with no trauma." She toasted Sophie with her glass. "I bet you didn't even get your clothes mussed."

"I lost it to Chad Berwick in Iowa, one month before school was out, my junior year," Sophie said, trying to keep her voice even so she wouldn't spit on Clea. "I thought I'd con him into taking me to prom because I wanted to be 'in' just once, and nobody was more in than Chad. Except it was awful, and when I got to school on Monday, everybody knew. And when I went to the cafeteria at lunchtime, his best friend came up and stuck his finger in the pie on my tray and scooped out this big, gloppy cherry and said, 'Heard you lost this, Sophie.' And then everybody laughed." Sophie kept her voice flat, but she felt sick all over again as the memory came back; smelled the bread-and-butter smell in the cafeteria, saw the gray linoleum floor and turquoise wall panels, and heard the smothered laughter.

After a minute, Amy said, "Jeez."

"I knew better," Sophie said, trying to sound offhanded. "Mama warned me about the town boys. They had to be nice to the girls they knew, so they'd go after the outsiders like me instead. And then I thought I'd be so smart, trick this town boy into taking me to prom." She shook her head. "Clearly *not* my father's daughter. Can't even run a decent con."

"I didn't know," Amy said, sounding miserable for her.

"You were ten," Sophie said. "I didn't feel like sharing. But I did make Dad leave us in the next town we stopped in so you and Davy could finish growing up in one place. And by the time you were a high-school junior, you belonged." She smiled at Amy to reassure her. "To the wrong crowd, of course, because you're a Dempsey, but still."

"And then I ended up with Darrin Sunderland," Amy said.

"I can't do everything," Sophie said. "You have to pick your own guys."

"Well, that explains why you were so cold to Phin Tucker," Clea said.

Sophie frowned at her. "What?"

"Town boy." Clea gestured with her glass. "The high-class town boy to end all town boys. You're making him pay for Chet Whosis."

"Chad," Sophie said, thinking of Phin Tucker and his perfect face and perfect body. "Chad was tall and blond, but that was it. The mayor doesn't look anything at all like him."

"Doesn't matter," Clea said. "Frank's still the guy I lost, and any town boy is going to be the guy who fucked you over. That's history. It keeps repeating on you."

"So you're making this film to get Frank back?" Sophie said, trying to get the conversation off town boys and Phin Tucker.

"No." Clea shuddered. "Did you see him today? What a fathead he grew up to be."

"We noticed." Amy sounded a lot more concerned than the occasion warranted. "You still want to do the video, right?"

Clea nodded. "All I need is film that shows I'm still bankable. When I talked to Leo, he sounded interested because he has this sequel he wants to make, but I don't want to do that."

"He wants to make a sequel to *Always Tomorrow*?" Amy asked doubtfully.

"I thought you were dead at the end of *Always Tomorrow*," Sophie said.

"Not *Always Tomorrow*," Clea said. "Look, all you guys need to do is make me look good on tape."

"That's not hard," Amy said. "As long as we get the light right, you still look great."

"Thanks," Clea said, as if she wasn't sure that was a compliment.

"And I'm still up for murder," Amy said. "Although I think Chet in Iowa deserves it more. Maybe we could go on a spree. We knock off Frank, and then on the way to Iowa to kill Chet, we find Darrin and break his kneecaps." She stopped, caught by a thought. "You know, that would make a great movie."

"Chad, not Chet," Sophie said. "And that was fifteen years ago. I'm over it."

"You're never really over it." Clea looked out into the night. "You just learn to live with it." She sighed. "Don't you wish you knew then what you know now? Don't you wish you could go back and fix it?"

"I'm not sure I'd know what to say even now," Sophie said. "'Get your finger out of my pie' doesn't seem enough."

"How about 'Yes, and he was lousy'?" Amy said. "You could at least make sure Chet didn't get any more."

"Chad," Sophie said. "It's all right. Really. *I'm over it.*"

"And what would you do if Chad showed up in the path of your speeding car?" Clea asked.

"I'd run him down like the dog he was," Sophie said. "And his little best friend, too."

"Well, don't get confused and go after the mayor instead," Amy said. "At least not until the video is done."

"I won't do anything to the mayor." Sophie thought of him as she said it, so carelessly confident that he was barely conscious. She found herself gritting her teeth, so she relaxed her jaw, took a deep breath and added, "No matter how appealing that might be."

While Sophie was drinking cider punch, Phin had gone home to his mother's brick house on the Hill and found his little blonde daughter waiting for him on the spacious, empty porch, her hands on her nonexistent hips.

"You're very late," Dillie told him in her precise, Tucker voice as he climbed the white stone steps. "Dinner is waiting."

"I apologize," he said. "Did you take your vitamin today?"

Dillie sighed with the exaggerated patience of a nine-year-old. "Yes. A Wilma. Jamie Barclay doesn't have to take vitamins."

"Jamie Barclay is going to be sorry about that someday." He kissed her on the top of her head and let his cheek stay there for a minute before he said, "Who is Jamie Barclay?"

"Jamie Barclay moved in two houses down across the street on Monday. Jamie Barclay gets to walk lots of places alone. I'm old enough to do that. I could walk from here to the bookstore by myself." Dill stuck her chin out, and her long pale hair fell away from her odd little pointed face.

"Don't even think about it."

"Well, when *can* I walk by myself?"

"When you get your driver's license."

"You always, always say that." Dillie scowled at him. "That's when *everything* happens."

"It's going to be a busy day," Phin agreed. Since he wasn't

planning on letting her get her license until she was twenty-one, he wasn't worried.

"Well, I already know about babies so we won't have to do that," Dillie said. "Grandma told me some stuff a long time ago, but then Jamie Barclay told me a lot more today."

Phin bent down to look at her. "Is Jamie Barclay a boy or a girl?"

"A girl." Her voice was full of admiration. "She knows *a lot*."

"Wonderful." Phin straightened again. "I thought I told you not to talk to strangers. And she's probably wrong, so don't worry about it."

"Okay. I have an idea," Dillie said, switching gears on him. "A *good* idea."

"Okay," Phin said cautiously. The Tucker porch didn't have any chairs because the Hill was not the kind of place where people sat on their front porches and chatted, so he sat down on the top step, and Dillie sat down beside him, a feather-weight in a white T-shirt and tan shorts.

"I was thinking," Dillie said, "that you and I could go live over the bookstore. Where you used to live."

"Dill, there's only one room that's livable up there. The rest is storage. We couldn't get all your stuff in there, let alone mine."

"I could get rid of some of my stuff." Dillie stuck her chin out nobly.

"That would be tragic."

Dillie shifted in her chair. "It could be just us. We could be . . ." She stared into space, searching for the right word, narrowing her gray eyes and pursing the cupid's-bow mouth she'd inherited from her mother, and Phin felt the instinctive parental ache that still took him by surprise after nine years: *How was I lucky enough to get this child, and how can I ever keep her safe enough?* He hadn't wanted to get married, he hadn't wanted a baby, and he sure as hell hadn't wanted to be a single father. And now he couldn't imagine life without her.

"We could be *private*," Dillie said finally.

"We're not cramped here," Phin pointed out. "There are fourteen rooms. It's a wonder we don't lose each other."

"We have to be with Grandma Liz all the time," Dillie said. "I really love Grandma Liz but I would like it to be just us family. If it was just us, we could have hot dogs. And paper napkins. And dessert when it's not the weekend." She put her hand on his arm, and said, "Please?" looking up at him with intense gray eyes, and he looked down to see a smear of purple on his shirt sleeve.

"Blackberry?" he said.

Dillie pulled her hand back. "Grape. I had toast 'cause you were late." She turned her hand to look at the jam-smeared edge of it. "It was goopy."

"So it was." Phin handed her his handkerchief. "Paper napkins, huh?" This wasn't one of Phin's priorities, but if it had come to loom large in his daughter's life, it had to be dealt with.

"That's just an example." Dillie licked her hand to dissolve some of the jam and then scrubbed at it with Phin's handkerchief.

Phin sat back and considered the situation. It had made sense to move in with his mother when Dillie was born because somebody had to take care of the baby. But Dillie wasn't a baby anymore. And it must have taken a lot for his preternaturally polite daughter to say, "I want out."

They could rent a house, he supposed, but since he owned the house by the river his mother-in-law lived in, and the bookstore house, and Liz had this semimansion on the Hill, it seemed like a waste of money. And if he and Dillie moved, who'd take care of her during the day while he ran the bookstore? She'd end up back here on the Hill with Liz anyway, which was the way his mother wanted it. "She'll be a Tucker," she'd told Phin when he'd brought the baby home from the hospital. "Leave everything to me."

Thinking about it now, he could see Dillie's point. Being a Tucker was often a pain in the ass.

"Compromise," he said, and Dillie sighed. "How about if we stay at the bookstore one night a week? Like a sleepover. We'll have hot dogs and dessert and no napkins. And we can try to put the overstock into two rooms instead of three so you can have your own room."

Dillie tilted her head, considering it, looking pensive and delicate in the evening light. Phin knew she was a tough little kid, he'd seen her on the softball field, but still her thinness shook him. "You looked just like that when you were her age," Liz had told him. "You were six foot at fourteen and didn't stop then. She'll fill out when the time comes."

"How about," Dillie said in her patient, measured voice, "if we try that for a little while and then if I'm good, we always stay there?"

"How about you take what you can get?"

Dillie exhaled. "It needs to be just us."

"Why?"

"Because I need a mom."

Phin went very still. "A mom."

"Jamie Barclay has a mom. Jamie Barclay said her mom said I needed a mom, too."

"Jamie Barclay's mom is wrong," Phin said grimly.

"I don't think so." Dillie's voice was thoughtful. "I think I need one. I think I'd like it. But I don't think I want my mom to be Rachel."

"Rachel?" Phin's temper flared. "Who—"

"Grandma Liz says Rachel is just like a mom when she baby-sits me," Dillie said. "And Rachel's mom keeps saying maybe someday she'll be my grandma and won't that be nice. But I don't think Rachel's *practical* enough to be my mom. And I really don't want her mom to be my grandma because her mom is mean to Grandma Junie all the time." She fell into her maternal grandmother's southern Ohio drawl as she added, "She's just *naasty*."

"Rachel's not going to be your mom," Phin said. "You can stop worrying."

"Well, I don't know." Dillie sighed and straightened. "That's what Grandma Liz wants, and if we stay here, that's what'll happen because we always end up with what she wants."

"Trust me, Dill," Phin said. "There's not a chance in hell that Rachel will be your mom." He heard his mother call, "Dillie?" and he raised his voice and called back, "We're out front."

Liz came around the house from her garden, her gloved fist clenching blue-violet roses, her pale hair refusing to move in the summer breeze. The Tuckers did not let nature push them around. "Why are you sitting out here?"

"Because it's nice," Phin said. "What did you want to talk to me about?"

Liz stopped at the foot of the steps. "I want you to spend more time with Stephen Garvey instead of turning your back on him and rushing off like that. You'll never build a consensus giving him the cold shoulder."

"I don't want to build a consensus, I want to run a bookstore," Phin said. Dillie poked him and he added, "And eat hot dogs with my kid. Dillie and I are going to have a sleepover at the store tomorrow night."

"What?" Liz frowned at them both, two ridiculous children. "She can't. Her piano lesson is at six and then there's dinner, and she has to be in bed at eight-thirty. There's no point in her sleeping there."

"Friday, then," Phin said.

"Ballet," Liz said. "I don't understand this at all."

"What night don't you have a lesson?" Phin said to Dillie.

"Mondays," Dillie said glumly.

"That's the only night?" Phin turned back to Liz. "When did that happen?"

"You stay at the bookstore past six most nights," Liz pointed out. "She's not missing quality time with you. And we want her to be well-rounded."

Phin looked down at his angular little girl. "She's rounded enough. We're staying at the bookstore on Monday."

"That's the first day of school so it would be impractical—"

Dillie looked at him anxiously and he broke in. "We like impractical. Dillie and I live on the edge."

Dillie beamed at him, joy radiating from every cell in her body, and he thought, *I have to spend more time with this kid. She's the best.*

Behind Dillie, Liz opened her mouth again and Phin met her eyes. "Monday we stay there."

"Very well," Liz said, clearly thinking it wasn't. "Just for this Monday, though. We have to be practical about school nights. Come on, Dillie, let's go get changed for dinner."

Dillie took one yearning look back at him, which would have wrenched his heart if he hadn't known what an actress she was. "All right," she said plaintively, and took her grandmother's hand, dragging her feet as she went up the stone steps.

"For heaven's sake, Dillie," Liz said, and Phin laughed.

Dillie jerked her head up and grinned at him, pure kid again, and then she went inside with her grandmother to go without dessert because it was a weeknight.

Diane would have given her dessert for breakfast, he thought, and then stopped, surprised that he'd thought of Diane at all. They'd been together for so short a time, he wasn't sure he could remember what she'd looked like. Round, he remembered, because that was what had gotten him into trouble in the first place. That, and she'd been so warm. Warmth had been in short supply at the Tuckers', especially when he'd come home to help his mother cope with his father's second heart attack and his father cope with his own mortality.

Then one night he'd gone to the Tavern to get away from all the manufactured optimism at home, and Diane had sat down beside him. "So you're Phin Tucker," she'd said. "Heard about you." He closed his eyes and tried to call up her face, guilty that he'd cared so little for her that he couldn't even get that back. Warm brown eyes, he remembered, and dark tumbling hair, and that cupid's-bow smile that Dillie could use to twist him around her little finger. He tried hard to put the features together, but instead of Diane, he saw Sophie Dempsey, who didn't look like Diane at all, her brown eyes wary and her dark hair twisted in that tense curly knot on top of her head. And her mouth was full and lush, not bowed like Diane's—

He felt a flush of heat thinking about her mouth and stood up, wondering what the hell was wrong with him that he could forget the woman who'd given him a daughter and get hot for a woman he didn't know and didn't like.

"Dad, *dinner*," Dillie said from the doorway behind him, and he went inside, dropping another kiss on the top of her head when he reached her.

"You are my favorite woman in the whole world," he told her, and she said, "I know," and led him into his mother's immaculate, air-conditioned, dessert-free dining room.

Chapter Three

On Thursday morning, Rachel Garvey went out to the Whipple farm, a woman on a mission: She had to get out of Temptation before she went crazy and became her mother.

Her plan was simple; she was going to offer Clea Whipple her services on the movie, and then she'd make herself indispensable, so that when Clea left, she'd take Rachel with her. Her mother was always telling her what a treasure she was, so now she'd be Clea's treasure. Rachel felt no guilt at all about deserting her mother. Her two older sisters were still in town and they could be treasures after she was gone. It was way past time for their turns anyway.

When she pulled up to the porch, Clea was sitting on the top step, beautiful in the sunlight. More than beautiful. Drop-dead, sky-eyed, magnolia-skinned beautiful. So when Clea said, "Hello?" in a voice that sounded like music, Rachel said, "God, I've never seen anybody as gorgeous as you."

Clea smiled and became more gorgeous.

Good start, Rachel thought, and went toward her. "I'm Rachel Garvey," she began, holding out her hand. "And I was thinking maybe you could use—"

"Garvey?" Clea lost her smile. "Any relation to Stephen Garvey?"

"I'm his daughter," Rachel said. "Um, I came out to see if you could use some help."

Clea shook her head, but before she could say anything, the screen door slammed, and Rachel looked up to see a red-head in tight jeans and a pink T-shirt knotted above her belly button.

"Hi." The redhead looked at Rachel with naked curiosity. "I'm Amy."

"I'm Rachel. I came out to help." Rachel held out her hand and then noticed that the redhead's hands were full of paint scrapers. "You're painting?" she said, hope rising.

Amy jerked her head to the right side of the porch. "Just the porch wall white for a background." She handed one of the scrapers to Clea, who looked at it as if she'd never seen one before.

"No," Rachel said. "First of all, the paint's almost off that wood, so it's going to suck up the first six coats of white paint you put on. You need a coat of primer."

"Oh." Amy squinted at her. "Listen, we don't want this to be a *good* paint job, we just want a nice background."

"Then you don't want white, either. White isn't very flattering." Rachel smiled sweetly at Clea. "You want something warm that will bounce color back at you."

"She's right." Clea reexamined Rachel, head to toe, and Rachel stood with her smile fixed, thinking, *I don't like you, but if you take me to Hollywood, I'll learn to deal with you.*

"So what do you suggest?" Amy sounded wary, and Rachel turned back to her, figuring she'd be easier to charm, anyway.

"I can get you a great deal on some peach paint," she told Amy. "We ordered a lot for a project that got changed in the middle. I'll get it for you at cost, and I'll help you for free. I just want to learn to do what you're doing." Rachel smiled up at Amy again, grateful Amy was on the top step so it was easier for Rachel to look small and innocent and appealing.

"You're hired," Amy said, and handed her the other scraper.

Rachel handed it back, sure of herself now. "You scrape, I'll go get the paint." She turned to go before Amy could argue, and Amy called, "Wait, do you need money?"

"Oh, no," Rachel said. "I'll set up an account for you at the store."

"Fantastic," Amy said.

"That would be Garvey's Hardware, right?" Clea said deliberately.

"What?" Amy said, and Rachel waved and left, determined to be such a treasure that Amy wouldn't dream of letting her go.

The peach paint turned out to be too dark for the porch, but mixed half-and-half with the white Rachel had brought, it was perfect, so pale it was more blush than peach. Rachel primed the wall, and while Amy and Clea talked out in the yard about reflectors and camera angles, she listened and learned and began to paint the porch rail. Peach for the posts and rails, blush for the spindles, white for the detailing.

"Wow," Amy said when she came up to the porch at noon. "That looks good. It's even pretty."

"Thanks," Rachel said, but she watched Clea closer because Clea was frowning.

"We should do the whole house," Clea said finally, and Amy said, "No, we should not. Are you nuts?"

"This film is a business expense," Clea told her. "Tax-deductible. This paint therefore becomes part of that business expense. And I want to sell this house." She nodded to Rachel. "Do the whole house."

"No," Rachel said. "We can do the whole front porch if you want to film on both sides, that won't take long. But I do not paint whole houses. I can call the Coreys for you, though. They'll paint anything."

"Are they expensive?" Clea said.

"It's a tax deduction," Rachel said.

"Let me think about it." Clea walked out to the edge of the yard to see the porch from a distance.

Rachel turned back to find Amy grinning at her. "I like you, kid," Amy said. "You remind me of me."

The screen door banged again and a brunette came out, saying, "If you want lunch—" She stopped when she saw Rachel, and Amy rushed to fill in the silence, saying, "This is my sister, Sophie," to Rachel, explaining Rachel's ideas and the paint to Sophie, all without ever mentioning the name Garvey.

Sophie smiled politely at Rachel. "Well, it's nice of you to offer to help, Rachel, but—"

Rachel went tense, but Amy said, "Wait a minute. Come here."

Amy towed her sister out into the yard, and Rachel thought she'd never seen two more different women in her life, Amy in tight pink and Sophie in loose khaki. Then Amy turned Sophie around and said, "Look at the porch."

Sophie folded her arms and studied the porch, and Amy did the same beside her, just like her big sister, and that's when Rachel saw how alike they were. Same big brown eyes, same curly hair, same full mouth, same incredible concentration, even the same white Keds, although Amy's had pink shoelaces and were painted with gold spirals. They stood close, leaning into each other a little, and Rachel was struck by how together they were. She'd never stood that close to her sisters, ever, but Sophie and Amy were a team.

"You think?" Sophie said.

"I think," Amy said.

"Your call," Sophie said. "The color is wonderful."

"Just one thing," Amy said. "Her last name is Garvey."

Sophie started and Rachel thought, *That's it.*

"Give her a chance," Amy said. "Why should she pay for her father's crimes?"

"Hey." Sophie stepped back. "Don't pull that on me."

"I'll work really hard," Rachel said from the porch.

Sophie came toward her. "I know you will, honey." She looked at the painted porch rail, gleaming warm in the sunlight, then nodded. "Come have lunch with us. Then you can paint the porch wall this afternoon and help Amy with whatever she needs. But if your father shows up, you're fired."

Rachel relaxed as relief flooded through her. "He won't ever know. And I'll be a huge help, you wait and see. I'll make things so much easier for you."

But after lunch, in spite of Rachel's best intentions, things got difficult because Rob Lutz showed up with his parents. Clea almost had a heart attack when she saw Rob, and Rachel could understand why, since it was hard to see he was a moron when you looked at that face. That was how Rob had talked

Rachel out of her virginity, by not talking, just by smiling at her with that face. There was a lesson learned, for sure.

Clea had said, "This is *your son?*" to Rob's dad, Frank, and Frank had grinned down at her like a dork, standing really, really close to her. That made Rob's mom, Georgia, mad, which Rachel could also understand except that if she'd been married to Frank, she'd have been *looking* for somebody to take him away. Then Clea put her arm around Georgia and called, "Sophie, meet Georgia."

Georgia squinted at the porch where Rachel and Sophie and Amy were standing, and she looked about twenty years older than Clea, probably because she'd been baking her skin into shoe leather all her life so she could be a Coppertone Blonde. That was what she'd said to Rachel every summer since Rachel had started dating Rob: "Come on and lay out with me, honey, and we'll be Coppertone Blondes. People will think we're sisters." *Right.*

Then Clea said, "Georgia and I graduated together, Sophie! Isn't that something?" and Sophie said, "And neither one of you has aged a day," and glared at Clea to make her behave, and Rachel liked her more.

Clea just laughed and called back to Rob, "Why don't you come up on the porch?" and that must have been the first time Sophie saw him because she said, "Oh, Lord."

"What?" Amy said.

"Look at the way he's looking at Clea," Sophie said.

Amy nodded. "Like she's whipped cream and he has a spoon."

Well, that was Rob for you. Always looking for sex. Rachel didn't know if sex in general was bad or it was just bad with Rob, but as far as she was concerned, Clea could have him.

Sophie moved to the top of the steps and called, "Come on up to the porch, we have lemonade," and when she had Clea,

Frank, and Georgia settled on the right side of the porch with a warning to stay away from the blush-painted wall, Amy began to shoot.

Rachel handed Rob a scraper and said, "We need to scrape the other side of the porch," and Rob said, "Cool." As he worked, he kept his eyes on Clea, who sat perched on the porch rail looking adorable. Clea watched Rob from the corner of her eye while Frank sat opposite her, laughing and flirting, and Georgia sat between them on the porch swing, looking like a Coppertone Toad.

Sophie had gone out into the yard to talk to Amy, and she looked concerned. Even after a few short hours, Rachel knew Sophie liked things calm and organized. So when Phin Tucker walked up behind her and said something, and she jumped a mile, Rachel could have told him that was a bad move. He and Wes had parked behind the Lutzes' van, and Wes had said something to Amy and gone in the house, but Phin went to Sophie and stayed. So he wanted something—three guesses what—but he was doing it all wrong. Well, he'd figure it out. Phin got everything he wanted sooner or later.

"Hey," Rob said behind her. "Get busy."

"Right," Rachel said, and crossed her fingers that Phin would do his usual good work.

Her future depended on it.

"I'm a little worried about Clea," the mayor had said to Sophie out in the yard. "I had nine stitches because of her. She could put Frank in the hospital."

Sophie watched Frank making a fool of himself on the porch in front of his wife, who looked homicidal. "Clea's not the only one who could hurt him." She turned back to the mayor. "How did she give you nine stitches?"

"I looked down her blouse and fell off my bike."

Sophie looked at him with contempt and he said, "Hey, I was twelve. She leaned over. Not my fault."

He was as immaculately handsome as ever in the sunlight, and it was even more annoying now that she knew he'd been a pervert at twelve. She started to tell him so and decided she didn't want to get personal, she just wanted to get rid of him. "Did you say you wanted to look at the electricity?"

"No," he said. "I said Amy wanted me to look at the electricity."

"Right this way," Sophie said, leaving Amy to handle the mess on the porch. Five minutes later, she was in the dark farmhouse basement, wishing she was back on the porch. At least in the sunlight she could see what the mayor was up to. "Uh, what are we doing, Mr. Tucker?"

"Phin," he said. "And this is your fuse box. We're looking at it to see if it's going to burn your house down."

"Where are the little switches?" Sophie squinted around his shoulder in the dim light. She'd expected to get a whiff of some expensive cologne as she leaned closer, but instead he smelled of soap and sun, clean, and she swallowed and concentrated on the fuse box.

There were no switches, just little round things that looked sinister.

"Switches would be circuit breakers," Phin said. "For which you need circuits, not fuses. This is the old way."

"Is this better?"

"No. But it's more exciting."

"I don't want exciting." Sophie took a step back. "I want functioning, nonshocking, neat little switches. I've always depended on the kindness of strangers. You do it."

"That's the problem with you city folk. No sense of adventure. Let me explain how this works."

"No," Sophie said firmly. "I don't want to know. I want switches. I know how they work."

"You can't have switches. Get over it."

Sophie shook her head. "I've heard about these things. You stick pennies in them, and they shock you."

"You do not put pennies in them." He sounded as if he were trying not to laugh. "If you put pennies in them, you deserve to be shocked. Not to mention have the house burn down. Do not put pennies in them."

"Not a problem. I'm not going near that thing." Sophie started up the stairs. "Thank you very much, but no." When she realized he wasn't following her, she stopped. "You can come up now. The electricity lesson is over."

He grinned at her in the light that filtered down the stairs from the kitchen. "Quitter," he said, and her pulse skipped a little at the challenge in his voice.

"Only on the stuff that will get me electrocuted," she told him. "I believe in safety first." She escaped back up the stairs and put on *Dusty in Memphis* to calm her nerves.

Phin followed a few minutes later.

"They're all working," he told her, washing his hands at the sink. "If you have trouble, yell, and Wes or I will come out and fix it."

Sophie blinked at him. "That's extremely nice of you."

"We're extremely nice people." Phin smiled at her, and Sophie had a brief moment where she thought he might be a good guy after all before he said, "So tell me about this movie," and she took a step back.

"I told you, it's just an audition tape," she said. "It was Clea's idea, and she hired us because we did such a good job filming her wedding. Amy's shooting it on the porch because it's easier to light." Even as she said it, the lights in the kitchen went out, and she heard Amy out on the porch say, "Oh, *damn*."

"If there was a switch," Sophie said, "I could go throw it now."

"But there's a fuse instead." Phin pointed at the basement door. "So you can go replace it. Like an adventurous adult."

"Not in this lifetime," Sophie said, and Phin sighed and went downstairs, shortly after which the porch lights evidently came back on because Amy called, "Thank you!"

"You do very nice work," she told him when he came back upstairs, trying to be nice since he wasn't Chad. Exactly. "For that, you get lemonade."

"You know, a little adventure in your life wouldn't kill you," he said as he sat at the table. "Especially if it's just replacing a fuse."

"I had enough adventure as a child," Sophie said firmly as she poured. "I'm having a staid adulthood to make up for it."

"That's a waste," Phin said. "Do you make staid movies, too?"

Sophie slapped a glass of lemonade down in front of him so that some of it slopped out on the table. "What is it with you and this movie?"

"What is it with you and this hostility?" He got up and pulled a paper towel off the roll by the sink and mopped up the spill. "You've been tense from the minute I said hello."

"It was the way you said it," Sophie said. "And I've told you. The movie is a short, improvised film for Clea which Clea asked us to do because she likes Amy's work."

"Not your work?" Phin sat down and sipped his lemonade. "This is very good. Thank you."

"Don't patronize me, just drink it," Sophie said. "Clea wants Amy because I don't do improvised. I shoot all the necessary parts of the wedding and manage the business, and Amy gets the weird stuff around the edges and cuts the video. She's the artist."

"'Weird stuff'?" Phin said.

Sophie folded her arms and leaned against the sink. "People can get the stuff I shoot from any video company, but they can't get the stuff that Amy finds. But if they only got what Amy shoots, they'd be mad because people like things like their vows in their wedding videos. So we work together."

"And why is Clea making this video?"

Sophie scowled at him. "Why do you care so much about this movie?"

"As long as you're out of here before Wednesday, I don't."

"Well, we're out of here on Sunday."

"Fine," Phin said. "And I wasn't patronizing you, the lemonade really is good."

"Thank you," Sophie said, feeling slightly anticlimactic.

"And for whatever I did in a former life to make you so damn mad, I apologize." Phin smiled at her, clearly used to charming everyone in his path. "Now, will you please stop spitting at me?"

"Considering that former life, an apology is not nearly enough. 'My name is Inigo Montoya' on this one."

"Who?" Phin said.

Sophie picked up the pitcher and said, "Lemonade?"— sounding more threatening than she meant to.

Phin pushed his glass back. "No, I've had enough, thank you."

He got up and went back to the porch, and Sophie felt a little guilty for taking her frustrations out on him. She put his lemonade glass in the sink and went out onto the low, wide, back porch to calm her nerves. If she could get just get rid of that constant feeling that something awful was bearing down on her—

Something furry brushed her leg and she looked down and screamed.

There was an animal there—a big one, it came halfway up to her knee—and it had matted red-brown fur on its barrel-like body and short white legs with little black spots on them, and Sophie had never seen anything like it in her life. It was crouched now that she'd screamed, in the attack position she was sure, and when it moved, she leaped back against the wall of the house and screamed again.

Phin slammed the screen door open as he came out onto the porch. "What?" he said, and Sophie pointed down. He let his shoulders slump. "You're kidding. You scream like that for a dog?"

That's a dog? "They bite," Sophie said in her own defense. It seemed feasible.

"Some do," Phin said. "This one appears not to."

Sophie followed his eyes down to the dog, which had rolled over on its back with its four stumpy white legs in the air. "It looks weird."

"It's built like a Welsh corgi." Phin craned his head sideways to get a better look at the prostrate animal. "And a few other things mixed in to keep it interesting." He squinted at it. "God knows where the black spots came from. It's probably a highway dog."

"A highway dog." Sophie looked down at the dog, which was now looking up at them from its back. It was splashed with mud and quivering, possibly the ugliest living thing Sophie had ever seen. Its huge, black-ringed brown eyes stared at her pathetically, and she felt bad for thinking it was ugly.

But dear Lord, it was.

"People dump the dogs they don't want along the highway," Phin said, a thread of anger in his voice, neatly repressed like everything else about him. "They think the dogs will be free and wild, but most of them get hit right away, looking for their owners' cars."

"That's terrible." Sophie stared down at the dog, outraged, and the dog stared up at her, upside down with those huge, melting brown eyes, comic and pathetic. "Is it hungry?"

"Probably, but if you feed it, you'll never get rid of it."

But there were those eyes. Sophie watched the dog for a minute while it watched her back, still upside down, and then she went into the kitchen to get some ham.

Five minutes later, Sophie was sitting on the back-porch steps, cautiously feeding ham to the grateful dog. "I never had a dog," she told Phin.

"We always did." Phin leaned against the porch post. "My dad never turned a highway dog away. If we had too many, he found homes for the ones we couldn't keep."

Sophie held out another piece of ham, and the dog took it gently. It looked up at her with the ham dangling from its mouth like an extra tongue, and she laughed because it looked so funny and sweet with its brown snout and black-ringed eyes. "Too much mascara, dog," she told it, and the dog opened its mouth and barked at her, dropping the ham. "Goofus," she said, and fed it again while the dog looked at her adoringly, completely ignoring Phin. Sophie held out another piece of ham.

"That dog's a real politician," Phin said. "Goes right to the pork barrel and hunkers down."

"Maybe I could keep him a couple of days, until we leave."

"Sure," he said. "Just don't name it. That's always fatal."

"Okay," Sophie said. "Here, dog, have some more ham."

Phin's voice was casual when he spoke again. "So do you take care of the whole world, or just dogs and Amy?"

"Just Amy and my brother." Sophie fed the dog again.

"And who takes care of you?" Phin said, and Sophie looked up, startled. "You're here because Amy and Clea want to do the video, and you're feeding ham to a dog you're not sure you like. Who takes care of you? When do you get what you want?"

"I take care of me," she said, scowling at him. "I take very good care of me, and I always get what I want." *Back off, buddy.*

"Of course you do." Phin straightened. "Lots of luck with the dog."

He went back to the front porch, and Sophie felt guilty for driving him away again, but then the dog nudged her hand with his nose, and she went back to feeding him. When the last of the ham was gone, Sophie patted the dog gingerly on the top of the head and the dog looked at her as if to say, *You're new at this, aren't you?* "I never had a dog," Sophie told it, and it sighed and settled in next to her, smearing mud on her khaki shorts. She patted it again and then went back into the kitchen and opened her PowerBook to block out a plan for the video now that the Lutzes were creating some story conflict on the front porch. The dog sat outside the screen door and watched her, and she sat behind her PowerBook and watched it back.

She couldn't remember ever having wanted a dog. It would have been impossible on the road anyway; the last thing she and her mother had needed was something else to take care of. And then she'd been stuck in that little apartment at seventeen, trying to raise Davy and Amy, and a dog was *really* the last thing she'd needed.

But there was something in the patient way this dog looked through the screen door at her, not trying to get in, just watching her. From the outside.

It rolled over on its back outside the screen door so all she could see was four stubby white feet pointed to the sky. "Okay," Sophie said, and let him in. "But you're covered with mud, so don't get on the furniture or anything." The dog sighed and lay down at her feet, and when Amy called her name and she went out to the front yard, it followed her.

Amy was standing behind the camera, talking to Phin, but she stopped when she saw Sophie coming. "We've got a problem," she said as Sophie got close, and then she saw the dog. "Cool. A dog." She looked at it more closely. "I think."

The screen door slammed as Wes came out. "You now have a new bathroom showerhead," he said to Amy as he came down the steps. "But the shower drain still needs work. I'll come back tomorrow."

"Oh, well—" Sophie began, but Amy said, "Fantastic."

"Your guests need work, too," Phin said, and Sophie turned to look at the porch, where the Lutzes were having one of those intense, whispered conversations that married people have before they kill each other.

"Yeah, that's the problem I called you out here for," Amy said to Sophie. "We may have pushed this too far."

"I'm blaming this on you," Phin said. "Before you got here, they only did this when they'd had too much to drink."

"Good," Sophie said. "Now they're out in the open. We're clearing the hypocrisy out of Temptation."

"A little hypocrisy never hurt anyone," Phin said.

"So were you born a politician?" Sophie started off for the porch. "Or did you have to work to achieve this level of immorality?"

"Oh, I was born to it," Phin said, sounding a little grim.

Sophie went up the porch steps to the Lutzes, with the dog at her heels. "We were so grateful that you were helping us with the filming that we forgot to feed you. Can I make you a sandwich?"

"Oh." Georgia straightened a little. "Oh, no, we have to be going anyway. But how nice of you to offer."

"Well, we're supposed to cater to the talent." Sophie smiled at her, and Georgia flushed with pleasure and smiled back.

"That's a good one." Frank looked at his wife with contempt.

"Amy says you both looked great on camera," Sophie lied. "Maybe you can come back out tomorrow."

"You bet." Frank perked up, and even Georgia began to look less fried around the edges.

"We'll do anything we can to help." Georgia looked at Sophie with unqualified approval. "And maybe you can use Rob, too."

Sophie looked into the yard to the minivan, where Clea was laughing up at a dazzled Rob. "I'm sure we'll be using him," she said flatly.

"That was kind of you," Phin said, when the Lutzes had gone and Sophie was sitting on the porch steps with the dog at her side surveying the yard as if it belonged there, its mascaraed eyes half-lidded in complacency.

"I'm a kind person," Sophie said, her chin in the air.

"You know, all evidence to the contrary, I think you are." He leaned over to pat the dog, his face was close to hers, and Sophie's pulse kicked up. "What I can't figure out is why you're so damn nervous."

"I've been under a lot of stress." Sophie scooted up a step, and the dog climbed to stay with her. "And I come from a very tense family." She thought about her father and Davy and Amy, all of them absolutely nerveless, and honesty made her add, "Well, some of the Dempsey women have been high-strung."

"A weekend in the country should take care of that," Phin said, still watching her as he scratched the dog behind the ear. "There's nothing stressful in Temptation."

Just you, Sophie thought, and he grinned at her as if he'd read her mind.

"Nice seeing you, Sophie Dempsey," he said, and straightened to go out to the car where Wes was waiting for him.

"Same to you," Sophie said, as her pulse slowed again. "And if I don't see you again, thanks for all your help."

"Oh, you'll see me again," Phin said without turning around.

"Terrific." Sophie watched him go, appreciating the fact that he was leaving while admiring how good he looked from behind.

Amy came to enjoy the view with her. "Helluva day, huh?"

"Explain to me again," Sophie said, "what happened to 'just the three of us'?"

Amy shrugged. "You're the one who invited the dog."

Sophie looked down at the dog who looked back up with its Cleopatra eyes, adoring her.

"The dog stays for a while," Sophie said. "The mayor goes."

When Sophie took her shower that night, blessing Wes the entire time for their new flexible showerhead, the dog put its feet on the edge of the tub and whined. It was covered with dried mud and looked so pathetic that Sophie said, "Oh, okay," and hauled him in with her, hosing him down while he squirmed in ecstasy under the water, and then sudsing him up with eucalyptus-and-lavender shampoo. Half an hour later, they both sat blow-dried in the kitchen, enjoying the semicool night air that came in through the screen door, the dog keeping one eye on the Dove Bar Sophie was eating. Sophie licked the ice cream and worried again about the accident, the movie, and the mayor.

She was still obsessing when Amy came down the stairs in her baby-doll pajamas, looking a lot like she had when she was ten. She sat in the chair across from Sophie and drew her knees up to her chin.

"We need a love scene," Amy said. "Clea wants one."

"A love scene." She should have figured on that, it was so like Clea. Sophie gave the wallpaper a dirty look in place of Clea. "I can't write a love scene. Especially not with those damn things staring at me."

"You cannot blame writer's block on giant mutant cherries," Amy began. Then she stopped, and said, "Oh. Cherries."

"What?" Sophie said, and Amy said, "You know. Cherries. And Chet."

"Chad," Sophie said, but she sat back, a little jolted. "I'm sure that's not it." She should ask Brandon. He knew everything about her subconscious. She frowned at the wall phone. She should have called Brandon before now, but she kept forgetting him.

Amy shifted uneasily. "Clea's decided that Rob is the love interest. She says it's better for what she has in mind."

"I bet it is." Sophie thought about it and nodded. "So she comes back to meet her old boyfriend and falls for his son. Lot of conflict there." She thought it through. "Oh, hell, *a lot* of conflict there. Frank's going to have a fit."

"If we do this right, he'll never know," Amy said. "Just write a nice seduction scene, and we can finish this up."

Sophie sat up and tapped her PowerBook out of sleep mode. "Who seduces who?"

"Are you kidding? Clea's an old-fashioned girl. He seduces her."

"So we're not doing a documentary." Sophie began to type in the scene log line, and Amy jerked away and stood up. "Hello?" Sophie said. "What?"

"Nothing," Amy said.

Sophie pointed at the chair. "Sit."

Amy sat, her feet on the floor this time.

"I've been very patient," Sophie told her, "but there's something you're not telling me which is dumb because you know I'll stand behind you no matter what you want. What are you doing?"

"I'm making a documentary," Amy said.

Sophie sat back. "You're making a documentary about Clea coming home to Temptation?"

"No, I'm making a movie of that. I'm making a documentary about making the movie." Amy leaned forward. "This is so cool, Soph. I didn't want to tell you because I wanted you to be natural in the footage—"

Footage? "Wait a minute."

"—but you wouldn't believe how great this is already. That virginity stuff we talked about last night came out great—well, a little dark, but very moody with Clea all lit by those candles, and I can use the stuff she said as a voice-over—"

"Amy!"

Amy stopped and Sophie reminded herself to be supportive. "You filmed me on the porch last night?"

"All of us," Amy said. "I set up the camera in the bushes. It's good stuff, Soph. And then today I interviewed Frank and got him to talk to the camera and he really comes across as the butthead he is."

"Is that fair? Did he realize—"

"He knew he was on camera. He signed a release. And we're going to have so much stuff to cut together, it's going to be great."

Sophie leaned forward. "Amy, you're conning these people. They're signing releases because they think they'll look great, and you're—"

"I'm not conning them," Amy said, indignant. "And even

if I am, I'm not taking anybody's money. I'm just filming what they say. I'm not changing their words. I'm just getting what I want."

"You have to think about other people," Sophie said, and Amy said, "No, that was you and Mama, trying to save everybody. Davy and Daddy and I, we know you can't save anybody so you might as well take care of yourself. And I'm not hurting anybody here. They all *want* to be in this movie."

She was so much like their father—all redheaded innocence, suckering people in with the Dempsey smile—maintaining to the end that it wasn't his fault if they trusted him, and that he never, ever lied.

But everybody he met lost something to him, just the same.

"Sophie, this is real filmmaking," Amy said, leaning closer, radiating sincerity. "Doing the wedding videos has been great, but it's been seven years, and I've learned everything I can from them. This is what I want to do now. This is my chance to get out. Maybe the only chance I'll get."

Amy's heart was in her eyes, and Sophie took a deep breath and thought, *I knew she'd get tired of those dumb weddings someday.* The thought of Amy leaving was painful, life without her was almost unimaginable, but the thought of her staying when she wanted to go was worse.

"I want to cut the documentary and go to L.A. and use it to get work there," Amy was saying. She looked as if she were holding her breath waiting for Sophie to say something.

Are you out of your mind? wouldn't seem supportive. "L.A.'s a tough town."

"I know." Amy bobbed her head up and down, eager to agree. "But Davy's out there. He can help me. It's his turn anyway." Her smile faded. "So what happens to you, now that I'm leaving?"

Sophie shrugged. "I don't know. I guess I'll have to think

about what I want for a change." *After I get finished worrying about you.*

"Don't you have any dreams?" Amy said. "Isn't there something—"

"No," Sophie said. When she thought about it, it was sad. Thirty-two years old, and she had no idea what she wanted from life. She thought of Phin on the back porch. Maybe his question hadn't been so smart-assed after all.

"Are you going to sell the business?" Amy said.

"Probably," Sophie said.

"Can I have half?"

Sophie blinked at her. "Of course. What were you thinking?"

"I was thinking you needed the money more," Amy said. "I'm going to have a career. You're sort of stuck."

Ouch. "Take half the money," Sophie said. "I can get myself unstuck."

"Thank you," Amy said. "I mean it. Thanks."

"You're welcome," Sophie said. "Now get some sleep."

Amy stood up, hesitating as if there was something else, and then she bent and wrapped her arms around Sophie's neck.

"I love you so much, Soph," she whispered.

"I love you, too, Ame," Sophie said, patting her arm as she tried to breathe. *That's the only reason I'm letting you go.*

When Amy had gone upstairs, Sophie sat back and thought about her future. She wasn't worried; smart, organized people who worked hard always found jobs. But she didn't want a job, she wanted what Amy had, a career that fulfilled her.

It occurred to her that the reason she'd never figured out what she wanted to be was that she'd spent so much time concentrating on what she didn't want to be: a Dempsey. She let herself think about doing what Davy did, conning slightly crooked rich people out of their shady gains, but it held no appeal. Well, that was good. But maybe if she opened her mind, she could channel the Dempsey genes into something productive and fun, like Amy had, getting people's weak spots on film.

Maybe if she just opened herself to life, she could have fun. There must be something in her life that was recreational. She thought of the mayor, smiling lazily at her, detached and undemanding and her pulse kicked up. *He'd be fun.*

It was a dangerous thought, so she only entertained it for one rebellious minute before straightening herself out and heading up the stairs to bed, the dog on her heels.

The last thing she needed was the mayor.

On Friday, Phin's hassles started early.

First his mother gave him grief at breakfast because he'd been out to the Whipple farm twice.

"Associating with those movie people can do you no good," Liz had told him across the white linen expanse of her dining-room table. "Stephen has mentioned it to me several times already. Don't give him any leverage, Phin."

"What's 'associating'?" Dillie said around a mouthful of bran muffin.

"Hanging out with," Phin told her.

"Do not talk with your mouth full," Liz told her. "It's rude and disgusting." She transferred her attention back to Phin. "Don't go out to that farm again." She didn't add, "It's rude and disgusting," but the implication was clear.

"I did not associate," Phin said as he buttered Dillie another muffin. "I went out on Wednesday with Wes to see about the accident, and I went back yesterday because Wes roped me into looking at their electricity." Liz started to say something, and he added, "And I would also like to point out that I'm over twenty-one, so you can stop hassling me about my peer group. Talk to Dillie about this Jamie Barclay. I have grave doubts about Jamie Barclay." He grinned at Dillie and handed her the muffin.

"Jamie Barclay is an *excellent* person," Dillie said, taking it. "I should associate with her."

"Jamie's stepfather is the new vice president at the Third National," Liz said. "Her mother joined the Ladies' Club and is very nice. Dillie is allowed to associate." She smiled at Dillie and leaned forward to wipe the butter off her granddaughter's chin. "You missed your mouth," she told her, and Dillie grinned back. Then Liz turned back to Phin. "Now about these movie people—"

"I have to go to the bookstore now." Phin pushed back from the table. He kissed Dillie on the top of the head and said, "Behave," but Liz followed him out onto the broad front porch before he could escape.

"I didn't want to discuss this in front of Dillie," she said, "but I know you and women. It's one thing for you to conduct most of your liaisons out of town, another thing to do it here with a woman we know nothing—"

"'Liaisons'?" Phin turned around, incredulous. "I replaced a fucking fuse, for Christ's sake." Okay, he'd lusted after a hostile woman, too, but he hadn't done anything about it.

"Don't look so outraged," Liz said. "I know you, and I worry about you. It's past time you settled down. Dillie needs a mother, and I want to see you married to a decent woman this time. You're almost forty, Phin."

"I'm thirty-six," Phin said. "And I have no intention of getting married again, and if I did, it wouldn't be to Rachel Garvey, which I know is where you're going with this. Which reminds me, stop talking about Rachel in front of Dillie. You're upsetting her."

"I never said anything to Dillie," Liz said.

"Well, she has big ears, and she's not stupid. Just forget the whole Rachel idea." He shook his head at her. "What is it with you lately? You never used to be this nuts."

"I think you should get married before the election," Liz said. "Weddings are popular. And—"

"Have you been hitting the cooking sherry?"

Liz stopped, two spots of color high on her cheeks. "Phineas Tucker, that is no way to talk to your mother."

"Well, this is no way to talk to your son." Phin met her eyes, and she had the grace to flush. "Have you listened to yourself? You want me to marry a woman I don't love so you can win the next election and get a grandson to win the one that'll come up thirty years from now."

Liz's blush deepened. "If you'd find somebody acceptable on your own, I wouldn't interfere. But I don't see the problem. You like Rachel, she's a lovely girl, she's very intelligent, and she's wonderful with Dillie."

"Dillie doesn't think so, and Rachel has no more interest in marrying me than I do her, so knock it off."

"Rachel's mother says she does." Liz moved in for the kill. "She says Rachel is shy, but she cares about you."

"Rachel is shy?" Phin laughed. "Rachel is a barracuda. And she does not want to marry me. If I know Rachel, what she wants is to get away from Virginia and Stephen."

"Nonsense," Liz said. "Rachel is very close to her parents."

"That's why she wants to get away." Phin turned to go down the Hill. "I'm going to work now. Try to regain your sanity before I come home."

"I just want what's best for you," Liz called after him.

"The words every son hates to hear," he called back.

It was a good thing he loved his mother, he thought, as he walked down the Hill to the bookstore. If he didn't, he'd have put her in a home for the politically deranged long ago. The problem was, she'd bought too far into the Tucker legacy. His dad had been hipped on it, but that was at least understandable since he'd been raised with a box of *Tucker for Mayor: More of the Same* posters as a booster seat. But Liz was a Yarnell. Hill people. She should have had some proportion on politics.

Except that she'd loved his father so very much. Phin slowed a little as he remembered them together, so wrapped up in each other and politics that they'd almost forgotten they had a son. He could remember a few times he'd had his parents' full attention—like the day he'd told his kindergarten class he wanted to be a fireman; they'd spent hours with him that afternoon—but mostly it had been the two of them, together against the world.

And now she was alone. He turned to look back at her and was distracted by the water tower, thrusting through the trees behind the houses.

It was bright, bright red.

"Oh, Christ," he said, and walked faster to the bookstore to find out what had gone wrong this time.

Chapter Four

It looks like the Whore of Babylon," Phin told Wes later that afternoon as they sat on the bookstore porch at closing time.

Wes said, "You should hear Stephen. He came into the station and told me Hildy had conspired with the Coreys to humiliate him."

"Yeah, I can see Hildy meeting two high school kids in a dark alley just to give Stephen heart failure." Phin sighed. "Which, unfortunately, he didn't have."

"Hey," Wes said. "I told you. No death."

"I don't want him to die," Phin said. "I just want him sick enough to resign from the council and take his rubber stamp of a wife with him. He's still trying to block the new streetlights because they're too expensive."

"He'll resign when they pry his cold dead hands from around his campaign posters," Wes said. "Which will now read, *Paint the Water Tower White and Buy Cheaper Streetlights.*"

"Forget the campaign," Phin said. "Tell me something new."

"I watched Amy's tape," Wes said, and the way he said it made Phin pay attention. "There were a couple of interesting things on it."

"I don't need any more suspense in my life," Phin said.

"The Garveys ran their stop sign, too," Wes said. "Clear as day on the tape; they didn't even do a rolling stop, just went right through."

"And they hit the Dempseys, so Sophie had the right of way," Phin said. "Although they both ran the signs, so fry them both, that's my advice."

"Well, there's one other thing," Wes said. "Stephen wasn't driving, Virginia was."

Phin frowned at him. "Why would they lie about a thing like that?"

"Don't know," Wes said. "I'm looking into it. But it's interesting, isn't it?"

"I don't want 'interesting,'" Phin said. "I want boring and calm." He looked away from Wes and caught sight of the water tower again, glowing like a bloodred bullet in the sun. "Why did the Coreys paint the tower red, anyway? I couldn't find them to get any answers."

"They're out painting the Whipple farmhouse," Wes said. "And they painted it red because Stephen gave them the cheap stuff the school buys in bulk for the athletic department, and the white wouldn't cover."

Phin leaned back in his chair and put his feet on the porch rail. "You know, I think I like it red. Perks the place right up. And it annoys Stephen. I can't see a downside here."

"Amy and Sophie are perking the place up, too," Wes said, and Phin kept his face expressionless.

"Yeah, my mother thinks so. Have you got anything out of Amy yet?"

"I'm biding my time," Wes said.

"I meant about the movie," Phin said. "Your sex life is your business."

"It appears to be a love story," Wes said. "Frank seems to think he's the lead."

"And he's not?"

"Judging from what I saw Amy shoot today, that would be Rob."

Phin winced. "Frank's going to be real unhappy about that."

"Yeah," Wes said. "The perfect start to your midlife crisis: Your son sleeps with the woman you always wanted and takes your part in the movie you've been waiting for all your life."

"But are they shooting porn?"

"I don't know," Wes said. "If they are, I hope they let me watch."

"That'll be a major consolation if Stephen uses that to throw me out of office," Phin groused. " 'At least Wes got to watch,' that's what I'll say."

"You're being irrational," Wes said. "You haven't even voted in the permit yet. And you said yourself, Sophie doesn't look like the type."

"I changed my mind," Phin said. "Sophie is capable of anything except changing a fuse and reading. She's obsessed with film. I don't think she's ever picked up a book."

"The movie-quote thing? Amy says she does that when she gets nervous. It was a game they used to play when they were little." Wes leaned back. "I get the feeling that they didn't have a great childhood."

"I can tell you that sometime during it, somebody like me did a job on Sophie," Phin said. "She spits every time she sees me."

"Maybe she just doesn't like you," Wes said, and Phin said, "Thank you. I'm sure that's it."

Wes stood up. "Got you mad, did I? Good. Let's play pool. Maybe I can beat you, now that you're distracted."

"Don't count on it." Phin stood up. "You going to look into this Stephen thing?"

"Have to," Wes said. "Insurance companies like to have the whole story. And so do I. I'm thorough. Which reminds me, we're going to the Tavern tonight."

"On a Friday?" Phin thought about the development crowd that came in on Fridays. He liked his bars quiet and dark. "I don't think so."

"You're driving," Wes said. "So you can leave and strand me there, and I can catch a ride home with Amy."

Phin closed his eyes. "I have to go through this hell so you can get laid?"

"No," Wes said. "I just want to get closer."

"She's leaving on Sunday," Phin said.

"She's just going back to Cincinnati," Wes said. "I can drive an hour to make my move. Nine o'clock. You can tuck Dill in and then go play with Sophie."

Sophie. "And I'd want to play with Sophie because she's so warm and cuddly? No."

"Just play with her until I hook up with Amy," Wes said. "We're buddies. You're supposed to come through for me."

Sophie. And that mouth. "I'll pick you up at nine," Phin said. "No earlier. There's only so much Tavern and Sophie I can stand."

• • •

When Rachel got home, her mother was sitting at their red-checked-plastic-covered kitchen table, snapping beans, waiting for her as always.

"Hello, baby," Virginia said, "I ran into Georgia Lutz today," and Rachel thought, *Uh-oh.* "She told me what a good job you were doing at the Whipple Farm. I'm not sure that's a good place for you to be." Rachel started to protest and Virginia added, "But your father seems to think it's a good idea, so I guess it's fine."

"Daddy does?" That couldn't be right.

"I called him after I talked to Georgia, and he said we should let you go out there. He seemed pleased."

That *definitely* couldn't be right.

"And that nice Sophie said they were going home on Sunday," Virginia said. "So you won't be out there that much anyway."

Rachel eyed her mother and risked her next move. "Sophie's going back to Cincinnati, but Amy's not. I'm sort of hoping Sophie might hire me to take Amy's place in their video business."

Virginia's hands stilled over the beans, and Rachel rushed on. "Wouldn't that be wonderful, for me to get a job so close to home?" She had no intention of ever coming back to Temptation, but her mother didn't have to know that.

"I don't think so, dear." Her mother smiled as she began to snap the ends off the beans again. "Your father wouldn't let you go that far."

I'm twenty, Rachel wanted to say. *I can go wherever I want.*

"And besides, he needs you at the store." Virginia stopped to smile lovingly at her. "And I just don't know what I'd do without my baby. I'd worry so much if you left. You don't want me to worry, do you?"

Rachel felt a flush of resentment. "What if staying here

makes me unhappy? You don't want me to be unhappy, do you?"

"Your father and I know what's best for you, Rachel. You've always wanted things that weren't good for you. Remember when you used to ask for two cotton candies at the fair? And we never let you have two because we knew you'd get sick."

"This isn't cotton candy," Rachel said, trying to keep the desperation out of her voice. "This is my life."

"Why don't you find something here in Temptation?" Virginia put the last of the beans in the bowl and stood up. "Let's see, what could you do? Not something too demanding because you'll be raising your own children soon." She picked up the bowl, and Rachel revised her plan.

"I suppose it's possible Sophie will stay here and work," Rachel said, watching her mother from the corner of her eye. "Phin's interested, you can tell, and if he decides he wants her, she'll have to stay."

"That's ridiculous," Virginia said, clutching the bowl to her breasts. "The two of you are practically engaged."

"Mother." Rachel took a deep breath. *Now or never.* "Look, Phin and I were never engaged, we never wanted to be engaged, and we're never going to be engaged." Her mother's eyes narrowed, and Rachel backtracked fast. "And anyway, I'm sure he's after Sophie now. He gets that look in his eye whenever she's around. He never gets that look for me." *Thank God.*

"That's just physical," Virginia said primly. "He made that mistake with that Diane but he won't do it again. Liz'll see to that. I'll call her and tell her about this Sophie and she'll put a stop to it." She nodded at Rachel. "You're the right one for him, and Liz knows it. The two of you have known each other forever. That's a real foundation for a marriage. Now, come peel potatoes, and then you can do some weeding."

"Fabulous," Rachel said, more determined than ever to get out of town.

By nine, the Tavern was as bad as Phin had thought it would be: Too many people determined to have a good time if it killed them, and Billy Ray Cyrus on the jukebox. He and Wes took their beers back to one of the initial-scarred booths along the back wall; half an hour later, he had a second beer and a headache, and he was ready to strand Wes for real.

"It's after nine," he told Wes. "They're not coming. Let's go back to the store and play pool."

Then Wes smiled past him, and he turned and saw Amy in a blue tube top.

And behind her was Sophie.

Sophie's hair was in loose, dark ringlets on her shoulders, and her cheeks were flushed, and she was wearing a short pink dress that fit tightly under her breasts, and it wasn't until Phin had taken it all in that he realized he had no idea what she'd been wearing the rest of the week. Something brown, he thought. Nothing like this.

He hadn't even noticed she'd *had* breasts until this. Just what he needed, something else to think about besides her mouth.

"Now what?" she said, looking at him warily as he tried to keep his eyes on her face.

"Cute dress." He slid over to make room for her since Amy had already taken a seat on the other side of the booth next to Wes.

"It is not cute." Sophie slid in beside him and put her drink on the pitted table. "I am never cute. But thank you for the compliment anyway. I borrowed it from Clea. She wore it in high school." Sophie stared down at herself doubtfully. "I think it was in style then."

"If you don't like being called cute, don't wear pink." Phin looked down the scoop neck of her dress. Excellent cleavage.

Sophie tugged up on the neck. "It's not pink, it's magenta. Or maybe watermelon."

"It's pink," Phin said. "As is your bra, I see."

"Those nine stitches didn't teach you a thing, did they?" Sophie gave up on the neck of her dress and picked up her drink.

"What is that?" Phin said, fearing the worst.

"Rum and Diet Coke," Sophie said. "And no cracks about what a wimpy drink it is. I like it."

He was sitting next to a woman with such lousy taste in alcohol that she'd mix good rum with aspartame. He looked across the table at Wes, who shrugged and made a small motion with his head that said, *You can go now.* Amy was talking a mile a minute about lights and camera angles, and Wes went back to listening to everything she said, his arm draped behind her across the back of the booth. One happy police chief.

Sophie was looking around the bar as if it were a zoo. " 'No point in mentioning those bats,' " she said to Amy, and Phin frowned. Then she added, " 'The poor bastard will see them soon enough,' " and he said, "Oh. Hunter S. Thompson."

Sophie frowned at him. "That's Johnny Depp. Who's Hunter S. Thompson?"

"Author," Phin said. "*Fear and Loathing in Las Vegas.* Great book. Who's Johnny Depp?"

"Actor," Sophie said. "*Fear and Loathing in Las Vegas.* Mediocre movie."

"So you're nervous," Phin said, and tried not to watch while Sophie wet her lips with her tongue.

"Me? What do I have to be nervous about?" Sophie said, and spilled some of her drink.

Phin pulled a wad of napkins from the holder and dropped them on the spill, just as Wes patted his shirt pocket and said to Amy, "I've got something for you." He pulled out a glasses case and gave it to her.

She opened it and said, *"My sunglasses,"* the way another, less interesting woman might have said, *"My diamonds."*

"I found them on the dashboard," Wes said. "Seemed like the least we could do to make up for such a lousy welcome."

"You're kidding," Sophie said, as she mopped up the last of her drink.

Amy put the glasses on. They were bizarre: thick pink plastic cat's-eye frames studded with rhinestones in the corners. Even the lenses were pink.

"You got pink lenses!" Amy was so delighted she was almost in Wes's lap.

He looked pretty delighted, too. "I couldn't tell what color the old ones were," he told her. "But Mindy at the optometrist's said pink would be best."

"Mindy is a genius," Amy said from behind her glasses. "These lenses are *much* better than the old ones."

"Got those turned around pretty fast, didn't you?" Phin said quietly to Wes as Sophie leaned forward to see the glasses better.

"I sent Duane to Cincinnati to one of those one-hour places," Wes said, not taking his eyes off Amy.

"You sent your deputy to Cincinnati so you could get— *ouch!*" Phin rubbed his shin as Sophie leaned back and smiled at Wes.

"You are obviously one of the good ones," she told him. "We're very impressed here."

"We certainly are," Amy said. "These are *great*."

Phin's work as a best friend was done. A smart man would leave. He turned to ask Sophie to scoot over so he could go, and look down her dress again.

On the other hand, if he left too soon, the whole setup would look as contrived as it was. It wouldn't kill him to stay a couple of minutes longer so Amy wouldn't catch on. "So how's the movie going?" he asked Sophie over the din, and she shot him a suspicious glance.

"Just fine, thank you," she said, and sipped her disgusting drink.

"You never did tell me what it's called."

"*Return to Temptation.*"

"Catchy title. I don't suppose I could talk you out of using the name of the town."

Sophie shook her head as she looked out over the crowd, and he watched the way her curls bounced on her shoulders. "I don't think so. Who are all these people?"

"People who live in Temptation," Phin said. "What did you think, we bus them in on Fridays?"

"I didn't think there were this many people *in* Temptation."

"Over two thousand," Phin said. "And every one of them contrary and stubborn as mules."

"And you know them all," Sophie said. "Who's the cute guy in the green windbreaker over there, talking to Georgia?"

Phin bent closer to her to see where she was pointing, trying to ignore how her hair smelled like lavender. "Pete Alcott. He's part of their theater group. He moves a lot of scenery."

"I can understand that. He looks really strong."

"Not that strong."

"He's built very well."

"He can't play pool worth a damn. No position play at all.

Fixates on whatever ball is in front of him." Phin looked down to see her frowning at him. "Sorry. Of course you don't know pool. Amateurs just knock the balls in one at a time. Pros use position play which means they always know not only how they're going to play the ball in front of them, but how they're going to play the next two or three balls, too. That way every shot they take positions them for the next one."

"And Pete Whatsis takes it one ball at a time." Sophie nodded at him, her eyes wide. "That's very interesting. Thank you."

She smiled at him, full wattage, and every political instinct he had went on alert. He looked down into her big brown eyes and said, "What are you up to?"

"Nothing." She nodded over to where Frank stood at the bar with his back to his wife and his front to Clea. "How's Frank play?"

"He likes trick shots," Phin said, still wary. "Bank shots, combination shots. Frank plays in the moment. He thinks pool is a performance. And he loses a lot."

"How about Rob?"

Sophie pointed over to the neon blue jukebox where Rob was arguing with Rachel.

"Rob tries to think ahead, but he never practices the basics. So he plans ahead four balls and then miscues on the second one and that throws him off so much that he panics and just starts banging balls around."

"You play with Stephen Garvey?" Sophie asked.

"Why are you so interested?" Phin said.

"Because I never thought about pool like this." She sounded sincere. "It's so smart of you to figure this out. That you could tell what kind of person somebody is by the way he plays pool. I'd never have thought of that."

"That's because you can't," Phin said. "Some people are very sharp, but they never learned to play the game right. So they screw up, but it's not a function of personality."

"But Rob and Frank learned right?"

Phin nodded. "My dad taught all of us. And Ed Yarnell plays us, too. Good training."

"So how does Stephen Garvey play?" Sophie said, smiling at him, lush and warm and round in the dim light, and Phin gave up trying to figure out what she was up to.

"He plays position, but he hits the ball too hard. The harder you hit the ball, the smaller the pocket gets, so it's easier to miss. He thinks it's macho to slam the cue into the ball which is why he loses a lot."

"But not always," Sophie said thoughtfully.

Phin shrugged. "Sometimes you have to hit the ball hard. In those cases, he wins."

"Sophie!" Georgia slid in beside her and jammed her into Phin.

"Sorry," Sophie said to him. "Easy, Georgia, we're a little cramped here."

She shifted to make more room, and Phin could feel the warm length of her thigh against his. *Thank you, Georgia.* Not that he intended to do anything about it, that would be dumb, but having Sophie pressed up against him even briefly was a pleasure. He let his arm fall along the back of the booth.

"Amy showed me some of the tape today," Georgia was saying as she beamed across the table at Amy. "I was *so* impressed. There I was, right there on the television. You have to come back from Cincinnati to tape our theater productions from now on."

"I'm not staying in Cincinnati," Amy said, and Phin winced at the look on Wes's face. "I'm going to drive to L.A. as soon as I have the tape edited." She leaned across the table to Sophie. "I forgot to ask. Can I take the car? To L.A., I mean?"

"Oh." Sophie looked taken aback. "Sure."

And what are you going to use for transportation? Phin wanted to say, but the last time he'd suggested she think about herself, she'd gotten hostile.

"Well, *you* have to come back here to visit," Georgia was saying to Sophie. "We just really like you a lot."

"That's very sweet of you, Georgia. I like you all a lot, too." Sophie looked up at Phin, imploring instead of hostile: *Get me out of this.* Then she drained her rum and Coke.

Phin thought about offering her a ride home and decided to keep her trapped there a while longer. For one thing, she felt really good pressed up against him, which was selfish of him but fortunately, he didn't have a problem with selfish. For another, if she got tanked, maybe she'd come across with more information about the movie. He looked down her dress again. It was a real shame he wasn't in a position to encourage her to come across with some other stuff, too. That was the trouble with dangerous women: They were almost always attractive. "The devil's candy," he remembered. "Women who would ruin you as soon as look at you."

Sophie looked up at him pitifully, but before he could say anything, Georgia bellowed, "Frank!" and Frank turned around from Clea to scowl at her. "Sophie needs a drink, honey."

"No, really," Sophie said, but Frank nodded and came over a minute later with another rum and Coke.

"Clea said this is what you're drinking," he told her, delighted to be reporting that he'd had conversation with Clea, and Phin thought, *Frank, you're a moron and your wife is going to kill you.*

"Thanks," Sophie said. "But really, you shouldn't have."

"Well, we're all so pleased you're here." Frank smiled at Sophie and Amy.

"Yes, we are." Georgia toasted Sophie with her drink and spilled some of it on the table in the process.

"And that you brought Clea back to us," Frank finished.

Georgia put her glass down.

Frank looked back at Clea and Rob. "That boy of mine," he said. "He's so starstruck, he doesn't know which end is up."

Phin looked around Frank and saw Rob at the bar being dazzled by Clea, who looked pleased to have him there.

"If he's not careful, Rachel's going to get jealous," Frank said. "I better go tell him to take care of what he's got."

"Good advice," Georgia said, but Frank was already heading back to the bar. She turned to Sophie, "I'm sorry, but Clea Whipple is a fucking bitch from hell."

Phin winced, but Sophie just said, "Cheers," and drank another slug of rum and Diet Coke.

"She's still trying to get him, that bitch," Georgia said. "She's never gonna learn. She tried to get him in high school, bet she didn't tell you that, did she?"

"Uh, yeah, she did," Sophie said into her drink, but Georgia wasn't listening, which was about par for Georgia, Phin thought. Center of the universe, at least in her own mind, that was Georgia.

"Thought she was going to get him, but she didn't. I fixed that. I fixed that good." Georgia drank again. "You gotta keep men in line or they'll just run all over you."

Phin spared a moment of sympathy for Frank until he looked back and saw him at the bar, leaning into Clea's cleavage. *Get a grip, Frank*, he thought, and then he looked down Sophie's dress and thought, *Never mind, Frank*.

"But I got what I wanted," Georgia said. "You can get what you want, too." She squinted at Sophie. "What do you want?"

"World peace," Sophie said, and tried to move away from Georgia a little.

Since that pressed her up even closer to Phin, he tried to think kinder thoughts about Georgia, but it was hard.

"I got everything I wanted," Georgia said. "Except a little girl. I never got my little girl. Boys aren't the same."

"This is true," Sophie said, and shifted on the booth seat again.

Very true, Phin thought gratefully, as the lavender in Sophie's hair drifted up to him again. Of course, if he'd been born female, there'd be blood in his brain right now, but a little light-headedness seemed a small price to pay for the rush he was getting every time Sophie moved. He tried not to think about that, but that was hard, too. Everything was hard.

"I really wanted a little girl," Georgia said. "I really did. But we never got one. When that bitch got her big Hollywood break, Frank said we could try, and we tried and tried but I never did get my girl. And I had the *cutest* clothes already bought for her."

"Oh, God," Sophie said into her drink. When Georgia went on in detail about the cute little dresses—"smocked with little tiny roses"—Sophie let her head fall back against Phin's arm, and he started calculating square roots so he wouldn't lunge for her mouth.

"He's still mad because we had to get married," Georgia said, looking back at the bar. "That's why he's doing this. That's why."

"You didn't have to get married," Sophie said.

Georgia straightened. "No, we certainly did not."

Phin had heard all about Georgia's eleven-month pregnancy when Diane's rabbit had died. "She's lying just like that Georgia Lutz," his mother had said, but when Ed confirmed it, even Liz had been defeated. Too bad Frank hadn't had a Liz in his corner.

"We did not have to get married," Georgia repeated, staring now at Frank and Clea. When she turned back to Sophie, her face was tragic. "You do what you have to do," she told Sophie quietly, not sounding drunk at all. "You fight for what's yours, for your family, for the family you were meant to have. And they never forgive you for it, *they never do*. You just keep paying and paying."

Sophie put her drink down. "Are you all right, Georgia?"

Georgia looked back at the bar. "I'm just fine. I've got everything I want. And nobody's going to take it away. I'm Frank's leading lady, he needs me." She straightened. "Did he tell you we're doing *Carousel*? I'm the lead, of course, and . . ."

For the next two hours, Georgia rattled on, and Phin watched Sophie knock back her third and fourth drinks. She was pressed up warm against him, her curls brushing soft against his arm, and he'd long ago given up caring about the movie and was now seriously reconsidering his stand on dangerous women. It wasn't just Sophie's cleavage and her mouth; when she tilted her head to talk across the table, her neck curved so beautifully into her shoulder that it made him dizzy. The temptation to lean down and bite into that curve was becoming overwhelming, to lick his way up her throat and take that mouth, and then Wes said something and she laughed and turned her face up to him to share the joke, and he fell into her huge, warm, brown eyes and his mind went blank.

"Are you all right?" she said.

"Nope." He caught his breath and drained his beer. "Hot in here."

At midnight, when Sophie reached the bottom of her fourth glass, she put it down and said, "I didn't need that."

She was drunk, he realized; not obnoxious drunk like Georgia, but still too drunk for him to move on. He didn't mind seducing women whom drink had made cheerful, but he drew the line at those whom drink had made stupid.

Amy leaned forward. "You can't drink worth a damn, Soph. You ready to go?"

"I can walk it." Sophie nudged Georgia with her hip. "It's not that far."

"Honey, it's dark out there," Georgia protested, but she moved out of the booth.

"I have Mace," Sophie told her as she slid across the seat. "And I'm not afraid to use it."

"Tell you what." Phin slid right behind her, chasing her heat. "I'll take you home.

"You sure?" Amy said. "I'm almost done here."

Phin smiled at Amy. "No problem. If you'll take Wes home when you're ready to go, I can drop Sophie off."

Amy nodded, and Phin steered Sophie to the door. "Give me the Mace," he said. "I don't want any accidents."

"Wimp." She walked away from him toward the door, and she looked as lush from behind as she did from the front.

I am a civilized man, he told himself as he followed her out the door. *I am not going to touch that inebriated woman.*

At least, not tonight.

The rum had made Sophie's knees loose, and as she sat in the dark in Phin's car—he had a Volvo, of course, tastefully expensive and understated—she was terrified the problem might spread to her lips and she'd say something stupid. Like, *Take me.*

She stole a glance at him as he drove down the main road

in the dark, his hand draped over the wheel, oblivious to her there beside him, and she felt a little shiver at how dark it was and how close he was and how damn sexy he was.

That was not a good thought so she tried to squelch it, but the fact was that she was in the dark with a powerful man, a *town boy*, and he was gorgeous and Not Her Kind and it was a real turn-on. She squirmed a little with guilt and pleasure, and Phin said, "You okay?"

"Sure," she said. "Why wouldn't I be?"

"All that rum and Coke," he said. "If you're going to throw up, let me know and I'll pull over. I just had the upholstery cleaned."

"Oh, that's romantic," she said, and he shot her a startled glance.

Right. They weren't supposed to be romantic. See? This was what loose lips did for you. "That's not what I meant. I meant that wasn't polite or something. What's the word I'm looking for?"

"I have no idea," Phin said, as he slowed to turn into the farm lane. "Your thought processes elude me."

"Oh, really?" Sophie knew that was lame, but she'd left her verbal skills in the last rum and Coke. "I fail to see why my thought processes are of any interest to you at all." There. That was pretty good.

"They're not until they interfere with my town," Phin said as the Volvo bumped down the short lane. "This movie of yours is disrupting things."

"Hey, *not* our idea," Sophie said. "*We* did not ask for volunteers from the populace. They just"—she waved her hands, almost smacking Phin in the eye—"showed up on their own."

Phin had ducked to avoid her hand. "Right." He pulled the car up in front of the porch and cut the ignition, and Sophie could hear the crickets creaking in the darkness. Lovely.

"You okay?" Phin said, interrupting the crickets.

"Will you quit saying that? I'm not drunk." Sophie swung open the door and almost fell out. "I'm just not used to alcohol. It'll evaporate off in a minute."

"No, it won't." Phin got out and came around to her door while she was trying to get her bearings. "Give me your hand."

"Why?" Sophie said belligerently.

"So you don't fall on your ass," Phin said.

"Nice way for a mayor to talk." Sophie took his hand. It was warm and firm and strong—he almost lifted her out of the car with that one hand alone—and when she was standing, she found herself inches from a broad chest that blocked out the moonlight. "You're like a total eclipse," she said, and tried to detour around him.

"Yeah, I get that all the time." He let go, and she began to walk toward the house, escaping before she did something *really* stupid.

"Thank you for the ride, Phineas," she called back over her shoulder. "You may go now."

The wind rustled through the trees and made her shiver because it was so warm and alive on her skin. When she stopped to feel the breeze, she heard the wash of the river and thought how good it would be to cool off listening to the river in the wind in the moonlight. She turned and headed for the path at the side of the house.

"A little higher and to the left," Phin called after her. "You're missing the porch."

"All part of my plan," she called back. "Good night."

"Oh, great." She heard the car door slam behind her. "Where are you going?"

"Not your concern," she said. "I'm not disrupting anybody. You can go home now."

She rounded the corner of the house and it was dark, the

trees blotting out the moonlight as effectively as Phin had, and she shivered because she was alone in the gloom.

"What are you doing?" Phin said from behind her. She started and tripped over a tree root, and he caught her arm before she could fall.

"I've told you a million times, stop sneaking up on me like that. I'm going to see the river in the moonlight." She pulled free and headed for the path again.

"Oh, good. The river. Excellent place for a woman who can't walk without falling over."

Sophie came out behind the house into a silvery blue landscape that fell away to the water like a movie set. "Oh," she said and stopped so that Phin bumped into her from behind. She spread her hands apart to frame the scene, flexing her fingers so that her rings glinted in the moonlight. "This is beautiful."

"Yeah," Phin said. "It is." For once he didn't sound exasperated or bored, and she looked over her shoulder to find him watching her.

"You get this all the time," she said. "You live in this movie set of a town, and you belong absolutely and everybody loves you and I bet you don't even appreciate it because you're too busy being cool and powerful."

"Do you have *any* idea of what you're talking about?" Phin said.

"Yes." Sophie started down the slope to the river. "I'm talking about what you have and what I don't. All you see is politics and problems. I bet right now you're thinking about how liable you'd be if I drowned."

"Well, I wasn't until you mentioned it," Phin said. "Try not to fall in."

"Maybe I will." Sophie turned around and walked backward so she could face him while she argued. "Maybe I'll just walk right in to see what it feels like."

"It feels cold and wet," Phin said. "Much like your bathtub, only with fish stink." He reached out and grabbed her dress at her stomach.

"Hey!" she said, but he had her stopped in her tracks.

"Two more steps and you'll be wearing the fish stink," Phin told her. "We haven't had rain for a while and the river's low. It gets muddy here." He tugged her closer to him but took a step back at the same time, a semi-gentleman. "Stay on the grass."

"You're no romantic," Sophie said, as she pulled his fingers off her dress.

"I certainly am," Phin said. "When the occasion calls for it. This occasion calls for the rescue squad."

"Prove it." Sophie looked around for a dry place to sit and headed for the dock. No mud there.

"Fall in the river," Phin said from behind her. "I'll pull you out."

"No, prove the romantic part. Tell me one thought you've had out here that didn't have to do with lawsuits or fish stink or river hazards." Sophie stepped up on the dock, kicked her shoes off, and went to sit on the edge.

"Julie Ann," Phin said. "And I was kidding. Do not fall in."

Sophie eased her feet into the cool, cool water and sighed before turning her attention back to Phin. "Julie Ann is somebody you had sex with here, I gather. That doesn't count. Romantic is not sweaty."

Phin sat down on the dock behind her. "It is if you do it right. Julie Ann's from a song. My grandma used to sing me to sleep with it."

"My mom used to sing us to sleep with 'I Only Want to Be with You.' It's pretty when you sing it slow." Sophie leaned back on her hands and looked up at the stars. "Was 'Julie Ann' a pretty song?"

"Yes," Phin said from behind her. "One line was about Julie

Ann in the moonlight, with her silver rings on her hands. When you held your hands up, your rings picked up the moonlight."

"That is romantic," Sophie said. "I concede. Sing the song."

"No," Phin said.

"So much for romance." The sky overhead was dark as velvet, and the moonlight was luminous blue. "Why was she out in the moonlight?"

"Her lover betrayed her and she wandered off into the mountains."

That sounded lovely, wandering off into the dark, looking for a dangerous, hot lover to replace the old, boring one. "Did she find someone in the mountains?" She leaned back farther just to feel her body stretch.

"A bear."

Sophie jerked her head around to look at him. He had stretched out on the dock with his hands behind his head, and he was looking at the stars, too, pretty much ignoring her.

"She fell in love with a bear?"

"No, a bear ate her." Phin rolled his head to look at her. "Appalachia is not big on silly love songs."

"A bear ate her." Sophie shook her head. "Leave it to you to think that's romantic."

"The song's beautiful." Phin looked back at the stars. "It ends with her ghost wearing a crown of sorrow. Very romantic."

"Dead women are not romantic," Sophie said flatly.

"Okay, she's not dead," Phin said. "The bear ate her, and she came her brains out."

Sophie felt her laugh spurt before she could stop herself. "Oh, *very* nice. That's not romantic, either."

"It is if you do it right."

Sophie thought about it. "I must not be doing it right."

"It wouldn't be you that isn't doing it right," Phin said. "It'd be the bear."

"No picking on the bear," she said. "Liberated women take care of themselves. 'I've read *The Second Sex*. I've read *The Cinderella Complex*. I'm responsible for my own orgasm.'"

"Why?"

"What do you mean, 'Why?' That's a line from a movie. *Tootsie*. It's a famous line. I can't believe you didn't recognize it."

"I don't watch movies," Phin said. "I read. And I repeat, why would your orgasm be your responsibility during oral sex?"

Sophie sat up a little. His tone was matter-of-fact, but his subject matter wasn't. "I don't think I want to talk about this."

"Okay," Phin said.

Sophie splashed her feet in the river and tried to think of something else. Talking about oral sex with Phineas T. Tucker was not something a smart woman would do. If you talked about sex with men, they often took it as a sign you wanted to have some. And then where would she be? She let her mind slide off that one fast, and it ended up back on his question.

Of course she wanted to be responsible for her own orgasm. She was an independent woman in control of her own life. She wasn't about to throw herself at some man and self-ishly demand that he satisfy her while she just lay back and *enjoyed* herself—

No, that wasn't right, either.

"It's because I'd have to depend on somebody else to give me what I want," she said, and Phin rolled his head to look at her. "I'd be one of those clingy women like Virginia Garvey or Georgia Lutz who just wait for men to take care of them and then are disappointed when they don't. If I take responsibility, then I can't be disappointed with anybody but me. I have control."

"And you see that as an improvement."

"It's empowering," Sophie said uncertainly. The rum and Coke were wearing off and so was the river. It still sounded and felt wonderful, but the fish stink was there, too. Reality, making its usual appearance just when she was getting somewhere.

"'Empowering.'" Phin didn't sound impressed.

"Well, it's better than just lying back and hoping for the best." Sophie kicked the water.

"Ever tried that?" Phin said.

Sophie kicked the water again. "I don't want to talk about this."

"Okay," Phin said, and went back to watching the stars.

The amount of water she was splashing was ruining the peaceful effect of the river so she stopped and let it flow past her ankles. The silence stretched out until all she could think of was Phin lying behind her. He wasn't that attractive. He was a pain in the butt. He probably thought she was uptight just because she was independent. He didn't even know what he was talking about. Her heart pounded harder the more she thought about him.

"Sex isn't what's important anyway," she said loftily. "It's the relationship that matters, and relationships take work." He didn't say anything, so she went on to fill the silence. "I mean, sure, it sounds good to just hand everything over to somebody else, but that's not how it works in real life." She felt angry about that, which was totally inappropriate, and she was pretty sure it was the rum and Coke betraying her, but it might have been her life.

"Depends on the version of real life you're using," Phin said.

"Well, in my version, you have to be careful all the time

and you get nothing for free," Sophie said waspishly. "Especially orgasms."

"Then you need another version."

Sophie lost her breath as the silence stretched out again. Well, if he made a pass, she'd say no. She'd just turn around and look at that great face and better body, and say no. Who did he think he was, anyway? She certainly knew who she was, and she wasn't the kind of woman who—

"Come here," Phin said, and Sophie felt his voice in the pit of her stomach.

She shook her head.

"You've got nothing to lose," he told her. "Day after tomorrow you're gone, and we'll never see each other again. This is your one shot at being selfish. Let somebody take care of you for a change." She swallowed as she tried to get her breath, and he said, "Come here and let me give you an orgasm you don't have to work for."

The heat spread fast and low in her, and Sophie bit her lip and tried not to feel anything. *Don't be dumb*, she told herself. *You are not this kind of woman, this is not what you want*, but her breath came faster and it was what she wanted, *he* was what she wanted. She opened her mouth to say no, but what came out was, "Why would you want to do that?"

"So I can touch you," he said. "I've wanted to since the first time I saw you on the porch."

There definitely wasn't enough air by the river. The heat was driving it away. If she turned around and looked at him, she'd probably asphyxiate. "You didn't even know me on the porch. You don't know me now."

"That's the beauty of it," Phin said. "No guilt. No responsibility. Just pleasure."

She did turn to look at him then, and he met her eyes

coolly. He had propped himself up on one elbow, but there was no tension anywhere in his body—she closed her eyes because he had such a beautiful body—no pressure there on her at all. He could have been offering her dinner and his voice would have sounded the same.

"You wouldn't care if I said no, would you?" Sophie said, and he looked surprised.

"It wouldn't ruin my evening." He sat up slowly. "Okay, not a good idea. I apologize. Let me walk you back to the house, and we'll forget—"

"I'd have to be depraved to say yes to something like that," Sophie said, and her voice sounded thick. "I'd have to be . . ."

She stopped because she couldn't get the words out, and he watched her for a moment and then he leaned closer. "Wild," he said, softly. "Reckless." He was so close his lips were almost touching hers, and she knew he was going to kiss her. But then he whispered, *"Satisfied,"* and bit her lower lip, and the ache made her moan, and then he did kiss her, tasting her mouth as if she were candy, easing her down onto the dock as she clutched his shirt and arched into him, depraved and abandoned after all.

Chapter Five

Phin's mouth was hot on hers where Sophie had been sure it would be cool, and she tasted the beer he'd been drinking and something else that she thought might be the intoxicating promise of sex without responsibility, or maybe it was just Phin. Then he pulled her hand off his shirt and put his hand on her breast, and the world swung around.

She broke the kiss and tried to catch her breath even while she clung to him. The river gurgled away under the rough boards of the dock, and the breeze was warm, and his hand was hot on her, and when he kissed her again, this time teasing her lips with his tongue, she opened on a quick breath and let him take her mouth completely.

This is wrong, she thought, but she couldn't remember why anything that felt this good would be wrong unless it was just because it felt so good. He kissed his way down the curve of her neck, into the hollow of her shoulder, and found a nerve there she didn't know she had and brought it alive as he pressed her onto the dock with the hard length of his body, and when she rocked under him, she heard him suck in his breath and that made her hotter, too.

Then his hand was on her thigh, and she felt him slide the short skirt of her dress up, and the slipperiness of the fabric and the weight of his hand and the prickle of her skin made her shudder. He kissed her again, and his mouth was as hot as before, his tongue as tantalizing, but his fingers were moving across her hip, under her dress, and she couldn't concentrate on his mouth anymore. He eased the elastic of her underpants down, and then his fingers slid against her, between her legs, and she went mindless.

She closed her eyes at his touch and said, "Oh"—too hot to feel embarrassed—and he kissed her again as he stroked her over and over. Then he slid his finger inside her and made her body jolt from the pure pleasure of it. "Tell me when it feels good," he whispered in her ear, and she said, "Oh my *God*," and he laughed—the first time she'd heard him laugh—and said, "No, when it feels *really* good," and moved his finger to curve it inside her. "Here?" he said, and she shook her head, wanting to tell him that the clitoris wasn't inside, that he'd passed it on his way in, but he said, "Wait," and slipped a second finger in. He moved higher this time until he hit something so good that Sophie jolted against him and said, "Oh, God, *there*."

"I'll be back," he said and slid down her body, shoving her dress up at the same time so that the breeze that had been so warm chilled her stomach. And then he bent and licked into her, finding her clitoris with no problem at all, while his fingers made her crazy from inside.

She gave one fleeting thought to panic, and then she crossed her arms over her eyes and let her body take her where he wanted her to go, living in the heat of his mouth and the rhythm he built in her and the shudder and the shake of her breath as the tension twisted tighter inside her. He pressed her down, holding her to the dock as she moved mindlessly against his mouth and hand, letting him do it all, and the pleasure built and built and built until she felt the first surge in her blood. She cried out in the darkness, shuddering against his mouth, and he brought her back again and again while she did absolutely nothing at all, and it was glorious.

When he finally stopped, she lay there, letting her mind seep back in, feeling every muscle and nerve in her body celebrating. He pulled her underwear back up and kissed her stomach, and she felt the nerves there jump, and then he smoothed her dress down with the flat of his hand, and the weight of it felt wonderful, and through it all, she lay there thinking she should be feeling guilty, should be feeling grateful, but instead feeling too damn good to move.

Phin stretched out beside her, and she rolled her head to see him, almost surprised that it was him. The mayor, no less. "So, it's you," she said, her voice thick and satisfied.

"Yep," he said. "It's me. How soon we forget."

It was odd, not feeling the need to take care of him after sex. No relationship to foster. No ego to stroke. She looked back up at the stars, content to float in postorgasmic mindlessness. "Well, you were gone for days."

"I had work to do," he said. "Everything okay up here?"

"It was incredible," she said politely.

"I know," he said, and she thought about how nice it was that they weren't in a relationship so she wouldn't have to kill him for being arrogant about being right all the time.

"I think this is the part where you say something nice about me," Sophie said, not really caring.

"Why?" Phin said. "You didn't do anything."

Sophie smiled dreamily up at the stars. "I like you after all. You're consistent. And competent. You know, you don't get stars like this in Cincinnati."

"There's a lot of stuff here you don't get in Cincinnati," Phin said. "In fact, you just got some."

"I could tell Br—" Sophie began. "Oh, *no*." She sat up, cold with guilt, sandbagged by reality once again.

Phin sighed. "What now?"

"I just cheated on my significant other," Sophie said. "I didn't even *think* about him, I just invited you right on in and cheated on him. I'm scum."

"You didn't cheat on him," Phin said. "Although you might have mentioned him sooner."

Sophie looked at him with all the scorn she felt for herself. "Like you care."

"I don't," Phin said. "I just like having all the information I can get." He turned his head to meet her eyes. "And the damnedest thing, Sophie, I always have this feeling you're holding something out on me."

"Clearly I wasn't holding out tonight," Sophie said, not liking the look in his eye or the turn the conversation was taking. "I can't believe I cheated on Brandon. I am *not* a cheater, but boy, I sure rolled over for you."

"Many women have," Phin said. "And you didn't cheat, so stop beating yourself up. Unless you enjoy it."

"How is this not cheating?" Sophie demanded. "We had sex. Right here on this dock. I was here. I remember."

"We didn't have sex," Phin said. "I was here, and I didn't have sex. You're too drunk to have sex. I'd be taking advantage of you."

"What? That's the dumbest thing I've ever heard." Sophie stood up and closed her eyes as her body remembered what a good time she'd just had. Which was wretched of her, she reminded herself, and then she stretched a little so her muscles would remember some more. "We had sex," she said, and her body telegraphed back, *Sure did.* She looked down at Phin, still stretched out on the dock, and the thought of what his body could do for her made her want to kick him. And then jump him. She looked away. "And now I'm going to call my lover and tell him what a scum I've been and hope he'll forgive me. Thank you very much for a lovely evening. Let's not do it again."

She walked off the dock and felt the cold grass on her toes just as Phin said, "Hold it, Julie Ann. Nice exit, but you forgot your shoes."

She turned and watched as he rolled to his feet and picked up her shoes. He strolled toward her and held them out, and she met his eyes and saw heat there and wanted him again.

Sophie took her shoes. "I'm not Julie Ann. I'm still alive and I'm staying that way." She looked into his eyes one last time, and then she turned back toward the house, toward safety and away from temptation.

"Maybe," Phin called after her as she walked away from him. "But the bear got you just the same."

Sophie closed her eyes and kept walking. The devil wasn't inside her after all. He was back there on the dock, making her crazy.

The dog greeted her with rapture when she came in, which made her feel even worse, keeping him shut up inside while she was having sex on the dock. She was a terrible mother. She took him outside and told him what a wonderful canine he was, and then she went upstairs for a long shower to scrub away the guilt. It didn't work; she could still feel Phin everywhere. *And hooray for that,* her body said, *let's do it again.* Then she put Dusty on for comfort and crawled into bed to call

Brandon so guilt would give her some perspective. It worked pretty well: When he said, "Hello," she felt like throwing up.

"It's me." She swallowed.

"Sophie?" Brandon sounded as if he'd been drugged.

"Brandon, I'm a horrible person," Sophie said. The dog jumped on the bed and she patted its solid little barrel body.

"No, you're not," he yawned. "What happened?"

"I had sex," Sophie said. "Of course, he says it wasn't sex, but it was, and now I've called you and made you feel awful in the middle of the night so I won't feel so guilty, and that's worse."

"What do you mean, 'he says it wasn't sex'?" Brandon said, not yawning. "Who was this?"

"A guy I met here. The mayor. We were talking and then he kissed me, and then things got . . . out of hand."

"If all he did was kiss you, he was right. You didn't have sex." Brandon sounded a little grumpy, which wasn't quite the reaction she'd been expecting. "Look, I know you think I haven't been paying enough attention to you and I should have called before this but—"

"You've been paying plenty of attention to me," Sophie said. "And it was more than one kiss. It was—"

"You're just tired of walking the straight and narrow." He sounded exasperated. "So you went for a little harmless excitement by necking with an authority figure."

"Excuse me?" Sophie said.

"You didn't even give this man a name. You said he was the mayor. That's obviously more important than who he is as a person."

"His name is Phineas Tucker," Sophie said. "And I think you're missing something key here."

"I'm not missing anything," Brandon said. "You're rebelling against the oppressive social structure that's made your family outcast, by corrupting its most powerful and popular adherent. And now you're sending me a wake-up call—literally—that I'm not paying enough attention to you."

"I don't think this is about you," Sophie said. "Brandon, I came all over that dock. Guilt and all, and I still came."

"Guilt can be an aphrodisiac," Brandon said automatically.

"Brandon, pay attention here. He went down on me and I loved it. I wanted to . . ." Sophie searched for the words that would make him pay attention and finally borrowed Phin's. "I wanted to *fuck his brains out*." Her voice rose as she thought about it, and anger made her honest. "As a matter of fact, I still want to fuck his brains out. Really, I do. And call me crazy, but I think this is a bad sign for our relationship."

"You don't have to shock me with language to make me pay attention," Brandon said, and Sophie wanted him dead. "When you get back home, we'll have a long talk and get you straightened out."

Sophie gritted her teeth. Maybe she didn't want straightened out. Maybe she liked being bent. Maybe she'd go find Phin and invite him to bend her some more. "And we did have sex. I came, that's sex."

"You come with a vibrator, too," Brandon said. "Stop dramatizing yourself."

Sophie gripped the receiver until her knuckles went white. "I'm telling you, I had sex!"

"Good for you," Amy said from the doorway. "Who are you bragging to?"

"Brandon," Sophie said.

"Yes!" Amy plopped herself down at the foot of the bed, bouncing with satisfaction, and the dog moved closer to Sophie, the epitome of annoyed canine. "Sorry, dog. This was Phineas T., right?"

Sophie nodded.

"And now Brandon is explaining to you why you did this, and he isn't mentioning lust and satisfaction."

Sophie nodded again.

"Who's talking to you?" Brandon said.

"Amy," Sophie said. "She just recapped your entire conversation."

"Oh, yes, your sister, the psychological genius." Brandon sounded annoyed for the first time. "Definitely listen to her."

"Let me get this straight. You don't care that Phin went down on me, but you're jealous that I'm listening to my sister instead of you?" Sophie gave up. "Brandon, I think this is an indication that this relationship isn't working for us."

"*Yes,*" Amy said.

"Of course the relationship is working for us." Brandon sounded really annoyed now. "You're just acting out a little—"

"'A little.'" Sophie shook her head. "I'm not acting out *a little.* I'm getting my brains blown out by the river by a guy I hardly know."

"I *love* this," Amy said.

"Sounds like acting-out to me," Brandon said. "Go get some sleep and sober up. You'll be back to normal in the morning."

"Wait a minute—"

"Good night, Sophie," Brandon said, and hung up.

"I don't believe this." Sophie stared at the receiver.

"Who cares about him?" Amy said. "You had great sex."

"Not according to Phin and Brandon." Sophie put the receiver back on the cradle. "It's not sex at all, according to these yahoos."

"Wait, I get it. You only had oral sex." Amy rolled her eyes. "How Clintonesque of them."

"Well, it's an out for me," Sophie said. "Evidently I didn't cheat, after all. And Brandon says when I get home, he'll straighten me out."

"Does he now?" Amy's voice was cold, and Sophie said, "Yeah."

"I don't like Brandon," Amy said. "The mayor, however, I might approve of. On a short-term basis only, of course."

"I don't," Sophie said, and thought about Phin in the dark, and his hands and his mouth, and she shivered all over. "I just want him again. Only this time, I want the whole thing, the entire phallic variation."

"The Phallic Variation." Amy grinned. "Sounds like a techno-thriller. Tom Clancy's *Phallic Variation*. I think you should go for it."

"I can't." Sophie slid down into her pillows and tried not to think about going for it and thought about it anyway. "I can't cheat again. But, oh God, Amy, it was good."

"You know, I never heard you say, 'God, it was good' after Brandon," Amy said. "And now here's the mayor, who seems to know his thumb from a clitoris."

Sophie felt her lips quirk in spite of herself. "Oh, yes. He went places no man has gone before. He also seems open to direction."

"Your future is clear." Amy grinned at her. "Dump Brandon and move on to the Phallic Variation. Of course I'd emphasize that it's a variation, and he has to slide down your stomach first before he gets his."

Sophie stopped smiling. "I can't. Phin was sort of a kinky fantasy, sex with a guy I don't know, swept away in the dark by the river, all that stuff—" She felt a little dizzy just thinking about it. "But I'm not even sure I like him—" *Although I like what he does, dear God, I do.* Sophie dug herself deeper into the bed and shoved all thoughts of Phin away. "He probably won't even come back. I don't think he had that phenomenal a time. Mostly we argued."

"You have so much to learn about men," Amy said. "If he

talked you out of your pants, he had a good time. And even if you're all right in the morning, you'll be wanting him again in the dark. That's what the dark is for. Wanting guys like Phin."

"Good *night*," Sophie said, and Amy laughed and left the room.

Guys like Phin. Sophie thought of him again, so relaxed next to her, careless and cool, and then she thought of the way his mouth had moved down her body and made her shudder, thought of his hands hot on her, his fingers inside her, thought about what he would feel like moving hard into her—

Sophie put her pillow over her head.

He'd been so hot. *She'd* been so hot. That was so wrong of her. But, oh God, it had felt so *good.* After an hour, she gave up and relived the whole thing all over again, dwelling lavishly on the moments that were particularly perverse and unlike her, fixing the awkward parts. By the time she'd reviewed it a couple of times, it was so glossy, it could have been a hot scene in a movie.

Hello.

That would be wrong, she told herself, but her mind clicked along, rewriting her night, and after a few minutes, she gave up and went downstairs and opened her PowerBook, the dog sighing and following her to lie down again at her feet.

"Sorry," Sophie told him.

And then she began to type.

"Beautiful morning," Phin said when he came down to the breakfast table. He kissed Dillie on top of her head. "You gonna beat 'em today, kid?"

Dillie straightened her softball shirt. "Yep. I'm ready."

"The Tuckers are always ready." He sat down, picked up

his glass of orange juice and met his mother's narrowed eyes. "What?"

"Good time last night?" she said.

He put his orange juice glass down. "I beg your pardon?"

"I said, did you have a good time last night at the Tavern with the movie people?" Liz said.

Dillie frowned. "You didn't say all that."

Liz handed Dillie a buttered muffin. "Eat, please." She turned back to Phin and smiled her cobra smile.

"Yes," Phin said, returning her smile with an equal lack of warmth. "An excellent time. What else did Virginia have to say?" He snagged a muffin and buttered it while he reoriented his brain from smug satisfaction to defense alert.

"She suggested you take Rachel to the movies."

"I don't go to the movies," Phin said. "Especially with Rachel. I have a major softball game this morning, and it needs all my attention."

"It's just the Blue Birds," Dillie said. "We can beat them no problem."

"Never let your guard down, Dill," Phin said, keeping one eye on his mother. "The ones that look harmless are the ones that take you by surprise."

"You really thought nobody would talk?" Liz said.

"Not before breakfast," Phin said. "It's Saturday, for Christ's sake."

"You're the mayor," Liz said. "You have standing. People are interested in what you do. You have a *responsibility* to this town."

"Lucky me. Could I have some eggs?" He handed Liz his plate, and she filled it while she talked.

"As I said, it's not a good idea, associating with the movie people. Virginia's told everybody by now—"

"Told everybody what? That I had a couple of beers at the

Tavern? There's breaking news for you." Thank God, Virginia hadn't been on the Whipple dock. "What does she—" he began and then froze at the belated memory of where the Whipple dock was.

Across the river from the Garveys'.

Not directly across. Upstream a little. But still too close.

"What else did Virginia say?" he asked his mother.

"That was it." She handed him his plate. "I gather she missed something?"

Phin sat back in his chair, stared at the ceiling, and regrouped. He must have been out of his fucking mind. Three or four beers and Sophie saying, "I'd have to be depraved" with that mouth, and he'd forgotten where he was and who he was and lunged for her.

Of course, she'd forgotten she had a boyfriend, so he wasn't alone. Lust could play hell with a person's memory. And morals. And common sense.

"What did you do?" Liz said.

Phin sat up and ate a forkful of eggs. "Excellent breakfast. Thank you."

Liz closed her eyes. "Am I going to be hearing something horrible?"

"Nope," Phin said. "You'd have heard it by now."

"What's horrible?" Dillie said.

"Nothing," Phin said. "Everything's great. But I still think you'd better watch those Blue Birds."

"Stephen will make capital of this," Liz said.

"Stephen sleeps with Virginia," Phin said. "He has to find something to do for excitement."

"Don't get cocky," Liz said. "Don't give him *any* advantage. And stay away from those movie people."

The phone rang, and Phin escaped to get it. When he came back, Liz said, "Who was it?"

"The movie people," Phin said. "They need fuses. I'm taking some out to them this afternoon."

"Don't do this," Liz said, with an edge in her voice.

"Don't push me," Phin said, just as sharply.

"Can I have more muffin?" Dillie said, and when he looked at her, her eyes were anxious.

"If you have more muffin, will you throw it up on third base?" he said.

"No." Dillie looked from Phin to Liz and back again. "Are you guys fighting? You never fight, but this sounds like a fight, and I don't like it."

"It's okay, Dillie," Liz said. "Your father is being a dummy, but we're not mad."

"Grandma's not minding her own business," Phin said. "But we're not mad. We don't get mad. We're Tuckers."

"Okay," Dillie said. "It sounded mad, though."

"About the Blue Birds," Phin said, and distracted his daughter with softball strategy.

Across the table, his mother regarded him coldly, not distracted at all.

When Sophie came downstairs again, it was almost noon. She'd shoved the memories of the night before away, tried to call Brandon and got his machine, buried the pink dress in the back of the closet, and resolved to be A Better Person now that the sun was up.

"Late night last night, huh?" Amy said, as Sophie came into the kitchen. She was eating toast slathered with butter, sitting at the worn wood table where Clea was reading pages of script. Dusty was singing "Mama's Little Girl" in the background, the sun shone through the kitchen windows, and the dog looked up, panting, and wagged his stubby tail when he saw Sophie.

It was hot as hell, but Sophie began to feel better. "Hello, baby," she said to the dog, and bent to pet it. Then she went to the fridge to pour herself a glass of juice. "I was up until about four—" She stopped, realizing what Clea was reading. "Oh, about that. It's—"

"It's phenomenal," Clea said. "My God, I had no idea you could even *think* like this."

"She's right." Amy opened her eyes wide. "You were obviously *inspired*."

"Don't start," Sophie said.

"Of course, we can't *film* this—" Amy said, and Clea said, "Well, maybe—"

"—but Clea and I were just talking," Amy went on, "and we think you should write another one, a full love scene this time." Amy took a huge bite of toast and then said, with her mouth full, "Like a Phallic Variation, you know?"

"We have no time to film a Phallic Variation," Sophie said crushingly. "We're going home tomorrow. We have work—"

"Not really," Amy said, and Sophie stopped with her juice glass halfway to her mouth. "I sort of canceled everything before we left," Amy said. "But it's okay, I got everybody booked with other places, I just—"

Sophie sat down hard. "Other places." All that work. All that income. Gone.

"I wanted time to do this right," Amy said, talking faster. "And now we can take our time and film a really great Phallic Variation. You can, uh, write it tonight."

"No," Sophie said.

"Amy's right," Clea said. "We need to build to a big finish." She held up the script. "This is good, but it's not the whole nine yards, you know?"

"I know," Sophie said. "Believe me, I know." She watched Amy, who concentrated on her toast, defiantly cheerful about having dismantled their business. "But this is a *short, nonpornographic* movie. It does not need a sex scene." She tried to take the script pages from Clea, who put them behind her back.

"Don't be a prude, Sophie," she said. "Sex is not necessarily porn."

Amy said, "Yeah, don't be a prude, Sophie. Maybe that's something else about you Brandon can straighten out when you get back to Cincinnati."

Then a car door slammed outside and Clea said, "Rob," and evaporated through the door.

"So you shut down the business," Sophie said.

"I set you free," Amy said. "If I hadn't, you'd have tried to go back and do it all alone. Now you're free to figure out what you want—"

"Thank you," Sophie said. "I want to be employed. Don't do me any more favors."

"Hi!" Rachel bustled into the room, making Sophie drop her toast. "Guess what I found!" She dumped a paper bag on the table and a tub of wallpaper paste rolled out, endangering Sophie's juice. "The rest of the wallpaper!" Then, to Sophie's horror she pulled out eight rolls of ancient wallpaper. "When you said Clea's mom had taken it back, I figured it had to be to our store, so I went and looked in the old stock and it was there. Isn't this great?"

Rachel looked so pleased that Sophie said, "Absolutely," and tried to smile. Just what she needed. A whole kitchen of snotty mutant cherries.

"Wait a minute," Amy said, picking up a roll. "These aren't cherries."

"I know," Rachel said. "The label on the roll says, *Apple Blossom Time*. But it had *Whipple* written on it, and how many rolls of kitchen wallpaper could Clea's mom have bought?"

"Apples?" Sophie studied the wall. "Those are apples? No, those are cherries."

"No, they're not," Amy said, squinting from the roll to the wall. "They're apples. This is the same paper. The ones on the wall just faded. The yellow went, for some reason, so they're sort of a blue-pink. That's why you thought they were cherries."

"They're not cherries?" Sophie opened a roll and spread it out. Definitely apples on the roll. Ugly, orangey red apples, but still apples.

"Whatever," Rachel said. "You can do the whole kitchen now, and then you can write."

She looked so pleased with herself that Sophie didn't have the heart to disappoint her. "Thank you, this was very sweet of you, Rachel."

"My pleasure," Rachel said. "Oh, and somebody else is here, too."

"The Coreys," Amy said. "Clea hired them yesterday to paint the house. You gotta see 'em. They look like Laurel and Hardy in high school."

"No," Rachel said. "The Coreys are already out there. This is some new guy who pulled up in a black Porsche just as I came in. I didn't see him—"

Sophie's heart sank. "Zane."

"Oh, no," Amy said.

"Zane Black, the anchor guy?" Rachel said. "Cool."

"You have a lot to learn, Rachel," Sophie said and headed for the front porch.

Sophie thought she'd seen all she'd needed to of Zane Black when she'd filmed his wedding to Clea, but now, as he came toward the porch across the sunbaked yard, a newscaster's smile pasted on his lips in spite of the fact that Clea was glowering behind him, she was struck by how much he looked like Frank. He was better-looking and not as smarmy, but the resemblance was still strong. "I'm starting to see a pattern here," she murmured to Amy, who said, "Yeah, add in Davy and Rob and you've got a four-pack of dark-haired guys you can't trust."

"Stephanie!" Zane said.

"Sophie," Sophie said.

"Right, right, Sophie." He came up the steps and took a deep breath. "Nothing like country air."

"That's dead fish," Amy said. "We haven't had much rain lately and the river's low," but Zane had already lost interest, staring past her, his smile widening.

"And who have we here?"

Sophie turned. Rachel stood inside the screen door, looking like a blonde cupcake. "Oh. This is Rachel, our production assistant."

Rachel's tentative smile for Zane spread all over her face when she heard her title. "Hello, Mr. Black," she said, but her smile was for Sophie.

"Call me Zane, everybody does," Zane said.

"Not everybody," Amy said under her breath. "Some of us call you 'dickhead.'"

They followed Zane and Clea in, as Clea said, "I told you not to come."

"Don't be ridiculous," Zane said. "You're my wife."

"You should have thought of that before you took my money and slept with the weather girl," Clea said, and went into the kitchen.

"Weather girl?" Amy said.

Zane followed Clea, a stiff smile pasted on his face.

"Okay, we should go out onto the front porch now and let

them have this argument in private," Sophie said to Amy and Rachel.

Out in the kitchen, Clea began to tell Zane what she thought of him. She had a nice turn of phrase and the delivery of an auctioneer.

"Or not," Sophie said, and the three of them sat on the couch and listened, the dog at their feet with his head cocked, too.

About ten minutes into Clea's list of Zane's offenses, which included theft, adultery, not waiting for Clea to come, preventing her from reestablishing her career, and not providing her with a warm, nurturing environment, Amy said, "This would be better if we had popcorn."

Five minutes later, as Zane was explaining that it was Clea's fault that he'd cheated on her because she was cold and withholding which was not what he expected from his wife because he wanted a warm, nurturing environment, too, Sophie said, "This would be better if we had alcohol."

And shortly after that, at the height of the argument, when Zane told Clea that she'd never see her money again if she left him, Amy said, "The hell with the popcorn. Let's get Sophie's Mace and take the bastard out."

"My mom thinks he's the coolest," Rachel said. "Wait'll I tell her about this."

Out in the kitchen, Zane was taking the righteously indignant route. "I can't believe you thought I'd spend that money. Hell, I'm not that damn Dempsey guy you used to be with, I'm honest."

Sophie straightened on the couch, and Amy said, "Easy, girl."

"Yeah, well, I should have stayed with him," Clea said. "He never took anything from me, and he took care of me, too. Only you said you could do it better, remember? And I was such a fool I went for it."

Amy said, "See? She's sorry," and Sophie relaxed.

"I've taken care of you," Zane said. "For God's sake, Clea, you live in one of the biggest houses in Cincinnati."

"How is stealing my money keeping me safe?" Clea shrieked at him.

"Not to mention the weather girl," Amy said.

"I didn't steal it," Zane said. "I told you, I've got it in an offshore account, and it's going to stay there until I move it, so if you want it, you're going to stay my wife."

"That's it, isn't it? You knew I was tired of your crap, so you hid the money so I couldn't leave."

"You're my wife—"

"Well, it's not going to work," Clea said. "Because my lawyer is going to make you give it up. And I'm selling this farm, too, and Frank says—"

"Oh, God, not Frank again," Zane said. "Frank the Great. Frank the Wonderful. Get over high school, Clea, he's not—"

"He's a developer here," Clea said. "He bought land from my dad before, and he said he'd give me seven hundred and fifty thousand dollars for the rest of the land around the farmhouse. When I get back what you stole, I'll have almost three million dollars, and when I send this tape to Leo—"

"*Leo?* No wife of mine is going to work for Leo Kingsley."

"He seems to be missing something key here," Sophie said, as Clea said, "Zane, I'm not your wife anymore. We're over."

"Not unless you want to give me half of that three million," Zane said, and this time there was a long silence from the kitchen.

"You wouldn't," Clea said.

"The hell I wouldn't," Zane said. "If you'd left me before

you got the money, you'd sure as hell have taken half of *my* assets. Well, I get half of yours, too, sweetie." When Clea didn't say anything he went on. "Now, there's nothing to be upset about, I have all the money safe in an offshore account. If we ever need it, it's just a phone call away."

"Prove it," Clea said. "I want to see a bank book or something. I want—"

"What good is that going to do you?" Zane said. "God, you know nothing about finance. Trust me."

"Oh, please," Amy said.

"You need me, Clea," Zane wheedled on. "You think you can take care of yourself? You never have. There's always been somebody around to be your daddy. And I'm the best one of the bunch. You think Leo is going to take care of you? The only reason's he's even talking to you is because he wants to make *Coming Clean Two.* You want to do that?"

Sophie frowned at Amy and said, "*Coming Clean Two?*"

Amy shrugged.

"No, I don't want that," Clea said. "But there are other projects I can do with Leo. Sophie's written some great stuff and she's going to write more. She—"

"Sophie couldn't write for *Sesame Street,* let alone Leo Kingsley," Zane said, contempt dripping from his voice. "Hell, look at her, she's about the least exciting woman we know. She's so repressed, she's sexless."

Sophie felt herself flush. "Definitely the Mace."

"Besides, I told you, my wife does not make movies for Leo Kingsley," Zane was saying to Clea. "Now you go get packed. I'll wait for you on the porch, and then we'll go home together."

They heard Clea stomp up the kitchen stairs and then her bedroom door slammed.

Zane came into the living room, looking mad as hell but triumphant. "Did you get all that?" he asked them, and Amy said, "Pretty much, but we have a few questions. About the weather girl, did—"

"You can pack up your video shit," he said. "My wife is not making this damn movie, she's coming home with me."

"Oh, *no*," Rachel said, and Sophie said, "We'll just wait to get the good word from her."

Zane shook his head. "My wife does what I tell her to. Someday you'll understand that."

"'And someday you'll drop dead and I'll come to your funeral in a red dress,'" Sophie said.

Zane snorted and went out on the porch.

They heard a car come down the lane, and Rachel got up to look. "It's the Lutzes."

"Nothing but good times ahead," Amy said, clasping her hands in front of her.

They sat on the couch and listened to Frank and Georgia fawn over Zane on the porch—"A real celebrity right here in Temptation," Georgia said over and over—until Rob came in from the porch looking annoyed. "That guy," he said, and Rachel nodded.

"We know." She made room for him on the couch.

"What a loser," Rob said as he sat down.

Sophie waited for him to elaborate, but he seemed to feel he'd said it all. Okay, so Rob wasn't deep. Looking like that, he didn't need to be. Except someday he wouldn't look like that, and then he'd be Frank.

"You know, Clea might be up there packing," Amy said, but then Clea came down the stairs in her red-and-white dress, ready to film, and smiled at Rob when she saw him.

"Well, hello there," she said, and he leaped from the couch, elbowing Rachel in the process.

"You look great," he said.

"So we're still making a movie?" Amy said.

"Well, of course," Clea said, and went out onto the porch with Rob to torment her husband.

And more power to her, Sophie thought, loathing Zane more than she ever had in her life.

An hour later, Sophie was exhausted from watching all the raging egos in the dusty yard. Georgia flirted obnoxiously with Zane (keeping one eye on Frank), while Zane flirted obnoxiously with Rachel (keeping one eye on Clea), while Rachel politely did not tell him he was a jackass. Through it all, an oblivious Frank continued to drool on Clea, who flirted obnoxiously with Rob and kept an eye on everybody else to make sure she was the center of attention. It gave Sophie a headache, but Amy filmed it all with delight, including shots of the now bright red water tower. "It looks like a lipstick with a nipple," she told Sophie. "Very female." Sophie looked at Clea and said, "I've had enough 'female' for a while," and went back into the house.

She sat at the kitchen table with the dog at her feet and tried to work on the Phallic Variation, but Zane's voice kept interrupting her thoughts.

"She's sexless," she heard Zane say again, and she thought, *You son of a bitch, I am* not *sexless.* Okay, maybe she wasn't exciting, but she wasn't sexless. Zane should talk to Phin, that's what he should do.

Although what would that prove? As Phin had pointed out the night before, he'd done all the work. She hadn't exactly taken a walk on the wild side. It was more like she'd been walked.

Which didn't mean she couldn't take a walk over there, it didn't mean she couldn't be sexy and exciting. When she thought about it, Temptation was the perfect place to go to the devil.

Thinking about the devil made her think about Phin, and thinking about Phin made her sure. That's what she'd do. The hell with Zane, she'd just go find Phin. And be exciting.

She got up to call Brandon to tell him things were definitely off, and got his machine again. Well, she'd just work on an *exciting sex scene* for now and call him later.

Two hours of anguished composition later, she'd tried to call Brandon four times and erased the words on her screen six times because they were so stupid, which proved Zane was right, damn him. Plus the temperature had risen at least ten degrees, and she was drowning in her own sweat. Even the dog had rolled over on its back and was panting heavily. Sophie looked at the words on her screen and thought, *And that's the only heavy breathing this garbage will ever hear*, and deleted it all again.

The problem was trying to write a love scene and stay a lady at the same time. It wasn't possible. The minute you started thinking that writing sex was cheap and disgusting, your mind froze up and you wrote boring dreck. It was sort of like having sex. You either threw everything you had into it, or it wasn't worth the bother.

Which was probably why most of the sex she'd had up till now hadn't been worth the bother.

She sat back and stared at the wall as she contemplated this new thought, and the cherries sneered back again. Evidently they hadn't gotten the good news they were apples.

"Amy called and said you needed these," Phin said from behind her, and Sophie leaped in her chair.

"I *hate* it when you do that," she said, trying to get her heart out of her throat.

Phin dropped a box of fuses on the table and pulled out a chair. "Why are you so nervous?"

"I'm not nervous." Sophie refused to meet his eyes. "I'm annoyed. I hate those damn cherries, and now it turns out they're apples. If you want to bring me something I really need, get me a gallon of white paint."

"If you don't like them, don't look at them," Phin said. "Look at me."

"The cherries are beginning to look better," Sophie said, staring at the wall.

"You want to explain why you're mad at me?"

"I'm not mad at you," she said, and made the mistake of looking at him.

Even sitting in an ugly kitchen in the heat, he was gorgeous: cool and immaculate in another one of those damn perfect white shirts.

"Good," Phin said. "Amy says you're coming to the Tavern tonight. Of course, this time you'll be drinking Diet Coke without the rum."

Sophie forgot how gorgeous he was. "I'll be drinking whatever I want. And give me one good reason why I'd want to go back to that dump."

Phin grinned at her, and Sophie's heart betrayed her and kicked up a beat. "You had a good time last night, didn't you?" he said.

"Why do you give me an opening like that?" She turned back to her PowerBook, trying to ignore the sizzle that was making her dizzy. "You're just begging me to say something crushing."

"You won't." Phin leaned back in his chair. "You're too honest."

She wanted to wipe that smile off his face, to tell him it had been lousy, tell him he was entirely forgettable, tell him that she wasn't honest, that she came from a long line of crooks and liars and deviants, that she'd been *using* him. . . . But when she met his eyes, she couldn't do it. "Okay. It was phenomenal."

"I know," Phin said.

Sophie's irritation rose again. "You know, women don't find arrogance all that attractive."

"Giving me pointers on my technique?"

"It could use some work."

"It got you on your back last night."

Sophie lifted her chin. "'When you first came in for breakfast, when I first saw you, I thought you were handsome. Then, of course, you spoke.'"

"So I make you nervous," Phin said.

"Not at all."

"Because that's a movie quote, right? You know, if you do that with books, people think you're intelligent."

Sophie lowered her chin. "If this is your pathetic attempt to seduce me again, you're failing miserably."

"I don't seduce women." Phin shoved back his chair and stood up. "They just fall into my open arms."

"Clumsy of them," Sophie said, feeling relieved and disappointed that he was going. She turned back to her empty screen and hated it that Zane was right. "A guy just called me sexless," she blurted.

"He's wrong," Phin said. "So, I'll see you at the Tavern tonight?"

There he stood, tall, blond, and capable of giving her not only the Phallic Variation and all the intense satisfaction that went with it, but also her love scene. And she wanted him. She was not sexless. She was practically hyperventilating because he was standing next to her. She was *hot*.

"Yes." Sophie swallowed. "We'll be there." He started to

leave, smug as ever, so she said, "By the way, love the water tower. Looks like a giant lipstick with a nipple."

He turned back. "What?"

She smiled at him. "The water tower. It looks like a lipstick now. Except there's that bump on top."

"Catwalk," Phin said. "It was harder to see when it was peach."

"It's not hard now," Sophie said. "In more ways than one. Gotta love it."

"Glad you like it," Phin said, and left, not nearly as smug.

Sophie went back to her PowerBook. She should be able to put all this heat to good use. *Concentrate*, she told herself, and tried to write the sex scene again.

At seven, she put her head down on the kitchen table in despair, which was how Amy found her a few minutes later.

"Not going well?" Amy said. "Not to worry. I asked Phin if he'd fix the slow drain in the kitchen sink tonight after the Tavern. And once you get him in the kitchen, how hard can it be to lure him upstairs?"

"I don't lure."

"Concentrate, Sophie," Amy said. "Your insignificant other will be back tonight. What are you going to do about it?"

"I have no idea." Sophie thought about Phin, and blushed in the heat. "Maybe he'll just take over like he did last time. And the earth will move, and then we'll both look beautifully moist without being too disheveled."

"You don't want to have sex," Amy said. "You want to have sex in the movies."

Sophie thought about it. "No, I want to have sex. I've been trying to call Brandon all day to break things off so I can have the mayor tonight without guilt, but he won't pick up the phone."

"He knows you too well," Amy said. "He knows you won't

cheat, so if he doesn't give you the chance to dump him, you'll have to be faithful."

"I don't have to be faithful." Sophie thought again about the night to come, and began to have doubts. After all, this would involve taking her clothes off in front of a semi–complete stranger. "But I probably will be anyway. I have no moves, and I don't see the mayor making one on his own. He's not the aggressive type. The only reason he moved last night was that we were sort of talking dirty."

"So do that again," Amy said.

"I don't think I can," Sophie said, looking at the mess on her screen. "I can't even *write* dirty."

"It's easy. Just say, 'Fuck me.' He'll take it from there."

"'Fuck me.'" Sophie tried to imagine saying that to Phin. It sounded so unlike her. "I'll think of something else."

"Simple ways are best," Amy said. "Go with 'Fuck me' and get that scene."

Oh, right, Sophie thought. Then she thought of Zane. The least exciting woman he knew, huh? Then she thought of the dock. And Phin. And the heat rose again. *Fuck me.* "Fuck me," she tried out loud.

"There you go," Amy said.

"Fuck me," Sophie said again, and went upstairs to practice while she put on Clea's pink dress.

Chapter Six

At nine that night, Phin sat in the booth across from Wes and watched Sophie, stuck at a table with the rest of the crowd from the farm. She looked as fuckable as ever.

"Amy's over there," Wes said. "We should—"

"No," Phin said, still watching Sophie. "As soon as Amy realizes she needs you, she'll come over here and we won't have to put up with Frank and Georgia. Although since you gave her that showerhead, she may not realize that anytime soon. Never give a woman an appliance that replaces you. She'll use it and turn on you."

"She's smart as hell," Wes said, ignoring him. "And she's funny and sharp, and she lays it right on the line. I like her."

"Try to think about something else," Phin said.

"I went to see Stephen Garvey this afternoon," Wes said obediently. "He said he was going to take care of the Dempseys' car to avoid negative publicity before the election. He seemed to think I was there because you'd sent me."

"Me?" Phin frowned at him. "Why would I—"

"He said he knew if he went after the Dempseys, you'd be vindictive and use it against him, you being so closely tied to the movie people."

"'Closely tied'?" Phin said, his mind drifting to rope and Sophie.

"His words, not mine. He's up to something and it's got something to do with that movie."

Across the room, Sophie stretched, and Phin lost interest in Stephen. "Maybe if I ask nice, Sophie will tell me about the movie."

Wes rolled his eyes. "That's good. Concentrate on the important stuff. What happened to her being a dangerous woman to get involved with?"

Phin watched Sophie nod at Frank. *Forget him, come over here to me.* "I'm not talking about getting involved with her. I'm talking about seeing her naked."

"I'm against you using Sophie for sex," Wes said. "I like her. Also, I think she's dangerous as long as Stephen's got this movie thing going. Besides, she has a boyfriend back in Cincy. Amy says he's a big-shot therapist."

Phin took his eyes off Sophie to frown at Wes. "That was a real hot conversation you had with Amy. Conversations like that will get you in the sack about in time for Y3K."

"Amy also said that, based on what Sophie tells her, the guy is extremely boring in bed. So you might be able to talk her into the naked part, but it would be a really stupid thing to do since she's going to leave tomorrow."

"Since when did you become the Chastity Patrol?"

"I like Sophie," Wes said. "Do not seduce and abandon her or I'll arrest you for something."

"Police brutality," Phin said. "Which reminds me, if I get lucky with Sophie, can I borrow some handcuffs?"

"You've still got the last ones you borrowed. Phin, I'm not kidding. Sophie deserves more than your hit-and-run, and Stephen's too damn pleased that you've been out there twice. Just stay away from her."

"Hey," Amy said, as she bounced into the booth beside Wes. "What's new in crime and government?"

Phin watched Wes turn toward her, his world a better place. *Great*, he thought. *She's going to leave and break his fucking heart.*

Across the bar, Rachel was standing, and Sophie looked unhappy.

"Later for you two," Phin said to them, and went to see what Sophie needed.

Half an hour earlier, Frank had sat down across from Sophie, friendly-drunk but not reeling, and said, "So how's it going?"

"Just great," Sophie had said, pretending not to notice Georgia crawling into Zane's lap beside them. It was difficult because she was also pretending not to notice Phin sitting across the room. She'd planned to play hard-to-get, but if that got her Frank's conversation and Georgia's seduction in stereo, she was going to get a lot easier very soon.

Georgia said loudly, "You really are some man, Zane Black, you really are," and Frank shrugged at Sophie and gave a little laugh.

Five minutes, to be polite, and then I'm heading for that booth. "And how's your life?" Sophie said, trying to make conversation, realizing too late that it was a dumb thing to ask at that particular moment.

Frank drank some beer. "Oh, pretty good." He started to peel the label off his bottle. "That's all I ever wanted anyway. Pretty good." He let his eyes drift over to Clea at the bar, laughing up at his son.

"'Pretty good''s not bad," Sophie agreed, wishing there was someplace she could look that didn't have evidence that Frank's life was pretty terrible.

"You know, growing up, I knew exactly what I wanted," Frank said, expanding into contemplative used-car salesman mode. "A good job, a nice house, a pretty wife, a son, and two cars, a Jeep and a big luxury car to take the wife places. I had it all planned out by eighteen."

"Well, you got that," Sophie said. "Of course, I'm guessing on the cars."

"I got it all," Frank said. "And it is not a bad life, not at all. Except . . ." He looked over at the bar again and took another swig of beer. Then he leaned forward, and Sophie leaned forward a little, too, to get farther away from Georgia. "Did you ever one day look up and realize you'd been staring at the ground when there was a whole sky on top of you? Just one day, realize that there was more out there than you could have imagined?"

"No," Sophie said. She'd always known there was more out there than she could imagine, that was why she was so careful not to look up. Bat country.

"By the time I was a senior in high school," Frank said, "I had it all lined up. Even the job with my future father-in-law." He stopped and stared at the bar. "And then one day there was Clea." He shook his head. "Sure, she's beautiful now, but you should have seen her at eighteen, Sophie." He leaned back. "We were in the school play together, you know."

Sophie nodded to be polite, and stole a look at Phin. He was talking to Wes, looking as detached as ever. She wondered if anything ever made him sweat, and then she thought, *I could.* No matter what Zane thought.

Frank was still talking. "And after the last performance, she said, 'Let's go out to the Tavern, Frank,' and we sat out in back, with a thousand stars over us, and she said, 'We could be like that, Frank, we could be stars. We could go to Hollywood.'" Frank laughed, a little shamefaced. "Yeah, I know it sounds corny."

"Not as much as you'd think," Sophie said. "Everybody needs dreams."

"Yeah, but Hollywood?" Frank leaned forward, serious again. "The thing is, I believed her, Sophie. When I was with her that night, I believed *I* could make it. I mean, I'm a damn good actor, and I have a really great voice. I might have . . ." He looked back at Clea. "No, I wouldn't have. *She* didn't even make it, really. But, boy, it was a hell of a night. We were going to have it all."

"I heard you got it all," Sophie said.

Frank looked down at his beer. "She told you that?" He shook his head. "Finest moment of my life when she said, 'I want it to be you, Frank.'"

Sophie frowned. This story was not the one Clea had told. She let her eyes slide to the booth in the back and saw Phin watching her and her pulse kicked up.

"You know . . ." Frank looked back at the bar and Clea. "It wouldn't be so bad if I hadn't thought, for just that one night, that there was more. You know? If I just hadn't seen what . . . It's like losing something you never had. You can't really be sorry, but you can't ever really forget it, either. Even when you've got everything you ever really knew you could get. Sometimes, it still comes back."

"In this case, literally," Sophie said, looking at Clea, who was flirting with Rob, oblivious to the carnage at the table behind her.

"Yeah," Frank said. "I was ready to go to Cincy to make the land deal, but she said she wanted to come here. And I thought . . ." He sighed. "Oh, hell, you know what I thought." He drained his beer.

"Yeah," Sophie said. "I know what you thought."

"Dumb," Frank said. "Jesus, I'm dumb."

"Well, human," Sophie said.

"No, dumb." Frank finally looked the other direction, away from Clea and toward Georgia, now hanging all over Zane.

Sophie opened her mouth to say something comforting, but she couldn't think of anything. The man's lost love was at the bar moving on his son, his wife was molesting a TV anchorman, and he was stuck nursing a warm beer in an ugly bar in a creepy little town. About the best thing that could happen to Frank would be a direct hit from an asteroid.

"We'll be gone in a week," she said finally, and Frank said, "That calls for another beer," and got up.

Rachel slid into his seat, looking miserable.

"Are you okay?" Sophie said.

Rachel rolled her eyes. "Oh, yeah, I'm great. I'm in Temptation, how bad can it be?" She was trying to come on cool, but she sounded a little shaky.

"Yeah, I heard you want out of town pretty bad, Rachel," Zane said, as he leaned toward her across the empty chair between them. "I told you, if there's anything I can do—"

Rachel leaned back.

"Want to trade places with me, Rachel?" Sophie said. "I have Mace."

"You wouldn't need it," Zane said.

"What are you *talking* about?" Georgia nudged Zane with

her shoulder and batted her eyes at him. "Go on, now. You were telling me about being a news anchor. I just think that's so *sexy*."

Zane leaned back and began to talk about the joys of being a celebrity, and Rachel looked even more miserable, so Sophie leaned forward and said, "Okay, what's wrong?"

"I want out of this town," she finally said. "I was lousy at college and I'm not good at anything else, and my mom and dad are hipped on me getting married and living next door to them forever, and if I don't get out of Temptation I'm going to go crazy, and I'm not kidding."

Sophie nodded. Given Rachel's parents, she wasn't exaggerating.

"And I thought, like, maybe the movie thing would get me out, but you're going back to Cincinnati, and Amy said no, and Clea hates me." She shot a look of loathing across the table at Zane. "And I talked to *him* about it for maybe two seconds, and he stood real close and put his hand on my butt and told me we could talk about it in private."

"Stay away from him," Sophie said. "He's a complete loss as a human being."

"I know," Rachel said. "But he's telling people how much I want to leave, just like I told him, only he's making it sound like I offered him something that I didn't. And he keeps touching me."

Sophie picked up her purse and took out her Mace. "Just in case he goes deaf when you say no," she said, and handed the lipstick-sized can to Rachel.

Rachel cheered up a little bit as she turned it over in her hand. "I've never had Mace."

"Well, now you're armed and dangerous," Sophie said. "And I'd be so delighted if you used it on Zane. Really. Use all of it."

Rachel grinned at her, almost back to normal. Sophie let

her eyes drift back to Phin. He was looking at her with a half smile on his face.

Sophie's pulse give a little surge of lust and panic.

Okay, there was no reason to get rattled just because he was looking at her as if he wanted her. She wanted him, too, right now, no waiting. That sounded slutty, so she told herself it was for the movie. It really wasn't sex—she took her eyes off Phin so she could think better—not sex, that would be depraved, it was work. That was it. She had work to do tonight. Important work to do tonight. *Imperative* work to do tonight. And it was just *sitting* over there *waiting* for her—

"Sophie?" Rachel said.

"We'll think of something for you," Sophie told her, babbling a little. "We've got an extra week, we'll think of something."

"Really?"

Sophie looked back at Phin. "Absolutely."

Frank came back to the table and put another rum and Diet Coke in front of Sophie, and Georgia said loudly to Zane, "Tell me more about being a big TV star." She pressed her breast against Zane's arm, and Sophie thought he was going to say something rude. Then he smiled and said, "What do you want to know?" and she realized what he was doing.

"Georgia, would you show me where the bathroom is?" Sophie said, and Georgia jerked her thumb over her shoulder.

"Behind the bar, sugar."

Zane leaned closer to her. "Sophie wants you to go with her so she can tell you what a bad man I am."

Georgia widened her eyes and giggled. "I *love* bad men."

"Georgia," Frank said quietly. "You're drunk."

Georgia leered at him. "Oh, you're a real rocket scientist tonight."

"I think I'll go home," Rachel said, and stood up.

"Wait." Sophie nodded to the bar where Rob was leaning close to Clea, clearly not leaving soon. "Rob brought you, didn't he? How are you getting home?"

"I can walk," Rachel said, and Sophie stood up and said, "No, you can't. I'll get the keys from Amy."

"I'll drive her," Phin said from behind them. "You want a ride home, too?"

Sophie turned and caught her breath. "Oh. Yes. Sure. If it's on your way." *Of course it's on his way. Jeez, Sophie.*

"I've had about all the Tavern I can stand for one night," Phin said. "We can take Rachel home and then go back and fix your kitchen."

"Sounds good." Sophie looked across the room at Amy, who waved her on and turned back to smile at Wes. Clea and Rob were practically in each other's laps. Georgia was whispering something in Zane's ear. Frank looked confused and sad.

"Get me out of here," Sophie said, and Phin said, "Thought so," and gave her a gentle push toward the door.

Half an hour later, Sophie leaned on the kitchen sink with a glass of wine and tried to calm her pounding heart while Phin worked on the plumbing. With his head under the sink, she could scope out his body without having to face the distance in his eyes, and, having reacquainted herself with how very nicely he was put together, she felt a lot better about having fallen the night before, not to mention her plans to fall again tonight. Clearly this was quality stuff. If she could just get him to shut up, he'd be perfect.

"That's it," he said, pulling his head out from under the sink. "Turn on the water."

She walked over to the sink and turned on the tap. "Very

fast," she said as the water swirled down the drain. "Nice job, Mayor."

"Yeah, well, we do it all." He got to his feet. "Now, I'll have some of that wine."

She poured him a glass while he washed his hands, and then sat at the table with him in uncomfortable silence while he took his first sip. "Interesting," he said, looking at the glass. "Did you make this in the basement?"

"We bought it at the grocery," Sophie said.

"The grocery here in Temptation?" Phin said, appalled.

"It's the only one," Sophie said. "Of course, the grocery here."

He started to laugh. "What, you couldn't afford the Ripple?"

"Fine, don't drink it." Sophie reached for his glass, but Phin held on to it.

"I'm sure it'll be fine once I get used to it." He took another sip and shuddered. "Never mind," he said, and passed it over to her. "So tell me about the movie."

"No." Sophie looked at him with naked exasperation. "That's all you ever ask about, and I've already told you everything. What is it with you?"

Phin shrugged. "Okay, tell me about your life. How did the therapist take the news last night?"

Sophie raised her eyebrows. "You know he's a therapist?"

"This is Temptation," Phin said. "Stay long enough, I'll know everything about you. Of course, since you're leaving tomorrow, you'll get to keep most of your secrets."

"We're not leaving tomorrow," Sophie said. "We're going to shoot some extra footage for the movie, so we're staying over until next Sunday."

"Really." Phin's face was as impassive as ever. "And how did the therapist take that?"

"I didn't tell him." Sophie sipped her wine and gathered her courage. "I told him I wanted to fuck you, and he told me I was trying to shock him with language." There, that was the ticket, just say it really fast, like swallowing medicine or pulling off a Band-Aid.

Phin frowned his disbelief. "You told him you wanted to fuck him, and he yelled at you for talking dirty?" He shook his head. "This guy is dead below the waist."

"No." Sophie picked up his glass and moved to the sink to dump it. Then she swallowed and said carefully, "I told him I wanted to fuck *you*, and he said—" She stopped because this time he'd gotten it. "That wasn't a pass," she said, backing up a step. "I was merely—"

"The hell it wasn't." Phin stood up, and Sophie thought, *Oh, jeez, it's working, now what do I do?*

"Well, not really." She backed up again and bumped into the wall. "It was more . . ."

He followed her to the wall and bent to look her in the eye. "Sophie."

"What?"

"That was a pass."

She shrugged. "Maybe, subconsciously, a small one."

"Sophie."

She shut her eyes. "Okay, it was a pass, but—"

He kissed her, and she didn't have to finish the sentence, which was a damn good thing because she had no idea where she'd been going with it. She kissed him back, clutching at his shirt, and he broke the kiss to say, "Don't wrinkle the cotton," and pried her fingers off. She thought, *Well, the hell with you.* Then he pulled her close again, and she pressed herself against all that lovely muscle and bone and thought, *As long as he shuts up, this is going to be good*, and then his mouth was on hers again, and she stopped thinking at all.

Ten minutes later, when her dress was unbuttoned and so was his shirt, and she was dizzy and tight with the heat and even he looked a little mind-whacked, he said, "Where's your bedroom?"

"What?" Sophie blinked at him, coming back from all that good lust.

"Bed. Room," Phin said distinctly, sliding his hand inside her dress. "Or we can do this on the kitchen table, but I'm pretty sure I just heard somebody pull up outside. I don't care if Wes and Amy watch, but having Zane in the room would definitely put me off my stroke."

"Oh, no." Sophie stepped back, and he followed her, his hand tightening on her waist. "That would be bad with people . . ." She looked around vaguely. ". . . here." She caught sight of the phone and said, "Oh, *damn*, I have to call Brandon."

Phin looked at her incredulously and took his hand out of her dress. "Now?"

"I have to break up with him before I fool around with you," Sophie said. "That's only right."

"You're a little late." He gestured to her open dress. "The fooling-around is pretty much under way. Come here." He reached for her again, and she ducked away to grab the phone. "I don't believe this," he said, and sat down on the edge of the table, disheveled and gorgeous, looking at her as if she were demented, while she dialed and then waited for Brandon to pick up the phone.

"Brandon?" she said when it finally clicked, but it was his machine again. "Listen, Brandon, I did not want to leave this message on your machine, but since you're avoiding me—" She looked back over her shoulder at Phin, who was shaking his head at the ceiling. "—I think we should break up. And see other people. So that's what I'm doing. Seeing other people."

Phin put his head in his hands.

"Of course, they're not sensitive, understanding people like you," Sophie said pointedly.

"You want sensitive and understanding, stick with the therapist," Phin said. "You want great, headbanging sex, get off the fucking phone and come with me."

"I have to go now," Sophie said breathlessly into the phone. "I'm sorry if this hurts you but I don't think it will. You always seemed sort of clinical anyway."

"Oh, yeah, that'll soften the blow," Phin said. "Remind me never to get involved with you."

"Um, have a nice life," Sophie said brightly, and hung up. She walked over and boosted herself onto the table next to him, willing herself to stay cool, and reached for her wineglass again. "So you're not getting involved?"

He took the glass away from her. "No. I'm just going to have cheap sex with you and then run like hell."

"Chicken," she said.

He stood up and put her glass in the sink, and then he came back to stand in front of her, parting her knees with his body. He said, "You bet," and she lost her breath again.

He kissed her, sliding his hand into her dress to cup her breast, and she thought, *A semi-complete stranger is groping me*, and smiled against his mouth.

"What?" he said, and she gave in to the devil and wrapped her legs around his waist.

"It feels good," she said, and he said, "Well, that's why I do it," and kissed her again, running his hands down her back to lift her off the table.

"Where's the bedroom?" he said, and she said, "Second door on the left upstairs."

"Upstairs?" He put her back on the table. "Then you walk. And make it quick, before the therapist calls back."

She was going to argue, but she heard Amy and Wes on the porch, so she slid off the table and headed for the stairs and all that headbanging sex she'd been promised.

Twenty minutes later, she was suffocating on top of him in the heat of her unair-conditioned bedroom, the ancient box springs squeaking under them like a bad accordion, and her head was unbanged because the sex was lousy.

It wasn't Phin's fault. He was as thoroughly competent at the Phallic Variation as he'd been orally the night before. *So it must be me*, she thought, as he moved under her, doing absolutely nothing for her. She felt embarrassed by the whole situation. Zane had been right. She just wasn't the type for headbanging sex. She was too detached. She was too prissy and straight. She was doing this to write a sex scene for a movie she wasn't even sure she wanted to make. She was hot and sticky and she could feel her hair kinking in the heat even as Phin breathed under her, so she knew she looked awful. She was *unexciting*. Whatever the reason, it didn't matter, she was never going to get anywhere at this rate.

She thought briefly about faking it, and then dumped the idea when she realized that Phin would probably see through it and make fun of her performance. That pretty much left her with no option except tapping him on the shoulder and telling him to play on through because she was out of the game. *Sorry*, she'd have to say. *I'm not even close.* Or she could let him figure it out on his own, except guys never did. They just—

"You're not even close, are you?" Phin said, breathless below her, and she refocused back on him.

"What?"

"Hi, I'm Phin Tucker, and I'm inside you. I know how these things slip your mind." He didn't sound annoyed, but she felt bad anyway.

"I'm sorry," she said, and he slid his hand down her back and rolled to one side so that they lay face-to-face on the damp sheets, the springs protesting under them.

"Don't apologize." He brushed back a curl that was stuck to her forehead. "Thinking about the therapist?" He moved against her to bring her closer, and her nerves kicked into gear.

"Who?" she said, trying to figure out what the hell he was talking about.

"Well, at least you forgot us both," Phin said. "That was very democratic of you." He used a corner of the sheet to wipe sweat off her forehead. "Remind me to get you an air conditioner before we do this again. I'm dying here."

She wanted to say, *What are you talking about, AGAIN? This is a disaster*, but it didn't seem polite. "Maybe we should just call it a night," she said, and moved back from him, and he followed her to stay inside her, and that made her shiver under his hands.

"Maybe we should give it another shot," he said as she trembled. "That's at least one nerve you've still got working." He kissed her in the damp curve where her neck met her shoulder, and she took a ragged breath and moved against him again without thinking. "And that one always works. I noticed that last night."

"Last night was different," she said.

"Yeah, you came," Phin said, and she laughed in spite of herself.

"Not that. I'm distracted tonight. It's not your fault."

"Do me a favor." Phin slid his hand down her sweat-damp back again. "Don't be understanding. There's nothing worse for a guy's ego."

"Your ego is in fine shape," Sophie said crushingly. "Along with the rest of you. Really, this isn't going to work. Could we go watch TV now or something?"

"No." Phin kissed her in the curve of her neck again, and she shivered and said, "Stop that."

"See?" he said in her ear, which made her shiver, too. "Progress. Now tell me your fantasies."

"What?" She tried to squirm away and he rolled again, trapping her under him. He was heavy and sweaty, which should have been a turn-off, but her body rocked against his, independent of her mind, and she closed her eyes as he slid deeper into her.

"I think it's time we got to know each other," Phin said, laughter in his voice. "What do you think about when you masturbate?"

"Okay, I'm out of here." Sophie tried to roll out from under him, but he pressed down on her with his hips, and she stayed just to feel him hard inside her.

"What do you think about, Sophie?" he whispered in her ear, and she said loudly, "I don't think about anything."

"You are such a lousy liar." He rolled again, this time so that she was on top, his body sliding slickly under hers, and Sophie felt herself flush.

"Bondage?" he said, his voice husky as he rocked against her, his hands on her hips, and she caught her breath and said, "You come near me with a rope, and I'm history."

"Okay, later for that," he said. "Rape fantasy?"

"Tacky," she said, and he said, "Not if you do it right. You want to dominate?"

"Oh, yeah. Like you'd let me." She started to laugh, only to stop when she heard people in the kitchen downstairs. "Shhh."

"Why?" Phin stopped moving. "It's just Wes and Amy."

"Yeah." Sophie looked over her shoulder at the door.

"Did you lock it?" Phin said in her ear, and he sounded amused.

"I forgot." She tried to pull away from him, but he rolled and trapped her again, sliding deeper inside her and making her gasp. "Stop it," she said breathlessly. "I'm not even sure it's closed all the way. Let me go lock it and I'll come back."

"Bothers you, huh?" Phin started working his way down her neck again as he pulsed inside her, and Sophie felt the heat spread low as her blood pounded.

"No," she lied.

"They could walk in anytime." He nibbled on her shoulder, and she twitched under him and felt her breath go. "Walk right in and find us naked." He slid his hand up to her sweat-dampened breast, and the heat rolled across her as she moved to his rhythm. "Find *you* naked. With me inside you. *Nothing* you could do about it."

She caught her breath and said, "*Stop* it," and he said, "Nope, I think we're getting somewhere."

She squirmed under him to get away, and their bodies slid together. He said, "Oh, God, yes, do that," and she smacked him on the shoulder because he was so impossible, and arched into him at the same time because he was so hard moving inside her and he felt so good.

"Maybe I can get . . . somebody else . . . to open that door," he said in her ear, and she said, "No!" a lot louder than she meant because it was part moan. She heard Amy say, "Sophie?" downstairs, and she tensed. Phin laughed down at her, his face as damp as hers.

Beautifully moist, Sophie thought. *Be careful what you wish for.*

Amy called her name again, and Phin said, "Excellent." He rocked higher into her, and she bit her lip to keep from moaning and then moaned anyway. "Louder," he said, and she shook her head as the heat built and his rhythm began to make her mindless.

"Then it's up to me." He sounded breathless. "The guy always has to do everything."

He leaned over her to the bedside table, and she bit into his shoulder from the sheer pleasure of feeling him against her. Then he stopped, and she looked up to see him holding the alarm clock.

"I'll buy you a new one," he said, and threw it against the wall.

"What are you *doing*?" she screamed as it crashed and went off clanging. Amy called up, "Sophie?" and Phin moved again, rocking harder, and she shuddered under him and gasped, "*Stop* it."

"This close? Not on your life." He was moving faster now, and she clutched at him and breathed hard as the pressure built. She said, "No . . . no . . . we're not . . . close," and he rolled across her again, making her jerk against him. He picked up the dolphin lamp, yanking the cord out with it, and she realized what he was doing and shrieked, "No!" just as he threw it against the wall.

It shattered and fell on top of the clanging alarm.

"Sophie?" Amy called, and started up the stairs, and Phin said, "This is it," and moved high into her, grabbing her wrists and holding them over her head, sliding hot on top of her, rocking hard inside her, whispering in her ear that Amy'd catch them, any minute, any minute, any minute, now, now, *now*, and Sophie twisted under him, caught in the heat and the slide and the panic and the throb he was pounding into her, and then Amy said, "Sophie?" and pushed open the door, and Sophie cried, "Oh, *God*," and came so hard she almost passed out.

"Oh," Amy said, and shut the door.

Sophie heard Amy go down the stairs, with only a fraction

of her attention. The rest was consumed with how good she felt everywhere as the aftershocks made her twitch, how much she needed her breath back, and how she was going to strangle Phin when he let go of her wrists and she was done feeling incredible. And even as she had the thought, he shuddered on top of her and let go, collapsing with his face in her pillow.

"You *pervert*," she said minutes later, when she could talk.

"You came," he said, his voice muffled by the pillow.

"I don't *believe* you did that."

"I don't believe you're not grateful."

"Grateful?" Sophie struggled to sit up, and for once he let her slide out from under him, rolling to get rid of the condom as she moved away from him. "*Look* at this." The alarm clock was smashed next to the baseboard, and the dolphin lamp was in a million pieces, and it was just a *mess*, but try as she might, she couldn't work up any real indignation. Total satisfaction did that, she supposed, just sort of made everything else irrelevant. Still, he'd been impossible, so she concentrated on the carnage while she used the sheet to blot the sweat from her happily throbbing body. "I mean, just look at it!"

Phin draped his arm across her shoulders and pulled her back down on the bed, his face still in the pillow. "Did you come?"

Sophie crossed her arms over her breasts and glared at the ceiling, ignoring the hot weight of his arm across her and all the cheering her body was doing. "Yes."

"Did you like it?" he said, his voice still muffled by the pillow.

She started to grin in spite of herself. "Yes."

"Say, 'Thank you, Phin.'"

"Oh, please."

"Say, 'Thank you *very* much, Phin.'"

"I don't think so."

"Say, 'You are a great lover, Phin.'"

"I'm out of here." She rolled to swing out of bed, and his arm slipped down to her waist and pulled her back against him.

He felt good, solid against her back, and she had to concentrate to remember she was annoyed with him for making her come.

That couldn't be right.

He pulled his face out of the pillow and rolled to cuddle her to him from behind, kissing her damp hair and holding her close. "Discovery fantasy," he said, and she relaxed into the hot curve of his body.

"What?"

"You have discovery fantasies. Very common among women." He yawned in her ear. "Men don't have them. We like to watch."

"I do not have discovery fantasies," Sophie said. "That's kinky."

"You're kinky."

Sophie tried to pull away in outrage. "I am *not* kinky."

He sighed. "Sophie, your soul is a corkscrew." He held on to her and kissed her neck again, and she gave up to stay curled in his heat, guiltily flattered that he thought she was kinky. Not sexless after all. In fact . . .

"So . . . I'm exciting?"

"Heart-stopping," Phin said into her neck. "And you definitely have discovery fantasies. I foresee us having a lot of sex in public places." He yawned again and shifted on the bed. "Anyplace would be more comfortable than this mattress. Not to mention quieter."

"I don't see us having a lot of sex anywhere," Sophie said, trying to get her control back. *But I'm exciting.*

"That's because you're repressed," Phin said. "Which is why God sent me to save you."

"God did not send you," Sophie said. "The devil sent you. And we're not having sex in public."

"Sure we are," Phin said. "You want to know why?"

He kissed her neck again and her pulse kicked up again. "No."

"Because you like it," he whispered in her ear, and she shivered against him.

"I don't think so," she said, and put her hand on the edge of the bed to push herself out of his arms before he talked her into sex on the kitchen table.

He caught her right hand to stop her, and then he brought it close to their faces to look at it. "Your ring has writing on it." He sounded sleepy, and she gave up trying to escape, enjoying the way his voice felt in her ear.

"They both do," Sophie said. "One says *free will* and the other one says *destiny*. They were my mother's." She looked at the ring in the moonlight, and at Phin's fingers intertwined with hers, and thought, *That's nice*.

Phin turned the ring until the *destiny* was centered on her finger and yawned. "Free will and fate?"

He didn't sound as if he cared, and Sophie rolled in his arms so she could look at him. He smiled when she turned, a sleepy, lazy smile just for her that had nothing to do with politics or charm, and she thought, *Wow*. She almost rolled closer and kissed him, but that would make things more complicated, so she concentrated on his question.

"There are things you can change . . ." Sophie held up her left hand with the *free will* ring to watch it glint in the moonlight. "And things you can't change." She pulled the *destiny* hand free from his.

Phin recaptured the hand with *destiny* on it. "I don't believe in destiny," he said, as he pulled her hand down. He kissed her knuckles, and Sophie shivered at the heat from his mouth.

"Mama said that family is your destiny," she said, trying not to fall again, "because they shape your life."

Phin shrugged against her. "Maybe at first—"

Sophie shook her head, her curls brushing his chest, and watched as he caught his breath. It was such a little thing, but she thought, *I did that.* "Your worldview is established by six," she said, watching him. "You don't have any choice in that. You just get it." *I think I want it again.*

"And then you grow up and move away. You have free will." Phin met her eyes and looked a lot less sleepy. "You can choose whatever you want. I choose this." He began to work his way down her neck again, his lips tickling hot on her skin.

Sophie's pulse kicked up. "Well, that was Mama's point," she said, her voice a little higher than before. "Your family is your destiny, and then you make what you can of that." She thought about her mother for a minute, about all those dreams lost because of her bad choices, and she pulled away. "And then sometimes, destiny comes along and slaps you again anyway."

Phin stopped. "What happened?"

"There was a car accident," Sophie said, remembering the sound of the crunching metal, now confused with the sound from the Garveys' accident, so it seemed new all over again. "She died. She'd spent all those years following Dad around the country, waving her rings and saying, 'Everything will be fine,' and Dad saying, 'Nothing but good times ahead,' and then—" She stopped for a moment, and Phin pulled her closer. "One day there was the accident, and Dad stopped talking about the good times and it was pretty much the three of us and Dusty Springfield."

"That explains a lot," Phin said.

She lifted her chin and flashed her mother's rings in the moonlight. "So then I'd say to Amy, 'Everything will be fine,' and Davy would say to her, 'Nothing but good times ahead,' and Dad would tell us to shut the hell up and we'd be off again."

"Your dad was a salesman?" Phin said.

"Sort of," Sophie said, and rolled away.

He pulled her back against him. "But now everything is fine," he said in her ear. "Davy and Amy are grown up and you're all safe and happy. You made it come true for them."

Sophie nodded. *Just not for me.*

"So let me make it true for you tonight," he said, and when she turned to him, amazed, he kissed her, so gently that she gave herself up to him completely, no doubts at all this time. "Nothing but good times ahead," he said against her mouth, and began to kiss his way down her body again, fulfilling his promise with every move he made.

The phone rang the next morning just as Sophie was typing the end of the lamp scene. She hit SAVE and answered the phone, only to hear Brandon say, "I'm returning your call."

Sophie winced. "Oh. I'm really sorry about that. But you're really better off without me. I know it's painful—"

"But are you better off without me?" Brandon said.

Sophie looked at the phone incredulously. "What?"

"I don't think you've thought this through. You're going to be home this afternoon and we can—"

"Actually, we're staying another week," Sophie said.

"—discuss the situation and help you deal with your denial."

"*My* denial?" Sophie said.

"Another week?" Brandon said.

"Brandon, the only one in denial here is you," Sophie said. "Really, I think we just got used to each other. I think it's time we found other people who will meet our needs." She closed her eyes as she thought of some of the needs Phin had met, could meet, would meet in the next week with any amount of encouragement at all.

"We can meet our needs," Brandon said. "We've always met our needs."

"I think I've discovered new needs," Sophie said.

"If this is about sex, don't be childish. Tell me what you want and I'll give it to you."

"My freedom," Sophie said. "I'm trying to do this the civilized way, but I really want out of this relationship. In fact, I am out."

"I'll call you again at the end of the week," Brandon said. "I'm sure the thrill will be gone by then and we can talk."

"The thrill might be gone, but I will be, too. Really, Brandon—" Sophie began, but he'd already hung up.

"Is the new scene done?" Amy said from the door into the living room.

"Yeah." Sophie hung up the phone and shoved the Power-Book toward her. "That was Brandon. He thinks—"

"Shut up so I can read this," Amy said, and Sophie jerked her head up at the tone in her voice. She watched Amy read from the screen, looking a lot tenser than the scene deserved.

"This is great," Amy said when she finished, but she didn't look happy. "And this explains a lot. I couldn't figure out what all the crashing was about."

"He's very inventive." Sophie frowned at her. "What's wrong?"

"Nothing," Amy said. "I have to show this to Clea—"

"No," Sophie said and closed the PowerBook. "What happened?"

Amy bit her lip. "That dickhead Zane," she said finally. "He just told me that if I don't quit doing the video so Cleo will go home with him, he's going to tell Wes about my juvenile record." She swallowed hard. "So I told him to go ahead. I told him Wes already knew and didn't care."

"Does he?"

"No," Amy said. "And I think he'd care—he's a cop, isn't he? But I don't care. I'm going to make this video and the documentary no matter what, and I don't care what that dickhead does, but—"

"But Zane must die," Sophie said, nodding. "I understand. We'll think of something horrible to do to him."

"That would help," Amy said, cheering up a little.

"Too bad Davy isn't here," Sophie said. "He always did the best revenge."

"Let's call him," Amy said. "Because I want something really bad to happen to Zane. Which reminds me, Clea wants another love scene. And that's bound to piss Zane off, so—"

"We should play along." Sophie tried to look blasé. "You want me to sacrifice myself to the mayor again."

"From what I saw last night, it was no sacrifice." Amy managed a weak smile. "And see if he's got a letter sweater we can borrow. He looks like the type who'd have one."

Sophie frowned at her. "A letter sweater?"

Amy nodded, not happy. "Clea wants to do this thing where she's driving up the road on her way home remembering Frank in high school so that when she sees the real Frank, everybody will understand the shock. And then when Rob shows up as his son, it'll make sense that she falls for him."

"I still don't get the lett—"

"She wants Rob to play Frank in her high-school memories." Amy wrinkled her nose. "Corny as hell, but she's calling the shots."

"Right," Sophie said. "I'll ask the mayor for a letter sweater."

And great sex. She stopped breathing for a moment just thinking about it.

"Soon," Amy said.

Sophie tried to look noble. "I suppose I could go visit the bookstore now. He said he was going to be working there today. And maybe if I can't find anything in the books, he'll have some ideas." *I have some ideas.*

Amy looked down at the lamp scene. "I'd count on it." She still seemed down. "You're just toying with the mayor, right? You're not getting involved?"

"No," Sophie said, cooling off a little. "It's pretty much mutual toying."

"Because I don't need a scene if this is going to be another Chad thing," Amy said. "I really hate it that that happened to you. And the mayor has Chad written all over him."

"He's not," Sophie said. "He was very sweet last night."

"I hate Zane, too," Amy said, not really listening.

"We'll take care of Zane," Sophie said as she got up to go. "Really, nothing but good times ahead."

For once, at least for the rest of the afternoon, she was pretty sure that was true.

Chapter
Seven

That same afternoon, Rachel's father called her out of the garden onto the cement patio behind their house. She sat gingerly on the steel garden chair beside him, her weeding gloves on, wary of both the sun-warmed metal and her father's topic of conversation.

"So you're working on this movie," he said. "What are they doing?"

"Just shooting people talking on the porch," Rachel said.

"Oh." Her father seemed disappointed. Then he said, "You let me know what they're doing. It's important for the town."

"Why?"

"It's my civic duty to know what's happening in this town," her father said, puffing up a little. "These outsiders, they could be bad influences. So you tell me everything, you understand?"

"Yes, Daddy," Rachel said, having no intention of doing any such thing. "The Coreys are painting the house this weekend and after school. There's some news."

Her father didn't look interested. "Maybe I should drop by, see for myself. Phin Tucker's out there a lot, isn't he?"

"He showed Sophie how to change the fuses," Rachel said, although she was pretty sure that wasn't the only thing Phin was showing Sophie how to do. Even from the backseat of Phin's convertible the night before, Rachel had picked up on the sexual tension in the front seat. When her mother had met her at the door and said eagerly, "Was that Phin Tucker who brought you home?" she'd said, "Mom, he didn't even know I was there."

"So he's involved with the movie people," her father was saying, and without thinking, Rachel said, "Oh, yeah."

"Does that upset you? Does it upset you that I'm running against him in the election?"

"Why would I be upset? You do it every two years." Rachel stared out at the garden, the garden she'd have to go back to weeding soon, the garden she'd weeded every summer for her whole life.

She wanted to go someplace where somebody else did the weeding.

"I don't want you to be hurt if he's spending time with other women," her father said. "And I don't want you to think you have to choose between your father and your husband."

"*Husband?*" Rachel said. "Not in a million years. Mom's got it in her head that we're going to be together, but she's wrong."

"I'm sure she—" Stephen began, but Rachel cut him off.

"Look, Daddy, it's *Phin*, for God's sake. He taught me to ride my bike and stuck Band-Aids on me when I fell off, and he coached me in softball and yelled at me when I fell over third base in the tournament game. After that, it's kind of hard to get hot looking at him."

"Oh." Stephen looked uncomfortable, and Rachel added, "Sorry, Dad. More than you needed to know."

"No, no, you know you can tell me anything," Stephen said, but his expression added, *Just not that.* "It would be a good match. You could hyphenate your last name. Garvey-Tucker." He looked out into the distance. "Your son could take that name, too."

"Son?" Rachel said.

"Phin needs a son, and you need to stop running around and be settled."

"Running around?" The unfairness of this was criminal. "Where do I run around?"

"I don't like you going out to the Tavern," Stephen said. "You're underage. Of course, I know you go with Rob and he's a gentleman. Too bad his father's an idiot. You're not thinking about marrying Rob, are you?"

Rachel thought about spending the rest of her days in Temptation and the rest of her nights with Rob. "No."

"Well, you have to marry somebody," Stephen said. "You think about Phin. He's a good-looking man. You'd have good-looking sons."

Enough of this "son" talk. The last thing she needed was a baby, for cripes' sake. She was *twenty.*

Her father was still talking, nodding to the house to their right. "And you'd live right next door, so we could help you out whenever you needed."

"Phin wouldn't kick Junie Miller out of that house," Rachel said. "That would be mean."

"There's no reason for him to house his ex–mother-in-law," Stephen said, and Rachel cast a wary look back at the kitchen in case her mother heard. Her mother could go on for hours about how Diane Miller had made Phin buy the house next door to the Garveys just so she could rub their marriage in Virginia's face.

"Just don't wait too long to decide," Stephen was saying. "Or you'll end up like Clea Whipple, not getting married until you're over thirty, no children, living all over the place and never coming home until you're middle-aged. . . ." He went on, and Rachel thought, *God, that sounds great.*

Her father talked on, about family values and her living next door and how they'd see each other every day and how her son would grow up to be mayor, too, and Rachel decided that she was definitely going to L.A.

Whatever it took.

When Sophie peered through the glass front door of the book-store in the heat of the late afternoon, she saw Phin frowning at papers on the counter. Then he saw her and his face cleared, and he let her in. "Hello, Sophie Dempsey. What brings you here?"

"Amy needs to borrow a letter sweater. And I might buy some books." Sophie turned away so she wouldn't have to meet his eyes and discovered that she was in a really nice bookstore. It was the downstairs of a converted Victorian house, but it had been opened up with support columns so that what had once been four rooms was now one big room. There were a couple of comfortable chairs and four fireplaces, but mostly the room was filled with walnut bookcases, neatly labeled with copperplate signs. "It's beautiful," she said. "Really beautiful."

"Thank you," Phin said, without any of the cynicism that could make his voice grate on her. "My grandpa did it all."

Toward the back, there was an open doorway, and she said, "What's back there through that door?"

"My pool table," Phin said, and she went to check it out.

The kitchen and a breakfast room had also been opened into one big room, and the pool table sat in the middle of it.

"It's pretty," Sophie said when she saw it, knowing what a massive understatement that was. It was a magnificent nine-foot hand-carved oak table, with rosewood rails inlaid with pearl and gold silk fringe on the pockets. Phin winced at the "pretty," but he said, "Thank you," like the gentleman he was.

She went to the cue rack and put her hands behind her back so she wouldn't touch anything. The temptation was terrible. The rack was old and very beautiful, an Eastlake design that had *New England Pool Cue Company* lettered in gold across the top. "This is really pretty, too." She backed up a step and almost fell over a stack of boxes behind her.

"Careful," Phin said. "Campaign posters."

There were cartons of them stacked all along the wall. "You planning on running a big campaign?" Sophie said, and Phin said, "No, my grandma made a mistake."

"My grandpa wanted these for his second campaign, back in 1942. He told her to order a hundred of them. So she did, but she didn't notice that they came in lots of a hundred, so she ordered a hundred lots and Grandpa ended up with ten thousand posters. We've been using them ever since."

"You haven't changed posters since 1942?"

"Only once. After Gil Garvey beat my dad because he'd built the New Bridge." Sophie frowned and he went on. "Gil made a big deal out of what a waste of money it was because we had to buy that right-of-way from Sam Whipple to put the new road in, but by the time the next election came around, people had noticed that there weren't as many car wrecks and the driving was easier. So my dad had bumper stickers printed that said *He Built the Bridge* and he and my mom and I sat here one night and stuck them over the *More of the Same* part of the poster and then went out and hung them the next day."

"And he won," Sophie said.

"In a landslide." Phin stuck his hands in his pockets, a clear giveaway, Brandon would have said, that he was repressing his emotions.

"So what's the rest of the story?"

Phin shrugged. "He served his term, had a heart attack, served four more terms, had another attack, and died a year later from his third attack. He got the office back but he was never the same."

Sophie frowned. "I can't imagine wanting anything that much."

"I don't think it was the wanting," Phin said. "I think it was the years of tradition he felt he'd broken. And then he thought he had to play it safe after that so he wouldn't lose again. It finished him."

"Just because he lost one election." Sophie shook her head.

"Tuckers don't lose," Phin said. "Which is why I'd like to know if you're shooting porn out there."

Sophie blinked. "Porn? Good grief, no. I wouldn't do that." She looked down at the posters and thought, *I don't want to be his New Bridge.* "We're shooting a sex scene, though." *Maybe two, if this afternoon goes well.* "About at the level of the *NYPD Blue* stuff on TV. It's not porn, I swear, but some people might think it was."

Phin relaxed a little. "Not if it's something you could show on TV. If that's all you're doing, we don't have a problem." He smiled at her, and Sophie felt the heat kick in just because he was close.

"So I . . ." she began, and he moved closer, and she met his eyes and went dizzy at the heat there.

"Tell me what you want and you've got it," he said.

"I don't know what you're talking about," Sophie said, trying not to fall against him.

"I'm talking about that look in your eyes. I've seen it three times now, and it makes me cheerful."

Sophie looked at the ceiling.

"Forget it, Soph," he said. "You don't want to do it, fine, but don't try to tell me you don't want it."

She met his eyes. "Oh, I want it," she said, and he kissed her, running his hand up her side to her breast while she leaned into him.

Fifteen minutes later, she was stretched out beside the pool table with her blouse open, her zipper down and her body ready. Phin stopped to get his breath and said, "You know I have a bed upstairs," and then the front door opened, and she clutched at him.

"I locked that," he said. "*Fuck*, it's my mother."

Sophie grabbed for her blouse while Phin rolled to his feet and tucked his shirt in.

"Hey, Mom," he said as he walked toward the front of the store, and Sophie heard a cold voice say, "What were you doing back there? You've left papers all over the counter. People can see this mess from the street."

"It's Sunday," Phin said. "There are no people in the street. That's why you came in here?"

"I'm on my way to pick up Dillie, but I wanted to talk to you alone first."

I shouldn't be listening to this, Sophie thought. She tucked in her blouse and then, just as Phin's mother said, "Virginia Garvey came by," she stood up and walked toward the front of the bookstore, saying, as nonsexually as she could, "Well, thanks for the help." She let her eyes drift to Phin's mother, casually, no big deal, but when she got a good look, she froze in place.

Liz Tucker was tall, elegant, blonde, and expensive, but mostly she was terrifying. And with the chill she was radiating right now, if they could get her to sit in the living room at the farmhouse, they wouldn't need central air. Ever. Sophie took a step back.

"This is my mother, Liz Tucker, who is just leaving," Phin told her. "Mom, this is Sophie Dempsey. I like her, so be nice."

"How do you do, Miss Dempsey." Liz Tucker held out a perfectly manicured hand that had a diamond on it that could have paid off any young doctor's college loans. Sophie looked at her left hand. The diamond there was even bigger.

"Pleased to meet you," Sophie said faintly, and took her hand. It was cold and dry and the handshake Liz gave her was the equivalent of an air kiss, sliding away before any real contact could be made.

"You're one of the movie people," Liz said. "Virginia said you were working hard." Liz's eyes went to Phin. "And interacting with the community."

"You know, I should be going," Sophie said. "Lots to do."

"You're not going anywhere." Phin opened the front door. "Good-bye, Mom. Give my best to Virginia and tell her to get a life."

Liz looked as if she wanted to argue, but Phin opened the door wider and pointed to the porch, patiently staring his mother down until she gave up and went out the door, giving Sophie one last, cool look before she went.

"Boy," Sophie said when she was gone.

"She wasn't always like that," Phin said. "My dad's death hit her hard. She has a good heart."

Sophie wanted to say, *How can you tell?* But it was his mother, after all. "I'm sure she does."

"No, you're not." Phin came closer. "But I don't care. I was about to be in the middle of you. Pick a place, anyplace, and lie down."

Sophie caught her breath and took a step back. Anyplace. Something that would be good in a movie. "The pool table." That could make up for the bad rep pool tables had gotten in *The Accused*.

Phin stopped in his tracks. "Are you insane? Do you know what that would do to the felt?"

As a matter of fact, Sophie did, but she was surprised he'd think of it now. "So much for adventure," she said to him, and he said, "Any adventure you want, as long as it doesn't screw up my pool table. Let me show you the upstairs. You can pick out a letter sweater and take off your clothes."

The bedroom at the top of the stairs was sloppily comfortable, and the bed was wide and rumpled. "Is this where you live?" Sophie said, looking around, and Phin said, "Not anymore," and kissed her, taking her down into heat.

"I want something exciting," she said breathlessly, as she came up for air. "I want something exciting and different and depraved."

He laughed as he stroked his hands down her back. "Talk's cheap. Give me details."

He kissed her neck, finding that good place, and she felt dizzy. *Concentrate*. "I can't think of anything," Sophie said, which was true; her mind was going south again.

"Handcuffs."

"I don't think so."

"Just as well, I can't find them anyway." Phin tugged her toward the bed and tipped her onto the quilt. "Ice cubes. Feathers. Whipped cream."

"What?" Sophie scooted over on the bed, her heart pounding as he took off his shirt. "Never mind. No."

"I could call Wes over for a threesome." He stripped off his pants and rolled onto the bed beside her.

"No, you could not," Sophie said, and shivered as he put his arms around her.

"He wouldn't do it anyway," Phin said against her hair, as his fingers moved down her blouse. "Private kind of guy, Wes is. Why are you still dressed?"

"What?" Sophie said. "Oh." She sat up and realized she was unbuttoned again. "I was thinking of something more—" She shivered as he pulled her blouse off her shoulders and the air-conditioned air hit her.

"More what?" he said, sliding her zipper down, and she tried to organize her thoughts and said, "You know. Erotic but not embarrassing."

He stopped at that. "Let me get this straight. You want something exciting but not weird, different but not kinky, and depraved but not embarrassing."

"Yes," Sophie said, trying not to notice that he was naked. God, he was beautiful.

He sighed. "Can't we just have sex? It's not as if we've known each other long enough to get bored."

"No," Sophie said. "I'm learning a lot from you. This is like college." *Touch me.*

"College," Phin said.

"I never got to go," Sophie said. "And I always wanted a degree. So I'm getting it from you." *Give it to me.*

"In sex," Phin said.

"Well, you're a master at it, aren't you?" Sophie said, batting her eyelashes at him as she shoved off her shorts. *Take me.*

"Don't even try to charm me," Phin said, but he sounded distracted.

Sophie put her arms around him and pulled him close.

"Teach me something new," she said, and he bent her back onto the bed and she shivered as his body slid against hers.

"Okay," Phin said. "But pay attention, Julie Ann, there'll be a quiz."

Sophie woke up alone. She stretched, sliding across almond oil–soaked sheets, which was disgusting, but she felt terrific, so what the heck. She squinted at the clock beside Phin's bed and realized that she'd been asleep for over an hour. Those quizzes took a lot out of a woman.

She wrapped herself in the slippery top sheet and tiptoed down the hall until she found the bathroom, and then she showered until she was sure all the oil was gone. The stuff was everywhere, so it took her a while.

Then she went back to Phin's bedroom and dressed, and, because she couldn't stand the mess, she stripped the oil-stained bottom sheet and mattress pad from the bed. Something clanked as she pulled them off, and she stooped to look under the bed to see what had fallen.

Handcuffs.

She held them up, and they glinted back at her, and she thought grim thoughts about what Phin had been using them for and whom he'd been using them with.

It wasn't that she was jealous at all, she told herself.

It was just that he was a *perv*.

"Would these be yours?" she asked Phin when she got downstairs.

He turned from the register, looking sleepy and satisfied in the late-afternoon light, and said, "Oh, good, I've been looking for those."

Sophie held the cuffs higher, hoping to instill some sense

of shame, if not in him, then at least in herself. One look at him and she wanted him again. "I found them in the bed."

"That makes sense," Phin said. "That's where I lost them."

"I'd ask what you were doing with them," Sophie said, trying not to sound bitchy, "but I probably don't want to know, do I?"

"Sure you do. It was exciting and different and depraved." Phin nodded toward the stairs. "Go put them someplace we can find them, and I'll show you later. How do you feel?"

"Unsure," Sophie said, looking at the cuffs with growing curiosity.

"Not about them, dummy," Phin said. "This is the part where you get frosty and turn on me."

"What part?" Sophie said.

"The part after we have sex," Phin said. "When you remember that I'm a pervert, and you're not this kind of woman, and it's all my fault." He sounded pretty cheerful about it.

Sophie looked back at the cuffs, now definitely intrigued in spite of herself. There was no point in being disgusted with him; she'd loved everything he'd done to her. And if she was going to be honest, she was open to discussion about the cuffs. "I think we can skip the frosty part from now on. So exactly what do you—"

The front door opened, and Sophie tried to hide the cuffs, too late.

Wes looked more startled than she did. When he recovered, he said, "Those are mine, thank you." He took the cuffs from her and put them in his back pocket. "Why does it smell like salad in here?"

"I had plans for those," Phin said, at the same time Sophie said brightly, "Well, I've got to go."

She tried to sidle out the door, but Phin blocked her. "Wes

was just going back to the pool table," he said, and Wes said, "Right. I'll just go back to the pool table."

When he was gone, Phin said, "So we can skip that part from now on."

"What part?" Sophie said, and he bent and kissed her, gently this time, and she leaned into him and felt her breath go, just because he was so close and so gentle and so hot.

"We can skip the frosty part," he murmured against her mouth. "And go straight to the good stuff."

"Right," she breathed. "Absolutely." She slid her arms around his waist and pulled him closer, falling into his kiss again, and when he came up for air, he said, "You know, I don't have to play pool right now."

"Oh. Sure you do." Sophie stepped away from him. "I have to get back. I have . . . work to do."

"Work." He let his breath out. "Okay. So I'll see you tomorrow."

"Yeah," Sophie said, drifting toward the door. "Tomorrow's good." She closed the door behind her and stood on the porch looking dazedly out at Temptation's Main Street baking in the late-afternoon sun.

Nice little town, she thought. *Pretty.*

The door rattled behind her and Phin came out, holding a white sweater. "Forgot to give this to you." He handed it to her just as a car went past.

It slowed down, and Phin waved.

"Anybody we know?" Sophie said, shaking the sweater out. It had a large red *T* with a red-and-white basketball in the middle of it.

"I know them. You don't," Phin said, and Sophie thought, *Story of my life, town boy.*

"We'll be very careful with the sweater," she told him, and he said, "Don't bother, I have more."

"Of *course* you do," Sophie said, and started down the steps.

"Frosty," Phin said, and went back inside.

"Satisfied," Sophie said to nobody, and went back to the farm.

"I suppose you had to," Wes said when Phin went back to join him at the table.

"Pretty much. She seduced me."

"Yeah, right," Wes said. "She said, 'Please fix the kitchen drain,' and you interpreted that—"

"She said, 'Fuck me.'" Phin put two balls on the table and picked up his cue. "I interpreted that to mean she wanted sex."

"Oh." Wes picked up his cue. "That would have been my call, too." He squinted at the table. "Why would she have said that?"

"On a guess? Because she wanted sex." Phin bent to shoot, and Wes did the same. They stroked the balls to the opposite cushion and then watched them roll back. Both balls hit the second cushion, but Wes's stayed an inch behind Phin's.

Phin racked the balls for him and stepped away from the table. "She's not as uptight as she looks. She wants to be a straight arrow, but she's bent as hell."

Wes slammed the cue ball into the rack and the balls scattered, two finding pockets. "So you're helping her find the real Sophie."

"I'm pretty much doing whatever she tells me to," Phin said. "That's working out well for me. She called the therapist last night and broke it off, so you can forget giving me grief on that account."

Wes made the next ball and walked around to the other side of the table. "So thanks to you, her relationship is over."

"Is this going to be a long conversation?" Phin said.

"I just want to know why she's giving up a solid relationship for seven more days of sex with you." Wes stopped to chalk.

"I have no idea," Phin said. "I'm just grateful."

"You said that first day she was up to something." Wes pocketed the second ball. "I think you were right. And Stephen is very hot to find out what and link you to it, and Zane Black thinks he knows."

Wes chalked again as Phin said, "Zane Black?"

Wes nodded. "He came in today. Tracked me down on a Sunday to say I should look into Amy's background. He said I should close down the movie because he was pretty sure it was something we wouldn't like, and once I got a look at Amy's history, I'd know it for sure."

Phin felt his old unease about the movie come sneaking back. "Did you check?"

Wes nodded again. "She's clean. But I'm still worried about Stephen." He bent to shoot again, adding, "Especially since you appear to lose your mind every time you get near Sophie."

"So, you getting anywhere with Amy?" Phin said, and Wes miscued.

"You want to play pool or talk?" Wes said.

"I want to play pool," Phin said, and began to run the table, trying not to think about what kind of trouble Sophie could be getting into out at the farm with that damn movie. He'd just have to watch her more closely, he decided.

His civic duty.

The next morning, Sophie handed Amy the almond-oil scene.

"This is good," Amy said when she'd finished reading. "Almond oil, huh?"

"It wasn't so much the oil," Sophie said, "as what he did with it. I think he reads a lot." She paused and then added, "I met his mother, too."

"That bad?"

"Angela Lansbury in *The Manchurian Candidate*. I kept waiting for her to say, 'Why don't you pass the time by playing a little solitaire?' and then the last thing I'd see would be Phin's eyes glazing over."

"That would explain a lot about Phin," Amy said. "There's a considerable chill factor there."

"That would be because his mother is a Frigidaire," Sophie said.

"One of the Hill Frigidaires?" Amy said. "These old families sure know how to repel outsiders."

"Yeah," Sophie said, feeling a little depressed. "They sure do."

They heard a car come down the lane, and Amy went to look. "Who do we know that drives a blue BMW?" she said, and Sophie said, "Us? Nobody," but when the car stopped and a champagne blonde got out, she said, "Oh, no."

Amy squinted out across the yard. "Who is that?"

"Phin's mother," Sophie said, and pushed past her to go out onto the porch.

"My son is an important man in this town," Liz said carefully, when they were sitting on the swing alone, Amy and the dog having taken one look at Liz and retreated into the house. Sophie was melting in the heat—she could feel the sweat trickling between her breasts—but Liz wasn't even flushed, even in her silk suit. "The Tuckers have always been important here."

Sophie nodded. The woman had to be an alien.

"I'm sure that seems amusing to you, coming as you do from the city—"

"No," Sophie said. "I'm not amused at all. He told me about the New Bridge. I understand how important it is."

Liz nodded. "Thank you. That makes what I have to say much easier." She pressed her lips together. "I realize that you and my son are involved in a liaison, and that is none of my business. But the political well-being of this town is my business, has always been the business of the Tuckers, and it's my duty to make sure that it is not threatened. Your association with him is unfortunate from a political perspective. When are you leaving Temptation?"

Sophie drew back, stung in spite of herself. Well, what had she expected? *Welcome to the family?* "Next Sunday," Sophie said, holding her temper.

"Will you be seeing him in Cincinnati?"

Sophie took a deep breath. "We haven't talked about it."

"I see." Liz stared out across the barren yard, her face like stone. "But if he decided to pursue the relationship once you went back to Cincinnati, you would agree."

"I have no idea," Sophie said. "By this time next week, I may loathe him." She thought about Phin, and fairness made her add, "Or not."

"He doesn't have any money, you know."

Sophie jerked around to look at her, all the anger she'd been repressing breaking through. "What?"

"He doesn't have any money." Liz stared out at the yard. "The Tuckers have never had money. The money comes from my family."

I'm not after his money, you ice cube. Sophie shook her head, willing herself to stay calm through her fury. "You know, you're not thinking this through."

"Really, Miss Dempsey—"

"I realize your view is clouded on this because you're his mother, but he's gorgeous and smart and funny and kind and skilled. He's fixed half the stuff in this house. Do you know how attractive that is?"

"His father was like that," Liz said, taken aback a little.

"Then you know how attractive that is. But mostly, he's just sexy as hell." Liz flinched, and Sophie thought, *Good*. "Trust me, if Phin were standing on a street corner in a barrel, holding a cup with pencils in it, women would still be lying at his feet." Sophie stopped, caught by the image. "Okay, that's a little weirder than I meant it to be, but you get my drift. He doesn't need money to be attractive. In fact, he's a lot more attractive to me without it. Rich people are usually lousy human beings."

Liz raised an eyebrow at her.

"Well, you haven't impressed me much so far," Sophie told her. "I still don't know why you're here. If I was after him for his money, what would you do? Buy me off? I'm warning you, I'm expensive."

Liz smiled at Sophie and Sophie wished she hadn't. "I can offer you—"

"Forget it," Sophie said, cutting her off with pleasure. "You keep your money, I'm keeping him. As an investment."

Liz's eyes grew colder, if that was possible. "Don't underestimate me."

"Don't underestimate me, either," Sophie said, just as sharply. "I'm sure you're out here to protect your son, and I can sympathize. My family is important to me, too. But I'm tired of being insulted. So let's cut to the chase: I know he doesn't have any money, which is fine by me because it's not his money I want. We low-class women are like that. We just go for the cheap thrill. So the only thing you have that I want is your son. Sorry."

"Clearly I made a mistake by coming out here." Liz got to her feet. "I was hoping to make you see reason."

"No, you weren't," Sophie said. "You were hoping to intimidate me so I wouldn't try to get into your world. Well, you can relax. I wouldn't have your world as a gift."

"You don't get my world as a gift," Liz told her, her voice slicing through Sophie's bravado. "You earn the privilege of entering, so don't even try to get in on your back."

"That's it," Sophie said. "I'm tired of you. Go sell paranoid someplace else. We're all stocked up here."

"Good morning, Miss Dempsey." Liz drew herself up even straighter, if that were possible. "Have a pleasant trip back to Cincinnati. And don't even think about trying to trap my son. I'll see you in hell first."

When she'd gone, Amy came out onto the porch and said, "Wow."

Sophie nodded, trying not to shake. "Yeah. 'They'll see and they'll know and they'll say, "Why, she wouldn't even hurt a fly."'"

Amy nodded with her. "'We all go a little mad sometimes.'"

"Except Phin's not Norman."

"If that gave birth to him, he's not normal, either," Amy said. "Stay away from both of them."

"No, really, I think I might like her," Sophie said. "If I had some time to get to know her, bond, do the mother-daughter thing."

"Like, a thousand years," Amy said.

"Maybe not that quick." Sophie tried to relax. "God, she did everything but mention my good bag and cheap shoes."

"As long as she didn't invite you to the house for a nice Chianti and fava beans."

"She'd never let me in that house." Sophie shivered. "She'd fillet me on the front steps."

"Good thing we're leaving on Sunday."

Sophie thought of Liz Tucker and nodded, and then she thought of Phin, smiling at her with heat in his eyes, fixing everything she had that was broken and then making her laugh while he licked almond oil off her in bed.

"Yeah, good thing," she said.

After lunch, an irate Zane went back to Cincinnati and the news, and Amy took Rachel and Clea off to film the driving-into-Temptation footage, and Sophie went out to the kitchen with the dog to work. But once she was alone, all she could think of was Phin. She was pathetic, that's what she was. He certainly wasn't mooning over her. When she'd told him that night in the kitchen that she was staying another week, he hadn't even said, "Good." You'd have thought he could have at least given her a "Good."

Well, that was men for you. She glared at the cherries across from her. Took what they wanted and then—

It occurred to her that this thought wasn't getting her anywhere. It was the same thought she'd been having for fifteen years without any insight or growth, it was the thought that had led her into two years of mind-numbing security with Brandon, it was the thought that had kept her from having the kind of wickedly abandoned sex she'd been having since she'd met Phin. It was, in short, nonproductive.

Worse than that, it was boring.

"I'm through with you," she said to the cherries. "It's a brand-new day."

When Phin showed up at five-thirty, he found her teetering on an old ladder, wrapped in apple wallpaper, sticky from the paste and sweaty from the heat and frustrated because the old paper kept tearing.

"You've never looked better," he said as she shoved a paste-matted curl out of her eye. "What are you doing?"

"Hanging wallpaper," Sophie said waspishly.

He reached up and peeled a torn strip off her sleeve. "It's supposed to go on the wall."

"You know that 'frosty' part you were talking about yesterday?"

"Get off the ladder, Julie Ann," Phin said. "I'm good at this, too."

"Of course you are, you do everything well," Sophie said, feeling surly as she climbed down.

"My mother has a house with fourteen rooms," Phin said. "And one summer she decided to paper twelve of them. My dad called it the Summer from Hell. You know, I don't mean to be critical—"

"Then don't be."

"—but that is ugly paper."

"You can go now."

He smiled at her and her pulse kicked up even though she didn't want it to.

"I can't go." He picked up the paper. "You want to wallpaper, we'll wallpaper. Then we'll do what I want to do."

Sophie tried to ignore the heat his voice flared in her. "You have to be kidding. I'm hot and sweaty and sticky and I look like hell and—"

"I know," Phin said. "I don't care. Get out of the way so I can hang this wallpaper."

Sophie put her hands on her hips. "Listen, if you think I'm—"

She stopped because he'd put the wallpaper down and was trapping her against the wall, one hand on each side of her head, his face close to hers. He started to say something and then he closed his eyes and laughed.

"What's so funny?" Sophie said, but she already knew. She looked awful and he was laughing at her, and she didn't need this from him, she didn't need it from anybody but certainly not from—

"Me," he said. "Christ. I met you six days ago and you've got me so crazy, I'll hang wallpaper so I can touch you."

Sophie blinked. "What?"

"What do you want, Sophie?" he asked, smiling down at her. "Fuses, books, wallpaper, flowers, candy, diamonds—whatever it is, you get it, just as long as I get you."

She was pretty sure he was kidding, but not completely, not with that look in his eye and that heat in his voice.

"Six days," he said and shook his head. "Hell, one day. One minute. One look at that mouth. The devil's candy." He bent his head to kiss her and she ducked under his arm and away from him as she began to realize he was serious.

"Let me get this straight," she said, as she put the corner of the table between them. "You want me."

"In every way possible," Phin said, moving around the table to get to her, and she moved just as he did, beginning to smile as he came after her.

"You can't resist me," Sophie said.

"Not since I saw that mouth," Phin said, following her. "Come here."

"I had you at 'hello,'" Sophie said, still moving back, and Phin stopped and said, "What?"

"I *love* this," Sophie said, beaming at him. "I look like hell and you're chasing me around the kitchen. This is great."

"I am not chasing," Phin said.

Sophie undid the top button on her blouse.

"I'm chasing," Phin said, and moved faster than she'd

planned on. She'd made a dash for the stairs but he lunged for her, grabbing her around the waist and lifting her off her feet to drag her back against him. She lost her breath because he'd knocked it out of her, and then he turned and trapped her against the table and pushed against her with his hips and she knew exactly how much he wanted her. "We'll do the wallpaper later," he said in her ear as his hands moved to her breasts. She tried to squirm away and he whispered, "Oh, Christ, Sophie," and slid his hand under her shirt, pulsing against her from behind, and she closed her eyes because he felt so good.

"We should go upstairs," she said breathlessly, as he buried his face in her neck, making the nerve there go wild.

"Here," he said, and she felt his hand slide down her stomach to her zipper. "Right here, against the table, I'm going to fuck your brains out."

She shivered and said, "Don't talk dirty," and he laughed low and said, "I could feel you get hotter when I said it. You are so bent, Sophie."

He slid down her zipper and she said, "No, I am not," and tilted her hips into his hand, and then as his fingers went into her shorts and between her thighs, she put her hands on the table and pushed back against him, taking the sharp intake of his breath for the tribute that it was.

Then she lifted her head to tell him how good he felt and looked through the screen door into Stephen Garvey's eyes.

"No!" she said, and tried to get away from Phin, but he said, "Yes," into her neck and pushed back, sliding his fingers lower, and when she twisted to get away, he held her tighter, which would have been erotic as hell if Stephen hadn't just put ice water in her veins. "Stephen!" she said, and Phin said, "What?" and stopped long enough for Sophie to gasp, "Back door," as she tried to turn away and pull her blouse back together.

Through it all, Stephen stood there with his mouth open.

Phin didn't let go, although he did take his hand out of her shorts and swing them both around so she was shielded behind him. "Stephen, we're busy here," he said over his shoulder. "What the hell do you want?"

Stephen straightened, still looking confused. "I came to see Rachel, and I certainly didn't expect—"

"Well, we didn't expect you, either," Phin said. Sophie tried to move away again, and he tightened his grip on her. "Rachel's not here. Go away."

"I was wrong. This is exactly what I would have expected from you," Stephen said, and left.

"I think that was an insult." Phin slid his hand into her shorts again. "Although this is what I would have expected from me, too."

"Oh, no," Sophie said, and twisted away, and Phin said, "Oh, yes," and caught her again.

"Trust me, Stephen just killed *any* interest I have in discovery fantasies," Sophie said. "There's a shower upstairs. With a showerhead that Amy says is illegal in most Southern states." Phin stopped fighting her and she pulled him toward the stairs. "Imagine the possibilities."

"I want you to know," he said as he followed her, "that once I get laid, I'll be back in control here."

"Think so?" Sophie turned and kissed him, licking into his mouth and making him shudder under her hands.

"For at least fifteen minutes," he said against her mouth. "Then I'll need to fuck you again."

She shivered, and he laughed and said, "You are so easy."

"So are you," she said, and he said, "And there's our problem right there. We're both crazed until this wears off."

Sophie straightened. " 'Wears off'?"

"This stuff never lasts." Phin pushed her toward the stairs.

"We'll be sane again someday, so let's enjoy it while we've got it."

"Been here before, have you?" Sophie said, feeling cranky because she hadn't.

"Actually, no," Phin said. "Not like this. Get a move on, will you?"

"You have to say that," Sophie said, starting up the stairs. " 'No, Sophie, nobody else has ever been like you.' " She picked up speed because she was mad and because she still wanted him, and he hooked his fingers in the back of her shorts and pulled her down a step against him.

"Not like you," he said in her ear. "Which is why you scare me. But I keep coming after you anyway."

She leaned back against him and said, "I would like to be memorable, if that's possible."

"Try 'unforgettable,' " Phin said. "And no, I did not have to say that. Now, can I please have you?"

"Yes," Sophie said. "You can have anything you want."

Two hours later, Phin kissed Sophie good-bye in front of Amy, who was frowning at the kitchen wall, newly papered in apples.

"I've got to go," he told Sophie. "I'm late to meet another woman."

"That's a joke, right?" she said, and he said, "Nope."

" 'You men are all alike,' " she told him, deciding to believe it was a joke. " 'Seven or eight quick ones and you're off with the boys.' "

"What are you talking about?" he said, and Amy said, "Movie quote. You must know that one."

"I don't watch movies," Phin said. "I'm an intellectual." He kissed Sophie again and said, "Calm down. Stop quoting."

Then he left before she could think of something cutting to say, like, *You remind me of your mother.*

"So exactly what were you doing in the bathroom?" Amy said.

"Exactly what you thought we were doing," Sophie said, still trying to assure herself the other woman was a joke. "Remind me to thank Wes for that showerhead. Oh, and Phin swears the mildew on the shower curtain was watching us and we should get a new one."

"Did you mention his mother had tried to run you out of town?"

"No." Sophie sat down at the table and opened her Power-Book again. "Although she'll no doubt be buying a bigger rail to do it on tomorrow. Stephen Garvey caught us in the kitchen."

"How bad?" Amy said.

"Oh, bad," Sophie said, and then smiled in spite of herself. "And really, really good."

"Sophie, you're not getting serious about the mayor, are you?" Amy said. "Because that would be bad. He's not going to love you the way you deserve—"

"Nope," Sophie said, but she felt a chill even as she said it. "Not serious at all. I have it on good authority that this will wear off."

"Okay," Amy said. "Uh, well, then. In other news . . ."

Sophie tensed. "What?"

"We're getting some company tomorrow," Amy said. "Zane appears to have lit a fire under Clea and she called L.A. and that Leo guy is coming out here to see what we're doing."

"Leo Kingsley," Sophie said, her instincts breaking through her satisfaction. That was the problem with great sex. It dulled your survival tools. "Davy's old boss, the producer."

"Right."

Sophie considered it. "I don't see how this could be trouble." *But it will be.*

"I don't, either," Amy said and they looked at each other doubtfully.

"Let's assume it's not until something goes wrong," Sophie said.

"Good." Amy turned back to the wall, not looking cheered at all. "Now, explain why ugly apples are better than ugly cherries, and all my questions will be answered."

Chapter
Eight

T his is excellent," Dillie said that night at the bookstore as she and Phin stretched the new mattress pad across the bed. "Except that you were an hour late getting me, so I should stay up an extra hour even though it is a school night."

"Works for me," Phin said, knowing she'd be out like a light five minutes after her bedtime anyway. "We'll read in bed that extra hour." He snapped the bottom sheet across the bed and Dillie caught her end of it. "So what's new with you?"

"Jamie Barclay is in my room at school." Dillie tucked the elastic corner under the mattress like a pro. "Grandma fixed it for me."

"Grandma's not supposed to do that," Phin said. "No special favors for Tuckers."

"Dad," Dillie said. "This is my life."

"Right." He flipped the top sheet across and she caught that, too.

"And besides, Jamie Barclay is new and needs a friend so it's really for her." Dillie smoothed her side of the sheet down. "Do you have new friends?" She said it with such elaborate disinterest that Phin stopped.

"There are some people visiting in town," he said cautiously.

"The movie people?" Dillie smoothed the already smooth sheet, her chin in the air to show how unconcerned she was.

Phin picked up the quilt and shook it out before he flipped it across the bed. "What do you want to know, Dill?"

Dillie caught her side of the quilt and pulled it straight. "I just think it's nice that you have new friends."

She sounded so much like the way Liz talked to her, Phin laughed. "Thank you."

"Are they nice?"

He tugged the quilt smooth over the bed where he'd poured almond oil on Sophie and thought of her, hot and round and slippery in his arms. And then that afternoon in the shower—

It seemed wrong to have those thoughts with Dillie in the room, so he shoved the memory away. "They're very nice. Okay, this is your night. We have hot dogs, we have paper napkins, we have dessert, and it's not a weekend. What else?"

Dillie shot a look at the armoire across the room. "TV?"

"What is this, Go-to-Hell Night?" Phin picked up a pillow and tossed it to her and she caught it.

"Jamie Barclay watches TV," Dillie said. "*All* the time, not just for special things." She plumped the pillow and put it at the head of the bed. "She watches it with her mom." She looked at Phin out of the corner of her eye. "It would be nice to watch TV with a mom."

"I'm so glad Jamie Barclay moved here," Phin said, picking up another pillow. "Yes, after dinner you can watch TV. With a dad."

"Would you like to meet Jamie Barclay?" Dillie asked, much too innocently.

"Sure," Phin said cautiously.

"And then I could meet the movie people," Dillie said.

"No," Phin said.

"Dad." Dillie put her hands on her hips. "I should know your friends."

"They're leaving in a week," Phin said, tossing the last pillow to her.

"Well, I'm really glad the movie people came here," Dillie said as she caught it. "Friends are important. Don't you think?"

"What do you want on your hot dog?" Phin said.

After lunch on Tuesday afternoon, a cab came bouncing down the lane to the farm. "Company," Sophie called back into the house, and then went out to meet Leo Kingsley. He was bent over talking to the driver, and she waited patiently, but then the cab door opened again and somebody tall, dark, and Dempsey got out of the backseat.

"Davy!" Sophie shrieked, and threw herself off the step into his arms, and he swung her around and hugged the breath out of her. "I didn't know you were coming, why didn't you tell me you were coming, I'm so *glad* you came—"

He kissed her on the cheek, a big, brotherly smack that was loud and loving, and said, "I didn't know, either, until Leo called me. What the hell are you up to?"

"We're making a video," Sophie said. "Amy wants to come to L.A. I am *so glad* to see you."

He looped his arm around her neck and said, "I'm glad to see you, too, babe. Amy's not going to L.A. She'd hate it. Now, explain to me why you're making—"

"Don't let me get in your way," a mournful voice said from behind him. "Just because it's the Mojave here and I'm about to have a coronary, don't let that—"

"Leo, this is my sister, Sophie," Davy said, and Sophie looked around him to smile at Leo politely.

Leo Kingsley was an attractive man, healthy and fit in his middle forties, beautifully dressed and styled to the teeth. His hair was thick and brown, and he had kind eyes and a good face. But Leo Kingsley was also clearly a man who'd seen too much and wasn't getting over it.

"Welcome to Temptation," Sophie said, and he nodded sadly and said, "Catchy title. Nice to meet you. I need central air."

"Sorry," Sophie said. "It's primitive here."

"That figures," Leo said gloomily. "It's Ohio."

"Why don't you come in and have some lemonade?" Sophie said.

"Lemonade?" Leo said. If she'd offered him arsenic, he couldn't have been more appalled.

"Diet Coke?" Sophie said. "Peach brandy? Ice water? Beer? Ham sandwich? Dove Bar?"

"Ice cream?" Leo said, and Sophie relaxed.

"Right this way." She held the door for him and he went in, stepping neatly over the dog that had flopped down in the doorway, saying, "Look out, Lassie," as he did.

Sophie said, "*No*, don't name it," but it was too late. She looked down at the dog and said, "Lassie?" and it stood up and wagged its stubby tail.

"You have a dog?" Davy said.

"Is this a problem?" Leo said.

"No," Sophie said to both of them. In a way it was a relief. She'd been getting the sneaking suspicion that the dog's name was Dog, and that would have been much worse.

"So," Leo said. "Clea here?"

"Of course I'm here, Leo, darling," Clea said, coming in so on cue Sophie would have bet money she'd been listening in the kitchen. Amy trailed behind her as Clea embraced Leo gracefully if not warmly and said, "It really is good to see you." Clea ignored Davy completely, and he watched her with no expression on his usually mobile face.

Leo patted her arm and said morosely, "Nice to see you, too, kid."

Then Amy caught sight of Davy and shrieked, and Sophie pushed them both into the kitchen so Clea and Leo could talk.

"I can't *believe it*," Amy said and hugged him as Sophie got Leo's Dove Bar from the freezer. "I didn't think we'd see you until Thanksgiving."

"I didn't, either, until Leo told me you were making porn," Davy said, and Sophie dropped Leo's ice cream.

"What?" Amy said, as Lassie grabbed the bar.

"Getting the news that you two were making a skin flick brought me right home. Have you lost your minds?"

"Skin flick." Sophie sat down. "We're not making a skin flick."

"Clea wants Leo to distribute it," Davy said.

"Right."

"Leo only does porn," Davy said. "That's why they call him the Porn King."

" 'Porn King'?" Amy said.

"He doesn't look like a Porn King," Sophie said. "Are you sure?"

"Harvard MBA," Davy said. "They don't mention him much in the alumnae mag. So what's going on?"

"Good question," Sophie said, and went into the living room to find out.

"It's not real porn," Clea said when they'd cornered her in the living room. "You've been filming it, Amy, you know that."

"Okay, well, fine," Leo said. "So what the hell am I doing here?"

"It's a new kind of porn." Clea sat down next to Leo on the couch and smiled at him. She looked beautiful. He looked doubtful. "It's called vanilla porn and it's very hot right now, it's just flying off the video-store shelves, and I think you should make it, Leo, I really do. We've got a great story, about me coming home to meet my old high-school lover and being disillusioned, and then meeting his son, who seduces me and sets me free of my past, and I drive off into the sunset with him, getting everything I've ever wanted. It's a real woman's fantasy, Leo, you'll make a mint—"

"I think I should make *Coming Cleaner*," Leo said.

"What the hell is *Coming Cleaner*?" Amy said.

"I don't want to make *Coming Cleaner*," Clea said. "I want to make *Return to Temptation*. I swear to God, Leo, this is good stuff. You could make a lot of money here. Don't blow it by being old-fashioned."

An old-fashioned Porn King, Sophie thought. An old-fashioned Ivy League Porn King. Her world was getting weirder by the minute.

"What is *Coming Cleaner*?" Amy said again, and Davy said, "Clea's second film. Set in a car wash. Lots of soap."

"Oh, *bleah*," Sophie said. "Clea, how could you?"

"How do you think I met your brother?" Clea said. "Working for Disney?"

Amy rounded on Davy. "You were in a porn film?"

"No," Davy said. "I worked for Leo who made porn films. Forget about me. Concentrate. You're making porn."

"No," Sophie said.

"Yes," Clea said. "Porn about a woman achieving all her dreams. Classy porn."

"Sort of like 'military intelligence,'" Davy said.

"Shut up, Davy," Clea said without looking at him. "This is completely different. It's not gross stuff, it's straight-to-video erotica for women."

"No," Sophie said.

Clea exhaled. "Sophie, what's your favorite scene in *The Big Easy*?"

"'Your luck's about to change, *cher*,'" Sophie said automatically.

"And what's the only thing you don't like about it?"

"It's too—" She broke off when she saw where Clea was going.

"Short," Amy finished for her. "I got it." She cheered up some. "I like it."

"It'll be romantic, not crude," Clea said. "I was thinking maybe we should change the title, maybe to something like *Cherished*, because it's about emotion, not sex."

"You want me to do a movie called *Cherished*?" Leo looked at Davy. "Get the cab back."

"The cab's halfway to Cincinnati by now," Davy said. "Look at my sister's tape."

Leo sighed and moved to the monitor, and Sophie went to get him a Dove Bar, feeling sorry for him even if he was a porn king.

• • •

"It's going to need some work," he said, when the last screen was dark again. "But Clea was right, you've got a good start there. It needs a lot more sex, of course."

Amy looked at Sophie and said, "We have somebody working on that."

"No, we don't," Sophie said.

"And the score will add a lot," Leo went on, and Amy winced.

"I don't know how—" she began, and Leo waved her away.

"We can do that in L.A.," he said. "No problem. Along with the titles and credits. You just shoot the footage and let us handle the details."

"The sound is a detail?" Sophie said, but Amy shushed her.

"But mostly you need more sex," Leo said. "A lot more nudity."

"Leo," Clea said. "Don't forget what I told you. This is women's porn—"

"Oh, no," Sophie said, and Amy kicked her ankle.

"Don't get in Clea's way," she whispered to Sophie. "This is my chance."

"—so it's not going to be vile like the other stuff you do," Clea finished.

Leo sighed. "I need skin."

Sophie winced, and Amy whispered, "He's a real producer, Sophie, *please*."

"Jesus," Davy said. "The Dempsey morals at work again."

Leo smiled at Clea, which didn't look natural at all on him. "Now about *Coming Cleaner*—"

"Later, Leo," Clea said. "We're making *Cherished* now."

"*Cherished*," Leo said, and looked more depressed than ever.

• • •

Rachel was out in the front yard watering what little grass there was when Leo came down the porch steps. He didn't look like a big Hollywood producer. He was only a couple of inches taller than she was, and even though he was good-looking in a Hollywood kind of way, he looked tired and depressed. So when he said, "Are you the gofer around here?" she squeezed the water out of the front of her T-shirt and said, "That's me," without trying to be anything special.

"I need a place to stay," he said.

"Sure." She dropped the hose and started for the car. "Get in the car. I'll take you to Larry's Motel out by the Tavern."

"Larry's Motel."

She turned back and saw his look of pain. "It's all we've got." Rachel opened the car door for him. "Just be grateful you've got me for a driver because we don't have a taxi, either. You could be, like, walking."

"No, I couldn't," Leo said, and got in.

"So you know Clea from L.A.?" Rachel said when they were on the road.

"Yes." Leo peered out the window

"Cool. I want to be the next Clea."

"No you don't," Leo said.

Rachel flipped the neck of her damp T-shirt back and forth to get some breeze going there, too. "Why not? She's rich and successful and she got out. Sounds good to me."

Leo didn't answer, and she looked over in time to catch him staring at where her T-shirt was stuck to her chest.

He caught her eye and said, "Sorry," and she shrugged and said, "Hey, I was the one flapping the wet T-shirt."

"I still shouldn't be leering. Sexual harassment." Leo sounded mournful. "Life's no fun anymore."

"Tell you what," Rachel said. "You can sexually harass me

if you want. I'm having a slow summer anyway. Want to look down my shirt?"

Leo sighed. "So this is what it's come to, teeny-boppers doing me favors. Middle age is hell."

"I'm not a teeny-bopper," Rachel said. "I'm twenty."

"Oh, shit." Leo put his head in his hands. "Contributing to the delinquency of a minor."

"I'm not a minor," Rachel said. "I'm twenty. You can sleep with me and not go to jail. Of course, you have to, like, take me to L.A. first. I've had all the lousy sex in Temptation I can stand."

"But lousy sex in L.A. is okay?" Leo shook his head. "Lousy sex is lousy anyplace, kid." He stopped and considered. "I don't think I've ever had lousy sex."

"That's 'cause you're a guy." Rachel turned into the motel driveway.

Leo stared at the motel with distaste as she parked in front of the lobby door. "So who runs this, Norman Bates?"

"It's okay, the showers don't work anyway. Think of it as an adventure."

"I don't want an adventure," Leo said. "Adventures are for the young. Comfort is for the old."

"What time do you want me to pick you up, old guy?" Rachel said.

"Soon," Leo said as he got out. "Very, very soon."

"I'll pick you up at five, then," Rachel said. "Dinnertime."

Leo poked his head through the window. "Five is dinnertime here?"

Rachel sighed. "When is it dinner in L.A.?"

"No, no," Leo said. "Five is fine. I missed lunch anyway." His face changed suddenly from vaguely worried to downright apprehensive. "You do have restaurants here, right?"

"Sure," Rachel said. "There's a restaurant in town and a

diner, too. The food's pretty good. It's not fancy but it's good."

"Okay."

He still looked doubtful, so she smiled at him and said, "And if you promise to buy, I'll come have dinner with you in a blouse with the top button undone and you can harass me until dessert."

"Oh, yeah." Leo nodded as he straightened away from the car. "That'll go over great at Granny's Home-Cooked Restaurant. Forget it, Lolita. I'll eat alone."

For some reason, that hurt. "Okay."

She put the car in gear just as he put his head down next to the window again.

"Hey," he said. "I was kidding. I didn't mean to hurt your feelings."

His eyes were kind, and she was so surprised she let the car die. "You didn't. Really. I just wanted to eat dinner with you. And hear about Hollywood."

He nodded. "Okay. Pick me up at five with all your buttons buttoned."

"You don't have to—"

"At five, kid. I'll tell you what a big shot I am. You're the only one who'll believe it anyway."

Rachel nodded. "Okay. Thanks."

Leo waved her off, and she watched as he headed for the motel door, shaking his head as he checked out the turquoise panels near the entrance. He wasn't really upset, she realized as she pulled back onto the road. It was just his way. Like Eeyore. She should tell him that at dinner. "You're the Eeyore of L.A.," she'd tell him, and he'd have to laugh. Getting a laugh out of him wouldn't be easy, but she'd do it before dessert. He should take her back to L.A. with him just for the laughs—

She slowed the car. There was an idea. She could be his personal assistant and make him laugh and help him relax and drive him places and take care of him. Of course, he'd say no at first, but he'd said no to dinner and she'd talked him into that.

It really was a great idea. She could take care of him and he could take care of her.

And she could finally get out of Temptation.

When Phin pulled up to the porch that evening, he saw Sophie sitting on the swing with a good-looking guy whose curly dark hair and dark brown eyes reminded him of someone. *The therapist*, he thought, and it bothered him a lot more than it should have. After all, he had nothing permanent with Sophie. He just needed to touch her on a semiregular basis or he couldn't finish his sentences. It was just lust. It would go in time.

He was going to have to get rid of the therapist.

Sophie waved to him, and the dog barked from under the swing as he got out of the car.

"Come meet my brother, Davy," Sophie said, glowing with happiness.

"Your brother." Phin regrouped, sizing Davy up again as he patted the shaggy panting dog who had come out to greet him. Now that he was closer, Davy looked like Sophie's twin, same ivory skin and generous mouth, but a lot more jaw and more height. And his eyes were colder than Sophie's ever could be. "Good to meet you, Davy." Phin went up on the porch and held out his hand.

"This is Phin Tucker, the mayor," Sophie said, and Davy freed his arm from around her and stood to shake Phin's hand with a firm, dry grasp.

"Pleased to meet you," Davy said. "What's the mayor doing so far out of town?"

Phin raised his eyebrows. "Just being neighborly."

Davy looked at Sophie and then back at Phin. "That's real nice of you."

"I try," Phin said.

"Whatever you guys are doing, knock it off," Sophie said.

"You never learn, do you?" Davy said to her before he turned back and smiled at Phin. "So, can I get you a drink, Phil?"

"Phin," Sophie said. "Stop it."

"I'm fine, thanks," Phin said.

"I bet you are," Davy said. "Could I see you for a minute, Sophie?"

"No," Sophie said. "Go harass Amy. She's dating a cop. And remember, you brought Clea home and we never said a word."

"Good point." Davy opened the screen door to go inside. "I'll be right back, Phil. Don't do anything stupid."

"What the fuck was that all about?" Phin said, and Sophie pulled him down on the swing beside her, the dog at her feet again.

"We moved around a lot when we were kids," Sophie said.

"And he's still hostile about it today?" Phin said.

"We didn't have a lot of money and the rich kids weren't our pals," Sophie said.

"Sorry," Phin said. "I still don't see how I figure in here."

"I told you, we took a lot of grief from rich kids."

"I'm not rich," Phin said, as Davy came back out on the porch with a beer.

"You're not poor," Davy said. "Have a beer." He handed it to Phin who took it as the easiest move at the moment, and then Davy sat down on the porch rail and folded his arms and stared at Phin.

Sophie looked from him to Phin and back again. "Okay, stop it."

"I'm just saying," Davy said, "that I've paid less for entire suits than he spent on that shirt."

"Well, it's been swell," Phin said, standing up.

"Armani, right?" Davy said.

"Right." Phin handed the beer back to him. "Great meeting you."

"Davy."

"Okay." Davy got up and turned back to the door with the beer. "I'll go, Harvard. You stay. Sophie makes her own choices." He grinned at Sophie who ignored the pun and glared back. "Right. You try to do the brotherly thing and nobody appreciates it."

When he was gone, Phin said, "Interesting guy, your brother."

"You should talk," Sophie said. "Your mother gives me frostbite every time I see her."

"What 'every time'?" Phin sat down beside her again. "You've only met her once." Then he grew very still. "Haven't you?"

"Anyway, Davy's just protective," Sophie said. "He thinks all guys are only after one thing."

"He's right," Phin said. "So my mother dropped by, did she?"

"Social call," Sophie said. "So you only want me for sex?"

"No, I'm nuts about your golf game. What did my mother do to you?"

"Maybe I'll go inside." Sophie started to get up, but Phin caught her arm and pulled her back down on the swing.

"Okay, sorry about the golf crack. Give me the right answer and I'll say it. I'm too tired to come up with it on my own."

"'No, Sophie, it's not the sex,'" Sophie said. "'It's your

wit, your beauty, your warmth, your intelligence, the cute way your nose crinkles when you laugh, your sunny, funny face.'"

"Your nose doesn't crinkle," Phin said. "I'm good for the rest of it."

"But mostly it's the sex, right?" Sophie said.

"And you want me for what?" Phin said. "The third day I knew you, you lay down for me on the dock. The next night I came back with a plan to get you down again, but you said, 'Fuck me,' before I could make my move. The next day, I'm thinking about heading out to see you and you deliver to the bookstore before I can find my car keys. I won't even mention what you did with the showerhead yesterday because I'm grateful. Now, what is it you want me for?"

Sophie sighed. "The sex."

"So we're on the same page here."

"I doubt it," Sophie said. "You're wearing Armani."

"I really like your brother," Phin said. "Is he leaving soon?"

"Don't pick on my brother. Your mother thinks I'm after your money. I told her it was the cheap thrill."

"Oh, fuck," Phin said. "I'm sorry."

"Yeah, well, I'll forgive you your mother if you forgive me my brother. They're just looking out for us."

"Christ, it's not as if we're sleeping with lepers," Phin said.

"Well, in a way we are," Sophie said. "We're both with people who are Not Our Kind. Davy looks at you and sees every guy who pushed us around when we were kids. Your mom looks at me and sees every gold-digger who ever went after you because of your name and your shirts. How are they to know we're just using each other for the physical thrill and have no interest or affection beyond that?" She folded her arms and stared out across the dusty yard.

Phin sighed and sat back. "'Go out and see Sophie,' I told

myself. 'You've had a rough day, she always makes you feel great, treat yourself. Go out and see the woman.'"

"Human Valium, that's me," Sophie said.

"Hey," Phin said, and when she looked up, her beautiful lips parted to say something horrible to him, he kissed her, long and slow and deep, and she kissed him back, and he felt human again instead of harried, just because he finally had his arms around her and she was so warm and sure against him. "We're more than just the sex," he whispered, and she closed her eyes and whispered back, "I know, I know."

He kissed her again, and then rocked the swing with his foot, and she put her head on his shoulder and said, "So tell me about this lousy day," and he told her while they watched the sun go down, and everything that had been awful seemed funny when he told her about it. He listened to her laugh in the twilight and felt the tension seep away. When it was dark, he sighed and said, "I have to go," but he didn't want to.

"What about the sex?" Sophie said. "Usually you have me naked by now."

"Davy's staying here, right?" Phin said, and when she nodded, he said, "I don't think so."

"You're kidding," she said, and he said, "Tell you what. Come on up to the Hill, and we can do it with my mother in the next room."

"Oh, God," Sophie said, and he laughed and kissed her and said, "I've got a council meeting from hell tomorrow anyway. I'll really need to release some tension after that."

"You're such a romantic," she said, and he kissed her again and then again until she laughed against his mouth, and he drove away feeling all the comfort he'd come for.

Maybe her brother would leave soon.

• • •

"You never fucking *learn*," Davy said when Sophie went inside.

"What?" Sophie plopped down on the sofa, and Lassie plopped down at her feet. "Thanks to you, he left early, so this is not a good time to yell at me." She looked at Davy, standing indignant by the fireplace, and had to smile. "I'm so glad you're here, even if you are being a butthead."

Davy came over and sat down beside her. "Let me explain to you again about town boys."

"Go away, Davy." Sophie let her head fall back against the couch and smiled, thinking about her town boy. "He's not like that."

" 'This can only lead to tears,' " Davy said in a comic voice, and when Sophie rolled her head on the back of the couch, he said, "*Anastasia*. The bat."

"Bat country," Sophie said. "What are you nervous about?"

"The way you look at him," Davy said. "The way he looks at you. You're in love. He's in heat. It's an old story and a lousy one."

"That's what I keep telling her," Amy said, coming in with three Dove Bars. " 'This is Chad all over again,' 'he's got "town boy" all over him,' but—"

"Chad?" Davy said.

"An old mistake," Sophie said, taking her Dove Bar. "And Phin is not Chad. And I'm not in love."

"I still think we ought to go to Iowa and make Chad pay," Amy said, and bit into her ice cream viciously.

"This would be Chad Berwick, right?" Davy shook his head and bit into his bar, too. "Not necessary," he said around the ice cream.

Sophie blinked at him. "How did you know—"

Davy looked at her with affectionate contempt. "I was a freshman in the same school, dummy. Everybody knew."

"Oh, *ouch*," Sophie said, and ate more Dove Bar for comfort.

"Yes, but the last month of Chad's senior year was not a good one," Davy said. "Poor guy."

Amy collapsed cross-legged on the rug in front of them with her ice cream dripping, looking about ten. "Ooh. Ooh. What did you do?" She licked the drips away and grinned up at Davy adoringly, moving her ice cream as Lassie took an interest and waddled over.

"Many things," Davy said airily. "Too many to recall now."

"Come on, Davy," Amy said. "Sophie needs to know."

Davy leaned back on the couch and ate more ice cream as he thought. "Mostly little stuff. I taped a cheat sheet in his notebook and then snitched on him to the English teacher. I started a rumor he had head lice and put lice shampoo in his gym locker. I stuck a bunch of Hustlers in his regular locker and he got busted and had to see the counselor."

"That's it?" Amy sniffed, and ate her ice cream, holding the stick above Lassie's reach.

"Well, let's see, *was* there anything else?" Davy pretended to ponder, and Sophie started to grin.

"I love you, Davy," she said, and leaned into his arm.

Davy put his arm around her. "I love you, too, babe. Oh, yeah, wait. It's all coming back to me now. There was that cherry-red Camaro he got for graduation. His folks gave it to him early so he could take it to prom." He grinned and bit into his ice cream again.

"He was driving a clunker when I . . . knew him," Sophie said.

"He drove it to prom, too," Davy said. "I put shrimp in the Camaro."

Amy frowned. "Shrimp?" But Sophie started to laugh, hiccuping on her ice cream.

Davy nodded. "I put shrimp down in the seats, in the wheel well, shoved some down into the screw holes under the carpet, anyplace it would be hard to find them. Shrimp are small, you know." He began to smile, remembering. "And it was the end of May so we were getting some hot weather." He shook his head. "Chad never did get to use that car. For a week, whenever I went by the Berwick house, that car was sitting in the driveway with all the doors open. Then finally, it just . . . disappeared."

He laughed and bit into his Dove Bar again, and Amy said, "Oh, *yes*." Sophie thought, *I love my family, I really do.* "What else?" she asked Davy.

"He destroyed the guy's Camaro," Amy said. "What do you want?"

"Dempsey revenge, Ame," Sophie said. "A car is not enough." She looked at Davy. "Right?"

"Well," Davy said. "There was prom."

"Oh, tell us about prom," Amy said.

"He was dating this really hot senior girl named Melissa Rose," Davy said. "Boy, she was something. She wore this silky blue thing to prom that sort of slipped around whenever she—"

"I thought this was supposed to cheer me up," Sophie said.

"And because Chad was an asshole, he took a flask to prom," Davy said. "Big man around town, sneaking Boone's Farm into the gym. So around midnight, I put ground-up sleeping pills in it."

"So he went to sleep at prom and that's it?" Amy said.

"No," Davy said. "He got groggy at prom, and Melissa got disgusted because she thought he was drunk and made him take her home, except he was too out of it, and I just happened to be there in the parking lot. So I helped her." Davy shook his head as he finished his Dove Bar. "He got a little banged-up when we tried to get him into the backseat. Melissa was not a nice person, so she did most of it."

"Good for Melissa," Sophie said, entertaining her first thoughts about Chad that didn't involve guilt.

"That's good," Amy said. "That's enough—"

"Then we took him home and left him on his front-porch steps with his flask in his hand and his fly unzipped," Davy said. "Melissa suggested he should have something else in his other hand, and I just happened to have Dad's Polaroid with me. The pictures were a big hit at school on Monday."

Sophie was laughing into her Dove Bar now. "Thank you, Davy," she said, and his arm tightened around her.

"Okay, *that* was enough," Amy said. "You did good—"

"And then I drove Melissa home," Davy said. "And we were feeling warmly toward each other at that point, being sort of united in our distaste for Chad, so I asked if there was anything else I could do for her."

"And was there?" Sophie said.

"You weren't the only Dempsey who lost yours in the back-seat of that clunker," Davy said. "I remember Melissa fondly to this day. That girl knew things. Wonder what happened to her?"

"Something wonderful, I hope," Sophie said.

"She already had something wonderful," Davy said. "Me."

"Beyond that," Sophie said. "I like a woman who knows how to get even."

"So do I, as long as she's not getting even with me," Davy said.

Lassie whined at their feet, and Sophie looked down into his pathetic brown eyes. "Poor baby," she said, and then he rolled over with his legs in the air and she laughed and leaned down so he could lick the rest of the ice cream off the stick.

"Con dog," Davy said.

"What?" Sophie said, still smiling at her baby.

"Con dog," Davy said. "Look pathetic, make the mark feel superior, get what you want. He just ran a con on you for that ice cream."

"My dog conned me?" Sophie said.

"What the dog is doing to you is not your problem," Davy said. "It's what the mayor's doing to you that worries me. Which brings us back to now. If I have to fill a Volvo with shrimp, I will, but I'd just as soon you wised up."

Sophie stopped smiling. "I'm wise. He's not a Chad. I'll be fine."

"Yeah," Davy said, "Right. Well, I'm telling you now, when he screws you over, I'm kicking his butt."

"I love you, Davy," Sophie said.

"I love you, too," Davy said. "You dumbass."

The council meeting the next day went so badly that Phin was still reeling from it when his mother cornered him in the empty council room.

"About this woman," she said. "You can't see her again."

"I did my damnedest to stop that permit vote, and Stephen got it through anyway because *you* turned on me." Phin sat down on the council table, fuming. "What the *hell* were you thinking of?"

"That movie company can do us no good," Liz said. "Zane Black visited everybody on the council this morning, trying to get them to stop the filming, and that's made everybody suspicious. I don't want us to do anything that aligns us with them. You cannot go back out there. That woman—"

"I like that woman," Phin said. "She's a hell of a lot more comfort than you are. You knew damn well—"

"Will you at least think of Dillie?" Liz said.

Phin frowned at her. "What's Dillie got to do with this?"

"You might think of her future while you're unzipping your pants," Liz snapped.

"You have to be kidding me," Phin said. "If every parent thought about his kid before sex, the race would die out."

"What happens when she finds out about this? What happens when she wants to meet this woman?"

"She's not going to meet her," Phin said. "And I get to have a life, too, you know."

"You put your child first," Liz said flatly.

"You never did," Phin said, just as flatly, and Liz took a step back, as if she'd been struck. "And you know it," he said when she didn't say anything. "You didn't even know I was there if Dad was in the room. And when he wasn't, I only had half your attention because you were waiting for him to show up."

"Phin," Liz said.

"It's all right." Phin sat back, trying not to take his frustration out on his mother, no matter how much she deserved it. "The older I get, the more I envy what you and Dad had. I'd watch him come up those steps at night, looking old and tired and miserable, and then he'd see you, and his face—" He stopped because Liz's face had crumpled and he thought she might cry. *It's about time*, he thought, and when she didn't, he said, "You made the world go away for each other."

Liz tightened her jaw. "Don't."

"I thought I was going to get that, too," Phin said. "I thought it just came with the wedding ring, that feeling that the world was all right because two people were together." He laughed shortly. "Found out I was wrong about that."

Liz rallied. "That was not your fault. That was—"

"That *was* my fault," Phin said. "I thought what you had

was easy. Now I know better, and I'm not settling. I get what you had or I don't get married. Which doesn't mean I can't have a good time while I'm waiting for the right woman."

"Damn few people get what we had," Liz said. "And you pay for it. You pay a lot for it."

Phin shook his head. "So you just gave up."

"I never gave up," Liz said. "We're still—"

"Not 'we'," Phin said. "I'm not talking about the fucking courthouse. I'm talking about you. You just cut that part of your life off completely. There are great guys in this town, but you won't even look at them."

"I have no intentions of getting married again," Liz said.

"I don't either," Phin said. "But you're pushing me at Rachel Garvey just the same." He leaned closer. "You really think if I marry Rachel, I'll start to love her? That she'll love me?"

Liz swallowed. "People do come to care for—"

"Is that how it happened for you? Is that what you and Dad had?"

Liz shut her eyes tight, and then the tears did start. "I'm sorry, Phin. I just can't stand thinking about it. I just can't. I've lost everything except you and Dillie and—"

She broke off and he said, "And that's not enough. We're a lot, but we're not enough. You need your own life."

Liz sniffed and said, her voice strangling with pain, "I just want him *back*."

"I know." Phin walked around the end of the table and put his arm around his mother, and then she did start to cry. "I know you do. I know." He patted her shoulder until she stopped crying, which was about thirty seconds, and then he said, "Listen, I don't know what's going to happen with Sophie. It's only been a week, so who knows?"

"I knew right away," Liz said, pulling back a little and

wiping her eyes with her fingers. "The minute I saw your father in high school, I knew. If you don't—"

"Yeah, well, that's easier in high school," Phin said, handing her his handkerchief. "Nobody has any sense then."

"But I knew," Liz said. "And so did your father, he knew, too. And if you and this woman—"

"Her name is Sophie," Phin said as he sat on the end of the table. "And there's something there, because I do not want to be involved with her, but I am still going back out there tonight."

"That's sex," Liz said, almost her old self again.

"Don't knock it," Phin said. "You guys used to do all right there as I remember, so don't even try to tell me you were above all that."

"No," Liz said. "We weren't above anything."

"I don't want any details," Phin said. "I got enough just walking into rooms at the wrong time. If I had a nickel for every time I caught Dad with his hand on your butt, I'd have a lot of nickels."

"That's enough," Liz said, but she gave him a watery smile.

"You had a good marriage," Phin said. "Respect and passion and good times and love."

"Yes," Liz said.

"Well, Sophie gives me respect and passion and good times," Phin said.

"No," Liz said. "Listen to me, that woman is all wrong for you. She's low and she's rude and she's callous. She's *terrible* for you."

"Talked back to you, did she? I don't blame her. You probably started it."

Liz froze up on him again, and Phin said, "You know, you were almost human there for a minute."

"Just because I'm looking out for the people I love—"

"Don't." Phin stood up. "Obsess about the election if you must, but don't even try to pretend you're doing it for me and Dillie. For some reason, you've got it stuck in your head that it's the most important thing in your life, and I'll be damned if I know how to talk you out of it. So I'm not going to try. Just back off and let me live my life."

"I will do *anything* to protect you," Liz said, all her tears gone. "Anything."

"You know, when you talk like that, you scare me," Phin said. "Knock it off. I'll go get Dillie. You get a grip."

He left her sitting there then, alone in the marble council room, under the portrait of his great-grandfather, and his grandfather, and his father, because he didn't know what else to do.

He just hoped he never found out exactly what *"anything"* meant.

While Phin fought the good fight, Sophie was brushing Lassie on the dock and trying to get her life back on track. Somewhere back at the beginning of time, she'd had a plan, but now Amy was out front with Rachel filming Clea and Rob in what was turning out to be a porn flick while Davy watched and shook his head. Georgia was planning to do God-knew-what with Zane when he came back that night, Leo was planning to talk Clea into *Coming Cleaner*, and the Coreys were painting the house a lighter version of the water tower. Amazing. "A cast of thousands," she told Lassie, bending down close to him. "But that's it. We don't let anybody else in."

"Are you talking to that dog?"

Sophie jerked her head up. A pale, thin child with long

blonde hair stood at the end of the dock in neatly pressed blue shorts and an immaculate white T-shirt. "Where'd you come from?" Sophie said.

The girl pointed across the river. "My grandma's house is over there."

"Not the Garveys."

"Certainly not." The little girl examined the end of the dock and evidently found it satisfactory because she sat down. "My grandma Junie."

"Oh. Does she know you're here?"

"She's napping." The girl stared at Sophie, and Sophie felt a little uneasy. "I'll go back before she wakes up. If you don't mind that I visit, that is."

"Oh. Sure." Sophie gestured to the yard. "Visit away."

"Because you said you weren't going to let anybody else in," the little girl pointed out. "You said that to the dog."

"Well, you're just visiting, not staying." Sophie tried to find her place in the conversation. "I'm Sophie."

"I know," the little girl said. "That's why I came."

"Okay, now you're weirding me out," Sophie said. "Who are you?"

"Dillie Tucker," the girl said, and Sophie said, "Tucker? Are you related to Phin?"

"He's my daddy," Dillie said, and Sophie lost her breath.

"Your daddy." Sophie regrouped and tried to keep her voice light. Well, Amy and Davy had warned her. Always listen to family. "And how's your mommy?"

"She's dead," Dillie said, and Sophie tried hard to feel sympathetic about that instead of relieved. The poor kid was motherless, for heaven's sake. "She died a long time ago," Dillie went on. "I was a baby. It was very sad."

"Oh," Sophie said. "Yes, I'm sure it was. So, uh, you live with your dad." *There's something he might have mentioned.*

"And my grandma Liz," Dillie said. "But I would like to move." She turned to look at the farmhouse, and Sophie had one strange moment when she thought Dillie might be house hunting. She seemed organized enough for it.

"How old are you?" Sophie said.

"Nine," Dillie said. "How old are you?"

"Thirty-two," Sophie said. "Explain to me again why you're here."

"Don't you want me?" Dillie made her eyes huge and pitiful, and Sophie said, "That's pretty good, kid, but you're out of your league, I grew up with a pro. What are you up to?"

"What's a pro?" Dillie said.

"Dillie," Sophie said warningly.

"Jamie Barclay says her mother says that she heard that you're my dad's girlfriend," Dillie said. "Are you?"

"No," Sophie said. "Who's Jamie Barclay?"

"Because it's okay if you are," Dillie said. "I can stand you."

"That's very generous," Sophie said. "I'm not his girlfriend."

"Why not?" Dillie said.

Sophie decided there was nowhere the conversation could go that wouldn't be dicey. "How about some ice cream before I walk you back to your grandma's?"

"Yes, thank you," Dillie said, and then she grew very still as Sophie stood up, and Lassie got to his feet and yawned.

Sophie watched Dillie watch Lassie. "Are you afraid of dogs?" she asked gently.

"No." Dillie stuck her chin out and just for a moment she looked so much like Phin that Sophie sucked in her breath. "I'm just not accustomed to them."

"This is a very nice dog," Sophie said. "His name is Lassie Dempsey. But if you're unaccustomed, I can make him stay out here while we go inside."

"No." Dillie seemed uncertain. "What kind of dog is he?"

"A con dog," Sophie said. "It's all right, Dillie. I promise he won't hurt you."

"All right," Dillie said, and then Sophie walked off the dock with Lassie close behind her as always and stopped next to the rigid little girl.

"Do you want to pet him?"

"Maybe." Dillie swallowed and gave the dog a gingerly pat. Lassie looked up at her with his *You're new at this* look. "His legs are short."

"But his heart is large." Sophie held out her hand. "Come on. We'll get you a Dove Bar and walk you home to your grandmother."

"What's a Dove Bar?"

"An insanely good ice cream bar."

Dillie looked at her for a long moment and then took her hand. "There's no hurry," she said, and they went up to the house.

An hour later, after extended conversation about school, softball, Dillie's driver's license, dessert, Lassie, Jamie Barclay, Grandma Junie, Grandma Liz, Dillie's dad, her hopes, her dreams, her past, her present, and her plans for the future, Sophie had a new respect for Phin. The kid never shut up; clearly nobody had ever turned on her and told her to put a sock in it. That took massively patient parenting skills. Phin really was good at everything.

Dillie also ate like a horse. When they'd gotten to the kitchen, Dillie had looked at the bag of potato chips on the table and said, "I missed lunch, you know." Sophie made her a ham sandwich, followed by potato chips, followed by an apple and a banana, washed down with lemonade. "This is excellent," Dillie said, reaching for another chip. "Is it time for dessert?"

They were finishing up their Dove Bars and singing along to the sixth replay of "I Only Want to Be with You" so Dillie could learn the words and Sophie wouldn't have to hear any more about Jamie Barclay, when Amy came into the kitchen.

"It's hot as hell out there," she said, and Sophie said, "Meet Dillie Tucker and stop swearing."

Amy blinked at Dillie. "Hello."

"Dillie is Phin's daughter," Sophie said.

"*Hello.*" Amy sat down at the table. "I knew it. I told you so."

"This is my sister Amy," Sophie told Dillie. "Ignore her."

"I don't have any sisters," Dillie said around the last of her Dove Bar. "Or a dog. It's very sad."

"Tragic," Sophie held her stick down so Lassie could lick the last of the ice cream off.

Dillie turned huge gray eyes on Amy. "I don't have a mommy, either."

"That's a relief," Amy said, sitting back, and Dillie looked shocked.

"I told you," Sophie said. "We're pros. Don't try it on us."

"Well, it is sad," Dillie said in her regular voice. "I love Grandma Liz, but I've had enough."

"I sympathize," Amy said.

"I'm not following here," Sophie said. "What do you want?"

"I want to live with my dad by ourselves," Dillie said. "But he says we have to live with Grandma Liz because somebody has to take care of me."

"Couldn't he get Nurse Ratched?" Amy said. "That'd be a step up in warmth."

Dillie concentrated on Sophie. "So then Jamie Barclay said you were Daddy's girlfriend."

"I'm not," Sophie said. "We're leaving next Sunday."

"You don't have to," Dillie said. "You could stay here. I like you. And I think I need a mom." She surveyed Sophie, who was trying to think of something to say, and added, "Maybe you. I don't know."

"Don't get confused because of the dog and the Dove Bar," Sophie said. "I'm really not mom material."

"I don't know," Amy said. "They might be pretty good indicators."

"You're not helping," Sophie told her.

"She raised me, you know," Amy told Dillie. "She was great."

Dillie frowned. "I thought you were her sister."

"My mother died when I was little," Amy said. "It was very sad."

"Don't try that on me," Dillie said. "I'm a pro, too."

"I like you, kid," Amy said. "Was your mom a Dempsey?"

"No, a Miller," Dillie said. "Her name was Diane. She was very pretty. Grandma Junie has pictures. She looked like Sophie."

"Time to go home," Sophie said, suddenly feeling depressed.

On their way out, they ran into Davy. "This is my brother, Davy," Sophie said.

"I don't have any brothers," Dillie said, looking up at him. "It's very sad."

"Not necessarily," Sophie said. "This is Dillie. Phin's daughter."

"Is it?" Davy smiled down at Dillie. "Very nice to meet you, Dillie. And how's your mama?"

"She's dead," Dillie said. "It's very—"

"The mayor gets to live another day," Davy told Sophie. He smiled down again at Dillie. "I was just going to teach this dumb dog how to play Frisbee. Want to help?"

"Yes," Dillie said, and then looked at Sophie.

"Ten minutes," Sophie said. "Lassie's legs are so short, that's all she's going to last anyway."

"That's about my attention span, so it should work out nicely," Davy said. "Come on, kid. Let's see what you've got."

"Davy?" Sophie said, and watched her brother take her lover's daughter out to play.

She had the sinking feeling Davy would be critiquing Phin's parenting technique all through dinner.

When Phin picked Dillie up from Junie's, her T-shirt had a chocolate smear on it. "What happened?" he said, and chunky little Junie said, "She must have found some chocolate while I was napping. She won't say."

"She won't, huh?" Phin looked at his daughter, who stuck her chin out.

"I'll tell you about it when I get my driver's license," she said.

"Get in the car," Phin said. "You'll tell me about it now."

But in the car, Dillie stonewalled him. "You have lots of stuff you won't tell me about. So now I do, too."

"Dill," Phin began warningly, but Dillie began to hum to drown him out. She had no musical ability whatsoever, so he couldn't tell what she was humming. "You know, you're asking for it here," he began, but then she threw back her head and belted out, *"Now listen, honey,"* to really drown him out, and he pulled off the road.

"Where," he said, "did you learn 'I Only Want to Be with You'?"

Chapter
Nine

Sophie met Phin at the door that evening, still not sure how she felt about that afternoon. "Hello, Dad."

"It never came up," Phin said. "Or I'd have told you."

"She's a pretty big deal to never have come up," Sophie said.

Phin looked past her into the living room. Amy and Davy were on the couch, listening with a great deal of interest.

"How you doin', Harvard?" Davy called. "Or is this a bad time to ask?"

"Can I talk to you alone?" Phin said to Sophie, and she said, "Anyplace but a bedroom," so they went down to the dock.

"It's all right," Sophie said when they were sitting, watching the river muddy by. "It was just a shock. Especially when she said I looked like her mother. I mean, it explains a lot about why you—"

"You don't look like her mother," Phin said. "Diane had dark hair, but she was shorter than you are, and younger than you are, and her face was different. Most of the pictures Dillie has are from far away. She just sees a woman with dark hair."

Sophie turned away. "I didn't even know you had a wife. I know you Tuckers are detached, I know you're going to forget my name before I'm back on the highway—"

"I married Diane because she was pregnant," Phin said, his voice flat. "She got pregnant because she thought I had money."

Sophie drew back a little. "Women don't get pregnant all by themselves. Men help. And of all the men I've slept with, you are the most Johnny-on-the-spot with a condom—"

"She told me she was on the pill and I believed her." Phin drew back, too, until they were sitting apart like strangers. "I don't make the same mistake twice."

Sophie's temper flared. "You think I'm trying—"

"Of course not." Phin bit off the words. "Christ, Sophie." He took a deep breath. "I don't think about her much. We were only together a couple of months, and she died in an accident three months after Dillie was born."

"An accident," Sophie said. "The Old Bridge?"

"No." Phin stared out across the river. "She died over there. She came home in the middle of the night and fell down the porch steps and hit her head and bled out before her mother woke up and found her."

"It must have been awful for Dillie."

"Dillie never knew her," Phin said. "Diane had complications after Dillie was born, so I took the baby home to my mother. Diane never came after her when she got out of the hospital."

"You weren't living with her?"

Phin closed his eyes. "My marriage lasted about two months,

and they were the worst two months of my life. When my dad died, I moved back to the Hill to stay with my mother because she collapsed. I thought I was going to lose them both."

Sophie thought of Liz's frozen face. "That could explain a few things."

"And I never went back. Mom was rocky, and Diane was happier without me as long as she could keep the river house." He shook his head. "She'd moved up with the in people. She didn't want me, she just wanted my name and my house."

Sophie said, "I'm sorry."

"It's all right," Phin said. "I didn't want her, either. I was stupid, and I paid. But I got Dillie, so I'd do it all again in a heartbeat. Dillie's worth everything."

Sophie nodded. "I can't believe Diane didn't want her baby."

"She wasn't the maternal type," Phin said. "And I think there was another man by then. She was spending a lot of money and she wasn't getting that kind of cash from me."

Sophie felt awful. Some guy that soon, right after . . . She straightened. That couldn't be right. No woman wanted to date right after she'd given birth. "*Right* after the hospital? And you never heard who the guy was?"

"No. I didn't care. I don't care now."

Sophie looked at him in exasperation. "Phin, this is Temptation. Everybody in town would have lined up to tell you who the guy was."

"Sophie, I didn't care. I had a mother who was half crazy with grief and a baby I didn't know how to take care of and a brand-new job as mayor to fill out my dad's term. Diane was the least of my problems."

"She was the least of your problems once she moved back to the river house and let you alone."

He frowned at her. "What are you talking about?"

Your mother bought off your wife. "Never mind. It doesn't

matter what you did nine years ago." Sophie stared at the river. "So Dillie told you she came to visit. Are you upset?"

He nodded, and she felt like hell. "It makes things more complicated. She's decided she needs a mother, and I don't want her getting attached and thinking you're it."

"I think I want to go in now," Sophie said. "This conversation is depressing the hell out of me."

"I know," Phin said. "It's not doing a damn thing for me, either."

Neither of them moved.

"So other than that, how was your day?" Sophie said.

"Stephen got the porn permit pushed through," Phin said. "It's the first time I ever opposed something that the council still voted for. He's also managed to convince damn near everybody that I'm involved in this movie, so if anything goes wrong out here, you're taking me down with you."

"Good to know," Sophie said.

"And my mother thinks you're the new Diane. She warned me Dillie would find out. That's the thing about my mother. She's always right."

He made it sound as if he'd been doing something vile, and Sophie flinched. "You know, nobody's forcing you to come out here and play with the unclean. Nobody's making you cross the tracks."

"I think I'll go home now," Phin said and stood up. "I'll call you."

Sophie nodded and didn't turn to watch him walk away, trying hard not to cry. She didn't turn at all until Lassie poked her cold nose at her. "Hey," she said, blinking tears back fast, and turned to find Davy standing there with the dog and two unwrapped Dove Bars.

"Want me to beat him up?" he said, handing her one of the ice cream bars.

"No." Sophie sniffed once and took the bar, patting the dock with her free hand. "Sit down and stop talking big."

Davy sat beside her, and the dog took her other side and looked longingly at the Dove Bar.

"He was mad because you met his kid, right? You're good enough to screw but not to bring home to the family." Davy bit into his Dove Bar as Sophie winced. "Okay, that hurts," he said around his ice cream. "But cop to it now while there's still time. He's not right for you."

"Nobody's right for me," Sophie bit into the sweet chocolate and let it melt in her mouth. It was a great comfort, but it wasn't enough. She thought of Frank saying, "It wouldn't be so bad if I hadn't thought, for just that one night, that there was more." *Right there with you, Frank.*

"Are you okay?" Davy said.

Sophie nodded. "I know you're right. If he's that upset about me seeing his kid, he doesn't deserve me."

"I don't want to be right, I want you to be happy," Davy said.

"I don't think that's one of the choices at the moment," Sophie said, and finished her Dove Bar in silence, leaning on Davy's shoulder, concentrating on the good stuff she could have instead of the great stuff she'd just lost.

For the next three days, Sophie watched as Rachel threw everything she had into convincing Leo to take her with him while avoiding her mother, who had begun to drop by frequently. At the same time, Amy threw everything she had into the video. Amy was the most successful. On Thursday, Leo had gone back to L.A. alone with the rough cut of *Cherished*— "Gotta change that title," he said on his way out the door— and Amy was deep into cutting her documentary. "I'm going to call it *Welcome to Temptation*," she told Sophie. "Just like the sign when we came in."

"Cute," Sophie said. Then Zane cornered her and threatened to tell Phin all her secrets if she didn't stop the movie so Clea would go home with him. Since the only exciting or deviant things about her were the things she'd been doing with Phin, she wasn't worried. Of course, he could tell Phin they'd been shooting vanilla porn, but if he did, then at least Phin would have to call. She hadn't heard from him since the afternoon on the dock, so clearly he'd decided that his kid was more important than great sex, a decision Sophie applauded in the abstract but resented in the specific.

So when Amy blew fuses, Sophie took a deep breath and went down and changed them the way he'd showed her. Then she cleaned the house to distract herself, putting the ugliest of the furniture in the barn and airing out the rooms. It was a lovely little place, she discovered, as she cleared it out. The rooms were cozy and the windows were wide and she couldn't help but picture it painted and papered and beautiful. It was already beautiful on the outside; the Coreys had finished painting, and the house glowed blush and peach in the sunlight. Sophie looked at it and thought, *I'm going to lose this, too.*

Even so she asked Rachel to get her some green paint for Saturday, something that matched the leaves in the wallpaper. "I just want to see one room done before I go," she said, and on Saturday they papered halfway up on the other walls and added two apple green stripes for a border, and then painted all the woodwork and cabinets apple green, too.

"It's pretty," Rachel said, when they were done. "I didn't think it would be, but it is." She began to pack the empty cans and used brushes into a garbage bag.

"Yeah, it is," Sophie said, and then pulled herself together. "Have you heard from Leo?"

"Oh, yeah, he calls every day, but it's always about business, and what's going on here. I mean, he never says he misses me."

"Rachel, if he calls every day to talk about business, he misses you. There is no business in Temptation."

"Well, he's not saying, 'Rachel, honey, come out to L.A., I need you.'"

"You may be asking for too much," Sophie said.

"Just a job. I'd be a great personal assistant."

"Oh, just a job," Sophie said, feeling sorry for Leo.

"It'd be a great job and I'd get out of here." Rachel dropped into a kitchen chair and surveyed her green-stained manicure. "My mother is driving me nuts because of all the rumors about you and Phin. That's why she keeps dropping by here. That and to see Zane." Rachel rolled her eyes.

"Rumors," Sophie said, feeling the chill again.

"The town knows you're doing it," Rachel said, and then added hastily, "Phin hasn't been bragging or anything or taking you to dinner to show you off. It's not his fault, he's kept you real quiet."

Yes, he has, Sophie thought, and then kicked herself for feeling wounded. She hadn't wanted to go to dinner anyway.

"But my mom is hipped on me marrying him so she hates you," Rachel finished. "That's why she keeps showing up here."

"Oh. Well, tell her she can stay home. Phin's lost interest. Doesn't call, doesn't write, what the hell."

"That can't be right," Rachel said frowning. "Phin's not like that. He's a gentleman. He wouldn't just walk off. And he really wants you. The last time I saw you guys together, he looked like he was going down for the third time."

"Well, his mother threw him a rope," Sophie said, getting mad just thinking about Liz and the rest of the insiders.

"You should talk to him," Rachel said. "He'll probably be at the Tavern tonight. You should go."

"Maybe," Sophie said, wanting to see him again, which was too pathetic for words.

"Definitely you should go," Rachel said.

Outside, thunder rumbled in the distance.

"Okay," Sophie said.

Back in town, Phin flipped over the CLOSED sign and thought about Sophie. Davy had made it acidly clear when Phin had called that Sophie never wanted to see him again, and when he remembered the things he'd said to her on the dock, Phin could understand that. But that didn't mean he couldn't seduce her back to him if he could just get her alone. Maybe he could drug Davy—

Somebody knocked on the glass door, and Phin turned to see Zane. Since it was unlikely that Zane had felt a sudden need to read, Phin opened the door with fair assurance that he was about to be the focus of Zane's next dumbass move to get Clea back.

"Heard you had a pool table," Zane said. "That's my game."

This should be good, Phin thought, and said, "Table's in the back."

Zane went past the table, picked up a cue and sighted down the length of it, scowling, then put it back and picked up another, settling on one wrapped with red tape.

"They're all good," Phin said. "But that's the break cue."

Zane nodded. "Good." He racked the balls, scrubbing the rack up and down on the felt until Phin thought he'd have to take it away and smack him with it. When he lifted the rack, the front ball was a sliver of an inch from the rest, but either Zane didn't notice or he didn't care. Then Zane went to the head of the table, put the cue ball a good six inches behind the head string, and bent to shoot, gripping his cue until his knuckles went white.

I'm playing with an idiot who doesn't even know you don't rack your own balls, Phin thought, and sat down, nodding when Zane's break bounced the head ball and left most of the balls barely scattered. Nothing went in, and he cushioned only three balls, two of them stripes that ended up near pockets. *And now I have to open that mess*, Phin thought, and picked up his cue again, but Zane said, "Stripes," and bent to shoot.

Phin sat back down again, wondering whether Zane knew he was cheating or if he just didn't know eight-ball. Both, he decided as he watched Zane flounder around the table, pumping his stroke from his shoulder and hitting the two stripes into their pockets at warp speed. On his third ball, the cue ball brushed Phin's two before it smacked into the thirteen, but Zane didn't seem to notice. *That was a foul and I have ball-in-hand*, Phin thought about saying, but it was more instructive to watch Zane bash the balls and the game around.

On his fourth shot, Zane jawed the twelve in the corner pocket and it bounced out. "Tight pockets," he said to Phin. *You're a moron.* "They can be," Phin said, and picked up his cue. "Solids, huh?" He scanned the table, which Zane had broken up for him with his blundering, chalked his cue, and began to pocket balls on plain vanilla draw-and-follow shots.

"I think there are some things about that video you should know," Zane said as Phin played. "Especially since you put in that film permit."

Phin ignored him and pocketed the six.

"It's pornography, Phin," Zane said. "I know you don't know that because I know Sophie lied to you. Her whole family is crooked. Davy's a con man out in L.A. Amy's got a juvie record that would turn your hair white. The cops want her dad on a fraud charge right now. Sophie's playing you—"

Phin straightened and met his eyes, not amused.

"I'm just saying," Zane said, stepping back, "that it would be smart of you to stay away from the Dempseys because people tend to lose things around them. Like money. And elections."

Phin shut him out, chalked his cue, and bent back to the table to work his way to the eight, concentrating so he wouldn't grab Zane by the throat.

"You don't believe me? Look up Leo Kingsley, that producer they've got out there. You know what his production company is? Leo Films. He only makes porn. You check it out. You'll see. She's lying to you if she told you that movie isn't porn."

Phin ignored him and put the one ball in the side pocket with a draw shot that brought the cue ball into position for the eight in the corner pocket. It was a lovely, simple shot, but then, the simple shots were always the prettiest, restoring his faith in physics and the world in general, something he needed right now since what Zane was saying was probably true. Anything that could be checked as easily as that had to be true. Except for Sophie playing him. She wasn't like that.

Of course, that's what every guy who'd ever been played had probably thought.

Phin chalked his cue and bent to put the eight ball in, and Zane said, "So you'll stop the movie?"

Phin pocketed the eight. "No," he said as he straightened. "That's game. You can go now."

"I'm thinking about your family," Zane said. "I can understand family, I'm trying to save my own here. My wife—"

"My family is fine," Phin said, putting his cue back. "Goodbye."

"Your wife isn't. She's dead." Zane leaned closer. "You

know, the police reports from her death are pretty interesting. A little more digging there, and I could have a real news story. And you could have a real scandal."

"And you could have a real lawsuit," Phin said. "My wife's death was an accident."

"The police chief was your father's cousin, and the coroner is a relative of your mother's." Zane put the break cue down on the table. "I start digging and you'll have no place to hide. You confiscate that video and send Clea home, or the Dempseys won't be the only family with a jail record."

"Don't fuck with my family," Phin said. "I will cut you off at the knees."

Zane stepped back and said, "Women can sure make fools out of smart men," and left, a lot faster than he'd come in.

Half an hour later when Wes showed up, Phin was sitting on the porch, sorting out the mess as lightning played in the sky and thunder growled in the distance.

"Looks like we're finally going to get that rain," Wes said as he dropped into his chair.

"Zane Black just tried to blackmail me into closing down the movie. Accused me of killing Diane."

Wes frowned. "He's not too smart."

"He also told me Sophie is lying to me and making porn."

"Hell. Is she?"

"I don't know. I've been warned to stay away from her."

"Her brother?"

Phin nodded. "And you and my mother and now Zane."

Wes sighed. "So knowing you, that means you're going to the Tavern to see her tonight."

The thunder rumbled again, closer this time.

"Oh, yeah," Phin said. "Got to."

• • •

Sophie didn't see Phin when she walked into the Tavern, but as she looked around the dim interior and recognized most of the faces there, she realized that in the past ten days, she'd become a regular without belonging there herself. It was sort of like being with Phin. She was there and interacting, but she wasn't a part of him, not somebody he'd introduce to his daughter or take to dinner.

She moved toward the jukebox, where Garth was singing "Baton Rouge," a perfectly good song, but too much like Temptation was before she got there and would be after she left. She started searching the song lists for Dusty, and after a minute she felt someone come to stand beside her.

"I've been looking for you," Phin said, and before she could stop herself, she said, "Don't stand too close. Your mother will find out." She flipped over another jukebox card.

"Forget my mother," Phin said. "Could you look at me for a minute? In fact, I'm the one who should be mad here. In the future, I'd appreciate it if you'd dump me in person instead of sending your brother with the message. That was downright—"

"What?" Sophie said, jerking her head up.

They stared at each other for a moment.

"Davy said you didn't want to see me again." Phin said. "And I was stupid enough to believe him."

"Oh." Sophie turned back to the jukebox. "Well, you sure gave up easy." She flipped over another jukebox card, and Phin took her chin and made her look at him.

"Talk to me," he said, looking her straight in the eye.

Sophie swallowed. "You made things pretty clear on the dock when you didn't want me near your kid. And then I realized that I'm not part of anything here, except now I'm part of the gossip, which is why you haven't been taking me to dinner, because you've been hiding us so Dillie wouldn't find out—"

"I haven't been hiding us," Phin said. "I just haven't been standing on Main Street shouting, 'I'm having great sex with Sophie Dempsey.' It didn't seem like a gentlemanly thing to do."

"You're right, you're right." Sophie turned back to the jukebox and flipped another card.

"Sophie, if I've screwed up, I'll pay for it, I'll even take you to dinner, but I'm damned if I'll pay for my mother and Davy."

He sounded annoyed which was cheering. Why should she be the only angry person in the bar? She flipped over another card.

He sighed. "What are you looking for?"

"Dusty," Sophie said. "I can't believe this stupid bar doesn't have—"

Phin took out some change and put fifty cents in the box. Then he punched in a number combination and said, "Can we go sit down now?"

The first chord sounded from "Some of Your Lovin'," and Sophie said, "Oh. Thank you."

"Don't mention it." Phin nudged her away from the box and toward the booths, and she moved away, swaying a little bit to the music, caught between misery and hope, but mostly glad just to be with him again, which was pathetic. One of the men by the bar caught her eye and smiled, and she stopped swaying. She was already enough of an outsider without calling attention to herself.

Phin put his hand on her back and said, "Over there," and she saw Wes and Amy in their usual booth, far back in the corner.

Dusty sang behind her, soft and low, and she thought, *No matter what I do, Liz and the others are going to hate me, and I'm going to be an outsider stuck in a booth in the back.*

"Sophie?" Phin said, and Sophie said, "I'm tired of this. Make your mother a happy woman. Go on without me."

She moved to the center of the dance floor and began to dance, losing herself in the gentle swing of the music until the guy at the bar got up. *Not you*, she thought, and turned away from him to see Phin shaking his head.

"Care to dance?" he said.

"That'll start talk," she said, and moved away from him.

"No, dummy." Phin slid his arm around her waist and pulled her back. "This is the part where you fall into my open arms and never stand a chance."

He smiled down at her, and Sophie relaxed into him, so glad to have his arms around her again that she didn't care what he said next. She moved with the music, and he pulled her closer.

"It's too late to stop the gossip anyway." Phin slid his hand down to the small of her back and moved his hips into hers. Sophie felt the heat start again and took a deep breath. "Anybody who's seen us knows we've been together," Phin whispered in her ear, making her shiver.

"That's how the gossip started. They just looked at us and knew."

"Oh." She moved with him, letting her cheek rest against his shoulder, and he held her tighter and her breath came faster. "This is the sexiest song in the world," she said a couple of minutes later, through so much heat she was blind with it.

"It is now," she heard him murmur, and when she lifted her face to smile at him, his eyes were dark and hot. "It's been four days since I've touched you. You're driving me crazy."

"Good," she said, putting her face against his shirt again, and he kissed the top of her head.

"Careful with that," she said.

"Hey," he said, and when she looked up, he bent and kissed her on the mouth, a quick kiss that turned into something longer, as rich and sweet as the song they were dancing to. He stopped moving and held her close, right there in the middle of the dance floor, and she forgot everything and kissed him back, clinging to him as the heat spread and her knees went weak.

When he broke the kiss, the music had stopped and he looked as mind-whacked as she felt. "If they didn't know before, they do now," he said, and then he looked past her shoulder, and his face changed. "Oh, Christ."

"What?" she said, still dizzy from his kiss, but he was already pulling her toward the crowd around the table where Frank and Zane were squaring off.

"Family values," Zane was sneering. "You and your town council brag about your family values, but you won't do a damn thing to stop a porn film right in your own backyard."

"I'm not making a porn film," Frank shouted back, and Sophie said, "Oh, no."

"And nobody wants to do anything about it," Zane said, talking to the crowd now. "You all just sit home, holding on to your secrets, pretending there's nothing wrong. Well, there's a lot wrong, and I know it all. I've warned everybody and nobody listens, so I'm telling you all now: You stop that damn movie, or none of you will have a secret left. Especially you, Lutz."

Frank stepped closer. "I told you, I wouldn't make porn. I support family val—"

"Your family values?" Zane's laugh spurted out. "Hell, your kid is fucking my wife, and your wife is fucking me."

Frank went white, and Phin said, "Okay," and pushed through the enthralled crowd to Zane.

"Not that she's any good," Zane said, looking at Georgia, and when she made a little cry of protest, he added, "Hell, Georgia, even Jell-O moves when you eat it."

"You're done," Phin said to Zane as he reached him. "Go home."

Zane toasted him with his glass. "And here's your mayor who is fu—"

Phin had him by the throat before he'd finished. "I said, go home," he said, and then Wes was there, too.

"Let go of him," he said, and Phin did, and Zane tried to say something through his bruised throat. "I wouldn't," Wes said to Zane and hustled him protesting to the door, making it look like no effort at all, and Davy followed them both out.

Frank was staring at Georgia as if he'd never seen her before, and Sophie went to her. "Zane lies all the time," she said to Frank, putting her arm around a still-frozen Georgia. "He—"

"He's not lying about you, is he, Georgia?" Frank said dully. He turned to look through the mass of fascinated faces. "Where's Rob? Was that true?" He looked at Sophie. "Was that true about Clea and Rob?"

"I don't know," Sophie said. "I really don't. I just know I wouldn't trust anything Zane says. He's awful, Frank."

"It's all true," Frank said, and left without a backward glance at Georgia.

"Frank!" she cried, and it came out like a mew.

"We'll take her home," Phin said from behind Sophie, and she nodded.

"Well, that was ugly," Phin said, when they'd dropped Georgia off at home and made sure she was marginally all right. It had started to rain as they left the Tavern, and Georgia had cried right along with it, the mascara running in black tracks down her face while the rain ran silver down the windshield and Sophie thought vicious thoughts about Zane.

"What is *wrong* with that man?" Sophie said now.

"He's trying to hold on to his wife," Phin said. "Men get tense when their women leave."

"Not Frank—Zane."

"I'm talking about Zane." Phin slowed to take the turn out of Frank's development and onto the main road. "Sophie, are you making porn?"

"No," Sophie lied, and felt like hell. The rain was sheeting down, and the wipers clicked back and forth, and she tried to concentrate on how happy she was to be back with Phin again, but guilt got in her way. "Zane just wants Clea's money," she said, to change the subject.

"He wants her, too." Phin squinted through the windshield. "I've never heard one man say 'my wife' so many times. He's all but branded her."

"She is spectacular."

"Yes, she is," Phin said. Sophie lifted her chin and he added, "Don't even try it. You know I wouldn't have her."

"Just wanted to hear it," Sophie said. "Not that I have any right to assume—" She broke off as Phin pulled to the side of the road and cut the engine. "What? Is the rain—"

Phin turned to face her in the light from the dash. "Okay, I know you've been mugged by my mother, but you've got to get past this. You want me to tell you I love you?" Sophie opened her mouth and Phin said, "Because I've known you ten days. That's too damn fast to start planning futures, don't you think?"

The rain pounded on the roof and Sophie felt lost. "Well, ye—"

"And you're mad because I wasn't happy you'd met Dill," Phin said. "Well, you're going off to Cincinnati day after tomorrow. I'm not happy about seeing my kid lose somebody she likes."

"She only spent a hour with me," Sophie said.

"You got me in the first minute," Phin said, and she flushed. "I'm so nuts for you, I'm not even asking the questions about that damn video that I should. I don't care. I just want you. Can I come see you in Cincinnati?"

"Yes," Sophie said, her heart racing as fast as the rain.

"Can I see you Monday before you go?"

Sophie smiled in the dark. "Yes."

"Can I see you tomorrow?"

"Yes."

"Can I see you naked tonight?"

"Oh, God, yes," Sophie said, and met him halfway for his kiss.

Several minutes later when they were both breathless and the car was back on the road, he said, "Listen, that stuff you said on Wednesday, about me crossing the tracks to get to you, that was just to annoy me, right?"

"Well, you're definitely crossing a river," Sophie said.

"Don't buy into that, Sophie. That's so damn dumb, I can't—"

"That's because you're the one on the Hill," Sophie said. "I understand from a very good source that you're either born there or you earn your way in."

Phin was quiet for a long moment. "I may be a little late coming to see you tomorrow," he said finally. "I'll be killing my mother first."

"Yeah, well, if I'm a little late coming to the door, it'll be because I'm disarming my brother."

"Still hates me, huh?"

"I cried some when you left."

"Oh, fuck." He reached for her hand in the darkness. "I'm sorry."

She laced her fingers with his and closed her eyes because

it was so nice to be alone with him again, in the dark, just talking. "Not a problem. Davy's not that good a shot anyway."

"Screw Davy. Are you okay?"

"Yeah," Sophie said. "I'm excellent, actually."

"That you are." He turned down the lane to the farm, taking his hand back to park in the sea of mud that was the yard. Then he curled his arm around her neck and pulled her close and kissed her again, and she fell into him, warm and safe. Everything she'd felt while they'd danced came back and she gave in to it, knowing it would only get better. "You do that *so* well," she whispered, and he said, "We do it well. Imagine if we practiced," and kissed her hard again.

An hour later, they were in her bedroom, damp from the rain that came in the open window and from each other, tangled in her sheets on her lumpy, noisy mattress, gasping in each other's arms. "We're getting good at this," Phin said between breaths, and Sophie nodded, too satisfied to do anything but agree. He stroked her back, and she stretched like a cat, feeling all her muscles because he'd made them throb. "I could stay like this all night," she said, and then realized what she'd said. "I didn't mean—" she began, and he cuddled her closer and said, "Good idea. How do you feel about sex in the morning?" She said, "With you?" and he said, "No, with Wes. Of course with me," and she smiled, but then somebody knocked on the door and broke the moment.

"Go away," she called, but Davy said, "Sophie, I have to talk to you."

"If he's trying to do the brotherly thing and warn you that I'm only after one thing, it's too late. I just got it." Phin drew the tips of his fingers down her back and made her shiver. "Get rid of him, and I'll try getting it again."

"Sophie, *now.*"

She'd never wanted to leave a bed less. "Hold on," she

called, as she rolled out of Phin's arms and grabbed his shirt from the floor.

"That's my shirt," he said, but she shrugged into it and held it closed as she opened the door.

"Amy has a problem." Davy's voice was low and his face rain-spattered and dead serious, and Sophie felt a chill. "Get rid of him and come with me. Fast."

"Okay," Sophie said, her heart pounding, and closed the door.

"About my shirt," Phin said. "Take it off and come back here," and Sophie slipped it off and threw it to him.

"All yours," she said, and picked up her dress. "Thank you for a lovely time—let's do it again real soon."

Phin sat up. "I was planning on doing it real soon. Where are you going?"

She threw him his pants. "I forgot, Davy and I have plans, and I can't stand him up just to have more incredible sex with you. That would be antifamily."

"What kind of plans?" Phin said, and she shoved his shoes closer to the bed. "So I gather we're in a hurry here?"

Sophie leaned over and kissed him, staying in the kiss a little longer than she should have because he felt so good. "I really have to go," she whispered against his mouth. "But I really do want this again. I missed you so much. I'll call you later tonight, I swear."

"The telephone is so impersonal," he said, and caught her to him, pulling her back down on the bed, and if it had been anybody but Davy and Amy who needed her, she'd have fallen. But it was Davy and Amy, so she said, "Thank you, I have to go," and rolled off the bed.

She left him sitting there, looking puzzled and not a little grumpy, and when she got to the landing where Davy was leaning against the wall, she whispered savagely, "This had better be good."

"Where's Harvard?" Davy said. "We need him off the premises."

"He's getting dressed," Sophie said. "And he's not in a good mood, so don't call him Harvard. And by the way, next time, *I* get to dump the guy I'm sleeping with."

"Later for that, we've got trouble," Davy said, and Sophie felt chilled again.

Phin came out of the bedroom, buttoning his shirt. "Just like the Waltons," he said, as he walked past them.

"No, we have better music than the Waltons," Davy said, and then held Sophie's arm until they heard the front door slam. "You can make it up to him later," he told her as he pulled her down the stairs and out the back door.

Sophie followed him as the instincts of disaster that had been dogging her from the beginning kicked into high gear. He led her around the side of the house in the pelting rain into the dark of the trees, and she saw Amy standing there, hugging herself.

"I'm sorry, Sophie," she said, looking like a soaked little cat. "Davy says this is a screw-up, but I didn't know what else to do."

"What?" Sophie said. "I still don't know—" Then she went cold as she saw the old blue-and-pink-fish shower curtain at Amy's feet, wrapped around something that looked horribly like a body. "Tell me that's not a—"

"That's Zane," Davy said, turning his collar up against the rain. "And thanks to Amy, he now sleeps with the fishes."

There you go, her instincts said. *Told you so.*

Chapter
Ten

Sophie said, "What??" and Amy said, "*No*, I didn't kill him. I just sort of . . . moved him."

"Moved him?" Sophie turned back to Davy. "What—"

"Amy found him on the dock," Davy said, his exasperation with his sister plain. "And being a Dempsey, she thought first of her own interests and realized that if she wanted to film a sex scene there tomorrow without the police, she'd have to move the body. So she dragged it up here, and I found her when she was wrapping it in the shower curtain."

"Oh, jeez, *Amy*." Sophie looked down at the rain-spattered bundle and saw Lassie sniffing it. "Lassie, get away from there." The whole situation was surreal. It couldn't possibly be true. She nudged the shower curtain gingerly with her foot. "Are we sure he's dead?"

"God, Sophie, you're worse than the dog. Don't kick him." Davy shoved Lassie away from the body with his knee. "I checked. He's dead." Davy sounded mad about that.

"Well, what did he die of?" Sophie tried to pull herself together. This was real. She had to think. Then she was going to be sick, but first she had to think.

"I don't know," Davy said patiently. "Here's what I do know: Zane is dead, Amy moved the body, and we should do something soon before people start to notice and make comments."

"Okay," Sophie said. "Okay." *There's a dead man at my feet.* "Okay." This was no time to panic. She could panic later. Panic later, plan now. The rain came down heavier, pelting them even through the trees. She cleared her throat. "Okay. We can take the body back to the dock and call Wes, we can leave it here and call Wes, or we can take it someplace else. I vote for the dock and Wes."

"No," Amy said, wiping the rain from her face, and Davy said, "As much as I hate to admit it, I vote no on that one, too."

Sophie said, "Why?" and he said, "Because they're going to know somebody moved the body. They can tell that, and they'll wonder why. Once she moved the body, we were screwed."

"Hey," Amy said, sharply. "We were screwed anyway. It's that dickhead Zane. Who else but us would want to kill him?"

"Half the town," Sophie said. "Moving a body is a felony or something, isn't it? This is bad."

"We have to put it someplace else," Amy said, her hands on her hips. "Some ditch maybe."

"Boy, dating the law hasn't taught you a thing, has it?" Davy said, exasperated. "We cannot put it in some ditch. And we're going to have to get this damn shower curtain off it, too." He turned to Sophie. "I'm assuming Harvard is acquainted with the shower curtain."

"Intimately," Sophie said. "He's had conversations with the mildew. Wes knows it, too. He fixed the showerhead." She looked down at the bundle again, trying to make the situation less surreal, but there was a body wrapped in that ugly shower curtain, the rain beading on the fishes. Vincent Price should be there. "Maybe Zane just had a heart attack. We could take him to an emergency room."

"Yeah, good idea," Davy said. "Except he's *cold*. He is obviously *dead*. They're going to wonder why we didn't notice that." He shook his head at his sisters, glowering at them through the downpour. "Generations of Dempseys must be rolling in their graves, watching you two."

"They're probably too busy hauling coal in hell to worry about us," Sophie said. "Okay, I'm against the moving the body someplace else, *really against*, moving the body. And I'm really, really against lying to . . . people."

Amy frowned at her. "Sophie, I need your help. How can—"

"Shut up, Amy," Davy said. "You're right, Soph. You're finally getting a life of your own and here we come to screw it up by making you lie to the mayor. Go back inside, we never should have dragged you into this."

"Wait a minute," Amy said.

"She doesn't even have a motive," Sophie said to Davy. "We could tell them—"

"Zane was leaning on everybody to confiscate the film," Amy said. "He tried everything to screw up this project while he was alive, and he's not going to do it now that he's dead. I'm going to finish this video. I'm moving him."

"Go back inside, Sophie," Davy said. "I've got this covered."

Right. "You want the head or the feet?" Sophie said.

"You sure?" Davy said.

Sophie nodded. "I think this is a mistake, but I'm damned if I'll let you do it alone. This is no time to break up the family."

"If you ask me, it's the perfect time," Davy said. "Amy, get the car and back it up as close to the trees as you can." When she'd splashed off into the yard, Davy said, "She's not going to make it in L.A."

"Thank you for sharing," Sophie said. "Can we worry about that when we've gotten rid of this body?"

Once they had Zane in the trunk, Davy said, "Okay, where?"

"Someplace where they'll find him fast," Sophie said, hugging herself against the downpour. "I am not covering up a crime if this is one."

"I'm pretty sure this is one," Davy said. "You need someplace dark with a lot of people. Temptation have a lovers' lane?"

"Oh, not there," Sophie said, and Amy said, "That's perfect. I'll drive."

Any lingering thoughts Rachel might have entertained about ever going back to Rob were vanquished after an hour and a half spent parked with him behind the Tavern with the rain drumming on the roof.

"You know, Rache," he said. "We're really not together anymore."

"I *know* that," she said. "I don't want you. But Zane was so awful—" She drank another slug of the scotch Rob had brought for her and wished for the four thousandth time that Leo wasn't out of town.

Rob frowned at Rachel. "I still don't get what happened."

"I told you, I went out behind the house to meet you, and he was there," Rachel said. "He was staggering and he grabbed me and—" She took another drink and sniffed. "Thank God my mom doesn't know about that. Thank God my *dad* doesn't know about that."

"He'd kill him," Rob said.

"I just need a chance to calm down," Rachel said. "I just need to be calm before I see my parents again because you know—"

"Yeah," Rob said. "But I think you should tell your dad."

"Why?" Rachel said, and then she got it and looked at him with contempt. "So he can kill Zane and you can get Clea. Get real." The idea was so dumb, she stopped shaking and took another drink. "You know, you have to get over her. She's going to eat you alive."

"She already did," Rob said, his voice smug with satisfaction.

"Oh, *gross*," Rachel said. Then, after a moment, she said, "So you're doing it."

"Yeah," Rob said.

"Fabulous," Rachel said. *You are such a dumbass.* Strangely enough, hearing about what a fool Rob was being was calming her down faster than anything. "So is she going to leave him for you?"

"If she can get the money back." Rob sounded truly disturbed. "If she can get the money, we can go anywhere, but without it, she's stuck with him." He pounded his fist on the steering wheel. "Man, I hate that guy."

"Whatever happened to true love being all you need?"

"We're talking over a million here, Rache," Rob said, sounding like a man of the world. "You don't just walk away from that kind of capital."

Rachel was willing to bet that was a direct quote from

Clea, and she had to admit it was a lot of money. But if she cared about somebody, she'd go with him without the money. If Leo got wiped out and asked her to go to L.A. to help him rebuild, she'd do it in a second, and she wasn't even in love with him. She could waitress to support them while Leo found his feet again.

Rob said, "So are you okay now? Because I got things to do," and Rachel gave up her rescue fantasy and said, "Yeah. Take me home. And thank you. For this."

"Hey," Rob said. "I owe you that much. I dumped you for Clea, and you're being great."

"Oh." Rachel thought about clueing him in to the fact that she'd already dumped him, and decided there was no point. "Well, if you love her, you love her."

"I love her," Rob said, and his voice was sure as he put the car in gear.

"Good luck," Rachel said. *You're gonna need it.*

Rob pulled out from the back of the Tavern through the sheeting rain, and the car bumped over something. "Shit," he said, and stopped the car. "I think I hit a dog."

"Oh, no." Rachel looked back, but it was too dark. "I didn't hear a yipe."

"Stay here." Rob slammed the door and she could see him splash around to the back of the car and bend down. Ten seconds later, he was back in the driver's seat, drenched and shaking.

"I hit Zane."

"What?" Rachel froze. "What do you mean, you hit Zane? I didn't see anybody! We didn't hit anybody!"

"I hit Zane. He's dead." Rob was sweating now. "Oh, God. They'll think I did it on purpose to get Clea."

"He's dead? Get us out of here," Rachel said.

"I just—We can't—"

Rachel grabbed his T-shirt and pulled him to her, nose to nose. "Get. Us. Out. Of here. *Now.*"

Rob nodded and put the car in gear. And when they peeled out of the parking lot, Rachel said calmly, "Slow down. We don't want Wes picking us up for reckless op."

Rob shook his head and slowed down. "What are we going to do?"

"We're going to do nothing." Rachel felt panic rise and stepped on it. There was already one loser in the car; they didn't need two. "We're going to go home and go to bed like good children. And we're going to be really surprised in the morning when we find out he's dead."

"I killed him," Rob said.

"Clea will be so grateful," Rachel said.

In the green light from the dashboard, she saw Rob's face change from panic-stricken to panic-thoughtful.

"There you go," she said. "Always looking on the bright side of life."

At eleven-thirty Phin was in bed, staring at the ceiling, listening to the drumming rain and waiting for Sophie to call, when the phone rang. He picked it up and said, "If this is an apology, you better be naked."

"It's not an apology," Wes said. "I'm at the Tavern. Pete Alcott just ran over Zane Black."

"Oh, Christ," Phin said. "I suppose Zane was too drunk to move out of the way."

"Too dead," Wes said. "He appears to have been murdered first. Ed's going to do a preliminary right away and an autopsy tomorrow."

"I'll meet you at the infirmary," Phin said. "Maybe Ed'll decide Zane died of a heart attack."

"I wouldn't count on it," Wes said. "There's a bullet in his back."

Zane didn't look good dead. He was damp and pasty and slack-jawed and squashed as he lay on Ed's table under the unforgiving fluorescent light.

"He was wearing your letter sweater," Wes told Phin when he came in.

"He can keep it," Phin said.

"A lot of people didn't like this guy," Ed said from behind the table.

"Nobody liked him," Phin said. "But I didn't think they'd kill him because he was an asshole."

"You taking this down, Duane?" Ed said, and Wes's deputy nodded. "Starting at the top of the head, there's a contusion on the left temple with wood fragments in it."

"Somebody hit him with a club?" Wes said. "What about the bullet hole?"

"Getting to that." Ed pointed to Zane's eyes. "Somebody also sprayed a corrosive at him. See the red patches around the eyes? Probably Mace, but not necessarily."

Mace. Sophie.

"And there are bruises on his throat where somebody choked him," Ed went on.

"That would be me," Phin said. "He was still alive after that."

Ed looked at him with the contempt he deserved. "Thought you'd gotten over that temper."

"He annoyed me severely," Phin said.

Ed nodded and went on. "Then there's the bullet hole in his shoulder. A .22. Which appears to have been fired at close range from behind and below."

"Close range? Somebody shot him in the shoulder with a popgun?" Phin shook his head, incredulous. "Why? To get his attention?"

"And there are also several cuts and scrapes on his arms and hands," Ed finished. "And his ankle is swollen. Looks like a bad sprain."

"That's not funny," Wes said.

"No, but it's true," Ed said. "And here's something else you're not going to like: None of that would have killed him. But he was definitely dead when Pete and somebody else ran over him."

"'Somebody else'?" Wes looked annoyed.

"Looks like two different tire tracks to me. Pete's truck and somebody's car."

"Then what *did* kill him?" Phin said. "The combination of wounds?"

"I'll do the autopsy tomorrow," Ed said. "My best guess right now, given the state of his clothing, is that he drowned."

Wes scowled. "Very funny."

"No. His clothes are damp clear through. He spent some time in the water."

"It's raining like hell out there," Phin said.

"No," Ed said. "He's been underwater, not just rained on."

"River or bath?" Wes said, and Ed said, "What am I? A magician? After the autopsy, maybe; when the lab report comes back, definitely."

"That'll be Monday, at least," Wes said gloomily. "Probably later. It's Labor Day."

"Okay, then," Ed said. "Here's a guess: The river. That would make sense with all the scratches, that he fell through some brush."

"Yes, but who'd do all this?" Phin said. "If you tried to kill somebody by shooting him almost point-blank and missed, you wouldn't drop the gun and reach for the Mace. You'd shoot him again. And if that didn't work, you wouldn't pick up a club. And you sure as hell wouldn't drown him."

"More than one attacker?" Wes shook his head. "Okay, Zane pissed off everybody in town, but I find it hard to believe they all decided to get even in the same two hours."

"Maybe they, like, planned it," Duane said.

"Conspiracy?" Phin snorted. "You couldn't get four people in this town to agree to kick him on the shin on the same day, let alone kill him."

"I heard he caused a ruckus at the Tavern," Ed said.

"A ruckus, yes," Wes said. "But nothing to make anybody shoot him."

Phin thought about Georgia, white with rage and shame. "Maybe."

Ed pulled the sheet back over Zane's body. "Could you two go argue someplace else? I have to operate on this guy in the morning."

Phin looked back at Zane lumped on the table under the sheet and felt a confusion of sympathy, regret, distaste, and exasperation. Zane had done nothing but make trouble since he'd come to town, but he didn't deserve to die for it. And now here he was, with people who didn't like him arguing over his body, and nobody to mourn for him. "Clea's his next of kin. Somebody should tell her."

"That'll be me," Wes said, standing up.

"Want some company?" Phin said.

"Oh, yeah," Wes said.

Sophie had showered and was knocking back her second cider and peach brandy when the squad car pulled up. She'd been okay until they'd unwrapped Zane, and then he wasn't a fish-covered bundle anymore, he was Zane, cold and stiffening with his eyes wide open, wearing Phin's letter sweater. They'd left him propped on the slope behind the Tavern in as lifelike a position as they could manage, but as they'd pulled away, Davy had said, "Damn. He fell," and Sophie had gone green again.

Davy looked out the screen door now. "It's Wes. And Harvard. The gang's all here. Suck it up, Soph. You're a Dempsey."

"Right," Sophie said, and hit the brandy again.

Phin didn't look happy to see her, and he didn't say much. Wes asked to see Clea, and when Amy went up to check Clea's bedroom, she was there, alone. That was so strange as to make anybody suspicious, but Clea's performance after that was so good that even Sophie had to give her points. She didn't play the grief-stricken widow, but she looked shocked, stunned, and all the other appropriate emotions on being informed that somebody she'd once slept with on a regular basis was now sleeping permanently.

"I can't believe it," Clea said. "He was always having those blackouts, but I thought that was just for attention." She put her hand to her eyes as if to block out the pain, and Sophie saw Davy's face twist just for a moment. *He can't still care about her*, Sophie thought, and then Wes took her attention again.

"Uh, we're pretty sure it wasn't a natural death, Clea," Wes was saying. "He was assaulted before he died."

"Assaulted?" Clea blinked up at him, her china-blue eyes opening and closing like an expensive doll's. "But why?"

"We're working on that," Wes said. "Right now we're just trying to get some information. When was the last time you saw him?"

"At the Tavern." Clea sniffed. "He was so awful, and I couldn't stand it anymore so I had Rob bring me here."

"And you didn't see him after that?" Wes was patient but not stupid.

"I saw him," Davy said. "About nine. I followed him back after that mess at the Tavern, but he was being a real butt-head, so I left him alone. He took that sweater and went out the back door and headed out past the dock."

"Toward the Old Bridge?" Wes said.

Davy shrugged. "Toward something. He wasn't wandering. He was going somewhere, although he seemed a little . . . sluggish."

"Sluggish." Wes nodded. "Like he'd been hit?"

"Or he was drunk." Davy shook his head. "I didn't get close. He pretty much walked through the house and out again."

Wes turned to Sophie and she thought, *I have the blood of a thousand felons in my veins. I can lie to the police.*

"Did you see him, Sophie?" Wes asked. Sophie shook her head and hugged Lassie to her. She hadn't seen him. That thing with the staring eyes hadn't been anyone she knew.

"I came back with Phin." She swallowed and said, "I can't believe he's dead. I hate this."

"I know," Wes said, and Phin told him, "We came back to the farm about nine-thirty and I was here until almost eleven. We didn't see him at all."

"You left before eleven," Wes said, and Phin turned to look at Davy and said, "Yep."

"I came and got Sophie," Davy said. "That dumb dog had jumped in the river again and was mud all over. So we put him in the bathtub and washed him off."

Phin got very still, and Sophie remembered her lie to him, that she'd forgotten something she had planned with Davy.

Next time she moved a body, she was going to make sure all the stories were straight.

"So the last time anybody saw Zane he was heading out the back door," Wes said. "About . . ."

"Nine-thirty maybe," Davy said. "Phin and Sophie came in after that, so before they came in, he left."

Sophie risked a look at Phin and met his eyes. He wasn't buying any of it.

"One other thing." Wes looked at Sophie. "Anybody here have Mace?"

"Mace?" Sophie blinked at him and clutched Lassie harder. *Rachel.* "Mace. No."

"Okay." Wes nodded. He began to ask Clea about Zane's life in Cincinnati, and Davy faded up the stairs as Phin crooked his finger at Sophie. "Could I see you a minute, please?" he said, and she went out on the porch with him.

Lightning split the sky and the thunder followed it as the rain pelted down. "What happened?" he said to her over the storm, and she thought, *I wish I could tell him everything.* But he'd have to tell Wes to protect his job and his family of politicians, and there was no way she was going to betray her family of felons. For the first time, she wished she didn't have quite so much family.

"Nothing. Davy and I washed the dog and that was it."

"You're lying," he said, not angry, and she shrugged. "Where's your Mace?"

"I don't have any Mace."

"You said, that first night at the Tavern—"

"It was a joke," Sophie said. "I don't have Mace."

Phin leaned down to her. "Believe it or not, I'm on your side."

She felt the tears start. "I know," she whispered, and he kissed her until she stopped crying.

"Yell if you need me," he said when Wes came out, and then they left.

When Sophie went back inside, Clea had gone back upstairs, and Davy was there.

"Her mourning was pretty much over when Wes left," Davy said. "What did Harvard want?"

Sophie said, "He told me to yell if I need help."

Davy leaned in the doorway and looked out into the stormy darkness. "He didn't believe a word we told Wes, and he never said a thing. He's got money, right?"

"No," Sophie said. "Forget him. Somebody killed Zane. Concentrate."

"Forget Zane, he's dead." Davy came to stand in front of her. "You concentrate. Harvard has money, right?"

Sophie flopped back against the couch. "No. He owns a bookstore but it can't make much, stuck out here. Don't even think about running a con on him."

"His shirts are Armani," Davy said. "And he drives a classic Volvo."

"His mother probably bought it all. Forget it."

"What are you talking about?" Amy said. "Zane—"

"He could take care of you, Sophie," Davy said, ignoring Amy. "He'd be good at it. He wants to do it. I've changed my mind. You can have him."

Sophie shook her head. "I don't need anybody—"

Davy nodded. "Yeah, you do. You're tired and you're not happy and you're still putting your butt on the line for us. It's time we set you free."

"Sophie doesn't feel that way," Amy said. "Sophie always says, 'Family first.'"

"He is family," Davy said. "He's her family—"

Yes, Sophie thought.

"—and she's not going to lose him because you and I are screwups. We've been dragging her down long enough." Davy nodded to Sophie. "It's time somebody took care of you, Soph, and that's Harvard. He was in real agony there, trying not to care tonight, covering your ass."

"Sophie?" Amy said. "He's wrong, isn't he?"

"I don't want to talk about this. I'm going to bed." Sophie stood up and then said, "Oh, damn, no I'm not. We have to do something with that shower curtain."

"You could just let Sophie run her own life," Amy said to Davy. "We did just fine after you left. We take care of each other."

Davy looked at her with contempt. "Oh, yeah, you take care of her. That's how she ended up making videos of other people's weddings and sleeping with a therapist and moving a dead body."

"Excuse me?" Sophie said. *"The shower curtain."*

"I'll take care of it," Amy said, ignoring Davy. "I got us into this, and I can get the shower curtain out."

When she was gone, Sophie said, "We're not going to put it back in the bathroom, right?"

"I'll take care of it," Davy said.

"You'll take care of it, just like that." Sophie folded her arms. "You know, while I was standing out there trying not to throw up, you were making *Godfather* jokes. That worries me."

"Well, somebody had to be cool," Davy said. "Would you just forget that? We have your future to fix now."

"That wasn't your first dead body, was it?"

"I've never killed anybody, if that's what you're asking," Davy said.

"I'm letting Amy go to L.A. because you're out there," Sophie said. "But if you're mixed up in—"

"You're not 'letting' Amy go anyplace," Davy said. "She's twenty-five, she can go anywhere she wants." He scowled at her. "Just not L.A."

"If you're there to watch out for her, I won't worry," Sophie said. "Unless you're getting rid of bodies—"

"I'm not going to be there," Davy said.

"What—"

"Okay," Amy said as she banged through the screen door, the shower curtain bundled in her arms. "I've got it." She looked at Sophie. "What do we do with it?"

"I'll take care of it." Davy took the curtain from her and looked back at Sophie. "For once, *I'll* take care of all of it. Everything's going to be fine."

Sophie shook her head, sure nothing was ever going to be fine again.

"So what's the plan?" Phin said to Wes as they headed back to Temptation in the rain.

"Look for a gun, a club, and a can of Mace and a car with some Zane in its tires," Wes said. "Try to figure out why the angle of that shot was so awkward. See if we can find somebody who will admit to seeing Zane after he left the farm but before Pete ran over him so we can narrow the time of death. And start checking alibis of anybody who might have a motive." He looked over at Phin. "Did Sophie come clean about the Mace?"

"Come on, Wes, you don't suspect Sophie."

"She might not kill him, but she'd use the Mace if he attacked her," Wes said. "Hell, that's why she carries it."

"But he wouldn't have attacked her," Phin said. "They'd known each other for years."

"Women are usually attacked by men they know," Wes said. "I'd bet anything the Mace was self-defense. It's such a lousy offensive weapon, it almost has to be."

"If it was self-defense, she'd have said so," Phin said. "No reason to lie. Maybe it was Amy's."

"I asked. She said no."

"Maybe Amy's lying."

"No," Wes said. "She isn't. Not about the Mace, anyway."

"About something else?"

Wes shrugged. "Oh, yeah. There's something big there. I haven't quite got it yet."

"I have to say," Phin said. "I don't think anybody we've talked to tonight has told you the whole truth about anything." *Including me, damn it.*

"Welcome to the wonderful world of law enforcement," Wes said.

Phin had a hard time sleeping, and things got worse when he woke to an increasingly stormy Sunday morning. The word had spread fast, and everybody in Temptation wanted to talk, even though the store was closed, but it was the strangers that got to him. The *Cincinnati Enquirer*, the *Columbus Dispatch*, the Dayton *Daily News*, and even some of the smaller papers, had sent reporters who'd slopped through the continuing storm, hoping for something juicy about the murder of a news anchor. "This is southern Ohio," Phin told one of them. "Nothing of interest ever happens here. Go away." But they stayed to dig dirt and gather gossip and by the end of the afternoon, Phin was sure they'd all have the scene at the Tavern at the very least and probably a line on the movie, too. None of that was good, but the worst was the original fact: Zane was still dead.

By late afternoon, Wes hadn't come by, which meant he was swamped, and part of being a best friend was the automatic obligation to dig out swamps. Phin turned the lock on the front door, but then he saw Davy with his jacket over his head against the rain, climbing the steps. He unlocked the door, and Davy shook out his coat and said, "Heard you had a pool table."

Phin said, "The last guy who said that got killed."

"Yeah, they said you were good," Davy said, and Phin let him in, wondering what he wanted and not caring much unless it was going to help solve the Zane mystery and get life in Temptation back where it belonged.

When Davy saw the table, he said, "Hello. *Beautiful* piece of furniture." His voice held real admiration as he walked around the table, and Phin tried not to like him for it. "Late nineteenth century, right?"

"Yep. It was my great-grandpa's."

Davy touched the rosewood rail. "It's like being in church. And you play on it every day."

"But I never take the privilege for granted," Phin said.

Davy met his eyes. "Harvard, you may not be a complete loss after all. What's your game?"

Phin shrugged. "Your choice."

"Straight pool," Davy said, and Phin thought, *Oh, hell, I don't want to like you.*

Davy added, "To fifty?"

"Works for me."

Davy went over to the rack, picked up a cue, bounced it on its end and checked the tip.

"They're all good," Phin said.

"So I see," Davy said. "Should have known. I beg your pardon." He sounded sincere.

Phin won the break, and Davy racked for him without comment, keeping the front ball tight against the rest and treating the felt with the respect it deserved, and Phin picked up the break cue, interested to see what Davy had going for him.

An hour later, the score was 32–30 with Phin in the lead, but that was pretty much meaningless. Davy's position play was flawless, and his concentration was complete: he'd been in stroke since his first shot. Even more impressive was his safety play. When he turned the table over with the cue ball frozen to the rail for the second time, Phin said, "Where did you learn to play?"

"My dad," Davy said. "He has few skills, but the ones he has are sharp and profitable."

Phin raised his eyebrows on the "profitable." "We playing for money here?"

Davy shrugged. "We can. Makes no difference."

Phin looked at the mess on the table. "How about twenty?"

Davy nodded. "Good bet. Enough to make you care but not enough to make you broke."

Phin studied the table and decided that a safety was the better part of his valor, too. "So your daddy was a hustler."

"Still is," Davy said. "And not just at pool. He's on the lam right now from a fraud charge."

Phin caromed the cue ball off the four and buried it in a cluster, and Davy said, "Damn."

"Thank you," Phin said, and moved away from the table. "Zane Black mentioned your dad was . . . uh . . . colorful."

"Zane did?" Davy looked thoughtful. "Now, why would he share that with you?"

"He was being helpful," Phin said. "Explaining why Sophie was a bad influence."

Davy's face darkened, and for the first time Phin realized that he wasn't just a slacker; Davy Dempsey might be dangerous. "Now that annoys me," Davy said softly. "He shouldn't have been talking about my sister."

"Well, he's dead, and I'm open to bad influences," Phin said. "You going to take a shot here?"

Davy bent to the table and did a bridge shot over the two ball, a beauty of a shot that did exactly what it was supposed to, and Phin shook his head in admiration. Then Davy picked up the cue ball and handed it to him.

"Foul," he said. "I brushed the two with my hand. That's what I get for letting Zane in my head."

Phin took the ball and said, "I didn't see it."

"I did," Davy said, and moved out of Phin's sight line.

Phin nodded and studied the table. If he could pocket the two, there was a possibility he could run the table. He put the cue ball down in position so that he could draw it back after he hit the two.

"That's what I would have done," Davy said ruefully from the side, as the two went in. "So you think my sister's a bad influence?"

Phin studied the table. "I think your sister's a hell of a woman, but I don't want to talk about her."

"Well, we're going to have to," Davy said. "Because that's what I came for."

"And I was hoping it was for the pool." Phin took his shot, but his ball missed the pocket by a fraction of an inch. *Concentration is everything*, he thought, and wondered if Davy had brought up the subject of Sophie to break his.

"Here's the deal with Sophie," Davy said as he took the table. "She's the finest person I know, so she should get everything she wants. Now, for some reason, she wants that ugly farmhouse, that stupid dog, and you." Davy chalked his cue. "None of which I would have picked for her, but then, Sophie has always walked her own path." He shot a plain vanilla draw shot with such elegance that Phin forgot about Sophie for a minute.

"It's a pleasure to watch you play pool," he told Davy, and Davy said, "I know. It's the simple shots that make you love the game."

"I really don't want to like you," Phin said.

Davy nodded. "I don't want to like you, either, Harvard, but we're stuck with each other because Sophie loves us."

"I went to Michigan," Phin said. "And Sophie doesn't love me."

"You know," Davy said as he chalked and shot again, "if you paid as much attention to your personal life as you do to your pool game, you wouldn't make these stupid mistakes. She's in love with you. And you'd better love her back."

"Is that a threat?" Phin said.

"Pretty much." Davy scowled at the table as his next ball missed the pocket. "And that's what I get for trying to talk and play at the same time. Look at that table. Don't say I never gave you anything."

"Davy, I care about Sophie, but that's it," Phin said. "And I never promised her anything at all, so you can back off now." Then he looked at the spread Davy had left him. "Christ, it's Christmas."

"Yeah," Davy said. "I had plans for that table." He sat down out of Phin's sight line. "I'll be over here in case you go blind and miss something. Now, about Sophie."

"I'm finished talking about Sophie," Phin said, and bent to make his shot.

"I'm not," Davy said. "She never told you about how we grew up, did she?"

"Yeah, she did." Phin made his shot and straightened to chalk his cue. "At least, she told me about your mom dying."

"She did." Davy seemed impressed. "So you know she's been taking care of us ever since."

Phin nodded.

"Well, it's time she found a man to take care of her, and you're the one she's picked. You're not my choice, Harvard. But you're Sophie's and you're going to marry her."

"No, I'm not." Phin bent to take his shot.

"Why not?" Davy said. "Think about it. You could go home to Sophie every night."

Phin looked at the ball, thought about Sophie at night, and miscued. Just a fraction of an inch, but pool is not a forgiving sport.

"Fuck," he said, and Davy said, "That was my fault, talking to you like this."

"No shit," Phin said, and walked away from the table, annoyed with himself for falling for it.

"Take another shot," Davy said.

Phin glared at him, and Davy said, "Right. I apologize for even saying it," and took the table back.

"It was the Sophie-at-night bit, wasn't it?" Davy said as he lined up his shot. "Sorry. It's what I miss most about her. That quiet bit at the end of the day when we talked about everything." He grinned at Phin over the top of his cue. "Of course, your nights with her are probably different."

Phin thought about the hours he'd spent talking with Sophie. Before he fell into bed with her and lost his mind. "Slightly different."

Davy nodded and began to run the table. When he was five balls from victory, he straightened and chalked his cue. "Here's the thing. I learned early that life is full of cheats and liars." He bent to the table and said, "I don't believe in Santa Claus," and hit his first ball into a pocket. "I don't believe in the Easter Bunny." Another ball went in. "And I don't believe in the innate goodness of mankind." A third ball went in.

"But I believe in Sophie."

He pocketed the fourth ball and straightened to chalk,

something that he should have done three times before but that would have ruined the effect. Dumb pool but interesting psychology.

"And that's why I'm going to make sure Sophie gets what she wants." He smiled at Phin. "And what she wants is you, God help her." He bent back to the table and said, "Game ball," and Phin watched as he lined his cue up for the easy draw shot into the corner pocket that would take the game. Then Davy moved the cue a fraction of a fraction of an inch to the right, and shot.

And the ball jawed and bounced out again.

"I should never talk while I play this game," Davy said philosophically, and walked away from the table.

Phin picked up his cue, chalked it, lined up the shot, and made the ball. Another rack later, he had the game. Then he turned to Davy, who was taking a twenty out of his wallet, and said, "On the very outside chance that we might play again, you should know that pool is the closest thing I have to a religion. Don't you ever throw a game with me again."

Davy went still and then nodded. "Fair enough. My apologies." He put the twenty back in his wallet.

"You really thought that would make a difference?" Phin said.

"Well, it seemed like a smart thing to do," Davy said. "Generally speaking, if you want something from somebody, it's best to give him something, not beat him at his own game. I just didn't realize who I was dealing with. Now I do." He nodded at Phin. "It was a damn good game, Harvard. Thank you."

Phin looked back at the table. "Yeah, it was. But I'm still not marrying your sister."

"Why?" Davy said, and Phin blinked at him. "You have a great time with her, the sex is obviously terrific, she's smart, she's funny, she's kind, she's a wonderful mother, your kid's crazy about her, and she loves you." He shook his head. "I don't see why you're fighting this. You can't say no to her anyway, or you'd have stopped coming out to the farm by now."

"You can go now," Phin said, annoyed.

"That would be best," Davy said. "I think my work is done anyway."

"And what work would that be?" Phin said as he followed him to lock the door behind him.

"I broke your concentration," Davy said. "Sophie was already in your head, you just weren't paying attention. Now she'll be there all the time."

"Don't come back," Phin said, and Davy laughed and went down the steps to the street.

Phin turned off the lights in the store and headed for the stairs to his apartment He was late to meet . . . Sophie. His steps slowed as he realized the rhythm he'd fallen into. Close the store, go out to the farm, kiss Sophie, and end the day. No wonder Davy thought he was the marrying kind. He was practically there already.

Well, the hell with that. Tonight he was staying home. Maybe Wes would want to play a little pool.

Oh, right, Wes would be dealing with the murder.

He picked up his car keys and went out into the rain to the police station, a little rattled that the murder wasn't the most pressing thing on his mind.

Chapter Eleven

E d got the autopsy done," Wes said from behind his desk when Phin came into his office. He didn't sound happy. "There's water in the lungs and it's river water, but Zane didn't drown."

Phin dropped into the chair across from him. "So what killed him?"

Wes tossed the report onto his desk. "Heart attack."

Phin leaned back. "That a joke?"

"No." Wes poked the folder with his finger. "It's in there. Necrosis in the heart muscle. Ed says his heart was a mess and probably had been most of his life."

"He had blackouts," Phin said. "Clea talked about them. She thought he did it for attention."

"He did it for oxygen," Wes said.

"So it's not murder?" Phin shook his head. "That can't be. A lot of people took a poke at this guy before he died. One of them must be responsible."

"Ed said to wait for the forensic report on Monday, but none of the attacks would have been enough to kill him, and we can't prove that any of them triggered the coronary, so we'll have a hell of a time getting a murder conviction." Wes's jaw was tight and he looked madder than Phin had ever seen him. "Which doesn't mean I'm not going to go after assault convictions, even though I have no clear motive, no weapon, and—oh, yeah—no fucking crime scene."

"He wasn't killed at the Tavern."

"No," Wes said. "That's the good news. We've narrowed down our options. He was killed somewhere in southern Ohio, but *not* behind the Tavern."

"You may be taking this too hard," Phin said. "Davy said Zane was heading out the back door. And Ed said he'd been in the river. Did you look at the dock at the farm?"

"What a great idea," Wes said flatly.

"Okay," Phin said. "If you're going to be surly, I'm going to leave."

"I checked the farm dock, the Garvey dock, your dock, and Hildy's dock, everything within walking distance given that Zane was drunk, and all points in between. Sent some samples to Cincinnati, but I'm not hopeful."

"My dock?" Phin said. "I don't—Oh, Junie's dock. I don't think Junie killed him, Wes."

"I think he went in on that side of the river," Wes said. "That would be consistent with the scrapes and cuts, if he fell off the high bank and through the brush. The bank on the farm side is just mud."

"So he went out the back door and took the Old Bridge to the other side?" Phin shrugged. "Easy enough, but why?"

"That's according to Davy," Wes said. "I don't think the truth is anything Davy Dempsey holds sacred."

"The only thing Davy holds sacred is his sisters," Phin said.

"Yeah," Wes said, and waited.

"Sophie was with me from nine at the Tavern to about ten forty-five."

"Pete ran over him a little after eleven-thirty," Wes said. "That gives her forty-five minutes, but it doesn't give her a motive. I ran a background check on everybody I could think of, which, by the way, solved our earlier mystery of why Stephen lied on that damn accident report. Virginia's been picked up for reckless op several times in Cincinnati. Evidently traffic in the city makes her nervous."

"Lot of points?"

"She'd have lost her license," Wes said. "So Stephen took the heat and tried to bully the Dempseys."

"Had he but known," Phin said. "Wrong family to bully. Why wasn't Stephen driving?"

"Don't know," Wes said. "I got the police report back on the Dempseys, too. Davy has a record."

"Since Zane wasn't defrauded to death, I think Davy's still in the clear."

"So you knew." Wes picked up a pack of cigarettes from the mess of papers on his desk and shook one out.

"I knew he was on the con," Phin said. "That didn't seem relevant."

"Anything is relevant." Wes lit the cigarette and inhaled. "As you damn well know. Amy has a juvie record which is, of course, sealed. But the cop I talked to in Cincy remembered her well. And then, just for the hell of it, I checked Dad, too. The guy has a record you wouldn't believe."

"Temptation has a 'no smoking in public offices' ordinance," Phin said. "And you kicked the habit two years ago."

"You got a real genius for the obvious," Wes said.

"So how do you feel about Amy's juvie career?"

Wes frowned. "Really turned on."

Phin nodded. "I'd have taken it that way, too. Still, falling for a bent woman is no reason to give yourself lung cancer. And since the Dempseys aren't violent—"

"If the Dempseys were being blackmailed, they could turn that way." Wes took a drag on the cigarette and then exhaled on a deeply felt sigh. "I used to think the Tuckers were crazed about family, but you guys can't hold a candle to those three out at the farm. I think Zane was blackmailing people, and they'd have been prime candidates."

"He tried with me," Phin said. "He wasn't too bright."

"What every town needs," Wes said. "A stupid blackmailer. I think he went after Frank, too. He was in today. He does not look good."

"Well, he's married to Georgia, who was fucking Zane," Phin said. "Although, evidently not very well. You know, if Georgia could have killed Zane at the Tavern last night, she would have."

"And, of course, there's always Clea," Wes said. "She's capable of damn near anything, and so far I haven't found that bank book everybody was talking about that she wanted so much and that I'm sure Davy was interested in, too. I'm going to Cincy tomorrow to look at Zane's apartment, talk to the people at his work, but if that book's not there, I'm going to have strong suspicions about Clea Whipple and Davy Dempsey." He took another hit on the cigarette and added, "Zane talked to your mom, too. Yesterday afternoon, right after your pool game."

"And we know this because . . . ?"

"Because that's what Frank came in to tell me," Wes said. "He also said Zane had talked to the Garveys and insulted Rachel and had something on the Dempseys. He was pretty much casting suspicion everywhere but at his family, although he did mention that Georgia was unstable."

"Like that's news," Phin said. "I don't suppose he mentioned his kid, who wants Zane's wife."

"No," Wes said. "Didn't mention that."

Phin shook his head. "Christ, what a mess."

Wes took another drag on the cigarette and then looked at it. "I wonder if we've confiscated any grass lately."

"You could go bust the Coreys," Phin said. "They paint stoned."

"Dangerous of them," Wes said. "The water tower is looking strange. Sort of bubbly. They're going to have to paint it again. Wouldn't want an accident up there."

"Taking their stash would be for their own good," Phin agreed.

"So what aren't you telling me?" Wes said.

Phin sat there for a long moment, balancing loyalties, and then he said, "I didn't leave voluntarily last night. I got kicked out when Davy came for Sophie."

"He needed help," Wes said.

"Or Amy did," Phin said. "My bet is Amy. She's the one they always rescue."

"Amy wouldn't kill anybody," Wes said. "I don't think. So, we talk to Davy Dempsey again."

"If you think you're going to break Davy, forget it. Especially if he's protecting Amy."

"Or Sophie," Wes said.

"Let's go bust the Coreys," Phin said.

Half an hour earlier, Sophie had been facing down Dillie through the screen door. "Dillie, your daddy *really* doesn't want you to be here."

"But don't you want me to be here?" Dillie said, looking rejected and heartbroken.

"Oh, honey, of course—" Sophie began, and then she frowned. "Nice try, kid. You almost had me."

Dillie looked exasperated. "Well, I know you want me here. You're just being difficult. Let me in."

"How come you're so sure I want you?"

"Because I'm delightful," Dillie said.

Sophie sighed and let her in. "You're father tells you this, I assume?"

"No, my dad tells me I'm spoiled rotten and not to pull that stuff on him." Dillie didn't look too abused by this. "My grandma Liz says it. She says, 'Dillie Tucker, you are the most delightful child in the world.' She thinks I'm smart, too. I'm a real Tucker."

"Lucky you. Dill—"

"I have a reason for being here," Dillie said hastily. "An important reason." She sat down at the table and fished a torn piece of notebook paper out of her back pocket. "Jamie Barclay and I made up a mother test."

"How cute of you," Sophie said. "No."

"It's just four questions," Dillie said, her cupid's-bow mouth drooping with disappointment. "Four little questions. *Please.*"

Sophie sighed. Maybe if she flunked Dill's test . . . "Shoot."

Dillie straightened in her chair. "Okay. These are multiple choice to make it easy."

"Thank you. We potential mothers appreciate all the help we can get."

"One. Should a nine-year-old's bedtime be (*A*) eight-thirty; (*B*) nine-thirty; (*C*) ten-thirty; or (*D*) whenever she gets tired?"

Sophie said, "(*A*). Or even earlier. Six, maybe."

Dillie nodded and made a mark on the paper. "Two. A child

should watch TV (*A*) only when there are educational specials on; (*B*) only on weekends; (*C*) whenever she wants."

"What happened to (*D*)? Shouldn't there be a 'never' on there?"

"Sophie," Dillie said, and Sophie said, "(*A*)."

Dillie made a mark on the paper. "Three. A girl is old enough to get her ears pierced when she's (*A*) ten; (*B*) twelve; (*C*) sixteen; or (*D*) twenty-one."

"(*D*). Or when she gets her driver's license, whichever comes last."

Dillie shot Sophie a look from under her lashes and then made another mark on the paper. "Four. When a girl grows up she should be (*A*) a ballerina, or (*B*) a mayor."

Sophie straightened, not amused anymore. "(*C*). Whatever she wants."

Dillie sat back. "Perfect score."

"What?"

Dillie nodded. "My dad picked the exact same answers. Even the different answer on number four."

"You gave your father a mother test?"

"No, I gave him a father test," Dillie said. "Jamie Barclay said I have to find a good match for him so he won't get divorced. She's had three dads so she knows. And since my dad likes you, I figured I'd start here." She looked at the paper. "We need to talk about some of this stuff, though."

Sophie stood up. "We're walking back to your grandmother's now."

"Without ice cream?" Dillie sounded truly distraught, so Sophie got two Dove Bars and several wet paper towels and took her down to the dock, Lassie on their heels. The river rushed past them, high and fast from the rain. "As soon as this is gone, you're gone," she told Dillie, who began to eat her Dove Bar slowly, chattering the entire time.

"My dad says that I'm his favorite woman in the whole world," Dillie said when she was finally licking the stick. "But I bet you're second." She thought for a minute. "Or maybe third. There's my grandma Liz."

"I'm just honored to be on the short list," Sophie said. "You have to go back now, Dill."

"But I just got here," Dillie said, imploring. "And it was a long way. My feet hurt. I'm just a child, you know."

"I have my suspicions about that," Sophie said.

"I shouldn't have come," Dillie said sadly. "It's because I don't have enough supervision. I need a mother. Really bad."

Sophie stood up. "Come on, Meryl Streep. We have to get you back before anybody notices."

Dillie ignored her to stare up the hill.

"Dillie?"

"Too late," she said in a small voice, looking genuinely pitiful this time.

Sophie turned and saw Phin coming toward them, looking like thunder. Dillie moved closer to Sophie and Sophie put her arm around her.

"I could have sworn," he said to Dillie when he reached them, "that I'd told you not to come here. You want to explain this to me?"

"You were unreasonable," Dillie said, sticking out her chin from the circle of Sophie's arm. "Sophie is my friend." She put her hand on Lassie's head. "And you won't let me have a dog, and she has one and I can play with him." She went into orphan-child mode. "This is probably the only dog I'll ever get to play with in my whole life. Ever."

"Where does she get this from?" Sophie said. "I can't believe she learned it from you or your mother."

"Her mother was one hell of an actress," Phin said grimly.

Dillie looked up, and Sophie said, "Well, she's damn good

at it, and it's a useful skill, once she learns to stop overselling it. Since you're here, can she stay a couple minutes and play with Lassie?"

"You want me to reward her for disobeying me?" Phin said.

Sophie leaned closer to keep Dillie from hearing, and whispered, "I want you to stop being such a tightass and let the kid play with the dog."

"Yeah," Dillie said.

"Don't push your luck, young lady," Phin said. "I told you not to come over here and you came anyway."

"Grandma told you not to come out here and you did anyway," Dillie said.

Sophie looked out across the river and pressed her lips together.

"Go play with the damn dog," Phin said, and Dillie went. "If you're laughing, I'm going to shove you in."

"Well," Sophie said, and then she laughed out loud. "I'm sorry, I'm sorry. But she had you on that one."

"She has me on all of them. Spoiled rotten kid."

Sophie watched Dillie run up the hill with Lassie. "You know, it'd be worth it to stay in Temptation just to watch you when she starts to date."

"She's never going to date."

"Not even when she gets her driver's license?" Sophie sat down on the dock and put her feet back in the rushing water. "She's a good kid."

Phin sat down behind her. "I know she's a good kid."

Sophie leaned back until she touched his shoulder. "I should warn you, she gave me a mother test which I tried to flunk. I passed."

"You pass all my tests, too," Phin said, and she turned her head just as he dropped a kiss in the curve of her neck.

"Hey," she said, alarmed. "Dillie."

"She just went around the house," Phin said in her ear. "Look at me."

She turned to him and he kissed her thoroughly. "I'll be back tonight," he said against her mouth. "Bed check. And you'd better be here."

"I thought your mother told you not to come here anymore."

"She's being unreasonable," Phin said. "You're probably the only Dempsey I'll ever get to play with in my whole life. Ever."

"Lucky for you," Sophie said, and he kissed her again, and she put her hand on his arm and felt safe and fine. "Is this what we're going to do tonight?" she said, her eyes still closed.

"No, we're going to wax my car," Phin said.

Sophie opened her eyes. "What?"

"Then I'm going to fuck you on the hood," Phin said, and took her mouth again.

"That was a *really* rude thing to say," she said a few moments later, trying to get her breath back.

"Yeah, but it turns you on every time," Phin said. "I go with what works."

"We have to stop necking on this dock," she said a minute later. "Stephen Garvey's probably taking Polaroids right now."

"See if you can get copies." Phin leaned toward her again, and then Lassie barked and they both jerked around to see Dillie coming down the hill, elaborately unconcerned with them. "Remind me to stay away from you," Phin said as he stood up.

"What did I do?" Sophie pulled her feet out of the water and drew them up under her.

"It's not what you do, it's what you are." Phin raised his voice and called, "Say good-bye to the dog, Dill. We have to get going."

"I could go out in front again," Dillie bargained, as she came up to the dock. "You could kiss Sophie some more."

"I had something in my eye," Sophie said. "We weren't—"

"I'm finished kissing Sophie," Phin said. "Say good-bye."

"Good-bye," Dillie said, the orphan child once more. "I had such a nice time, but it was too, too short."

"That's the good times for you," Sophie said. "They never last."

Leo came back Monday afternoon, splashing through the front yard and talking about arks and Labor Day traffic, and Rachel was so glad to see him she couldn't stand it. Her life was so awful, so out of control, but now Leo was back. She could tell him about the Mace and he'd tell her what to do. She'd wait until he was done at the farm and then—

He showed them his cut of *Cherished*.

"I changed the title, of course," he said as the video began to play. A cartoon lion in a smoking jacket appeared and the words *Leo Films* scrolled across him, and Rachel thought, *This is so cool, he's got to make me his assistant if I don't go to jail for giving Zane a heart attack.* But then the credits started.

Gone was Amy's carefully filmed approach to Temptation, panning up to the water tower. Instead two curvaceous-to-the-point-of-chunky legs straddled the words *Leo Kingsley Presents* which dissolved to flaming letters that read, *Hot Fleshy Thighs*.

"What?" Clea shrieked, " '*Thighs*'!"

But the title change was the least of it. Leo had kept most of the film, but he'd added some of the raunchiest sex scenes Rachel had ever seen, not that she'd seen many.

"I'm going to be ill," Amy said, when they'd hit the second one. "Look at that grain. It's not even the same film quality," and Rachel and Sophie looked at her in disbelief.

"Film quality?" Sophie said, her voice going up an octave.

"The fact that this is *pornography* doesn't bother you? My dog shouldn't be watching this."

"Leo, this is disgusting," Clea said. "Did you do this all the way through?"

"Of course," Leo said, not the least insulted. "This is what I sell. This is what makes money. This—"

Oh, Leo, Rachel thought, torn between anger and disillusionment. *This is so wrong.*

"I don't care about the money—" Sophie began.

"You ruined my film—" Amy began.

"Leo, you pervert—" Clea began.

He wasn't a pervert, Rachel knew, growing calmer even as the bodies flailed on the screen. He was a darling. He just wasn't thinking, that was all. Sometimes you had to point things out to Leo. The big sweet dummy.

"Now, look," Leo was saying. "You knew I wasn't Disney. And I told you it needed—"

Rachel turned off the television and popped the cassette out of the player. She took a red magic marker and wrote *Smut, Smut, Smut,* on it in big letters and handed it to Leo.

"Rachel, honey, be—" Leo said.

"This is *not* going to happen, Leo," Rachel said firmly. "We had a deal. You were going to try vanilla porn. You were going to be classy this time."

"Rachel, baby," Leo said, very avuncular. "You don't understand—"

Rachel pointed her finger at him. "Don't you 'baby' me. A deal's a deal. You don't put garbage like that in a quality film." She put her hands on her hips and stared down into his eyes, making him pay attention. "That's just wrong, Leo. You should be ashamed."

The silence stretched out until Amy said, "Yeah."

Leo sighed. "Look, you girls did a fine job, but you have to be practical. I couldn't sell what you made to high-school kids, it was that tame."

"So we'll make it hotter," Rachel said, making him meet her eyes again. "This is not a problem. But *we* make it hotter, not you. Jeez, Leo, what did you think? That we'd say, 'Oh, good, Leo put in some cheesy sex scenes for us?'"

"I thought you'd be reasonable," Leo said.

"You thought wrong," Rachel said. "Give us a week."

"Rachel—"

"A week. That's not too much to ask, Leo. Not after what you just did." Rachel stared him down, implacable, and Leo sighed again and said, "Okay, a week. But I need skin and I need sex. And if you don't give it to me, I'll cut it in myself."

"Deal," Rachel said, and then stepped back as she realized what she'd just done. "Uh, if that's okay with Amy and—"

"It's okay with me," Amy said.

"You can make all our deals," Sophie said.

"Especially with Leo," Clea said, looking at her appraisingly.

"Come on," Rachel said to Leo, feeling magnanimous now that she'd gotten her way. "I'll take you out to the motel and you can drop off your stuff. And then we'll go get something to eat, and you can tell me what this movie needs."

"I am not going to talk dirty to you in a restaurant," Leo said.

Rachel shrugged. "Then we'll go to Dairy Queen and eat in the car."

"Fabulous," Leo said, but he followed her out when she opened the screen door and gestured, just like she knew he would. He was a good man, really. He just needed to be *managed*.

Rachel got in the driver's seat. "Dairy Queen or the diner?" she asked, and Leo sighed and said, "You choose."

"Dairy Queen," Rachel said, putting the car in gear. "You

like their ice cream. And tonight we'll go watch the Labor Day fireworks, and you'll feel better. I'll take care of everything."

Beside her, Leo groaned, and Rachel thought, *Not a good time to tell him about the Mace.*

She'd just tell him later, then.

When they were gone, Sophie said, "I'd give her a raise but we're not paying her anything."

"Forget Rachel," Clea said. "She's bought us another week, but it's up to us to come through. We need sex scenes. And we're going to have to film them fast."

Sophie shook her head. "We signed that porn permit—"

"Sophie," Amy said. "For God's sake, this is my video. When we signed the permit, we weren't making porn. Exactly. And we're not filming on public property, so we're innocent."

"Amy, we're never innocent," Sophie said. "I said this place was trouble. Remember? That first day, when we *were* filming on public property?"

Amy looked back, unblinking. "You sorry we came?"

Sophie stopped and thought of Phin. "No." Then she thought of Clea and Zane's sightless eyes and the lying and making porn. "Yes." Then she thought of Phin again.

"No. Okay, we'll do this fast, but this is the end. No more." She met Amy's eyes. "I'm not lying to him again, not even for you."

"So much for family," Amy said, and stalked off into the kitchen.

At nine that night, Sophie stood with Amy on the bank of the river while Clea and Rob took their places on the dock. There wasn't much light from the quarter moon, so Amy had set up reflectors and side lights, and the dock looked like a carnival to Sophie. Trashy.

"This is too bright," Sophie said. "Way too bright, somebody's going to see."

"Stop whining," Amy told her. "Everybody's at the Labor Day picnic. We're going to shoot this very fast and get out of here before the fireworks are over. Right, guys?"

"Well, I like to take a little time," Rob said, and Clea said, "Very funny. Not tonight."

She stripped off her sundress and stood naked on the dock, looking even more beautiful in the moonlight than she did in the sun, and Rob said, "Whatever you say, Clea." He pulled off his shirt and threw it on the grass next to her sundress, and then unbuttoned his jeans, and Sophie turned away.

"I don't want to see this," she said, as she heard his jeans hit the ground, and Amy said, "Oh. Yes, you do."

Sophie turned around and blinked. It wasn't just youth that drew Clea to Rob.

Amy looked at her. "We're going to need a bigger dock," she said, and Sophie turned away again, trying not to laugh. Fireworks exploded beyond the trees, and she stopped to watch them sparkle gold and blue and red in the sky. Beautiful. Then she caught a glint from the trees across the river upstream. At first she thought a spark had caught a tree, but it wasn't that kind of glint, and she froze as she saw it again.

"Somebody's watching us," she told Amy quietly, and Amy clutched her camera tighter. "There, see that? Somebody's got binoculars or a camera or something. That's glass reflecting back light. Turn those lights off now."

"No, I can't." Panic made Amy's voice tight. "We can't stop, we have to get this. We're running out of time." She grabbed Sophie. "You have to go see who it is, maybe it's nobody, maybe nobody's there."

"Are you nuts?" Sophie pulled away. "Turn off those damn lights."

"*Please*," Amy said. "Just go see. And then come right back if somebody's watching and we'll stop, I swear, but it's probably nobody, and I don't want to stop if it's nobody."

"Amy, somebody just got murdered here. I'm not going—"

"It was *Zane*," Amy said. "Everybody wanted him dead— nobody wants to hurt you—just go look. Oh, please, Sophie." Sophie hesitated and Amy said, "*Please*. This is my chance, please help me."

Sophie closed her eyes. "If I get killed, I'm haunting you."

"Oh, thank you," Amy said. "Thank you, thank you, you always come through for me, Sophie."

And I'm getting a little tired of that, Sophie thought, as she headed for the main road and the other side of the river. The Old Bridge was just too creepy this late at night.

When she turned off the road and began to walk down the river path, she realized the whole place was creepy at night, thick with trees with the swollen river rushing below. *Just find out what that glint is and go*, she told herself. Once she knew for sure what was going on—

She stopped when she was behind the Garveys' house be- cause somebody was moving on the path above the dock. She stepped into the shelter of the trees and saw Stephen, binocu- lars ready, staring across the river.

They were screwed.

She bent to look through the trees to see the dock so brightly lit they could have counted Clea's freckles from the courthouse.

They were completely screwed.

Then her Dempsey instincts kicked in and she realized she wasn't alone, but before she could turn, somebody shoved her hard, and Sophie tripped and fell into the trees, smacking her head hard on a branch and toppling down the steep slope half-conscious, grabbing instinctively at branches that ripped at her hands until she plunged headfirst into the river.

She hit the water hard and went under, and it was cold, ridiculously cold, and that helped bring her back from the head blow. The pull of the current was strong as she fought her way to the air, shuddering and gasping as the river took her. She was past the farm dock by the time she surfaced. She saw Junie's dock off to her left, and kicked off her shoes and began to swim for it, cutting diagonally across the current, but the water was so cold and her head hurt and she missed the dock, slipping under the water twice as she almost lost consciousness.

I'm not going to die, she thought, and kept fighting her way across the current, and then the current was weaker, and there was another dock and she managed to get close enough to shore that the river took her against the pilings. She clung to the edge of the dock, feeling herself slip away, and then she thought, *No*, and pulled herself up, painfully, to collapse on the splintery boards. *You can't stay here*, she told herself, and put her hand to her head where it hurt the most. It was wet, she was wet all over, but when she brought her hand down, it had blood on it. *I'll get help*, she thought. *I'll get help in a minute.*

And then there was nothing.

Phin was opening the bookstore the next morning when Wes came up the steps. "I got the lab report and I'm heading out to the farm," Wes told him, biting off the words. "You coming?"

"I have this store I'm running," Phin frowned at him. "What are you so mad about?"

"The lab report." Wes stopped on the top step. "And the Dempseys. They're going to tell me the truth this time or

I'm going to fry them, and that includes your girlfriend. I don't care how banged-up she is."

He started down the steps, and Phin said, "What?"

"Sophie," Wes said. "She didn't call you? Somebody shoved her in the river last night. She's got the same wound on her forehead that Zane had. Ed's pretty sure they both hit their heads on the same tree."

Phin flipped the sign *Back at 4:30* over, slammed the door to the bookstore shut, and went down the steps past Wes. "Drive," he said.

When they got to the farm, Phin was out of the car and at the door faster than he'd ever moved in his life. He didn't bother to knock.

"Oh, hi," Sophie said from the living-room couch. She had a livid scraped bruise on her forehead and blue circles under her eyes, and she looked like hell. Davy and Amy stood over her, scowling at each other, but when they heard Phin come in, their faces smoothed out to bland.

"What the hell did you think you were doing?" Phin said to Sophie, not caring that everybody was listening. "It's *dangerous* out there."

"What?" Sophie frowned at him and then winced and put her hand to the bruise, and Phin wanted somebody dead. "Whoever killed Zane doesn't want me, unless you think you've got a serial killer on your hands, which doesn't seem—"

"If you ever do that again," Phin snapped, "you won't need a serial killer. I'll do you myself just to get the suspense over with."

"It's just a scrape," Sophie said. "It's no big deal."

"The hell it isn't," Phin said. "And you were in the river. Tell me Ed pumped you full of penicillin."

"Yes," Sophie said. "I'm *fine*."

She sat there with her chin in the air, and he said, "No,

you're not. You're too dumb to live," and went out and sat down on the porch steps and put his head in his hands and thought, *I almost lost her.*

Davy came out and sat down beside him.

Phin braced himself. "If you're coming out here to kick my ass because I yelled at your sister, go right ahead."

"No, I think you pretty much summarized the situation for her," Davy said. "She's just used to taking care of everything. Sophie's not one for waiting around if the family's in trouble."

"Wes said she says she just went for a walk." Phin raised his head and looked at Davy. "Tell me she's not *that* damn stupid."

"I wasn't there," Davy said. "As I understand it, they were shooting on the dock, and Sophie thought she saw somebody watching, so she went to see. Amy would like that to be Sophie's idea, but my bet is, Amy leaned on her. The movie is making Amy crazy, but it's family that makes Sophie stupid. You should be able to relate."

Sophie came out on the porch. "You still here? I thought you'd have gone back to the smart people by now. Davy, Wes wants us."

Phin looked at the bruise on her forehead and the misery in her eyes and felt like hell. "You are not allowed to leave the house again until you get your driver's license."

"I already have a driver's license."

"That's what you think," Phin said, turning to stare back across the yard. "I'm making Wes take it."

Davy stood up. "Don't scare the mayor again," he told his sister and went inside.

After a moment, Sophie sat down beside Phin. "I'm sorry if I upset you."

"You didn't upset me," Phin said. "You took ten fucking years off my life." She leaned into him a little, and he felt her warm weight against his shoulder. She was so close and so important, that he put his arm around her and kissed her, very softly because she'd been hurt.

She closed her eyes. "I'm sorry if I scared you. I scared me, too. I even lost my rings." Her voice shook a little and he kissed her again.

"I'll get you new rings," he said against her mouth, and then Wes came out and said, "I want Sophie in here now."

Phin sat on the arm of the couch with Sophie close against him, and Amy leaned on the fireplace and stared malevolently at him. *Warm little family you got, honey,* he thought and then remembered his mother. *Never mind.*

"A couple of things," Wes said. "Somebody filled Zane full of sleeping pills."

Sophie straightened against Phin, and he thought, *Great, now what did they do?*

"Enough to kill him?" Phin said, and Wes scowled and said, "No. But there's more." He turned back to Amy. "There was mildew smeared deep into that letterman sweater. I'd like to see your shower curtain."

Amy froze, and Davy said, "I made them get rid of it. It was so gross I couldn't stand it."

"You know," Wes said, "you're pissing me off." He looked at Amy. "You got anything you want to tell me?"

Amy stuck her chin out. "No."

Wes nodded. "I know damn well you moved that body, and I need to know where you found it." He never took his eyes off Amy's face. "Don't lie to me."

Amy flushed, and Sophie looked miserable.

Phin took her hand. "Sophie's sick," he said, and pulled her outside, away from her family. "Okay," he said, when they were back on the porch step. "You don't have to tell me a damn thing, but don't go down for them. There's a limit to what you do for family."

"I don't think there is," Sophie said miserably. "We didn't kill him, Phin, I swear, we didn't."

"Okay." He put his arm around her. "Don't get upset. How's your head?"

"It hurts," she said, and he kissed the scrape. "We moved the body," she blurted, and he looked back over his shoulder to see if Wes was close enough to hear. "I can't *stand* lying to you."

"That why Davy came for you," he said, and Sophie nodded.

"Amy wanted to film on the dock, but the body was there, so she moved it into the trees, and then we moved it to the Tavern."

"Amy's been leaning on you for too damn long," Phin said grimly. "When are you going to let her clean up after her own mistakes?"

"When are you going to let Dill?" Sophie said. "When she gets her driver's license? I don't think there's an age where you say to the people you love, 'You're on your own.'"

"No, but there's an age where you say, 'I'm on my own,'" Phin said. "And you're there. Can I tell Wes?"

Sophie closed her eyes. "I don't want to betray my sister."

"As long as she didn't shoot Zane, you won't," Phin said. "Wes isn't going to arrest her for moving the body, he's after bigger fish."

She shuddered. "That damn shower curtain. I see it in my dreams."

"You don't think she shot him, do you?" Phin said, and Sophie was quiet for too long.

"No," she said finally. "But I think she might have given him the sleeping pills. Davy got revenge once using sleeping pills, and we'd just been talking about it. I don't know." She put her hand to her head. "You know, this really hurts."

"You need quiet," Phin said and stood up. "Come back with

me. I'll have Ed give you some stronger pain stuff and you can sleep upstairs at the bookstore."

Sophie closed her eyes. "I can't leave Amy."

"You have to leave Amy," Phin said. "It's the only way you're going to survive."

The council meeting the next day was depressing, even more depressing than telling Wes the Dempseys had moved the body or leaving Sophie at the farm with her conniving sister. Stephen asked to table the streetlight vote for another week so he could present more evidence of Phin's fiscal depravity and neglect of civic duty. Then, during the new business, he tried to pass a formal thank-you to Phin for working so closely with the movie people, said thank-you to be printed in the Temptation *Gazette*. The motion went down when only the Garveys voted for it, the rest of the council viewing them with deep suspicion. Stephen fumed, his hands shaking, and then he played his last card.

"I have an announcement," he said. "I've talked to the people at Temptation Cable and they've agreed to preempt their usual programming so that we can show the "Return to Temptation" video at eight next Tuesday night."

"Uh-oh," Rachel said from beside Phin.

"Have you asked the people who made the movie, Stephen?" Phin said. "They have rights, too."

"I'm sure they'll be thrilled," Stephen said smugly. "Why wouldn't they be? A chance to preview their film to a receptive audience. And besides"—his voice dropped a little—"We should see what they've done. We gave them a permit, after all. I'm just doing my civic duty."

You *watched them film on the dock*, Phin thought. *What do you know?*

But he already knew.

They were making porn.

Half an hour later, Phin stopped by the police station and told Wes about the cable premiere.

Wes stubbed his cigarette out on the edge of one of the coffee cups that littered his desk. "They know about this out at the farm?"

"I doubt it," Phin said. "I haven't heard any screaming. Rachel will tell them when she gets out there. You want to go out?"

"No," Wes said, sourly. "Amy won't tell me anything anyway. When you go, find out if they have a .22."

"Everybody has a .22," Phin said. "Hell, I have a .22, or at least, my dad did."

"I know," Wes said. "I ran the registration forms. There are almost four hundred of the damn things in this county alone."

"An armed populace is a secure populace," Phin said. "Also, this is southern Ohio. What did you expect?"

"You have one, Frank has one, Clea's dad had one, which could mean it's still at the farm, Ed has one, Stephen has one, hell, even Junie Miller and Hildy Mallow have one—" He stopped, caught by an idea. "Your entire city council is armed."

"That, I didn't need to know," Phin said, standing up.

"I went to Cincinnati today," Wes said, and Phin sat down again. "No bank book anywhere, although Zane showed it to a couple of people on Friday."

Phin winced. Missing money and Dempseys were a no-brainer.

"Also, he had the whole council investigated." Wes tossed

a thick folder across the desk to him. "He had a crackerjack research team. The people at the station thought a lot of him. Evidently he was a damn good reporter. He'd been an investigative journalist before doctors found his heart problem and made him quit, but he trained the research team. They thought he was God."

Phin picked up the folder and began to leaf through it. The top sheaf of papers had his name on them: a list of everybody he'd slept with for the past ten years, with significant details. "Fuck you, Zane."

The next set of papers was Hildy Mallow's arrest record.

"Everybody at the station hated Clea, though," Wes was saying. "Said she was a conniving, manipulative bitch."

"That sounds like Clea," Phin said, still reading. "Hildy went to jail for protesting the war?"

"Often," Wes said. "She said Zane tried to talk her into stopping the video on the basis of family values, and when that didn't work he threatened to do her arrest record as part of a human-interest story. She offered him his choice of pictures of her behind bars from her scrapbook and asked him for a copy of the arrest records because she wants to frame them."

"Good for her." Phin flipped through her records, his respect for Hildy growing. "Man, she was busted everywhere. She—" He stopped when he came to the next set of papers: Virginia Garvey's record. "He knew about Virginia's driving citations."

"She says he never mentioned them, but he did come by the house. She said he asked Stephen to stop the video on the family-values grounds again, and Stephen said he'd look into it." Wes shrugged. "He probably didn't use the records because he didn't need them. They came on board without the threat."

"Did he have anything on Stephen?" Phin said, stopping

to frown at an invoice from an online video-porn distributor. "He didn't really think he was going to blackmail Ed for porn, did he?"

"He tried," Wes said. "Ed told him everybody in town knew he had the best porn collection in southern Ohio."

Phin flipped the invoices over and found a medical record. "What the hell? So Frank Lutz had a vasectomy in 1976. Who cares—" Then he heard Georgia again, talking about the little girl she didn't get. "Frank, you moron."

"Yeah," Wes said. "Frank's revenge."

Phin looked at the Cincinnati address on the top of the form. "Georgia would have left him if she'd known. How the hell did Zane find this?"

"Look at the next one," Wes said. "Stephen has Parkinson's disease."

"That's why his hands have been shaking," Phin said, reading the next medical record and feeling sorry for Stephen for the first time in his life. "They don't always, so I thought it was just rage." He looked up at Wes. "That's why Virginia was driving. He didn't want to have an attack while he was driving."

"It's more than that," Wes said. "He didn't want anybody to know because of the election."

"Why? I don't—"

"Because he thought you'd use it against him," Wes said, and when Phin jerked his head up, outraged, Wes added, "He'd have used it against you."

Phin sat back and stared down at the folder. "Christ, what a mess."

"You know, this might be pretty much the last chance for him," Wes said. "Parkinson's is progressive, and he's getting older. He only has to keep it a secret for another two months to win this time. But another two years, in this town—" Wes shook his head. "It's not like Temptation's ever given him a break before."

Phin winced. He'd never thought of it that way, and for the first time he wondered what it must be like to be Stephen Garvey in Temptation. While he'd been trapped under the weight of dozens of Tucker victories and one loss, Stephen had been carrying dozens of losses and one victory. What must it be like to be destined to strive for something you were lousy at, that your father had been lousy at, and his father before him? What would that do a man?

What would a man do to end that?

Phin met Wes's eyes. "So did Zane threaten him with the medical report?"

Wes shook his head. "Stephen swears it was all family values and agreement."

Phin spared one last sympathetic thought for Stephen and then flipped through the rest of the papers, through Davy's record, and a page on Sophie's relationship with the therapist that he definitely didn't want to read, and a much thicker sheaf of pages on a Michael Dempsey that had to be dear old Dad. At the bottom of the Dempsey stack was a final clip of papers, and Phin stopped when he saw the newspaper article on top.

Mayor's Wife Dies in Accident.

"He really was going after that, then," Phin said, shuffling through Ed's autopsy report and the police report with crime-scene photos and the newspaper report and Diane's obituary. He tried not to look at the photos, at her pale face lit starkly against the dark of the grass. "What did he find?"

"I don't know," Wes said. "But I don't think Zane bluffed anybody. I think everything he said was true. Had a real nose for secrets, Zane did, not that there's anything there to show Diane's death wasn't an accident."

Phin tossed the folder back on Wes's desk. "So what do you conclude from this?"

"There's a thorough report in there on all four of the Dempseys," Wes said. "And there are reports on you and all the council members. Except one."

Phin felt sick. "Maybe he just couldn't get anything on her. She's damn near perfect."

"Nobody's perfect," Wes said. "Not even your mother. If he took Diane's file to her and told her he was going after you—"

Phin thought of Liz saying, *"anything."* "What do you want?"

"Bring me your dad's .22," Wes said.

"Fuck," Phin said.

Out at the farm, Sophie stared miserably across the kitchen table at Davy while Lassie sniffed his suitcase by the door and Amy glared at them both. "You really have to go?"

"Yes," Davy said. "I'm catching a ride with Leo, but we'll both be back Friday, so stop looking so tragic."

"I'm not tragic," Sophie said, and Amy said, "Sure, go ahead, just desert us," but then the phone rang, and when Sophie picked it up, it was Brandon.

"Are you all right?" he said. "Amy called and said you'd fallen in a river. I think I should come down there."

Sophie glared at Amy, who looked at the ceiling. "No, you should not come down here. I'm fine. Brandon, you should stop calling. I appreciate your—"

"Sophie, I've been doing a lot of thinking, and I think you should come back home," Brandon said. "I realize you feel the need to act out your anger with this man—"

"Brandon, you're a wonderful man," Sophie said. "You

deserve somebody who loves you completely, not somebody who loves you comfortably. I—"

"Comfort lasts," Brandon said. "The kind of passion you're talking about doesn't. A year after you marry this man—"

"We're not getting married," Sophie said, looking at the pretty apples on the wall. "He's not that serious about me."

"This guy needs his ass kicked," Davy said, and Amy said, "Which one, Phin or Brandon?"

"Both," Davy said. "The two of you have terrible taste in men."

When the silence on the other end of the line lengthened, Sophie said, "Brandon?" and he said, "You deserve more than that, Sophie."

"I know." Sophie swallowed. "I'm working on it. But—"

"Sophie, I think Amy's right I should come down there—"

"I have to go, Brandon," Sophie said. "I'm sorry. Good-bye."

She hung up and said to Amy, "Do *not* call him again. Stay out of my life."

"At least he loves you," Amy said. "He's boring, but he's committed. The mayor doesn't even—"

"Yes, he does," Davy said. "He gets my vote. Now, let's discuss the stupidity of a Dempsey getting involved with a cop."

"I'm not involved," Amy said, trying to sound tough and only sounding more miserable because of it. "He hasn't even called since he yelled at me." She shoved back her chair. "It doesn't matter, I have real problems. I have to finish cutting a documentary. I don't have time to worry about some guy."

When she'd gone, Sophie sighed. "Do you really have to go?"

"Things to take care of," Davy said. "But I'll be back. Don't let her shoot anybody till I get here."

Sophie swallowed. "You don't think—"

"I don't know," Davy said. "I wish the cop would just take

her over. She needs a strong hand, and you've babysat her long enough."

"Hurry back," Sophie said.

Phin's next two days were lousy with problems and frustration, alleviated only by the time he spent with Sophie. Phin watched Wes move up to two packs a day and thought, *We have to finish this before he gets lung cancer.* It didn't help that his dad's .22 was gone from the locked gun cabinet. "Anybody could have taken it," he told Wes. "The key's on the top, up where Dillie can't reach it, but we weren't trying to keep anybody else out. I haven't looked in there for over ten years. It could have been gone that long."

"Great," Wes said, and turned down a pool game to obsess over his lack of evidence again.

The premiere took over the townspeople's attention, possibly because Zane had been such an outsider, probably because the video was more interesting because it was about them. Stephen suggested the schools assign it as homework. "I have to write a report," Dillie said on Friday, "so I *have* to watch TV. Jamie Barclay said I could watch at her house and then we could do our reports together—isn't that a good idea?"

"Oh, yeah," Phin said, and thought, *I hope to hell they've got a G-rated version of that video.*

"I'm going out to the farm," he told Liz, who looked at him with frozen contempt. He went out to the car, grateful that it had finally stopped raining, and then caught sight of the water tower on the Hill above him.

It was peeling.

"What the hell happened?" he said, when he'd tracked down the Coreys.

"It's that stupid cheap paint," the older one said. "When that hard rain hit, it just peeled right off."

"It's cool," the younger one said. "Looks like blood dripping off. The newspapers were here taking pictures."

Phin looked back up the Hill where the tower did indeed look like a huge bleeding phallic symbol. "Can you get that red off and paint it white?"

"Oh, yeah, like we're gonna strip the water tower," the older Corey said. "Just give it a couple of days and it'll be off anyway. The tower's gonna be a weird color, though. That red doesn't stick, but it stains."

That would explain why the tower looked rosier this time, even more like flesh than before. Wonderful.

He let the Coreys go and drove out to the farm for sanity and comfort, and by the time he'd slammed the car door, Sophie was on the porch. He went toward her, feeling better just looking at her, but she shook her head and whispered, "This isn't a good time."

"Now what?" His irritation married his frustration and made him snarl. "Amy build a bomb? Davy decide he hates me again? Or are you just playing hard-to-get because you want to go out to dinner? Come on, Sophie, I've had a lousy day. Fuck me."

Sophie winced, and he frowned at her, wondering when she'd turned into a prude. The screen door slammed as he said, "What's wr—" and then a fist slammed into his eye and he was on his back in the dirt, his head throbbing.

"*Brandon.*" Sophie said, and Phin looked up through the pain at a guy the size of a tank.

"You son of a bitch," the therapist said.

Chapter Twelve

Sophie moved in front of the guy, blocking Phin's view which was pretty hazy anyway. "All right, stop it, Brandon. He didn't mean it the way it sounded—"

"*Nobody* talks to you like that," Brandon said, and Phin sat up and tried to figure out how he'd ended up the bad guy.

"It's his idea of foreplay," Sophie said uncertainly, and Phin felt like hell.

"It's his idea of diminishing you so that you know you're not important to him," Brandon said. "He's abusive, and you're enabling him."

Wait a minute. Phin tried to stand up but the world swooped around him, so he sat back down in the dirt again.

"He's not abusive," Sophie said. "He's in a bad mood. He can be perfectly lovely when he wants to be."

"Ouch," Phin said.

"And what do you have to do to make him lovely?" Brandon said. "Sophie, I know he's been exciting, but if this is the way he treats you—"

"He treats me just fine," Sophie said, and Brandon looked down at Phin in the dust and said, "He treats you like a whore."

"Brandon!" Sophie said, and Phin leveraged his way up, grabbing the porch rail to keep what little sense of balance he had.

"I will never understand why women stay with abusive men," Brandon was saying. "Especially somebody like you. You're a sensible woman, Sophie. Surely—"

"Oh, not really," Sophie said, watching Phin warily. "Brandon, I think you'd better go."

"Sophie, you can't—"

"Yes, I can," she said to Brandon. Then she looked at Phin, frowning. "Don't move until I get back." She prodded Brandon over to his car, and he went, still explaining her abusive relationship to her. Phin squinted at the car. A late-model Toyota. Practical of him. Then Sophie stretched up to kiss the giant therapist good-bye, and Phin scowled, which hurt, and leaned against the porch post, which also hurt, until the enemy was gone.

"Let's get some ice on that eye," Sophie said, as she came back to him and took his arm.

"I don't like him," Phin said, still dizzy.

"I know, bear," she said. "He doesn't like you, either."

Fifteen minutes later, Phin was stretched out on the dock by the rushing river with his head in Sophie's lap, ice on his eye, and Lassie sniffing his ear.

"This is all my fault." She leaned down and moved the ice to kiss his bruised eye, and he felt some of his tension seep away. "I never should have told Brandon about you."

"Yes, you should have." Phin watched her face hover above him, concern wrinkling her forehead. *She's mine*, he wanted to tell Brandon, preferably on the phone. "You might have told me he was built like a truck."

Sophie put the ice back on his eye. "He played second-string football for Ohio State. He says he would have been first-string but he kept going to class."

"Don't tell him I played golf for Michigan. Although, if I'd had my four iron, this would have ended very differently."

Sophie's laugh bubbled out and he smiled at her because he loved her face when she laughed. "Why the hell did he hit me anyway? I thought you'd told him it was over."

Sophie's smile faded. "It was that crack you made about dinner and the . . . language you used."

Phin frowned and then winced as his face protested. "He doesn't want me to take you to dinner?" he said, as he moved the ice away from his eye. "Too damn bad, but that's not a reason to punch somebody. And you never minded my language before."

"He doesn't want you making me feel cheap," Sophie said. "I have a history of that."

He scowled up at her and said, "What?" and then he listened with increasing guilt as she told him about the louse she'd lost her virginity to.

When she'd finished, he said, "This is the town-boy thing." She nodded.

"Fuck. I'd have hit me, too. Maybe I can still catch him, and we can go to Iowa together. Beating up a middle-aged businessman would make us both feel better."

"Thank you, but no," Sophie said. "Davy took care of Chad a long time ago."

"Good for Davy," Phin said. "I'm sorry, Sophie."

"You didn't mean anything when you said it," Sophie said, smiling at him.

An "enabler," Brandon had said. "Call me on it when I'm being a son of a bitch," he told her. "Don't take that crap from me just because I'm tired and I can be nice when I want to be."

"Call yourself on it," Sophie said, a little waspishly, and he said, "Fuck," and moved the ice pack up to cover his eye.

"I'm sorry about Chad," he told her. "I'm sorry about every guy who ever fucked you over. God knows, I probably did it to some girl, too." *"Probably," hell. Definitely.*

"No, you didn't," Sophie said. "You married Diane."

"I used Diane to get what I wanted, and then paid for it," Phin said. "I don't think I get any awards for being a sensitive male on that one."

"I don't want a sensitive male," Sophie said. "I want you."

"Thank you," Phin said. "Damn good thing you have lousy taste in men or I'd be out in the cold."

"Oh, cheer up." She kissed him on the forehead and he frowned and then winced again.

"I'm sorry about the 'fuck me,' too," he said. "The therapist is wrong. You're important to me. You know that."

Sophie glared down at him, exasperated.

"Well, you do, right?" He squinted up at her again.

"Sure. Yeah." Sophie took a deep breath. "Forget Brandon. Let's make you feel better."

"The only thing that would make me feel better at this point is headbanging sex," he told her, guilt making him cranky. "But since Brandon pretty much banged my head for me, I think sex is out." *Probably part of his plan, the son of a bitch.*

"Well, then, talk dirty to me," Sophie went on, now relentlessly cheerful. "You like that. What about *your* fantasies? We never talk about you."

Phin stared at the sky. The last thing he needed right now was Sophie being chirpy. Under ordinary circumstances, he'd have told her to can it, but that "abusive" bit had stung. "My fantasies," he said. "Most of them start with you naked."

Sophie nodded. "Okay, then what?"

"Handcuffs, whips, chains, butter, the usual."

"Stick or tub?" Sophie said.

"What?"

"The butter."

Phin closed his eyes and gave up being sensitive. "Sophie, I know you're trying to be cute, but shut up. I have a headache." He felt his eye and winced and then tried to sit up.

"No, I'm serious." She put her hand on his stomach to stop him, and he stopped moving to appreciate it. "Tell me a fantasy."

He looked down at her hand. "About six inches lower."

"A *fantasy*."

He sighed, and her hand rose and fell with his stomach. "Okay. Let's see." He closed his eyes and let his head fall back into her lap. She was going someplace with this, so he went for something easy. "I'm sitting in a bar, being my usual cool, sophisticated self . . ."

"That's it," Sophie said. "A fantasy."

". . . and this incredibly beautiful woman sits down beside me."

"This has to be something I can do," Sophie said.

"Stop fishing for compliments. And she says, 'I want you, I need you, I must have you, and by the way I'm not wearing underpants.' And then we go someplace, and she fucks my brains out." Actually, that sounded pretty damn good, now that he thought about it. The pain receded a little.

"You have no imagination," Sophie was saying. "That's like the oldest cliché there is."

"Don't say 'like,'" Phin said. "You sound like Rachel."

"That one's even been in the movies a couple of times," Sophie said. "Don't you have anything—"

"Hey." Phin opened his eyes and glared at her. "You asked, I told. I have others involving hardware and dairy products, but you made mock."

"You're not taking this seriously."

Phin closed his eyes again. "Christ, no. You should never take sex seriously. Terrible idea. Do you have any aspirin?"

Sophie sighed. "Okay. Meet me at the Tavern tonight at eight."

Phin opened his eyes. "You're kidding."

Amy came out on the porch and called to her, and Sophie gritted her teeth.

"Tell her to take a hike," Phin said.

"She's having a rough time." Sophie lifted his head to slide out from under him. "Wes hasn't called since that day he yelled at her for lying to him. And then there's this cable premiere thing. She's under a lot of stress."

"Who the fuck isn't?" Phin said.

"You, tonight." Sophie bent over and kissed him as she got up. "The Tavern at eight, bear."

Phin let his head drop back onto the dock, missing her warmth. "Cool."

"Now *you* sound like Rachel," she said, and headed for the house and her sister, the problem child.

"Leo, I have to talk to you," Rachel said that night after she'd picked him up at the airport and they'd dropped Davy off at the farm. "This is really, really, *really* important."

"I'm not taking you to L.A.," Leo said automatically.

"I have to get out of Temptation," she began, and he said, "I know, I know," and she said, "Because I think I might have killed Zane."

"Pull over," Leo said, and Rachel did. "Tell me."

"I went out back of the house to meet Rob," Rachel said. "And Zane was there, sort of stumbling, and he grabbed me, and wouldn't let go and I had Sophie's Mace so I Maced him, and then I pushed him and he fell in the river and had a heart attack and died and I think it's my fault." She stopped, breathless.

"What were you doing meeting Rob?" Leo said, sounding cranky.

"He called me," Rachel said. "He wanted to break up with me because he's sleeping with Clea now. You're missing the point, Leo. What about Zane?"

Leo shook his head. "You're okay, kid. It was self-defense. They won't arrest you."

Rachel shook her head and leaned toward him. "He told people I was chasing him. He told people I offered to sleep with him to get him to take me to L.A., and I *didn't*. I know that's hard to believe, but I wouldn't have crossed the street with him—"

Leo put his arm around her as she started to shake. "I know, I know."

"—but nobody's going to believe that," Rachel wept into his shoulder, "because I've been chasing everybody, trying to get out of here, and they'll think he said no and I killed him because I was mad—"

"They won't." Leo patted her shoulder. "That's ridiculous."

"—and then we ran over him—"

Leo stopped patting. "You what?"

"Rob and I ran over him at the Tavern. We didn't know he was there. I don't even know how he *got* there—"

"Shut up for a minute," Leo said, and Rachel was so surprised, she shut up. He'd tightened his arm around her when he'd told her to shut up, and that felt good, too, to have him holding her that tight and sure, and, for the first time since Zane had grabbed her, she felt safe. If she could spend the rest of her life with Leo's arm around her, she'd be okay.

"L.A. is not your answer," he said. "We'll just go to Wes and tell him everything and you'll get points for being so honest."

Going to Wes sounded like a lousy idea, except he'd said "we'll go," and that sounded wonderful.

"But we should get there first, before anybody else. Who else knows about this?"

"Just you," Rachel said, feeling almost cheerful. "Rob knows about the Tavern because he was driving and he knows Zane grabbed me, but he doesn't know I Maced him and pushed him."

"You only told me?" Leo sounded amazed.

"You're the only one I trust," Rachel said. "Besides, you'll know what to do. You know everything." It sounded dorky when she said it, but it was true.

"Oh, great."

Leo tightened his arm around her, so she leaned into him a little more, and that felt so good she put both her arms around him and hugged him to her.

"I know I'm a pain," she said into his chest. "I know I drive you crazy, but you're the only one I—"

"Rachel, don't—" He let go of her but she held on.

"I need you," she said. "I need you and I trust you and I love you." She hadn't meant to add the last part, but there it was and it was true, and she felt wonderful as soon as she said it. "I know you think I'm just a hick kid, but I really love you. I just

didn't realize until this happened and you were the only one."
She swallowed and then raised her head so she could look in
his eyes. "I want to be with you. It's okay if you don't—"

"I'm not what you think I am," he said. "Nobody could be
what you think I am."

She shook her head. "You can be. You are. You're the best."

He closed his eyes, and she pressed closer, afraid of losing
him.

"I should let go of you," Leo said.

And then she kissed him.

Phin sat at the bar—the only guy in the Tavern in a linen
jacket—wondering if Sophie was going to go through with
her promise. He pressed his cold beer to his bruised eye and
thought about Sophie and his fantasy, such a great thing for
her to do, slink into the Tavern with half the town watching
and tell him she wanted him while he grinned down into those
big brown eyes. . . .

He looked at his watch.

Fifteen minutes past eight. Sophie was never late. She'd
chickened out. He tossed a ten on the bar to take care of his tab,
and then turned to go, and that's when she slid onto the stool
next to him. "Promptness is a virtue—" he began, but the rest
of his sentence died in his throat as he got a good look at her.

She was wearing a bright red tube dress that started low
on her breasts and stopped halfway to her knees, a narrow
red ribbon tied behind her neck holding it up. Her hair was
loose in dark ringlets on her shoulders, and her cheeks were
flushed, and she'd put on a lot of lipstick so that her usual
pink mouth was a red slash that matched the dress. The only
jarring note was the bruise on her forehead, and she'd mostly
covered that with makeup. He looked down at her breasts

again, stretching the red fabric of the dress far past any safe point, and his palms itched to jerk that dress down and set her free. "Very hot dress."

"Literally." Sophie tugged at the top, making everything shift beautifully. "It's Clea's. This stuff doesn't breathe and it *itches*."

"I don't think that was your line," Phin said. "Are you sure that's going to stay up?"

"No," Sophie said. "That's why I'm tense and forgetting my lines. Wait a minute." She frowned in concentration and he grinned at her, and she said, "Knock it off. You're not supposed to patronize me, you jerk." She took a deep breath, which he appreciated, and then she leaned closer to him, and he almost fell into her cleavage.

"I saw you across the room," she said throatily. "I want you, I need you, I must have you, and I'm not wearing—"

"Phin, I need to talk to you," somebody said behind him, and Phin said, "No, you don't," but Sophie had looked over his shoulder and was already sliding off the stool, taking her breasts with her.

"Are you all right, Georgia?" she said in her normal voice, and Phin shook his head to get his mind back to where it belonged.

"I just need to talk to Phin," Georgia said, as she looked at Sophie's dress, and then she hopped up on Sophie's stool and smiled at Phin.

"Oh." Sophie looked a little taken aback. "Uh, I'll just be over . . . here." She gestured behind her, and Phin looked past her to where several assorted townsmen were watching her with great appreciation.

"Do not talk to anybody," he told her.

She nodded, and went down to the end of the bar, and Phin craned his neck to see her go.

"Phin?" Georgia said, leaning forward to smile weakly at him and then she blinked. "What happened to your eye?"

Sophie's end of the bar began to get crowded as a general migration headed in her direction. "Make it fast, Georgia," Phin said. "I'm in the middle of something here."

"Oh," she said. "Okay. It's about Frank. I'm really worried—"

"Georgia, I don't do marriage counseling." He tried to see Sophie at the end of the bar, but there were too many people. Male people.

"I think he might have killed Zane," Georgia said, her voice shaking. "He wasn't home that night, he didn't come home at all, and he was so mad when he found out—" She dropped her eyes. "You know."

"I know," Phin said. "Try not to fuck other men, and he won't get so mad."

"Well, he was doing it with that bitch Clea," Georgia said, stung. "What was I supposed to do?"

"Not have sex with Zane," Phin said, trying to see around her. "Georgia, go home. Get some rest, talk to Frank, apologize, he'll probably tell you he spent the night at Larry's, and things will be fine in the morning."

"You think so?" Georgia hiccuped. "Oh, Phin. I'm so worried." Her voice dropped an octave. "And I hate that bitch Clea."

"Right." She started to lean into him, and he took her arm and helped her off Sophie's stool. "Good night, Georgia. Careful going home. Do not drive."

Georgia nodded and wobbled off, and Phin caught Sophie's eye. She sidled out from the group at her end of the bar and came slinking unsteadily back, teetering, he saw for the first time, on ridiculously high, red spike heels.

Her legs were flawless. And they went all the way up to where she wasn't wearing underwear, if she was telling the truth. Given how short that dress was, Phin wouldn't have been surprised if she'd hedged her bets on that one.

"Hello, gorgeous," she said as she slid onto the stool. "I saw you across the room—" She met his eyes and grinned, which shouldn't have been sexy at all but was, and he grinned back and thought, *Hell of a woman, my Sophie.*

"—and I want you—" She licked her lips and leaned closer. "I need you, I—"

"Phin, I have to talk to you," Frank said from behind him, and Phin said without turning around, "Get out of here, or I will hurt you."

"It's about Georgia," Frank said, and Sophie said in her normal voice, "I'll just be at the end of the bar."

"No you won't," Phin said.

"I'll just be at the jukebox." Sophie slid off her stool, and Phin looked down at her round butt in that tight dress and saw no panty line. In that dress, he'd have seen a birthmark, so she wasn't wearing underwear. And she was walking away from him.

"This better be good, Frank," he said.

Frank took her place on the stool, and Phin sighed, resigned to at least another two minutes of Lutz.

"I saw you talking to Georgia," Frank said. "And—" He frowned at Phin. "What happened to your eye?"

"Frank, what do you want?"

"What did Georgia say?"

"She's afraid you killed Zane," Phin said. "Why don't you go discuss that with her?"

"I think she did it, Phin." Frank looked pasty in the dim bar light. "I think she went after him after that Jell-O crack. She went for me with a knife when we were first married and I told her that it was okay to move in bed, and let me tell you, she wasn't kidding."

Phin watched Sophie at the jukebox. "I don't want to know this, Frank. Tell Wes. Human interaction fascinates him."

"And it was that time of the month, too." Frank shook his head. "Georgia and PMS are a bad combination. Plus she was drunk. She's a mean drunk."

"Frank."

"I'm just saying, you be careful believing what she tells you. She's crazy. And Zane, he was crazy, too. You wouldn't believe the lies he was telling. Probably told some about me." Frank laughed.

"That would be the vasectomy."

Frank closed his eyes. "Oh, crap, don't tell Georgia."

"I don't plan to," Phin said. *You stupid son of a bitch.*

"Jesus, if she knew," Frank said, leaning against the bar, going weak at the thought, "she'd kill me. She really is crazy, Phin."

"Well, the good news is, she'd kill you, not Zane," Phin pointed out.

Frank frowned, not seeing why that was good news.

"Zane's the one who died, Frank. If you were dead, she'd be a good candidate, but since you're still with us—"

Frank perked up a little, "Right."

"—she evidently doesn't know about the vasectomy."

Frank began to get a little color in his face. "Right, right."

In the background, the jukebox started playing "Some of Your Lovin'," and Phin lost what little interest he had in Frank. "Well, I have things to do. Go talk to your wife. Save your marriage. Whatever." He took Frank's arm and helped him off the barstool.

Frank nodded and wandered off, slightly happier than he had been when they'd started, and Sophie came back and boosted herself up on the stool, making everything bounce, including his libido. Then she leaned forward, stopping his heart with the view, put her hot little hand on his thigh (*Higher*, he thought), and said, "I saw you across the room—"

Then she stopped, caught by something from behind him.

He turned and saw Rachel searching the crowd with Leo close behind her. *No*, he thought, and then Sophie grabbed him by the knot in his tie, and he had to turn back to her to keep from choking.

"I'm not wearing any underwear," she said, nose-to-nose with him. "Want to fuck me?"

The room swung around as all the blood left his brain. "God, yes," he said, and pulled her off the stool to drag her to the door.

"I'm sorry, that wasn't your fantasy," she said from behind him.

"Not a problem," he said, dodging people like a demented quarterback with Sophie in tow. "Yours was better."

Behind him, Rachel called, "Phin!" but he didn't stop until he had Sophie at the car and he'd opened the door to the backseat.

"Backseat?" Sophie said, and he said, "I'll make this up to you later. Get in there and strip."

She slid across the seat and he slid in after her, reaching for her before the door slammed closed. He shoved his hands up her thighs, pushing her rubber band of a dress up as he went, and when his hands moved over her naked butt, he said, "I'm going to last about five seconds here." Sophie wriggled to slide under him, and he added, "Maybe not even that."

"Your fantasy, bear," Sophie said, twining her hands around his neck. "Do with me what you will."

He tugged at the top of her dress, and she let go of him to reach behind her neck and untie the straps so he could pull it down. Her breasts popped out as if they were as glad to be free as he was to see them, and when he'd filled his hands with them, and she'd arched her hips into his, he said, "I swear, I'll make this up to you later," and reached for his zipper for the best fast fuck of his life.

And then Sophie said, "Ack!" and slid out from under him, tugging her dress up and down at once.

"What?" he said, trying to pull her back and she said, "Window," and gestured with her elbow.

When he turned, Rachel was peering at them.

He rolled it down and said between his teeth, "Get out of here, Rachel, this is not the time," and she said, "Please, Phin."

"No," he said, and started to roll up the window, and she said, "I think I killed Zane."

He froze, a thousand thoughts colliding in his head, half of them to do with plunging hot into Sophie and the other half to do with Rachel in big trouble and the inevitability of the choice in front of him.

"We tried to find Wes, but he's out, and we don't have his pager number and we knew you—"

"*Oh* . . ." Phin searched for words vile enough to vent with and then banged his head into the seat in front of him and went for the classic, "*Fuck!*"

Rachel took a step back, and Phin took a deep breath. Then, in his normal voice, he said to her, "I'll call Wes. You follow us to the station." He rolled the window up and took another deep breath and then turned to Sophie, who was trying unsuccessfully to put everything back where it had been. "You know, before you came here, I never screamed like that."

Sophie put her chin in the air and tried to look superior, which was difficult considering her hands were full of her breasts. "You were repressed. Which is why God sent me to save you."

"It wasn't God," he said, watching her trying to stretch fabric where it would never go again. "It was the devil." He thought about just ripping the damn dress off her, but then he'd never get to the station, and Rachel needed him there.

"I have to go to the police station," he said.

"I picked that up. Uh, could I borrow your jacket? I don't think this is ever going to work again."

He took off his jacket and passed it over and watched as she gave up the good fight and the breasts he wanted appeared within reach again, only to be covered by his linen jacket. He thought about the smooth silk lining of the jacket sliding over all that smooth, warm flesh and felt light-headed again. "We have a minute," he said, and reached for her, and she blocked his hand.

"Rachel," she said, and he gave up and moved to the front seat to call Wes on the car phone and tell him about their latest disaster. "I'm sorry this didn't work out," Sophie called to him from the backseat.

"The night is still young," he said, trying to see her in the rearview mirror, and then Wes answered, and he concentrated on the problem at hand instead of the pleasure in the backseat.

The only part of Rachel's confession that Phin found even vaguely interesting was that Rob had called her to meet him exactly where Zane had turned up. From the look on Wes's face, that was the only part that interested him, too. When he'd sent Rachel off with Leo and a stern warning to tell the police everything from now on, Wes turned back to Phin and said, "I want to talk to that dumb fuck Rob."

"Me, too," Phin said. "But not now. I have unfinished business with Sophie."

"How's Amy?"

"Miserable. Call her. Hell, you knew she was bent."

"She lied to me," Wes said.

"She lies to everybody," Phin said. "It's part of being a Dempsey. You want the excitement and the tube top, you have to take the lies, too."

"I don't want them that bad," Wes said miserably, and Phin said, "Sure you do," and went out to find Sophie.

When he got to the farm, everything was dark and the door was locked. Given the turn the crime rate had taken in Temptation, that was smart, but it wasn't helping him get to Sophie. He stood out in the front yard and considered trying to climb the front porch to her window and rejected it for the moment. No point in killing himself for sex unless he had to.

Instead, he picked up a stone from the yard and threw it at her window. Unfortunately, it was open, but on his next one he got lucky and hit Sophie, who had come to the window.

"Ouch," she said as she stuck her head out. Her shoulders were pale and naked in the moonlight, and he realized she was wrapped in a sheet.

"Are you naked?" he said.

"You threw a *rock* at me," Sophie said.

"Think of it as foreplay," Phin said. "Come down and play."

"It's midnight," Sophie said, and pulled her head in.

Well, he'd tried. He sat down on the hood of the Volvo and decided to give her five minutes in case she changed her mind, but she surprised him by showing up almost immediately, wearing his jacket and nothing else, Lassie padding sleepily beside her.

"You're a biddable woman," he said, as she boosted herself up on the hood beside him, and the dog stretched out in the dirt and fell asleep.

"There's generally a payoff if I do what you tell me," Sophie said. "Also, it seemed weird tonight not arguing with you flat on my back, so this is sort of closure."

"Closure?" *She's leaving*, he thought, *she's going back to the therapist*, and panic kicked up his pulse even though he knew it was stupid.

"We never did finish your fantasy," she told him. "We were building to a climax there, and then you wandered off. How's Rachel?"

"Not guilty of anything but self-defense," Phin said. "How are you?"

Sophie smiled up at him. "I have a fantasy."

"If it takes a lot of energy, it may stay a fantasy," Phin said, and thought, *Anything you want.*

Sophie let his jacket fall open so that she sat pretty much naked on the hood of the car. " 'Right here,' " she said in a Brooklyn accent, patting the hood. " 'On the Oriental.' "

"It's a Volvo," Phin said, trying to be cool. "It's Swedish." Then he looked at how round and hot she was and gave in. "A naked woman on an expensive car. I think this is *my* fantasy. Without the movie quote, of course."

Sophie leaned closer and said, "Tell me where the quote's from, and I'll go down."

"Let me take a rain check," Phin said. "Plain vanilla is all I have the energy for."

"Also you have no idea where it came from," Sophie said.

"Don't bust my chops tonight," Phin said. "Are you really going to let me have you on the hood of this car in the front yard?"

"There's no moon," Sophie said. "Not much to see."

"Unless your brother looks out the window," Phin said. "Then I'm a dead man. How about the backseat?"

Sophie moved her knees apart and leaned back on her hands.

Phin sighed. "Or right here."

She leaned over and kissed him, and he felt a lot better. "If you could make this day go away for a while," he whispered. "I'd be really grateful."

"I thought that might be the case," she said, and climbed into his lap to straddle him, and he caught her to him, sliding his hands under his jacket and over all her smooth softness, and buried his face in the hollow of her neck.

"It's just you and me, bear," she whispered in his ear. "Nobody else."

And then she made everything go away.

Three hours later, Phin was sleeping like the dead beside her, and Sophie was trying to find a comfortable place on her mattress. There was one errant spring in particular that was torturing her. She tried to shift over, but Phin was taking up most of the double bed, and the rogue spring dug into her even as she tried to shift him.

Phin murmured something in his sleep, and she tried to climb over him. If he was that fast asleep, he could sleep on the damn spring. But when she was on top, his arms went around her, and even though she said, "No, go back to sleep," he rolled her to one side—the good side of the mattress—and kissed her, still half asleep, and she thought, *What the hell*, and kissed him back.

Half an hour later, with the mattress rattling like a tambourine under them, Sophie felt her blood boil and dug her fingernails into him and said, "Oh, God, *yes, now*," and he rolled so that he was on top, and the spring gouged into her again and cooled her blood on the instant. "Ouch!"

She tried to squirm so her spine was off it, but Phin was oblivious on top of her, rocking fast into her, making the bed bounce hard. She tried to bounce her hips over when he pulled back, but he was too fast, so they only hit the mattress harder in the same place. She said, *"Ouch"*—really loud this time—and tried to shove him away before her spine went, and Phin jerked up, finally hearing her, at the same time she heard a sharp *crack* with a whine behind it.

He rolled them both off the bed onto the floor, and she landed on top of him.

"Ouch," she said again, trying to sit up, and he pulled her head back down and rolled on top of her.

"Stay down," he said, breathless but not mindless anymore.

"What are you doing?" Sophie said. "Get *off* me—" and then Davy slammed the door open and said, "Sophie?"

"She's okay," Phin said from the floor. "I'd stay away from the window if I were you."

Davy stepped back into the hallway. "Sophie?"

"I'm okay," Sophie said from under Phin, as he stretched his hand to find his boxers. "What did I miss?"

"Sounded like a gunshot to me," Davy said from the hall. "I thought maybe the mayor had gotten tired of you." He was trying to keep his voice light, and failing.

Phin retrieved his boxers and stood up away from the window. Sophie pulled the sheet from the bed and wrapped herself in it.

"What are you doing?" she said as she propped herself up on one elbow, keeping an eye on the window. "If somebody shot at us—"

"At you—so you stay down," Phin told her as he put on his khakis. "Remember the river? Somebody may be trying to kill you. The only person who wants me dead is Davy."

"I've decided to let you live," Davy said, back in the doorway. "Where'd it come from?"

"I'm still not sure it was a shot," Phin said. "My mind was on other things." He looked around the room. "But it sure as hell sounded like one and it was in this room." He looked back at Sophie. "You stay there."

"Through the window?" Davy said, coming in and looking at the wall opposite the window. "I'm not seeing a bullet hole."

"Maybe it hit the mattress." Sophie crawled away from the window in her sheet to get her clothes, trying to unscramble her mind from interrupted sex and the new knowledge somebody had just tried to kill her. "Or maybe a car backfired," she said, going for normality.

"No," Davy and Phin said at the same time.

She had crawled almost to the door when she saw the hole, a little one, about two feet up from the floor. "There," she said, still on her knees, pointing to it, and Phin and Davy both bent to look.

Phin said, "Hold on," and went to the bedside table to rummage through the drawer. "Here," he said, going back to Davy, and handed him a pencil.

Davy put the pencil in the hole as far as it would go, and it stuck straight out.

"I don't get this," Sophie said from where she was sitting by the door, but they both ignored her to follow the line of the pencil.

"You're kidding me," Davy said, and they both moved to the bed.

Phin pulled up the quilt and said, "Nope."

Sophie squinted over at the bed. There was a hole in the side of the box spring.

"Go out in the hall," Phin told her, and they both went to the other side of the bed, while Sophie scooted out into the hall.

"No hole on this side," Davy said, bending over.

They grabbed the mattress at the same time and pulled it off the bed.

"No wonder my back's been killing me," Phin said, and Sophie craned her neck around the doorway to see a box spring so ancient, the top fabric had rotted to ribbons.

Davy looked at the wall and then back to the box springs and said, "Someplace about here." He began to peel the rotted ribbons of fabric from a section of the spring in line with the hole, and after a moment he stopped. "Son of a gun."

"Literally," Phin said.

Sophie stood and inched her way over to the bed, trying not to trip over her sheet. A small gun lay caught in the box springs, pointing toward the wall. It was so surreal, she felt detached from the moment, as if she were watching a movie. "Somebody booby-trapped my bed?"

"No," Phin said.

"Somebody stuck a gun under your mattress," Davy said. "And then you and Harvard fucked it into the box spring and set it off."

"Beautifully put," Phin said, looking at him with distaste.

"Somebody's trying to frame you, Soph," Davy said.

Sophie looked down at the gun again. "Well, somebody's not too bright. It's been decades since anybody looked under this mattress."

"So somebody's still waiting for this to be found." Phin looked at Davy.

"And getting anxious," Davy said, nodding at him. "So now what?"

"What do you mean, 'now what?'" Sophie said, fear making her cranky. "We call Wes."

"Quietly," Phin said. "Because we don't want anybody to know about this."

"You really think somebody's going to believe I killed Zane?" Sophie said.

"No, he really thinks somebody's going to go nuts waiting for the damn gun to be found," Davy said. "And the crazier somebody gets, the more likely it is he'll overplay his hand."

Sophie looked back at the gun. "I can't believe I've been sleeping on that."

Phin looked back at the mattress. "I can't believe I've been having sex on that. From now on, we do this in my bed."

"I don't want to know about this," Davy said. "She's my sister." He left the room without a backward glance, and Sophie looked back down at the gun.

"Somebody really hates me." The thought made her cold, and she drew in a long shuddering breath.

"Not necessarily." Phin picked up his shirt. "Somebody may just want you out of the way."

Yeah, your mother, Sophie thought, but even she couldn't imagine Liz sneaking into the house to plant a gun. "How'd it get in here?"

"Anybody can get in here." Phin buttoned his shirt and tucked it in. "The damn place is always full of people, and they all came upstairs to use the bathroom. Go sleep with Amy." He looked back at the mattress. "I'm assuming you're out of the mood."

"Maybe forever," Sophie said, picking up her shorts.

"Just until tomorrow," Phin said, and went to tell Wes.

"What happened to you?" Phin's mother said to him when he came down to breakfast after three hours of sleep.

"What? Oh, the eye?" He looked at Dillie. "I ran into a door."

"Really?" Dillie said, pushing back her softball cap.

"Sophie's ex-door," he told Liz, under his breath. "No cap at the table, Dill."

"You ran into a therapist?" Liz said, and Dillie put her cap by her plate.

"Yes, it surprised me, too," Phin said. "Next topic."

"What's a therapist?" Dillie said.

"Like a guidance counselor," Phin said.

"Sophie has a guidance counselor?" Dillie said.

"No," Phin began and then stopped as his mother's face darkened.

"Do you know Sophie, Dill?" she asked.

"Oh, ye—" Dillie began, and then stopped, just as her father had. "A little."

"You took your daughter to meet your . . . friend?" Liz said, her voice taut as piano wire.

"No," Phin said. "My daughter went to meet my friend on her own after talking with Jamie Barclay. I told you that kid was no good."

"Jamie Barclay's mother said that Sophie was Daddy's girl-friend so I went to see," Dillie said. "Sophie said she wasn't. It's perfectly all right."

"You went to see." Liz's eyes softened a little as she turned to her granddaughter, but she still wasn't happy. "All by your-self?"

"While Grandma Junie was napping." Dillie looked from her father to her grandmother. "It's all right. I'm perfectly safe. I've done it dozens of times."

"What?"

"You have not done it dozens of times," Phin said. "You've been there twice." After Dillie was silent for a moment, he added. "That I know about."

"This stops now," Liz said. "Dillie, you do not go back there. Ever."

"But—"

"Never," Liz said. "Do you understand?"

"No," Dillie said, and both Phin and Liz zeroed in on her.

"Don't tell your grandmother no," Phin said.

"Well, I *don't* understand." Dillie looked scared but determined. "Sophie's my friend. She likes me. She's *expecting* me. I go on Sundays and Wednesdays when I'm at Grandma Junie's and Sophie likes it. I play with the dog. We talk. And sing. She's *expecting* me."

"Life is full of disappointments," Liz said. "You're not going back."

Dillie turned tragic eyes on Phin, and he said, "Do you want to say good-bye?"

Dillie nodded, tears starting in her eyes.

"I'll take you tomorrow when I pick you up at Junie's," he said, and Liz said, "No, you will not."

"Excuse me," he said to his mother. "I'm talking to my daughter. And she's going to say good-bye to her friend because it's the polite thing to do. Tuckers are always polite."

Liz pressed her lips together.

"Thank you, Daddy," Dillie said, blinking back the tears. Tuckers didn't cry.

"You're welcome." Phin met Liz's eyes across the table. "Anything else you want to say about this?"

The phone rang again, and Liz said, "I will get it." When she was gone, Dillie leaned forward and said, "Daddy?" in a half-whisper.

"What?"

"Remember how you said we could have sleepovers every Monday, and then I didn't get them?"

Phin winced. "Yeah. Sorry about that."

"That's okay," Dillie said. "Can I have something else? Just for one morning? Not a sleepover? Just once?"

"Probably," Phin said. "What?"

Dillie hesitated a long time, but when she heard Liz hang

up the phone in the hall, she leaned forward and said fast, so the words ran together, "I want Sophie to come to my softball game today. It's my last one, and I don't get any sleepovers, and I want you and Sophie to come to my game. Please."

Liz came back in and sat down. "That was Virginia Garvey."

"There's a surprise." Phin finished buttering Dillie's muffin and passed it over, and Dillie took it, keeping her eyes on his face.

"Stephen's concerned you're up to something with those movie people," Liz went on.

"No he isn't," Phin said. "He *hopes* I'm up to something with those movie people."

"Well, you're going to stay away from them from now on," Liz said.

"Mother." Phin waited until Liz met his eyes. "You tell me what to do one more time, and Dillie and I are moving down to the bookstore."

"Phineas—"

"Back off or lose us." Phin watched her bite her lip, and then she got up from the table and went upstairs.

Dillie sat next to him, frozen, her muffin clutched in her hand.

"You okay?" he said to her.

She nodded. "Are we going to move?"

"Probably not. Grandma knows when to quit."

Dillie took a deep breath. "Can Sophie come to my game today?"

"Yes," Phin said. "At least we can call her and ask."

Dillie nodded and bit into her muffin, and Phin sat back.

"It will be exciting to have Sophie at my game," Dillie said around her muffin.

"You have no idea," Phin said.

Chapter Thirteen

The softball section of Temptation's tree-filled park had four neatly marked white diamonds, each with its own stand of seats, all filled with parents, grandparents, sisters, brothers, and friends of the family. It was like four Christmases without the turkeys, unless you counted some of the coaches and the more obnoxious of the parents.

"Bat country," Sophie said. "In every sense of the word."

"Yep," Phin said. "Temptation athletics at its finest."

Dillie nudged Sophie's arm. "Wish me luck, please."

She looked so determined in her red-and-white uniform, her red ball cap tilted over her little pointed face, that Sophie resisted to the urge to say, *You are cute as hell, kid*, and said, "You bet. Break a leg," instead.

"What?" Dillie said.

"It's an expression," Phin said. "One never used in athletics. Go do good."

"Okay." Dillie stretched up and Phin bent down to kiss her. Then she stretched up to Sophie, and Sophie bent down, too. Dillie's cheek was satin-smooth where Sophie kissed her, and she wrapped her arms around Sophie's neck and pulled her close for a moment.

"Thank you for coming to my game," she whispered, and Sophie whispered back, "Thank you for inviting me."

When Dillie ran off to join her team, Sophie turned back to the bleachers and faced a sea of fascinated faces, most of which were curious, some of which were disapproving, and at least one of which—Virginia Garvey's—was actively hostile. "Why is Virginia here?"

"Niece on the other team." Phin put his hand on the small of Sophie's back to steer her toward the bleachers, and Virginia flushed. Probably from the effort of trying to reach Liz by mental telepathy.

"So this is like dinner, only more so," Sophie said to Phin.

"This is dinner squared, cubed, and cloned."

"It's prom," Sophie said. "I finally made it."

Phin nodded. "They'll be talking about this ten years from now."

"They should get lives."

"They did," Phin said. "Ours. Go up to the top. We can see better up there."

Since the top was only a dozen rows up from the bottom, it was a short trip. It was also hot as hell, and by the middle of the first inning, Sophie was drenched in sweat.

Phin sat beside her, intent on the game, oblivious to the heat.

"So Tuckers don't have sweat glands?" she said, as she watched Dillie come to bat.

Dillie fanned the ball, and Phin winced and said under his

breath, "Watch the ball, Dill," and a second later, the coach stood up and yelled, "Watch the ball, Dillie!"

"Uh, this doesn't really matter to you, does it?" Sophie said.

Dillie hit a single, and Phin said to himself, "Okay, that's not bad, not bad." Then, evidently realizing she'd been talking to him, he turned to her. "What?"

"Oh, jeez, you're one of those Sports Parents," Sophie said. "It's not just a game, it's a reflection of you and all of those in your bloodline who ever picked up a bat. It's—"

"We like to win," Phin said. "It's the American Way."

"Right," Sophie said. " 'We're ten and one.' "

"What?"

"It's from a movie," Sophie said. " 'We're Americans, we're ten and one.' The 'one' being Vietnam. Never mind."

He frowned at her. "Stop quoting. What do you have to be nervous about here?"

Sophie looked around at the various curious and hostile faces, with Virginia glaring in their midst like a basilisk. "Let's just say I'm not feeling the love." She started to twist her fingers where her rings had been, and Phin put his hand over hers.

"You're okay." He folded one of her hands into his and moved it to his knee, and she sat there in the sun, holding hands with the mayor, while Temptation parenthood looked at them from the corners of their eyes and whispered.

It was probably a nice change from talking about the murder and the video premiere.

The next batter grounded out, and Dillie went to play third base.

The pitcher wound up and threw the ball with her eyes closed and it sailed over the head of the batter and into the backstop.

"Oh, Christ," Phin said under his breath. When Sophie raised an eyebrow, he leaned closer and said, "This kid can't pitch, but she has low self-esteem so her mother insists."

"You're kidding," Sophie said. "Why are we whispering?"

Phin pointed to a tense woman in navy shorts sitting two rows in front of them. "That's Mom. President of the PTA. Nobody to mess with."

The pitcher wound up again and threw the ball almost straight up in the air. "Concentrate, Brittany!" the woman two rows down yelled, and when Brittany got the ball back, she screwed up her face in intense concentration and flung it as hard as she could. It went west and hit Dillie smack on the temple.

"Ouch," Phin said under his breath.

Dillie picked herself up and rubbed her head, and her coach went out to see her. Dillie nodded, and then the coach motioned somebody in from off the bench, and Dillie came up into the stands.

"I'm really okay," she said to Phin, blinking tears from her eyes. "Coach just thought I should sit down for a minute."

"Let me see, honey." Phin looked in her eyes and held up two fingers. "How many fingers?"

"Two," Dillie said, focusing on his hand. "I can go back in."

She sniffed once, and Sophie said, "Oh, take a break. Come here." She opened her arms and Dillie crawled into her lap and put her head on Sophie's shoulder. "We could use some ice here, Dad," Sophie said to Phin, as she took Dillie's cap off. "If you can't get that, get a cold can of pop."

"Actually she should probably go back—" Phin began, but Sophie met his eyes and he stopped.

"Ice," she said, "or there will be a scene."

"Okay," Phin said, and went.

"It kind of hurts," Dillie said.

"I can imagine." Sophie kissed Dill's forehead where the bruise was starting to come up. "Now you match your dad. He has one, too."

"So do you." Dillie looked up at her, as if she were gauging the moment, and then she said, "The whole family matches."

Sophie caught her breath.

"Don't we?" Dillie said, pressing closer, and Sophie thought, with more certainty than she'd ever dreamed possible, *This is what I want.*

"Yes," she said, and Dillie said, "Excellent," and cuddled closer.

Phin came back with some ice in a plastic bag. "Let's see, Dill." Dillie straightened a little and then winced as Phin put the cold bag against her bump. "Just hold it there a minute and then you go back."

"I don't think so," Sophie said, holding Dillie close and watching the field. Brittany had just whiffled one past the new third baseman, who was looking very uneasy.

"Back off," Phin said to Sophie. "This is my kid. She's a fighter. Right, Dill?"

Dillie straightened and nodded. "I'm a Tucker, and Tuckers are brave. We don't quit."

"Yeah?" Sophie said. "Well, I'm a Dempsey and Dempseys are smart. We don't go back on the field until the coach pulls the pitcher who's trying to bag her limit on third basemen."

"I beg your pardon," Brittany's mother said from two rows down.

"Sorry, Catherine," Phin said at the same time Sophie said, "Teach your kid to pitch before you force her out on the field." When Phin turned to give her the universal *Shut the fuck up* look, Sophie added, "Well, I don't think maiming her friends is helping Brittany's self-esteem. Look at her."

Down on the field, Brittany was sniffing back tears. That

didn't stop her from pitching, of course, and with one mighty heave, she took out the new third baseman.

"I want to be a Dempsey," Dillie said.

"*What?*" Phin said, and Sophie said, "No, no, honey, you're a Tucker. You're just like your daddy. You need to defeat somebody on a regular basis or you'll start to twitch. Just wait until the coach disarms Brittany, and then you can go back."

Brittany's mother stood up, sent them a meaningful look, and stalked down the bleachers.

"Listen," Phin began, but out on the field, the coach was on her knees talking to Brittany, who was sobbing and nodding in what looked like relief.

"Yeah, sports are great for kids," Sophie said, and when the new pitcher came in, she said, "I don't know. This one looks wild, too."

Phin shook his head. "Tara Crumb. Her mother pitched the junior high to the semifinals and her father played high school baseball with me."

"Yes, but do they work with her?"

"Nightly," Phin said. "This one can pitch. Will you let go of my kid?"

Sophie opened her arms, and Dillie said, "Jeez, are we sure?"

"Oh, for crying out loud," Phin said, and Sophie said, "Yes. We have examined the family tree in detail, and they pass. You may go." She handed Dillie back her cap and added, "Put your cap on, though, it's hot out there."

Dillie nodded and started down the bleachers again.

"Clearly you do not understand athletics," Phin said.

"Clearly, I do," Sophie said. "Davy and Amy both played. And believe me, any pitcher who hit either of them lived to regret it. Dempseys get even."

"It's a game, not a war," Phin said, his eyes on his daughter as she went back on the field.

"Then why is your daughter wounded?" Sophie said, and then stopped.

Down at the foot of the bleachers, Brittany's mother was talking to Liz Tucker. While Sophie watched, Liz lifted her eyes to the top of the bleachers and stared, unblinking, at her son and the nightmare he'd brought to the game.

"Your mom's here," Sophie told Phin, who was still watching Dillie.

"I know."

"Boy, are you in trouble now."

He leaned back and let his arm fall along the rail behind her. "I've been in trouble since I met you. This is just more of the same." He squinted at the field as Tara pitched a strike. "You're a pain in the ass, but you're worth it."

"Oh. That's good to know." Sophie tried not to look at Liz.

When Tara pitched her second strike and Dillie pounded her fist into her glove on third, Phin said, quietly so his voice didn't travel, "Thanks for taking care of my kid."

"My pleasure," Sophie said.

"But try to avoid my mother."

"Absolutely," Sophie said, keeping her eyes off Liz.

"And fuck my brains out later," Phin said, still staring at the field.

Sophie turned to see if anyone had heard. Evidently not; they weren't coming for her with pitchforks. "Are you trying to get me killed by a mob of softball moms?"

"They didn't hear," Phin said. "And it's your fault. You're sitting there driving me crazy."

Sophie looked down at her damp blouse and reddening arms. "I'm soaked in sweat and cranky."

"Doesn't matter." Phin did look at her then, and the smile he sent her pretty much telegraphed to everybody everything he'd said before. "All you have to do is breathe, and I fall."

Sophie felt herself flush. "Oh." She swallowed. "You're definitely getting lucky later." She turned away from him before she fell into his lap right there.

Out on the field, Tara struck out the batter, and Dillie jumped up and down with joy.

And down at the bottom of the bleachers, Liz stared up at Sophie, not joyful at all.

Phin pulled up in front of the farmhouse after the game and said, "I have to work until five and then Wes is coming by at seven. I'll be late coming out tonight."

"Or I could come buy a book between five and seven," Sophie said, and he met her eyes and she thought, *Oh, Lord, take me now.*

"I'd appreciate it," Phin said. "But you deserve more time than that so I'll see you at five, but I'll still come out when I get rid of Wes." Phin leaned to kiss her, stopping when she moved back and jerked her head a fraction of an inch toward the backseat and Dillie.

"I could look out the back window so you could kiss Sophie," Dillie said.

Sophie smiled at Dillie. "Oh, honey, he wasn't going to—"

"Look out the back window, Dill," Phin said, and when Dillie turned around, he kissed Sophie hard. "I'll see you at five," he said in her ear, and kissed her again, and when they drove away, she thought, *But that's six hours.*

She jumped the gun and got there at four-thirty, wearing her pink dress, and Phin said, "What kept you?"

"I'll be upstairs," Sophie said. " 'Take me to bed or lose me forever.' " She headed for the stairs and heard him come out from around the counter, and then she heard the CLOSED sign smack against the front window. "I can wait until five," she called back, and he hit the step behind her and said, "I can't."

But upstairs, he got a bottle of wine from the refrigerator—"It's safe to drink," he told her. "I bought it out of town"—and when she had her glass, he flipped on the stereo, and Dusty started to sing "I Only Want to Be with You."

Sophie sat up on the bed, delighted. "Why, *Mr.* Robinson, are you trying to seduce me?"

"Because that's so difficult? No. I've just developed a taste for Dusty. And you." She laughed up at him, and he looked at her for a long minute, and said, "My dad would have loved you."

"Oh," Sophie said.

"Scoot over," he said, and she did. He sat down and kicked off his shoes. "So how was your day?" he said, and leaned back on the pillows beside her.

Sophie cuddled up to him and sipped her wine. Good stuff. "My favorite part was when the coach threw Brittany's mother out of the game."

"That was good." Phin nodded. "You probably missed the part where Brittany's mother complained to the head of the Temptation Athletic Association to have the coach removed."

"Oh," Sophie said. "Is the president reasonable?"

"That would be Stephen Garvey."

"Oh, jeez, is there anything we can do?"

"The coach is staying," Phin said. "Drink your wine."

"Fixed it, did you?" Sophie said, and drank her wine.

"Yep."

"Do you have any idea how sexy power used for good is?" Sophie said, looking over her wineglass into his eyes.

"Really?" He settled deeper into the pillows. "Did I ever tell you how I battled Stephen to get Temptation new streetlights?"

Sophie put her wineglass down. "Take me."

He grinned at her, and then he put his wineglass down and leaned over and kissed her, slowly, and when they were naked under the quilt together, he still moved slowly, even though she'd said, "We'd better hurry if Wes is stopping by."

"The hell with Wes," he'd said. "Stay a while." Then he touched her everywhere she loved to be touched and when her breathing slowed to match his, she touched him, too, and the afternoon dissolved into soft laughter and heat and bone-deep pleasure. And when he finally took her, he moved so deliberately that he stretched minutes into eternity, and she stayed with him, looking into his eyes and sliding against his body and living in his kiss until she was so flooded with heat, she glowed. Then, after eons, he whispered, "Now," in her ear and rolled to bear down on her, and the heat fused and broke and she clung to him as every nerve she had went incandescent.

And when she stopped trembling, he was still holding on to her, shuddering and breathless and spent against her. She buried her face in his shoulder and thought about the day she'd had with him, and the laughter and the pleasure and the solid rightness of it all, and she felt so safe and satisfied and *better* that she held him tighter and when they were both calm again, she told him the truth: "I love you."

His breath went out on a *whoosh*. After a very long time, he pulled away from her, and when he smiled down at her, he looked as if he were trying to sell her a used car.

"Uh, thank you," he said.

Thank you? "You're welcome," Sophie said, disappointment and annoyance breaking nicely through her satisfaction. "What's the matter with you?"

"Why are you in such a hurry? Three weeks and you're throwing commitment around."

"That wasn't commitment, that was emotion," she said flatly.

"That was commitment," Phin said, just as flatly. "You know I'm crazy about you, why—"

"Say the *L* word and I'll know."

"What happened to 'You Don't Have to Say You Love Me'?"

"I'm not a fan of Dusty's masochist period," Sophie said. "You have to say it."

Phin rolled out of bed. "You know, you were right, Wes is going to be here anytime. We should probably get dressed." He grabbed his boxers and headed for the hall and the bathroom.

"Was it something I said?" Sophie called after him, but he was already down the hall, and it took all her self-control to keep from throwing his alarm clock at the wall.

Okay, she'd been stupid. But she really did love him. The middle of great sex probably wasn't the best place to have that realization, since great sex did tend to cloud a woman's mind, but now that she knew it, she also knew it had been there for a while.

She got out of bed and picked up her bra, determined to think of a way to make him admit he loved her because, of course, he did, the dummy, she had no doubts about that. The fair way would be to confront him and make him talk about it, but she'd just tried that and look where it had gotten her.

So, time to be a Dempsey. Time to throw away all her conscience and pride. Time to cheat and lie and get what she needed. She sat on the edge of the bed and thought about Phin's weak spots. He had so few. Sex. Shirts. Pool.

Pool.

She heard the shower go on in the bathroom and thought, *This boy is toast.* Then she got dressed, made one quick stop in the bathroom while he was still in the shower, and went downstairs to show him exactly what he was dealing with.

When Phin came out of the bathroom, Sophie had gone, which made him feel relieved and guilty until he heard balls knocking together on the pool table. He put his khakis and his shirt back on and went downstairs with dread in his heart.

The last thing he wanted to do was explain why he didn't love her back although he *cared* about her, of course, more than any other woman he'd ever known, but not "I love you," not after only three weeks—was she insane? They had such a great thing going here, and it could lead to commitment in a couple of years, maybe when Dillie wasn't so vulnerable and his mother got used to her, and until then they could keep things going if they were just careful, didn't expect too much, but no, she had to say it. Christ, *women.*

Then he hit the bottom of the stairs and saw Sophie.

She was bent over the table, racking balls and humming "Some of Your Lovin'," looking very hot in her pink dress, and the memory of where they'd just been and what they'd just done lessened his annoyance considerably.

"Hey, you," she said, and came around the table to kiss him, no hassles and no nagging, and when she broke the kiss and smiled lazily at him, he smiled back.

"How about a game?" she said. "We've got time for nine ball."

"You know nine ball?" he said, and she said, "Everybody knows nine ball, although I'm not in your league, of course. Do you want to play?"

"Yes," he said.

"Davy said you were really good," Sophie said. "Try not to beat me too bad."

"I'll go easy," he said, planning on blowing a few shots. It really wasn't fair to play her straight-on when she wasn't as good as he was.

She smiled at him again. "This is a magnificent table," she said, and the last of his tension eased away as he watched her stroke the rosewood rails. "But then, everything about you is magnificent."

He felt a faint stir of alarm, but then she came to the end of the table with cue in hand. She took a stance that dynamite couldn't have shifted, gripped the cue firmly with her thumb and two fingers and bent to sight down it in perfect form. Phin tilted his head to see her better. Perfect form and the world's best butt in a short pink dress.

She looked up at him, still smiling. "You playing, here?"

"Yeah." He picked up his cue and bent to shoot for the lag, but she was close beside him in that pink dress, and she shook his concentration and took the break away from him.

"I'll be damned," he said. "Very nice."

"Rack 'em." She chalked her cue, and then, while he watched, her smile evaporated and she pocketed the seven on the break with a power stroke that banished "cute" from his vocabulary for her forever.

"I never told you this before," she said, after she'd chalked and taken aim on the one. "But I come from a long line of felons."

"Really." Phin watched the ball fall into the pocket without hitting the back.

Sophie stood and chalked. "My father's on the lam right now on a fraud charge." She bent and fell into perfect position again, and Phin stifled a sigh. "He's a recidivist. A big one." She pocketed the two with a follow shot that left her exactly where she needed to be, and stood to chalk again. "Then there's my brother."

"Davy." Phin watched her bend again.

"He makes his living defrauding people who defraud people." Sophie pocketed the three. "They're not really in a position to go after him, so he gets away with it, although there are a considerable number of people who don't like him."

"Can't imagine why," Phin said, and Sophie chalked again.

"Amy had a few small problems with the law, but in general she's pretty straight now."

"That's good."

"And then there's me," Sophie said.

She pocketed the four on a beautiful stop shot, and Phin said, "You."

"Yeah." Sophie nodded and chalked again. "I've been ducking my destiny, trying to go straight and be good. But you know—"

She bent to take her shot, aimed carefully, and followed through with such perfect form that Phin went a little dizzy for a moment.

"—that's not really me," she said as she straightened. "I was born to be bad." She smiled at him. "I learned that from you. Thank you so much."

Phin swallowed. "You're welcome."

Then Sophie put away the six, and he thought, *Hell, she could beat me.* It was a strangely arousing thought.

But there was a limit.

"Actually, I already knew about your family," he said. "Zane told me."

She had chalked and bent to shoot again, but now she hesitated. "He did?"

Phin nodded. "He seemed a little annoyed that I didn't care."

"Oh," Sophie said, and sighted down the cue to the eight. When she missed the shot, it was by such a tiny miscalculation, hitting the ball just a fraction too hard, that he was almost sorry.

But not sorry enough not to put the eight and nine away. This was, after all, pool. He chalked his cue and looked at the eight. She'd left him a cut shot, not an easy one, but one he could make. He bent to shoot, and she said, "There's something else you should know."

"What?" he said, without raising his head.

"I'm not wearing any underpants." She sat down out of his sight line, and when he turned his head to look at her, she smiled at him innocently with her legs crossed, the slender, curving line of her thigh disappearing into her short, clinging pink dress. "Sort of like your fantasy."

His cue wavered, and he straightened. "You really think I'm going to fall for that?"

Sophie shrugged. "Check your back pocket."

Against his better judgment, he did, and felt the slippery slide of nylon and lace. He pulled it out and held it up in front of him. Definitely Sophie's pink lace drawers. He shrugged. "Big deal." He stuffed them back in his pocket and bent to take his shot, and then he thought about her bending over the table, making draw and follow shots with such elegance, hitting that one stop shot that had been so simply beautiful that he'd felt dizzy just looking at her. All without underpants.

Steady, he told himself.

Then he thought about the incredible things she'd just done to him in bed, and for the first time in his life, he thought seriously about having sex on his pool table. The hell with the felt. Great-grandpa would understand.

"You going to take that shot anytime soon?" Sophie asked,

and he lined up the shot, thought of Sophie's naked butt, and miscued, just a fraction of a fraction of an inch, but a miscue just the same.

"So close," Sophie said as she stood up. "But then pool, like love, is not a forgiving sport." She went to the table, and he watched her make the cut shot with perfect draw and then pocket the nine with that stop shot that made his heart clutch.

"God almighty," Wes said from the doorway, and Phin looked up and said, "I know. It's a beautiful thing."

"Thank you." Sophie put her cue carefully back in the rack, and Phin followed the line of her back as she did, lingering on her naked-under-that-dress butt.

He had to do something to get some blood back to his brain. "I need to see you upstairs."

"I don't think so." She reached for his back pocket and pulled her underwear out as she walked past. "Turn around, Wes."

Wes raised his eyebrows at the underpants and then turned his back, and Sophie stepped into her drawers and pulled them up over her firm, round butt.

Phin said, "No, really. *Upstairs.*"

"No, really, *I can't*. If I go up there, I'll just lose my head and ask for commitment. So later for you." Sophie drifted past Wes, a vision of skill and sex, and Phin let his breath out as she went.

"I missed something, didn't I?" Wes said when she was gone.

Phin leaned on his cue, staring at the doorway where he'd seen her last, her pink dress imprinted on his retina. "I knew it. I knew it the first minute I saw her. The devil's candy."

"What?"

"She just fucked me six ways to Sunday."

"She beat you at pool, too," Wes said, looking at the table.

"That's what I mean," Phin said. "It's going to take me years to recover from this."

"It's just pool," Wes said. "She's leaving after the premiere on Tuesday. Get a grip. I need to talk to you."

Phin ignored him to replay Sophie's stop shot in his mind. Then he replayed her body in his bed. Then he remembered the way he needed to talk to her every night, and the way she'd stood up for Dillie at the game, and the way she laughed and made his heart pound harder every time she met his eyes, and he knew it wasn't just sex.

It wasn't even pool.

"Phin?" Wes said.

"I think I'm going to have to marry her," Phin said. "Dillie likes her. I could teach her to read. This could work."

Wes shook his head. "Your mind is clouded by pool. You've only known her three weeks. Wait until the game wears off and rethink this."

"Okay," Phin said, and thought about Sophie's stop shot again.

For that alone, he had to love her.

"Clea got to Rob," Wes told Phin, when they were sitting on the bookstore porch. "She's been telling him that the only thing standing in their way was Zane. She's got him convinced she's in love with him."

"Just like Dad," Phin said. "Helluva tradition, those Lutz boys."

"She gave him her cell phone and sent him out after Zane that night with instructions to call if Zane got into any trouble. She told Rob he was drunk and if he fell in the river, he'd drown."

"And Rob didn't get the hint."

"No, thank God. He followed him to the back of Garvey's, and then Zane stopped and waited there, so Rob called Rachel on the cell phone to come out and meet him."

Phin frowned, incredulous. "Why—"

"He thought Zane would make a pass and Rachel would scream and Stephen would come out and it would be all over. This is Rob, remember. No execution. For which we should all be grateful. So Rachel Maced him and shoved him in the river, and then Rob took her out to the Tavern and Zane climbed back to the path and met somebody with a gun." Wes sighed. "With the stuff I dragged out of Amy about the body, I've got a better time of death. Zane went into the water alive and unshot about nine forty-five. Amy came back from the Tavern and went upstairs a little after ten, but you and Sophie were . . . loud, so she went out to the dock to cool off and found Zane. Her best guess is ten-thirty."

"Forty-five minutes," Phin said. "Anybody have an alibi?"

"You and Sophie," Wes said. "Rob and Rachel at the Tavern. Leo in L.A. Hildy and Ed."

Phin raised an eyebrow. "Hildy and Ed?"

"Watching porn at his place," Wes said. "Police work turns up a lot of stuff you wish you didn't know."

"So that leaves . . . ?"

"Frank, who didn't go home. Georgia, who was home alone after you dropped her off. Your mom, who was home with Dillie in bed. Stephen, who was home, but who sleeps in a different room than Virginia."

"Christ, this guy can't catch a break," Phin said, and then thought about Virginia. "Or maybe he can."

"And Clea, Amy, and Davy," Wes said. "None of these people can find the guns that are supposed to be in their respective houses. All of them had access to Sophie's bedroom to plant the gun we found there, which, by the way, is now in Cincinnati for a ballistics test."

"Davy and Amy wouldn't put a gun under Sophie's mattress," Phin said.

"Amy might," Wes said. "She's used to Sophie carrying the can for her. And there was a good chance that gun would never be found. But Davy's the one I'm really interested in."

"I don't think Davy Dempsey is a killer."

"You're forgetting Clea. They were lovers five years ago until she dumped him for Zane, and I'm picking up some tension there now. It'd be like Clea to hedge her bets by sending two guys after Zane. What if she told Davy she'd made a mistake, that she'd come back to him if Zane were gone?"

"Davy Dempsey is not a killer," Phin said. "And if he decided to become one, he wouldn't shoot his victim in the shoulder with a popgun."

"Unless he knew his victim had heart problems," Wes said. "Then that becomes a smart thing to do. You can't be convicted of murder, but you can cause a man to die, just the same. That's devious enough for Davy. In fact, it's so devious I'm starting to think it can only be Davy."

"What are you going to do?" Phin said.

"Keep digging," Wes said. "Wait for the ballistics report on the gun in Sophie's bed. Watch Davy Dempsey. Pray for a miracle."

"You're doing a helluva job with this," Phin told him.

"One other thing," Wes said, and Phin tensed at the tone in his voice. "The gun in Sophie's bed was your dad's."

The worst part, Phin thought, was that neither of them was surprised. "I don't want to know this."

"Doesn't mean it's the gun that shot Zane," Wes said.

"No, but it is the gun that framed Sophie," Phin said. "I need to talk to my mother."

• • •

When Phin got home, Liz was waiting for him in the hall, glowering.

"Now what?" he said, and she said, "You took her to Dillie's softball game."

"Yes," Phin said, looking around for his daughter, and Liz said, "She's not here. I took her to Junie's so we could have this out."

"Good," Phin said. "You put Dad's gun under Sophie's mattress. A *loaded gun*, under Sophie's mattress. You could have killed her."

"I suppose she told you that," Liz stood stone-faced, framed by the big front door. "She lies. She's trying to destroy this family and you're letting her. You're going to have to choose. If you're going to continue to consort with her, you can't live under my roof. I won't let you destroy this family for sex."

"It's not sex," Phin said. "And I'm not destroying the family, but you might be."

"Choose," Liz said, and Phin said, "You're right. It's time anyway."

Her face relaxed and she smiled. "I knew you'd see—"

"I'll pack my stuff and move down to the bookstore tonight—"

"*No,*" Liz said, her face twisting.

"What did you expect? I'll get one of the bedrooms cleared out tomorrow and come back for Dillie and her things then."

"*NO,*" Liz said, and Phin said, "You can stop shrieking 'no' at me. This was your idea."

"If you have to move out to be with that—"

"Careful."

Liz drew a deep breath. "—that woman, that's your mistake, but you're not taking Dillie. You're not capable of—"

Phin took another step toward his mother so that he towered over her. "You have no idea of what I'm capable of when it comes to my daughter," he said softly. "Don't try to find out."

"You're being a fool," Liz said.

"You're being a bitch," Phin said, and Liz drew back as if she'd been slapped. "Stop harassing Sophie. I'll come get Dillie tomorrow." Then he turned and went up the stairs to pack, not looking back at all.

It took Phin and Sophie all Sunday to move the books from one of the bedrooms—the one with the window seat in the tower corner because Sophie insisted Dillie would love it—and when they were done, they were both covered in dust and sweat in spite of the air-conditioning.

"Dillie's going to go nuts for this room," Sophie said, wiping the sweat from her forehead and leaving a dirt streak behind. She looked at him cautiously. "Speaking of nuts, how's your mom taking this?"

"About as well as can be expected," Phin said, trying not to think about his mother. "Which is not well at all. Can I interest you in a shower?"

"I assume this is a twofer," Sophie said.

"Water conservation." Phin reached for her, knowing exactly how she'd feel against him and wanting her even more because of it. "Also sex. Come here."

"The things I give up for you." Sophie moved toward him into his arms. "Private showers, vintage mattresses, money, my reputation—"

"So you're not losing anything you really needed." He smiled down at her as she cuddled close, and then what she'd said registered. "What money?"

She stopped to look up at him, caught, her eyes wide. "Money?"

He moved his hands up to her shoulders, exasperated with her and loving her anyway. "Sophie, listen to me, if you know where Zane's money is—"

"Oh, I don't," Sophie said, meeting his eyes without hesitation, clearly telling the truth. She slid her arms around his waist and pulled him close, and she felt great against him, but not great enough to distract him. "About that shower—"

"About that money," he said. "Whose money, and where is it?"

Sophie sighed. "It's your mother's, and it's in her bank account. That day she came out to the farm, she tried to buy me off. But that was two weeks ago so—"

"Buy you off?" Phin looked down at her, incredulous. "Who the hell does she think she is?"

"Liz Tucker," Sophie said. "She's just trying to protect you. Now, can I have that shower?"

There was something in her voice; she was talking too fast. "No." Phin guided her over to the window seat and pulled her into his lap. "There's more. I don't give a damn what it is, I'll forgive you anything, but I want it all."

Sophie pulled away from him. "I didn't do anything, you butthead. You can go forgive somebody else."

Phin winced. "Sorry. But you're not telling me everything. What else did my mother do?"

"I don't know," Sophie said, standing. "I haven't seen her since that day, I swear to God. Now, I'm going to shower. If you want to come, too, fine, but I'm going to be naked and wet with or without you."

He followed her into the bathroom, still suspicious, but when she took off her clothes, he decided he could wait to grill her again until they were both clean and satisfied.

An hour later, buttoning up his shirt as he sat on the edge of his bed and trying to think of what he was missing about his mother and money, Phin stopped on the second button and thought, *Diane.* "She bought off Diane, didn't she?" he said to Sophie, and Sophie zipped up her shorts and said, "How would I know?"

"But that's what you think."

"But I'm often wrong," Sophie said.

He thought about Diane and Dillie and the whole miserable mess. "Christ."

"It's over," Sophie said, coming to him. "Whatever really happened, it doesn't matter. It's over."

He put his arms around her and thought, *It's not over.* Two women had come between him and his family, and the first one was dead.

Family values weren't supposed to be lethal.

"What?" Sophie said.

"I have to take you home," he told her, standing up. "It's time for a little Tucker family time."

Phin found his mother sitting at her desk in her air-conditioned office on the Hill. She nodded when he came in, and then turned back to her desk, punishing him with her silence.

"You bought Diane off," he said, and she stiffened but didn't turn around. He went to her, grabbed the back of the chair and spun it around on its wheels so that she grabbed the arms.

"Phin!"

"How much?" he said, leaning over her.

She pressed her lips together, stony-faced, and he waited for what seemed like hours. "Fifty thousand," she said finally.

Phin straightened. "Not bad. What was that for, the first year?"

His mother nodded.

"As long as she stayed away from me and Dillie." His mother nodded again.

"But she bought a car," Phin said. "New clothes, furniture for the river house. How long did it take her to run through it?"

"She was stupid," his mother said bitterly. "Thank God, Dillie got our brains."

"Right now, I'm wondering about yours," Phin said. "You really thought she'd leave us alone for fifty grand a year? Living right here in Temptation? She wasn't the only one who was stupid."

Liz flinched. "She was supposed to move away. As soon as she recovered from having Dillie, she was supposed to go away."

"And how were you going to make her do that?" Phin said. "Who do you think you are?"

"I'm your mother," Liz snapped. "I took care of you. That harpy would have ruined you. She made you miserable the whole time she was with you." She looked at him in disgust. "You're impossible when it comes to women. Diane was a greedy little slut and now this—"

"*Careful.*" Phin's voice cut across the space between them. "You really don't want to make me choose again."

"The whole town's talking," Liz said, her voice shaking. "That woman killed Zane. They found the gun under her bed—"

"What?" Phin said. How the hell had the gossips gotten hold of that?

Liz nodded. "You don't know her. She killed him—"

"She was in bed with me," Phin said. "Wes has got the time of death narrowed down to forty-five minutes, and she was naked with me the entire time. Where'd you get this crap?"

"Virginia," Liz said. "But everybody knows. And now you're protecting her—"

"Could you just once listen to me?" Phin said. "Instead of spitting paranoia at me?"

Liz clenched her jaw. "I'm not paranoid. You need me. I got you free of Diane. I saved you."

"I'm just wondering *how* free," Phin said, looking at the steel in his mother's eyes. "She died when Dillie was three months old. That must have been about the time she ran out of money. Did she come back for more?"

"Yes," Liz said, her disgust palpable, and then his implication must have registered because her eyes widened, and she said, "No."

"Did you shove her down those steps?" Phin said, sick at heart. "Did you watch her bleed to death? Did Zane find out? Did you shoot him?"

Liz stood up. "I've given you my entire life and you say this to me."

"I didn't want your life," Phin told her bitterly. "I wanted mine. And Diane and Zane probably wanted theirs, too."

"I didn't kill them," Liz said.

"That's a pretty damn big coincidence, Mom." He turned to go. "I wouldn't want to have to explain it."

"Are you going to Wes?" Liz said from behind him, no emotion at all in her voice.

"No," Phin said, refusing to look back at her. "You're still my mother. Just stay away from Sophie."

"I didn't kill Diane, Phin," Liz said. "It really was a coincidence."

Her voice shook a little this time, and he turned back. "Remember that day in the courthouse when you said you'd do anything for me?"

She nodded.

"Don't."

He turned and walked out of his mother's house and down the Hill to the bookstore, not stopping until he was in front of the pool table.

It was a beautiful thing, massive in its elegance, impressive in its tradition. Just like his family.

He really did not believe his mother had killed people. His mother might be unhinged from his father's death but she wasn't a killer. There was still a human being in there somewhere, a cold, driven human being, but still a human being. She hadn't become a monster when he wasn't looking.

"Oh, Christ," he said, and sat down hard on the edge of the table. She really hadn't. Not his mother.

And now she was trying to pin Zane's death on Sophie.

He got up and went to the phone and dialed Hildy Mallow. "Hildy?" he said when she answered. "I've got some gossip for you to spread."

"I don't spread gossip," Hildy said primly.

"You will this gossip," Phin said. "Somebody's spreading the rumor that Sophie killed Zane."

"I'd heard that," Hildy said. "Didn't seem likely but people are strange."

"She was in bed with me," Phin said. "The entire time. Tell everybody."

"Oh," Hildy said. "All right. Your mother's not going to like this."

"Good," Phin said. "Tell her first."

When Sophie got home, Amy was waiting for her. "Where have you been?" she said. "I need—"

"Get it yourself," Sophie said, and went upstairs.

Amy followed her up. "What's with you? I just wanted your opinion on the cable cut of the video."

"Get all the sex out of it and bleep the foul language," Sophie said. "After that I don't care. I'm worried about Phin and Dillie. They—"

"Oh, sure," Amy said. "Phin and Dillie."

Sophie looked up at the tone in her voice. "You're jealous."

Amy shrugged. "I just think family—"

"That's why you called Brandon," Sophie said. "You don't like him, but you'd rather I was with him because you know I don't care about him. But Phin—"

"I don't care what you do with the mayor," Amy said. "Screw him all you want."

"It's really Dillie, isn't it?" Sophie said. "I can only have one kid in my life, and that's you?"

Amy's eyes filled with tears.

"Amy, I will always be here for you, but you're not getting my life anymore."

"No, *they* get it now." Amy sniffed. "Well, no problem. I can take care of myself."

"Actually, you can't." Sophie tried to smile to take the sting out of the words. "I wish you'd apologize to Wes and get him back. This is a man who not only fixed your funky sunglasses, he made them funkier. And he gave you a flexible showerhead that you've been using for immoral purposes ever since we got here. He may be the only man in the world who understands you and gives you what you need even before you know you need it. But you're giving him up for a dirty movie? Come on, Ame."

"This is my career, Sophie," Amy said stiffly.

"This is a home movie, Amy," Sophie said. "An amateur,

direct-to-video skin flick. You are not Robert Rodriguez. Grow up and look at what matters in life."

Amy turned and walked out.

When Davy came up the stairs a few minutes later, he said, "What happened with Amy?"

"I picked Phin and Dillie," Sophie said. "Was that lousy of me?"

"No," Davy said. "It's past time for you to get a better plan than, 'I'll sacrifice my life for my grown brother and sister.' Way past time."

"What about you?" Sophie said.

"I have a plan of my own," Davy said, grinning. "Everything's going to be fine."

"Not for Amy," Sophie said, and Davy's smile faded.

"She'll be all right," he said, but he didn't sound convinced. The lights flickered, and he said, "Oh, great, she's plugged in all the computer stuff again. Didn't you tell her—"

"Over and over again," Sophie said, and got up to call down the stairs. "Amy? You're going to blow a—"

The lights went out downstairs.

"—fuse."

"I'll get it," Amy said coldly from the foot of the stairs. "How hard can this be if you do it?"

They heard her slam open the basement door and stamp down the stairs.

"You know, she needs to be smacked," Davy said. "Spoiled brat."

"She's just hurt," Sophie said. "She—"

The lights came on for a split second, and then there was a *crack* and they went out again.

"Amy?" Sophie said.

"*Amy?*" Davy ran for the stairs, Sophie on his heels.

• • •

"Somebody pulled loose a wire in the fuse box," Wes said, when Phin had come back from the hospital. "And poured water on the floor and set a trap for her."

"Not for her," Phin said, his voice grim. "Amy doesn't change the fuses. She doesn't do any scut work. She's the artist." He felt lousy even as he said it, remembering Amy's pale little face in the hospital bed, her fingers bandaged from the burns, her head shaved to stitch up the wound she'd gotten when the charge had blown her back against an old metal table.

"For Sophie," Wes agreed. "I got an anonymous phone call today. Somebody seemed to think there was a gun under Sophie's bed."

"Trace it?"

"The courthouse," Wes said. "Anybody in the world could have made it. And now this. Somebody wants Sophie out of the way pretty badly."

Phin closed his eyes. "I do not see my mother sneaking into a basement to fray a wire. Or putting a gun under a bed she knew I'd be sleeping in."

"Your mom is . . . upset that you moved out," Wes said. "Extremely."

"She'll get over it," Phin said. "So you going to the hospital to see Amy?" Wes turned away as he added, "She asked for you. I told her you were investigating the accident and you'd be out to talk to her later."

"She wants to see me?"

"Sounded like it," Phin said. "She pretty much got the spunk knocked out of her, and she's stuck in the hospital for the night. Good time to go talk to her."

Wes turned on him. "You think I'd ask her about Zane now?"

"I meant about the two of you," Phin said. "She's leaving tomorrow after the premiere."

"She'll be out that fast?"

"They're just watching her for the night. Go see her."

"Maybe," Wes said. "Is Sophie—"

"Sophie's staying with me tonight."

"I thought Dillie—"

"She's staying with me and Dillie," Phin said.

Wes raised his eyebrows. "Your mother—"

"Go see Amy," Phin said. "I'll take care of my mother."

When Wes brought Amy home from the hospital the next day, Sophie had the entire house cleaned, their things packed, and the car full of gas. "If you don't feel like leaving tonight after the premiere, we can stay," Sophie said, and Amy said, "Whatever you want," and went upstairs to bed.

"I'll come back later tonight," Wes told Sophie. "She's okay, she's just nervous about the video."

But when Sophie went upstairs to see her, she found Davy instead, packing his bag.

"You're leaving?"

"I've got a place I have to be, and somebody I have to finish things with." He closed the suitcase lid and locked it. "Harvard's watching your back here, probably better than I can. It's his turf, after all."

"I don't think—"

"Amy's okay and Clea's gone, so I'd say your problems—"

"Clea's gone?"

"Left about an hour ago," Davy said. His voice was light, but his face was grim.

"Is that why you're leaving?" Sophie felt sick. "You're not going off with her, are you? You don't want her back?"

"You ask too many questions." Davy sat down beside her and put his arm around her. "Listen to me: Marry the mayor and keep the dog and live happily ever after in this house. That's what you want. Forget about me and Amy and go for it."

"Just like that," Sophie said.

"Have you tried?" Davy said.

Sophie smiled faintly. "Well, actually, yeah. I kicked the mayor's butt at pool."

"Good girl," Davy said.

"By not wearing underwear," Sophie said.

"Even better," Davy said.

"I just don't think that's going to do it," Sophie said. "And I know that's not going to get me the house."

"I have a deal for you," Davy said, and Sophie said, "This should be good. Scamming your sister."

"No," Davy said. "This one's a promise. You stay here and marry the mayor and I'll get you this house."

Sophie blinked at him. "You have three-quarters of a million dollars?"

"Never ask people about money," Davy said. "It's rude."

Zane's bank book. Sophie went cold. "Where did you get three-quarters of a million dollars?"

"Sophie—" Davy said and hit her with the Dempsey smile.

Sophie sighed. "Call me for bail when you get caught."

"You have an attitude problem," Davy said, and kissed her cheek. "Don't go back to Cincy, stay here. I'll have the deed for you by Monday."

He picked up the suitcase, and she said, "Wait," and he caught her as she flung herself at him. "Be very, very careful," she whispered in his ear, not adding *especially with Clea*, and he held her tight and said, "Just for you, I always am." Then he kissed her cheek and was gone.

That night, Phin had just grabbed his car keys when Sophie knocked on the back door of the bookstore.

"I thought I was coming out to you," he said, letting her in.

"Amy is driving me crazy," Sophie said. "I left Wes to deal with her. She likes him better than me anyway." She slid her arms around his waist and he pulled her close and kissed the top of her head. "And unlike Amy, you are calm," Sophie said against his shirt. "I like that in a man."

"That's been harder lately," he said. "Dillie's at Jamie Barclay's. Want to come upstairs and watch TV in my bed?"

"I didn't even know you had a TV," Sophie said.

"ESPN2 has billiards on Wednesday nights," Phin said.

"Then of course you have a TV."

She piled his pillows at the head of the bed while he opened the cabinet that held his TV and flipped the channels to Temptation Cable, and when he turned, she was propped up waiting for him, looking fairly comfortable and really good, even if she was back in khaki.

"Do I get popcorn?" she said, and Phin looked at the kitchen clock and said, "We have five minutes before showtime. You may get something else."

"Oh, gee, a whole five minutes." Sophie rolled her eyes. "That's what I need, a guy with staying power."

He stretched out on the bed next to her. "Before I forget, *Prizzi's Honor*." He patted the bed. " 'Right here on the Oriental.' "

"How'd you get that?"

"Amy," he said. "I asked her when she was in the hospital. Of course, she didn't know what I was going to do with it."

Sophie laughed and kissed him, and he fell into all her softness and the heat of her mouth.

"Funny you should mention that," Sophie said as she snuggled closer. "I went to Hildy's today to take her Dove Bars as a thank-you for rescuing me off her dock, and she had this book of ballads."

"Good," Phin said, and bent to kiss her again, sliding his arm behind her head.

"And 'Julie Ann' was in there," Sophie said, ducking him a little so that he stopped. "And I think you had it wrong."

He lifted his head. "Wrong? My grandmother sang that song to me for years. You're telling me my grandma was wrong?"

"The last line," Sophie said sternly, "says that they never found Julie, and they never found the bear."

"Right," Phin said.

"So they both disappeared," Sophie said.

"Right," Phin said.

"So it's a pretty patriarchal assumption that the bear got Julie." Sophie turned away from him a little and slid her hand under the pillows. "I think Julie got the bear."

"Yeah, right," Phin said, and then he felt something cold snap on the wrist he'd put behind her head, and when he sat up, Sophie had him handcuffed to the headboard.

"Wes loaned them to me," she said. "I have to give them back later tonight, though."

Phin tugged once on the cuffs as he felt something closely akin to panic. "This isn't funny. Give me the key."

Sophie sat cross-legged on the bed and shook her head. "Nope. It's definitely Julie Ann's turn this time."

Phin closed his eyes. "At least tell me you *have* the key."

"Of course I have the key." He could feel Sophie leaning closer, and then he felt her working the buttons on his shirt open.

"Sophie, I don't th—" Phin began, but then her fingertips brushed his stomach, and every muscle he had tightened, and he shut up.

She popped open the button on his pants and said, soft and slow, "Let me give you an orgasm you don't have to work for," and he looked into her liquid brown eyes and said, "Just don't lose the key." She laughed and kissed his stomach, and then he forgot about the key, and the murder, and Temptation in general, and surrendered to Sophie's cool, searching fingers and her hot, hungry mouth.

Fifteen minutes later, he was staring contentedly at the ceiling, counting his blessings which now seemed numerous, when he heard somebody pound on the downstairs door. Sophie sat up beside him, and he tried to do the same, only to realize he was still handcuffed to the bed. "The key—" he began, and then he saw she was looking past him to the television, stunned. "What?" he said, and she said, "That's the wrong movie. That's *Cherished*."

He turned and saw Rob on-screen, naked, reaching for Clea, also naked, and heard him say, "'You definitely have discovery fantasies.'"

Phin froze as the dialogue rolled over him.

"'We're going to be having a lot of sex in public places,'" Rob said. "'You want to know why?'"

"'No,'" Clea said and stretched for the camera.

"'Because you like it,'" Rob said, and reached for her, and then the movie cut to grainier film of bodies writhing, and Sophie said, "Oh my God, that's *Hot Fleshy Thighs!*"

The pounding got louder downstairs, and Phin turned to her and said, "*Get me that key.*"

Sophie scrambled for it on the bedside table and unlocked the cuffs with shaking fingers while he watched the film go into such a tight close-up that it was almost impossible to tell what body parts were being filmed.

Almost.

Phin rolled out of bed and grabbed his pants. "Call Wes at the farm and tell him to meet me at the cable station."

"That's not our movie," Sophie said, as she grabbed the phone and punched in the numbers, "that's Leo's movie, I swear to God."

"I really don't give a damn, Sophie," Phin said. "My kid is watching that."

The picture flipped back to a naked Rob who said to a naked Clea, "'Your soul is a corkscrew.'"

"Phin—" Sophie's voice broke, and then the picture snapped and turned dark, and she shut up. Either his TV was broken, or somebody had stormed the cable station and shut it down. He flipped the channel and saw a blond teenager kicking the hell out of a vampire. His TV was fine.

His life, however, was broken.

"I'm sorry," Sophie whispered.

"Yeah, so am I," he said, and went downstairs to talk to the irate citizen pounding on the door.

Chapter Fourteen

Rachel sat across the table from Leo in Temptation's only diner, mired in misery, while Leo put on his glasses and read the receipt the waitress had just handed him with his Visa card.

He was leaving. He was going back to L.A. and leaving her stuck here in Temptation. And she loved him, damn it. That was the worst of it. It wasn't that he was leaving her in Temptation, although that was bad enough.

It was that he was leaving *her*. He didn't *love* her. She couldn't understand it at all. He'd kissed her that one glorious time, and he'd taken care of her when she'd gone to Wes, but that was it and now he was going and she was miserable.

Leo checked his watch. "The movie started fifteen minutes ago," he told her. "How long is it?"

"The clean version? About half an hour." Rachel leaned forward. "Leo, stop ignoring me."

Leo sighed. "I know you want to come to L.A., kid."

"I'm not a kid," Rachel said. "I'm a good worker. I learn fast. You're stupid not to take me."

"I'd be stupid *to* take you." Leo signed the receipt and pocketed his Visa. "Even assuming your father didn't come after me with a shotgun, I'd spend all my time looking after you. You stay here and have a normal life."

"I don't want a normal life," Rachel said. "If I wanted a normal life, I'd have done what my mother wanted and married Phin."

"Phin?" Leo scowled at her. "Phin's not right for you."

"I know that—" Rachel began, and then stopped as she realized somebody was standing by their table.

"You the guy that made that movie?" the man said, looking red in the face.

"No," Leo said. "Why?"

"Because whoever did that is a fucking pervert, that's why," the guy said.

"What?" Rachel said.

"Kids are watching that filth," the man said, and glared at Leo. "Are you sure you're not the guy?"

"I'm positive," Leo said mildly.

"Well, you should just be glad you took your daughter out for dinner tonight instead of watching that trash with her—"

"We have to go," Rachel said, getting up.

"My *daughter*?" Leo said, and Rachel leaned over and said, "*Now*, Leo."

Leo watched as the man stalked away. "She's not my daughter, you putz."

"*Leo.*"

"Showed the wrong movie, did they?" Leo said, and Rachel

said, "I think they saw the old *Cherished* instead of the clean cut that Amy made, and I need to talk to Sophie *now*."

Leo dropped his napkin on the table. "Okay. But I'd still like to hear—"

"*Now*," Rachel said, and dragged him from the diner.

"I bagged the tape and sent it to Cincinnati," Wes said two hours later when he and Phin were finally alone in the bookstore. "Maybe we'll get some prints."

Phin shook his head, more tired than he could ever have imagined. It took a lot out of a mayor to have to deal with that many screaming citizens.

"Phin," Wes said. "Pay attention. We have to find out who took the tape. He violated the FCC up, down, and sideways, and we'll get him."

"I can't even think," Phin said. "I've been explaining the unexplainable all night. Where the hell did that tape come from?"

"From the farm," Wes said. "According to Amy, it was Leo's cut of a tape they'd made. I gather they made several versions."

"So whoever took that tape knew which one would do the most damage." Phin felt anger rise, cool and clean. "Somebody at the farm—"

"Not necessarily," Wes said. "Amy said when Rachel saw what Leo had done to the movie, she took the tape and wrote '*Smut, Smut, Smut*' on it in bright red marker. Anybody who wanted to sabotage the movie would have picked that one up."

"So somebody went out there and sorted through the tapes—"

"No," Wes said. "Somebody went out there and took all

the tapes. As soon as the movie started, Amy went running to look. They're all gone, even the documentary she was working on. Somebody just backed up a car while we were all at the hospital this morning and took every one of them."

"Who?" Phin said, but even as he said it, he knew.

"Stephen's got this movie tied to your tail," Wes said. "This is a big break for him, just six weeks before the election. Six days would have been better, but six weeks isn't bad. And he's the only one I can see getting anything out of this."

Phin thought about Sophie. She'd gotten something out of it—out of making that damn movie at least. He heard his own stupid words coming out of Rob's mouth and felt like a fool.

Wes said, "You want to come to Stephen's with me?"

Phin thought of Stephen's smug, red face, and the pain cleared and his rage focused. "Yes."

"Thought so," Wes said.

Stephen answered the door, trying to look innocent and only looking smugger as a result. "I saw the premiere on television," he said to Wes. "That was a shocking thing. I certainly hope—"

"Forget it, Stephen," Phin said, as he pushed past him into the living room where Rachel sat on the couch in patent misery. "You knew all about it."

Across the room, Virginia looked up from the phone she was clutching and lowered her voice. Spreading the good word as usual.

Meanwhile Stephen was waxing indignant.

"What do you mean, I knew about it? You think if I'd known that kind of disgusting pornography was going to be broadcast to the people of this town—"

"Forget it, Stephen," Wes said. "The only voters here are the ones who know what really happened."

Rachel jerked her head up. "What did happen? I couldn't find Sophie to find out. That wasn't our film—"

"Young lady, you had nothing to do with that film," Virginia said from the phone.

"I worked on that film," Rachel said. "I'm proud of that film, but that film wasn't my film."

Virginia said, "I have to go," into the phone and hung up. "You had nothing to do with that disgusting movie, so you stop even pretending you did."

"I'm not pretending, I worked *hard* on that," Rachel said, and Virginia pointed her finger at her and said, "Enough. You've caused enough trouble acting up and from now on, you're going to be the daughter I raised. You're going to get married and settle down and be a good woman." Virginia's eyes slid to Phin.

"She's not marrying me," Phin said.

"She certainly isn't," Stephen said. "You're responsible for that porn going out to all of Temptation, corrupting—"

"Stephen," Wes said. "I told you. You can knock off the speeches. Everybody here knows you switched that tape—"

"Daddy?" Rachel said.

"That's the most ridiculous thing I ever heard of—" Stephen began.

"—and we're sending it to Cincinnati for a forensics check. The fingerprints will nail you if nothing else does."

"We'll just have to wait and see, then, won't we?" Stephen said, smug as ever, and Phin said, "Fuck. You wiped it before you played it, didn't you?"

"Phin!" Virginia said, and when Stephen said, "Well, that's the kind of language I'd have expected from somebody who'd consort with the *whores* who made that trash," Phin grabbed Stephen's throat and shoved him against the wall.

"About *Sophie*," Phin said, rage making his voice shake. "You damned near killed her, you bastard, and I never came after you for that—"

"I don't know what you're talking about," Stephen choked, wide-eyed.

"You shoved her in the river and almost drowned her," Phin said, gripping him tighter, and Rachel said, "Daddy!" at the same time that Wes said, "Let him go, Phin."

"You hurt her." Phin gripped his neck harder. "From now on, you come after *me*, you son of a bitch, not her, and not the people of this town—you do not show porn to kids to bring me down, do you understand? This is between *us*."

Stephen didn't say anything, but he turned blue, and from behind him, Phin heard Wes say calmly, "He's sick and smaller than you are and older than you are and not worth it. Let go of him, or I'll break your arm."

Phin looked into Stephen's sly, stupid, blue face and thought about all the crap Stephen had gotten away with because nobody had fought him—*because I didn't fight him, because I played it safe, because I was too damn lazy*—

Wes jerked Phin's left arm up hard behind him, and the pain knifed into his shoulder, and he let go of Stephen and his own pent-up breath at the same time.

"Thank you," Wes said, releasing his arm as Stephen slid down the wall, an interesting shade of purple.

"Ouch," Phin said, and eased his shoulder back.

"It would be bad if you killed him," Wes said. "Understandable, but bad." He looked at Stephen on the floor, trying to fill his lungs. "That 'whore' bit was a dumb move, Stephen. Don't do that again."

Phin rubbed his arm and watched Stephen get his breath back. "Well, at least the short-term pleasure was great." He leaned over and said softly to Stephen, "If you ever try to hurt Sophie again, I'll let Wes break every bone in my body before I let you go."

"I didn't hurt that woman," Stephen rasped. "I don't attack women. Have you lost your mind? Arrest him for assault, Wes. He's crazy. He almost killed me."

"I didn't see any assault," Wes said. "I did see two men in heated conversation but—"

"Well, my family saw." Stephen climbed to his feet. "Rachel—" He stopped when he realized Rachel was gone. "You better get a lawyer," he told Phin. "You're in big trouble."

Virginia stared at them from across the room, horrified. "You're a terrible man," she told Phin. "I'll never let you marry my daughter now."

"Well, at least something's going my way." Phin turned back to Stephen. "You shoved Sophie in the river, you stole that tape, and you played pornography on a public television station. Get your own lawyer, you son of a bitch."

"You can't prove any of that," Stephen said. "I wouldn't shove a woman anywhere." He looked genuinely insulted that Phin had suggested it, and Phin frowned at him. Then Stephen's face grew smug again. "And I certainly wouldn't show pornography to the good people of—"

"Here we go again," Wes said. "Stephen, we need the other tapes back. I don't think the women will prosecute if you give them their tapes back, but—"

"Nobody's going to prosecute me for anything," Stephen said. "You have no proof. And the last time I looked, you needed proof to arrest somebody, so—"

"Stephen," Phin said quietly. "Sophie came over one night when you were watching them film on the dock, and somebody pushed her into the river. Right here, at the end of your property." Stephen shut up and Phin watched him closely. "The river was high and she almost drowned. If she wasn't such a fighter, she'd have died."

"I don't know anything about that," Stephen said cautiously. "But I do know that the people *you* consorted with produced a *pornographic* movie in *clear* violation of the Temptation *film ordinance*—"

Phin tuned him out, and Wes said, "Okay, Stephen, you practice your speech, and we'll talk to you tomorrow."

"I want him arrested," Stephen said, and Wes said, "No, you don't, because if I arrest him, he'll get to explain why he went for you, and then people might get to thinking you'd played porn to their children just to get elected."

Stephen scowled. "That's ridiculous."

"No," Wes said. "That's the truth, and it's the lousiest thing I know about you. How many people had their kids in front of that TV set to watch Temptation in the movies? You set it all up. Anything to get elected. You and your family values."

"I didn't do it," Stephen said stubbornly, but his eyes slid away, and Phin gave up.

When they were back in the car, Wes said, "If you ever attack another citizen in front of me, I will break your fucking arm and then move on to your head."

"Fair enough," Phin said. "I can't think of anybody else I want to attack, anyway, so it shouldn't be a problem."

"Because you pretty much threw away whatever leverage I had," Wes went on. "He can file assault charges, you know, and they'll stick. So I'm not exactly in a position to lean on him for this tape thing."

"I'm sorry," Phin said. "But we did get something out of that."

"Yeah," Wes said. "He didn't push Sophie."

"So who did?" Phin thought about Sophie and the movie, and shoved it aside as too painful to think about. He went back to everything Sophie had told them about the river. Somebody had shoved her really hard, she'd said. "Who else would do that?"

"You got me," Wes said, and started the car. "I'll put it on my list of things to do along with, 'Find out who shot Zane and tried to electrocute Sophie,' and 'Try to nail Stephen for pandering porn.' Jesus, I'm lousy at this job."

"No, you're not," Phin said. "You're just up against it right now."

Wes pulled back out onto the road and headed for the station. "I hate to point this out, but so are you."

"Yeah, I think that pretty well wraps it up for me as mayor." Phin settled back, rubbed his shoulder, and thought about how good it had felt to grab Stephen. "Thanks for waiting so long to pull me off."

"My pleasure. You know, this wasn't Sophie's fault, that was Leo's cut. She must be upset about all this. She worked pretty hard making that movie."

Phin heard his own dialogue coming at him from the screen again. "You have no idea how hard she worked."

"Am I missing something here?"

"Yes," Phin said.

"Am I going to continue missing it?"

"Yes."

Wes sighed. "Fine, be that way." He pulled up in front of the bookstore. "Get out. I got work to do."

"What work? It's after eleven. Go home."

"I'm not the only one here missing stuff," Wes said. "You go mope. I have things to do."

"Wait a minute," Phin said, but Wes pointed to the door, so he got out and let him drive away.

Fine. Whatever. He wasn't moping, he'd just had his entire future shot out from under him, and there was nobody to vent his annoyance on. Wes was gone, his mother was somewhere committing hari-kari, the Garveys were no doubt celebrating the coming mayoral victory, and Ed was probably trying to get a copy of *Hot Fleshy Thighs* for his porn collection even as Phin stood there.

And then there was Sophie.

"Fuck it," he said, and walked around the back of the bookstore to his car. Wes was right. He had things to do. Like demand an explanation. Like ask her what the hell she thought she was doing. Like make her feel guilty for all the hell she was leaving behind her.

If she thought she was leaving town without a reckoning, she didn't know him at all.

Rachel found Leo in his motel room, packing.

"Thank God," he said. "My ride to the airport and out of here. That guy in the restaurant was only the beginning. Did you hear those people in the lobby? I don't think I've ever seen that many people angry over soft porn before. Imagine what they'd do if they knew the kind of stuff I do."

"They do," Rachel said. "You missed that part. My dad switched tapes and the town watched *Hot Fleshy Thighs*."

"Oh," Leo said. "Well. Even so, it was just a movie. They overreacted."

"Forget them," Rachel said. "They're history. Think about the future."

Leo eyed her cautiously. "You seem fairly calm about this."

Rachel leaned against the wall and shrugged. "It'll be okay. Everybody's mad right now, which is good for them because not much happens in Temptation so this'll give them some exercise. They're not bad people and they won't go after Sophie or anybody, and even if somebody really lost it and tried, Phin and Wes would take care of it."

"I doubt Phin's going to take care of it," Leo said. "From the way those people downstairs are talking, he just lost the next election."

Rachel shrugged. "He'll get over it. He loves Sophie, and he'll keep her no matter what. Phin's determined like that. Love'll do that to a person." She met Leo's eyes and he flinched.

"Right." Leo shut his suitcase. "Well, I'm ready. You want I should call a taxi so you don't have to—"

"No," she said, and pulled her dress over her head.

Leo took a step back. "Rachel, stop it."

"I know you think you're leaving me." Rachel lifted her chin so it wouldn't quiver because that would ruin what she was pretty sure was the magnificent sight of her in Victoria's Secret red lace. "But you're not. I'm the best thing that ever happened to you, Leo. And I mean professionally, too. I stopped and talked to Sophie on my way here, and we worked it all out. You can teach me to run that new vanilla-porn section." She took a deep breath. "I think you should call it Rachel Films and use a cat for the logo that's like the lion on the Leo stuff. And I can do a lot of the promotion that you can't do, because I'm a woman. Sophie thinks it's a great idea."

"Rachel—"

"And I'm smart, Leo," Rachel said. "And I learn fast. Sophie says so. I'm going to do a lot for you, you'll see."

Leo looked at the ceiling. "Could we talk about this with you dressed?"

"No," Rachel said. "Because I'm going to sleep with you,

too. I know you don't want to do this, but even just that one kiss with you was better than having sex with anybody else I've had sex with, and I'm coming after the rest of it now. And then we're going to go to L.A. and live happily ever after." She narrowed her eyes at him. "If you think I'm settling for anything less, you don't know me."

Leo closed his eyes.

"And you know me, Leo." She walked toward him while he kept his eyes closed. "Although, not nearly as well as you're going to."

Sophie was sitting on the porch swing waiting when Phin pulled up at the farm. Whatever he did, however much he yelled, she'd just take it. She deserved it.

When he came up on the porch and sat down beside her, he stopped the swing, and she curled her feet under her and sat there, suspended in air, not sure of where she was with him, or even where she wanted to be.

"Did Dillie see it?" she asked him, and he said, "No. Jamie Barclay's mother has a very fast hand with the remote."

"That was not our movie. That was Leo's movie. He took ours and cut the porn stuff into it."

"But you made a porn flick, didn't you?" Phin said, staring out across the yard.

Sophie thought about explaining vanilla porn and decided it was hopeless. "Yes. Not like that one, ours wasn't hard-core, and it was good, but yes."

"And you used the stuff I said in bed," Phin said.

"Yes," Sophie said.

"I wondered why you were so easy," he said. "Research."

"No," she said. "I was so easy because you were so good."

"Don't even try it," he said.

"You forget," she said. "We didn't start out like we are now. It was a game, remember? Julie Ann and the bear on the dock? You thought I was a one-night stand." She swallowed. "And I thought you were a safe chance to break some rules. I didn't think about writing that first scene until after you'd gone that night. And I didn't think you'd ever know. I didn't know you'd ever be important."

He closed his eyes. "You kept on doing it. When you knew we weren't a one-night stand."

"I stopped a long time ago," Sophie said. "Before Stephen caught us in the kitchen, even. Before it was more than you just exercising with me."

"Sophie, it was never just exercise."

"Well, you never told me that." Sophie felt her temper spurt even as she said it. "You make jokes and you stay cool and you do not get involved, and I'm supposed to feel guilty because I don't recognize your deep emotional involvement?"

"You're not supposed to betray the people you sleep with," Phin said.

"By the time I realized there might be something to betray, it was too late," Sophie said. "I owed Amy, too. And we didn't think anybody would ever know. Nobody does know, except for you and Amy. And now the tapes are all gone. There's nothing left of all that work." She lifted her chin. "So you're off the hook."

"Then why does it still feel like it's buried in my back?" Phin said.

He hadn't turned to look at her once, and she lost it and punched him hard on the shoulder so he jerked around. "What do you want from me?" she said. "An apology? I'm sorry, I really am. You want me to destroy the tapes? They're gone. You want me to feel guilty, to suffer? I do, I am. But you're part of this, too, you know. You never said, 'Sophie, you're important to me, Sophie, *this* is important to me.' You never even said, 'I love you.' You remember what you said when I said it on Saturday? You said, 'Thank you.'"

Phin turned away from her, and she said, "'Thank you.' Yeah, that was a clear indication that you cared desperately about the sanctity of our relationship. You arrogant bastard."

"Wait a minute," Phin said. "Why are you yelling at me?"

Sophie stood up, and Phin grabbed the chain as the swing bounced. She said, "Because you betrayed me ten times more than I betrayed you. You knew you cared and you didn't tell me, and now you come out here all wounded, saying it was more than just playing around and *I should have known that*?"

"I'm just saying," Phin said quietly, "that it's pretty much a basic rule that you don't make public what a lover says to you in private."

"What 'private'?" Sophie waved her arm at the yard. "We weren't private. You went down on me on the *dock*. You threw a *lamp* against the wall so you wouldn't have to be alone with me. You did me on a *car*. It was all *a game*. And now you change the rules and you want me to feel guilty? Well, I'm not going to, so there. I've changed my mind. This is your fault."

"My fault." Phin stood up. "*My* fault. That's rich."

"Oh, that's good." Sophie nodded. "Now you can feel indignant and go back into town and lord it over the council meeting tomorrow and patronize everybody and think about how lucky you are to not be involved with somebody as irrational as me because you are clearly the cool one in control and—"

"Sophie, shut up." Phin leaned against the porch post, looking more tired than she'd ever seen him. "I'm so far out of control, I don't think there's anything left of my life."

"Well, then, do something about it instead of standing there all smug," Sophie said. "You're playing so many balls ahead, you don't even know there's a game in front of you."

"You know, I knew you were the devil's candy," Phin said, as if he weren't listening to her at all. "As soon as I set eyes on you, I knew you'd bring me down. You and that mouth."

Sophie stuck out her chin. "And I knew you were a town boy, out to get my virtue and leave me crying." She waited for him to say something snarky about her virtue, but all he did was shake his head.

"We should have gone with our instincts," he said, and started down the porch steps.

Sophie stared after him, nonplussed. "So what did you come out here for?" she called after him. "Vindication? Validation? Revenge? What?"

"I don't know," he said, as he jerked open his car door. "But I sure as hell didn't get it."

"Well, that's the first time you came out here and didn't get what you wanted," Sophie yelled. "You're long overdue to go home empty-handed, as far as I'm concerned."

He stood inside the open car door for a minute and then he said, "Do you know who pushed you into the river?"

"What?" Sophie looked at him incredulously. "What are you talking about? We're in the middle of a fight here." When he stood there, waiting, she said, "No, I've told you a million times, I don't know."

"Because it wasn't Stephen," Phin said. "Which means somebody else is gunning for you."

"It could be anybody," Sophie said. "The whole damn town hates me."

Phin shook his head. "No, they don't. Most of them don't even know you, and the ones that do, like you. Nobody'd want to kill you."

"After tonight they all do," Sophie said.

"Oh, I think they're pretty much concentrating on me, thanks to Stephen." Phin looked grim in the moonlight. "And you're leaving anyway. I'm the one facing the music. And it ain't Dusty Springfield, babe. Have a nice life." He got in the car and slammed the door and started the engine, drowning out anything else she might say, like, *Come back here and fight this out, you bastard.*

When he was gone, Amy came out on the porch and handed her a Dove Bar. Sophie took it and followed her to the swing, which Lassie crawled out from under, now that the shouting had stopped.

"That's not over, you know," Amy said.

"It might be," Sophie said, trying not to sniff. "He's such an uptight jerk, it just might be."

"Nah," Amy said. "He's just trying to figure out what hit him. And what he's going to do with the pieces. He'll be back. He's like us that way. Gets what he wants."

They rocked in silence for a couple of minutes, and then Sophie said, "Are you okay with that? With Phin and me?"

"Yeah." Amy nodded. "Davy was right. And Wes likes him so he must be okay."

"What did Wes say about the video?"

"Not much." Amy bit into her ice cream. "He didn't care about the permit thing at all. He wants to know who switched the tapes and played porn to Temptation, and he wants to nail somebody for shooting Zane, preferably Clea or Davy. I don't know why he's so fixated on them, but he seems sure they know something."

"They're both gone, you know," Sophie said. "She left before he did. I don't think she even told Rob good-bye. So it's just us."

Amy nodded. "I'll stick with you through the council meeting tomorrow. And then I'm going to L.A. Unless we get arrested for violating the permit."

Sophie stopped the swing. "What?"

"Wes said it wouldn't be a big deal and we could come back to the farm. He said he and Phin would work it out because the whole permit thing was probably unconstitutional. But he also said we had to stay until they got it fixed. By Thursday, he said."

"Phin isn't going to fix anything for me," Sophie said. "And I was the only living Dempsey who'd never been in jail."

"Dad will be so proud," Amy said.

"There's a comfort," Sophie said, and rocked for a minute. "Phin said something else. He said Stephen wasn't the one who pushed me."

"And he got this information how?"

Sophie shook her head. "I don't know, but he was sure. And he hates Stephen so if he could have pinned it on him, he would have. So who did?"

"This doesn't make sense," Amy said. "I'd bet money Stephen switched the tapes. If he was out to get you—"

"Why would he be out to get me?" Sophie said. "Phin's the one in his way."

Amy stopped swinging. "So it really was somebody else?"

"Whoever it was, pushed me really hard," Sophie said slowly. "And then watched me fall into that river and get swept away. Somebody really had to hate me to do that. So who was it?"

" 'We all go a little mad sometimes,' " Amy said.

Sophie thought about Liz and Phin and Dillie, trapped together, tearing each other apart. "That has to end," she said. "I have to at least fix that before I go."

"You're not going to go see her, are you?" Amy said.

"I have to," Sophie said. "She's trying to kill me."

Chapter Fifteen

At noon the next day, Phin watched Wes climb the steps to the bookstore. "Good, it's you. I couldn't take one more person telling me how disappointed they were in me, what a loss I am as mayor to have let that happened, or how delighted they'll be not to vote for me in November. It's been a real stampede in here." He rubbed his neck. "And not one of them bought a book."

Wes sat down in his chair and put his feet on the rail. "So it's all over, huh?"

"Looks that way," Phin said. "I've still got six weeks before the election, but this is the kind of thing that sticks in people's minds."

"Yeah." Wes nodded sadly. "So how's Sophie?"

"Furious," Phin said, trying to sound detached about it.

"She's decided it's my fault." He shrugged. "It's better this way. If I'd talked her around, I'd have had to listen to Dusty Springfield every day for the rest of my life."

"Yeah, and there'd have been all that sex, too," Wes said. "That would have gotten old."

"You can shut up anytime now," Phin said.

"And she could kick your ass at pool, too," Wes said.

"So, Amy still going to L.A.?"

"Shut the fuck up," Wes said.

"We did real well, didn't we?" Phin said, giving up on detached. "Christ, I haven't seen a crash-and-burn like this since . . ." He shook his head at the sky. "I've never seen a crash-and-burn like this. We're *good*."

"Finest kind." Wes stood up, letting the legs of his chair hit the porch floor with a thud. "However, unlike you, I am not a quitter. I don't have a plan, but I'm not a quitter."

"I'm not a quitter," Phin said. "I just have no interest in going out there and having Sophie slam the door in my face to 'All Cried Out,' shortly followed by Davy trying to beat me up."

"He's gone," Wes said. "Hit the airport last night and flew to the Bahamas."

Phin straightened a little. "Did he, now?"

"Yep." Wes went down the steps. "So did Clea."

"And you let them go?"

"I can get 'em if I want 'em. I think they're both guilty as hell, but I can't figure out what they did. So I'm not sure I want them."

"But you want Amy," Phin said.

"I'll get Amy." Wes started down the street and then stopped and came back a couple of steps. "Almost forgot. The ballistics report came back. Zane's bullet did not come from your dad's gun."

Phin let his breath out. "Finally, something goes my way." Then he frowned. "So my mother used the gun to frame Sophie, not caring that the ballistics test would trip her up? That doesn't make sense. She's nuts but she's not stupid."

"I think the real gun's in the river," Wes said. "Everything about this yahoo so far says he's impulsive. It would make sense at the time for him to drop the gun in the water after he shot Zane. And with the current the way it's been, I don't think we're going to find it. If that's true, and somebody decided to frame Sophie as an afterthought, he'd have to get another gun. And if all he wanted to do was start gossip about Sophie he wouldn't care about the ballistics report."

"Or she."

Wes shrugged. "God knows, our women are as nuts as our men. Which reminds me, looked at the water tower lately?"

"The water tower?" Phin went down the steps to look up the Hill. "Oh. Nice."

The rain had done its work, washing off the bloody streaks of Stephen's cheap paint, but, as the Coreys had told him, red stains. It was flesh again, but it was a rosy flesh, a glowing flesh, round and full above the trees. Only, the catwalk at the top was still red. "A lipstick with a nipple," Sophie had said, but now it didn't look like a lipstick anymore.

"I like this even better," Wes said. "It's friendlier. And God knows I could use some 'friendly.'"

"Stephen's really going to hate this," Phin said.

"Yeah," Wes said as he started back up the street. "It's going to be some council meeting. See you there."

Phin thought about the meeting and his neck tightened even more. Stephen would be after his butt, his mother would be even more homicidal over the tarnished Tucker legacy, the entire population would want him barbecued for contributing to the delinquency of their minors, and Hildy would ignore it all to protect her new mammary water tower.

And after all of that, Sophie wouldn't give him the time of day because he was a dickhead town boy.

She's a fucking nutcase, he told himself, and concentrated on the stuff that mattered in his life.

He was going to lose the election to that moron Stephen in six weeks, there was something to look forward to. His dad at least had gone down over the New Bridge, something civic. He was going down over a porn flick. And if he hadn't gone down in the first place, he wouldn't be in this mess. The devil's candy, and he'd bit. He closed his eyes against the memory. " 'I coulda been a contendah,' " he said, to nobody in particular, and then walked back up the steps to the book-store.

"Wait a minute," his mother called from the street, and he turned as she reached at the bottom of the steps. "I'm on my way to Hildy's but I want to talk to you first."

"Oh, good," Phin said, and sat down.

"I realize we've had problems," Liz said, as she came up the steps. "But that's all behind us now that you're not going to see that woman again. Things are bad right now, but we have six weeks and if you stay away—"

"Mom, we're going to lose."

"We are *not* going to lose," Liz said. "Tuckers do not lose, we're not going to lose, I'm not going to lose you, we're going to—"

"What are you talking about?" Phin said. "You—" He stopped as what she'd said registered. "Fuck. *That's* what this is about?"

"Watch your language," Liz said. "Everything is—"

"Mom, You're not going to lose me," Phin said. "I'm not

going to die if I don't win. My heart is fine, and even more important, I don't give a damn about being mayor. I care about winning, but not about being mayor. I'm not going to die if I lose."

"Well, of course you're not going to die," Liz said, but her voice shook a little. "Of course not. Now, we'll get everything back to normal. Dillie will forget, and you'll be re-elected, things will be just the same. I think you were right about not getting married again, I won't bring it up anymore, we'll just go back to the way we were." She smiled at him, fiercely cheerful. "Just the three of us again."

Just the three of them. Trapped and frozen in the house on the Hill.

"No," Phin said, and Liz's smile evaporated and the cobra came back.

"Listen to me. I know you're blinded by your hormones on this, but will you just look at where this woman has left you?"

Phin nodded. "With nothing. She destroyed my life."

"Exactly." Liz bit off her words. "But we can get it back again. We—"

"Why the hell would I want to do that?" Phin shook his head at her startled face. "My life was a fucking wasteland; all Sophie did was clear the brush."

"What are you talking about?" Liz said.

"I don't want to be mayor," Phin said. "I never wanted to be mayor. I'll fight for the office this one last time, but don't expect me to give anything more for the Tucker legacy. I've already given too damn much for it."

"This is all because of that woman." Liz looked as if she were about to hyperventilate.

"Yep." *No more mayor*, he thought, and felt wonderful. No more council meetings, no more wrongheaded citizenry, no more fights over streetlights and bridges, just books and Dillie and pool.

And Sophie. The tension seeped from his muscles and he relaxed. Thank God for Sophie and her stupid fucking movie.

"She's corrupted you," Liz said, almost spitting in her frustration. "She's—"

"Well, it runs in her family," Phin said. "The rest of your grandchildren are going to be half-degenerate."

Liz froze.

Phin nodded at her sympathetically. "Yeah, I have to marry her. I'm sorry, Mom. I know this wasn't what you had planned. Any last words before you disown me?"

Liz swallowed and put on her Let's-be-reasonable-or-I'll-kill-you face. "You can't possibly be serious about marrying her. She's a known pornographer."

Phin nodded. "She beat me at pool, too."

"Oh, dear God," Liz said, and sat down on the step.

Sophie waited in front of the courthouse until Liz came into view. Then she got out of the car and said, "I need to talk to you."

Liz kept on walking. "I have *nothing* to say to you."

"Then I'll go to Wes," Sophie said. "He'll keep it quiet, but it would still be better if we just talked here. You know how this town finds out everything."

Liz stood very still for a long minute, her jaw clenched as she stared at Sophie. "In the car," she said finally. "I'd rather people didn't see us together."

Sophie nodded and got back in the car.

"Talk," Liz said, when she was in the car.

"I want you to stop trying to kill me," Sophie said, and Liz lost her frozen expression.

"What?"

"Somebody's been trying to kill me. And you're the only one in this town who hates me enough to do that."

Liz reached for the door. "That's ridic—"

"I understand. I'd do almost anything to protect my family, too. You want the best for Phin and Dillie, and I'm not it, and that's all right because I'm leaving." Sophie leaned forward, projecting sincerity and sanity. "But you have to stop attacking people, Mrs. Tucker. I think you should get help. I know a wonderful therapist in Cincinnati who is very discreet." Liz gaped at her, and Sophie said, "Look, I'm leaving, but sooner or later somebody else is going to get in your way, and this isn't a good method for handling it."

Liz found her voice. "You really think I'd try to kill you?"

"I think you'd do anything to protect Phin and win the election," Sophie said. "I'm not sure which you think is more important, and I don't like that part of you, but I can understand protecting Phin. Just not that way."

Liz sat back. "Exactly what's been happening to you?"

"Mrs. Tucker—"

"I didn't try to kill you." Liz's voice was so dry and matter-of-fact that Sophie began to have second thoughts. "If I'd wanted to hurt you, I have other ways. I'd never put my family in jeopardy by breaking the law."

"Oh," Sophie said.

"What happened?" Liz repeated, and Sophie hesitated and then told her about the river and the gun under the bed and the gossip and the electricity. "And you thought I'd be that stupid?" Liz said when she was finished. "To try to kill you that sloppily?"

"I knew you hated me that much," Sophie said uncertainly. "I didn't think about stupid."

"Whoever's doing this isn't thinking it through," Liz said. "He's stupid and impulsive."

"Stephen Garvey," Sophie said. "But he doesn't have a reason."

"Stephen wouldn't try to electrocute you." Liz stared into the distance, frowning. "He might push you in a rage, but he wouldn't *plan* to kill you. He's not insane."

"Well, nobody else hates me except for you and him," Sophie said. "I'm generally well-liked. Really."

The silence stretched out, and then Liz said, "No, there's somebody else who hates you."

Sophie swallowed. "Oh?"

"Do you know where Hildy Mallow lives?" Liz asked her. "Drive there."

"The Garveys will be here any minute," Hildy told them when they were sitting on her couch. "I still think this should wait until after the council meeting. Have you seen the water tower? There's so much—"

Her doorbell chimed, and Liz said, "Get it. We do this now." She sounded like Phin, and Sophie wasn't at all surprised when Hildy shut up and went.

Virginia Garvey came in, and Sophie could see past her to Hildy's porch, where Stephen checked his watch, bouncing on his heels in anticipation of his greatest council meeting ever. Virginia said, "Are you ready, Hildy? We're running a little—" and stopped dead when she saw Sophie. "What is she doing here?"

"Shut the door, Hildy," Liz said, and Hildy did, keeping her back against it. "Virginia, did you push Sophie into the river?"

"Liz!" Virginia looked outraged. "What a thing to—"

"I'll be damned," Hildy said. "Of course you did. It would be just like you. Impulsive and dumb as a rock. What did she do, wear white shoes after Labor Day?"

Sophie looked down at her white Keds and pulled her feet back a little.

"Hildy!" Virginia turned from one woman to the other. "This is ridiculous. I don't have to stand here—"

"Actually, you do," Liz said. "You tried to kill Sophie. Twice." The disgust in her voice was plain, and Virginia whipped her head around as if she'd been struck on the raw.

"Don't *you* defend her," she said. "You're on *my* side. You know what she is. If it hadn't been for her, Rachel would be married to Phin—"

"Phin is never going to marry Rachel," Liz said.

"Rachel was going to marry him until *she* showed up," Virginia said. "*She's* the one who introduced Rachel to that man who told her he'd find her a job in *Los Angeles*." The way Virginia spit the words out, she might have been saying, "Gomorrah," which was fair, Sophie thought. "She's the one who *seduced* Phin away from Rachel."

"I swear to God, he seduced me," Sophie said.

"You think it's funny." Virginia took a step forward, and Sophie sank back a little into the sofa cushions. "You ruined my baby's life. I made sure Phin coached her at softball, I made sure she baby-sat his daughter, I made sure she got a job on the council, *I made sure he was going to marry her.*"

"Oh, Christ," Liz said. "*Virginia.*"

"And then you come in and you take Phin and you tell Rachel she should leave, and she does." Virginia shook with rage. "She called me. She's in *California*. And *it's all your fault.*"

Virginia was breathing hard now, and Sophie tensed to duck if she came after her, no longer doubting that Virginia was the one who'd shoved her into the river. Virginia would have shoved her into Hell if she could have.

Then Virginia got a grip. "But I didn't try to *kill* her," she said to Liz, with a tense little laugh. "That would be . . . insane."

"Exactly," Liz said.

Virginia laughed again, buddies. "Liz, our kind of people don't do that kind of thing."

"There is no kind of people that includes you and me," Liz said. "I always said Stephen married beneath him."

Virginia went white, only two spots of color high on her cheeks.

"Did you push Diane?" Liz said.

Virginia drew herself up. "If I had, it would have been just what she deserved, grabbing your son like that, ruining his life. If I had, you should be thanking me now. But I didn't. Nobody pushed her. She was a slutty little drunk who fell down her own steps."

"Here's what I know," Liz said. "I know you took my husband's gun from my house because you're the only one who visited me there. I know you put it in Sophie's bed because you started the gossip that it had been found. I know you know the farm and could have frayed that wire in the fuse box with no trouble at all."

"That's not proof," Virginia said. "You don't have any proof because I didn't do anything."

"I know you were out there watching with Stephen the night Sophie was pushed in the river," Liz said. "You wouldn't miss something like that. Sophie saw Stephen right before she was pushed—so it couldn't have been him—so you pushed her in, and when that didn't work, you stole my gun and put it in her bed, and when that didn't work you tried to electrocute her. You *are* dumb as a rock, Virginia, but what I still don't know is if you shot that man."

"He met somebody on the river path," Sophie said. "Wes got that far: that Zane had an appointment to meet somebody behind the Garvey house."

"He was trying to blackmail all of us," Hildy said, helpfully. "He must have had something on her."

"He had a file on Diane's death," Liz said. "He brought it to me and tried to convince me she'd been murdered. He said if we didn't stop the video, he'd do a human-interest piece on it, investigate it, solve the mystery, create a scandal. Except I didn't push Diane, and neither did my son, so I sent him away."

"My God," Sophie said, watching Virginia's face. "You did push Diane."

"You just shut up," Virginia said. "You're just like her, but I did *not* push her."

"You met him on the path because he was trying to blackmail you, and you shot him," Liz said. "How did you get him to the farm dock? He would have been heavy. Unless . . ." Liz frowned in thought. "Unless you convinced him to let you take him home." She nodded. "That was it, wasn't it? You told him you'd take care of him and you rowed him across the river, and when he got out onto the dock on his own, then you shot him. You *mothered* him to death. That would be like you. And you got Stephen to cover your car accidents, and me to harass my son about Sophie for you, so you could certainly get that stupid man to travel to his own death."

"You shot him from a boat?" Hildy looked at Virginia with disgust. "That's why you missed at close range and why the angle was so off. You shot him while you were *standing in a boat*. What kind of idiot are you?"

"I have no idea what you're talking about," Virginia said.

"But I want you to know I'm deeply hurt by this. And I'm leaving."

She looked deeply enraged, to Sophie.

"Of course, we can't prove any of this," Hildy said gloomily to Liz, as Virginia reached past her to tug at the door.

She's going to get away with it, Sophie thought, and then she saw Liz smile her cobra smile.

"We don't have to prove it," Liz said. "We'll just talk."

"What?" Hildy frowned, and then brightened. "Oh. Yes. We will. We'll talk a lot, Virginia."

Oh, excellent, Sophie thought.

Virginia stopped tugging on the door.

"About how much you hate Sophie," Hildy went on happily. "About how you don't have an alibi for the shooting." Hildy let her eyes slide to Virginia's face. "About how Rachel ran to L.A. to get away from you."

Virginia's face went red. "She didn't. Rachel and I are very close. And—"

"We'll tell everybody what a lousy mother you are," Hildy said. "We don't have to take you to Wes. We're taking care of this ourselves."

"Unless," Liz said.

Virginia turned to her, seething.

"At the council meeting today," Liz said. "We're going to be watching your vote very closely."

"You can't—" Virginia began again.

"Yes, we can." Hildy was practically bouncing on her toes now. "One wrong vote and we hit the phones. And people will listen. They always listen, don't they, Virginia?"

Virginia's eyes darted from Hildy to Liz. She looked like a trapped mink, and Sophie would have felt sorry for her if she hadn't been such a miserable excuse for a human being.

"Cross me again and I'll destroy you," Liz said to Virginia. "Don't ever come after my family again."

"I didn't—" Virginia said.

"And that includes Sophie," Liz said.

Sophie felt a catch in the back of her throat.

"Right, that's the other part of the deal," Hildy was saying. "You have to stop trying to kill Sophie. She gets a hangnail, and we pick up the phone."

Virginia drew a deep breath in through her teeth and looked at Sophie like death.

"Don't even think about it," Liz Tucker said. "You touch her, you say one word against her, and I'll bring you so low not even Junie Martin will give you the time of day."

"Jeez," Sophie said.

Liz looked at Sophie for the first time since they'd arrived. "Don't ever cross a Tucker."

"No ma'am," Sophie said.

The council hall was full by the time Phin got there, and the crowd was clearly not a happy one, but only Ed and Frank sat at the council table.

Amy and Sophie came in and sat down in the front row.

"'This isn't the junior chamber of commerce, Brad,'" Sophie said to Amy.

Amy nodded, looking around at the marble and walnut. "'Thank goodness we're in a bowling alley.'"

Nervous, Phin thought, and couldn't blame them.

Sophie turned and saw him. She stuck her chin out, and he thought, *Oh, good, still frosty.* Then Stephen and Virginia came in followed by Hildy and Liz, and he ignored Sophie to concentrate on the problem at hand.

Stephen looked fat with satisfaction as he stopped to shake hands and nod to the populace, but Virginia looked tense and mad as hell. Hildy detoured around them and plopped down in the seat across from Phin. "'Fasten your seat belts, it's going to be a bumpy night,'" she said, but she didn't look nervous at all.

"What are you up to?" he said, and she beamed and said, "Oh, I'm going to *enjoy* this."

Phin frowned at her, but then his mother sat down and shook his concentration. She had that look in her eye, the one she got right before she mutilated somebody: implacable will mixed with certainty of triumph.

"Mom?" he said, and she shook her head and said, "It's all right, Phin," and he sat back, wary as hell.

"All right," Phin said. "Now all we need is Rachel and we can get started. Where—"

"She's gone," Virginia said through her teeth, and Stephen looked at her, startled. "That woman—" She broke off as Hildy leaned forward and met her eyes. "She's not here."

"Okay." Phin nodded to Hildy. "Keep the minutes, please."

"Of course," Hildy said. "Although I'm only going to write down the intelligent things, so if anybody here was going to make a stupid speech, he can forget about getting it into the record."

"Hildy," Phin said, and Stephen said, "I don't need the record. I've got the whole town here, or most of it. And the ones that aren't here will hear about it later."

"Don't count on it," Hildy said, and Phin wondered what the hell was happening under his nose. Besides his political ruin.

"The first item of business," Phin said, when they were all settled and the crowd had stilled in anticipation, "is the streetlight vote that Stephen Garvey wants recalled." A soft murmur of disappointment went up from the crowd, and Phin knew how the lions had felt in the Coliseum. "The motion on the floor is from Hildy Mallow, to purchase vintage reproduction streetlights for Temptation. Hildy, do you want to address this again?"

"Just what I've said before," Hildy said. "It makes a difference to people when they're surrounded by beauty. We owe it to Temptation to look to the future."

"Anyone el—"

"But we also owe it to Temptation to be fiscally responsible," Stephen said, and waxed eloquent on fiscal responsibility for five minutes.

Phin tuned him out and felt uneasy. The crowd was restless, but his mother and Hildy sat back, calm. That was wrong. "Anybody else?" Phin said, when Stephen had wound down. "No? Call the roll, Hildy."

"Garvey."

"Certainly not," Stephen said.

"Garvey," Hildy purred, and Virginia turned to look at her.

Across the table from Phin, his mother shook her head and Hildy nodded.

Virginia smiled. "No."

Hildy turned to glare at Liz, who looked taken aback. "We need a little consensus here," Hildy hissed at Liz, who whispered back, "Well, Stephen's convinced people they're too expensive."

The vote split, three to three—Frank voting with Hildy and Ed because fancier streetlights would make his development look better—and Phin broke the tie, saying, "Yes. Let's go with posterity."

"Oh, sure," somebody from the crowd called. "You care about our kids."

"That's progeny," Phin said. "Posterity is your kids' kids."

"Phin," his mother said, and he shrugged.

"New business," he said.

"The water tower," Stephen said, taking him by surprise. "We're going to have to paint it again. It looks . . . well, we're just going to have to paint it."

"I like it," Hildy said. "It's not as good as the original color, of course, but if somebody hadn't messed with it before, we wouldn't have this problem now. It's still pretty. Leave it be."

"You want that thing—"

"Can I have a motion?" Phin said.

"I move we paint the water tower *white*," Stephen said, and Virginia started to say, "I second," and then stopped.

"We need a second," Phin said to prod her.

"I second," Frank said. "What's going on here?"

"Call the roll, Hildy," Phin said, before Stephen could get into the water tower as a further corrupter of the town's children.

"Garvey," Hildy said, and Stephen said, "Yes!"

Hildy turned to Liz and whispered audibly, "It does *not* get painted."

"It looks *awful*," Liz hissed back.

"Hildy?" Phin said. "The roll?"

"Garvey," Hildy said, and Virginia looked down the table. Liz nodded and Hildy shook her head.

"Oh, for crying out loud," Sophie said from behind them, and Liz and Hildy flinched.

The vote split again, and Phin broke the tie by saying, "No, we're not spending any more time or money on the water tower."

"Just what we'd expect from a porn mayor," somebody in the crowd called out, and Phin said to Hildy, "How come you paint it and I get the flack?"

"Because I'm a sweet old lady," Hildy said. "Let's get to it, shall we?"

"Oh, sure," Phin said. "If there's no other new businesses—"

Stephen opened his mouth.

"—I have some. It has come to my attention that this council passed an ordinance that is unenforceable because of the vagaries in its wording."

Hildy blinked at him, and his mother looked alarmed.

Phin said, "I move that the council repeal the antiporn ordinance it voted into effect two weeks ago before we get sued for overstepping somebody's constitutional rights."

The murmur from the crowd sounded angry, but Ed's "I second," cut right across it.

It was the first motion Ed had seconded in thirty years, and Phin looked at him appraisingly.

"Good to see you got your thumb out of your butt, boy," Ed said.

"Thanks, Ed," Phin said. "Discussion?"

"I have discussion," Stephen snapped. "Somebody clearly violated that ordinance—"

"Can't talk about that, Stephen," Hildy said briskly. "We can only talk about the issue on the table."

"It didn't violate anything," Stephen said.

"Yes, it did," Phin said. "You can't make a law against something you can't define. And we didn't define pornography. Therefore the ordinance is unconstitutional. We could get sued. For the protection of the town's treasury, we have to repeal it."

"That is the biggest—"

"I'll call the roll," Hildy said. "Garvey."

"*No*," Stephen said. "This is—"

"Garvey," Hildy said over him, and turned razorlike eyes on Virginia.

Virginia looked down the table, and raised her eyebrows, as smug as her husband.

And Liz nodded with Hildy.

"Garvey," Hildy repeated viciously.

Virginia swallowed. "Yes."

"What?" Stephen turned on his wife, white-faced. "Have you lost your mind?"

"Virginia votes her conscience, Stephen," Hildy said crisply. "Now stop trying to intimidate a council member. Lutz."

"No," Frank said. "They ruined my life and I want them to pay."

"That's very adult of you, Frank," Hildy said. "Mallow— yes. Tucker."

"Yes," Liz said, and Phin thought, *I have no idea what's going on here, but I like it.*

"Yarnell," Hildy said, and before Ed finished his "yes," she said, "The motion passes."

"That pretty well wraps this up," Phin said, and Stephen said, "Oh, no it doesn't. Somebody showed pornography to our citizens and they should pay."

"And as soon as we find out who switched the tapes, Chief Mazur will arrest him," Phin said. "But until then—"

"What about the people who made the pornography?" Stephen said. "What about the person who *abetted* them? What about—"

"Okay, I've had enough," Sophie said, and Phin turned to see her standing up in the front row in her pink dress, looking like Gidget the Fury.

Don't do this, he thought, going tense in his chair, *We were almost out of here.*

"I can speak, can't I?" she said to Hildy. "As long as it's on the issue?"

"No, you can't," Stephen said, leaning forward to expound

at the same time Hildy said, "Sure, go ahead." Hildy turned back to Virginia and said, "Shut your husband up before he violates her freedom of speech."

Virginia stiffened and then said viciously under her breath, "Shut up, Stephen. This is all your fault anyway."

Stephen sat back, stunned, and Phin sympathized. He didn't know what the hell was going on, either.

Sophie cleared her throat, and Phin thought, *Keep it short.* He'd save her from the mob if he had to, but it would be a lot easier if she just apologized and sat down.

"My name is Sophie Dempsey, and I'm responsible for the tape you saw last night." The crowd began to murmur, and Sophie raised her voice. "I'm responsible, because I knew somebody had cut those obscene parts into the beautiful love story we made here, and I didn't destroy that awful tape. And because I didn't destroy it, somebody broke into our farmhouse and stole it and played it to you all last night. That was a horrible thing, an unforgivable thing, but I believe that your police chief will ultimately find out who was to blame. You have a terrific police force here." The majority of the crowd stared back, hostile, but a couple of people nodded, and Amy folded her hands and put two fingers out, smiling to herself.

"So I apologize for my mistake," Sophie went on smoothly. "You see, I love Temptation so much and I feel so safe here, I didn't even lock my doors so it was easy to steal from me. That was stupid of me and I won't make that mistake again."

A couple more people shook their heads at how dumb she'd been, but they looked vaguely sympathetic, and Amy extended three fingers.

"If I could, I'd show you the real tape because Temptation looked wonderful in it, but unfortunately, whoever stole that vile tape to sabotage the premiere, also took everything we had. *Cherished* is gone forever."

Thank God, Phin thought, and kept a wary eye on the crowd.

"However, to make it up to you, my sister and I would be more than happy to tape your next theater performance so that can be shown on your cable channel."

Frank sat up at that, looking vaguely cheerful for the first time in weeks, and Amy looked surprised. She looked down at her hand and extended her fourth finger.

"The most important thing now, though," Sophie said, "is to help the police find the pervert who thought it would be a good idea to show pornography to schoolchildren." Sophie sounded outraged, and Phin wondered if that was real or con. He was pretty sure the rest of it was a con, but at least the populace wasn't trying to lynch her.

"So what I'm asking you all to do, is to think about who has the most to gain from this," Sophie said earnestly, and one or two people began to look interested.

"The mayor did it," the heckler said from the back, and Sophie said, "Why? That would be political suicide, I've even heard some people are so shortsighted that they're talking about not voting for him, but they can't be thinking this through. He'd have to be crazy to play that tape."

"He is," the heckler shouted back, and Sophie said, "No, he isn't, and you should be ashamed of yourself for just shouting things out instead of standing up for what you believe in, the way your mayor does. The people of this town don't like cowards and they don't like cheats, which is why they're not listening to you and why they're going to find out who really did this. The people of Temptation are too smart to fall for this. You're all upset now, but pretty soon you're all going to be asking yourselves the smart question: Who has the most to gain? It's your *civic duty* to ask that question, all of you."

She let the silence hang there, and Phin thought, *Don't look at Stephen, let them get there on their own.*

Sophie nodded. "You all know this town so much better than I do, you'll figure this out, and then I know you'll punish the culprit properly. Thank you." She sat down abruptly, and Phin could see her hands shaking.

Amy held out five fingers and said, "You got everything but the smile."

"I can't work miracles," Sophie said, and Phin thought, *The hell you can't.*

Because she'd made porn, and she was getting away with it. Stephen couldn't get her for it because he'd stolen the tapes, and if he produced them to get her, the townspeople would know he had been responsible for the debacle the night before.

Hell of a woman, his Sophie.

Phin leaned over. "Not bad," he told her, and she lifted her chin, still shaking, and said, "I was magnificent."

"I want to know what she was getting at," Stephen was blustering loudly, and Phin leaned back and said, "No, you don't, that's the last thing you want to know. I declare this meeting adjourned."

Hildy said, "Works for me," and stood up. "You can all go home now," she told the crowd. "Show's over."

"Wait a minute," Stephen said, and Virginia turned to him with loathing.

"This is all your fault, all of it," she told him, and got up and left, leaving her stunned husband behind her.

"Some days are like that, Stephen," Phin said, as he stood up to go.

"Sit down, I want to talk to you," Liz said, and Phin nodded as he watched the crowd. Most of them were still throwing him dirty looks, but one or two looked at Stephen with some curiosity.

Sophie went out with Amy and Hildy, and nobody said anything to her, nasty or otherwise, so she was going to be fine. Better than fine, if he had anything to do with it.

Then Wes came to stand in the doorway and caught his eye, motioning to him as people filed out around him.

"Make this fast," he told his mother as he nodded to Wes. "I have things to do."

Rachel sat by the garden at Leo's house, marveling at where she'd ended up. It looked like paradise. Leo's tiled pool sparkled blue in the sunlight, and there were palm trees, real palm trees, and blooming hibiscus, and up by the hot tub there was a lemon tree that really grew lemons.

She couldn't wait for Sophie to see that. She could pick them right off the tree and make lemonade.

Leo came out and sat down on the chaise next to her, still looking slightly stunned, and handed her a glass of what looked like sludgy orange juice.

"What is this?" Rachel said, looking at it with deep suspicion.

"Vitamin citrus smoothie," Leo said. "Drink it. It's good for you."

Rachel sipped it. It wasn't bad. "It's great." She looked at Leo over the glass. "Thank you."

"I'm going to hell for this," Leo said, and Rachel knew he wasn't talking about the smoothie. "Your father is going to come after me with a shotgun."

"He doesn't have a shotgun," Rachel said. "He has a nice rifle, though." Which he would probably use if he had any idea of the things Leo had done to her in his bedroom. Amazing, the things older men knew.

Not to mention how much longer they lasted.

She grinned again, the silly, satisfied grin that she couldn't keep off her face even though it made her look like a dork. She was in L.A. now. She was supposed to be sophisticated. A producer's mistress wasn't supposed to grin like somebody who'd just had the first great sex of her life.

"Twenty years old." Leo shook his head.

"I am not the first twenty-year-old you've slept with," Rachel said. "Cut me a break. How dumb do you think I am?"

"No, but you're the first twenty-year-old I'm going to marry," Leo said. "How dumb does that make me?"

Rachel straightened. "Marry?"

Leo sighed. "Yeah."

"You're going to marry me?"

"I think it's best for the kids. Especially if one of them's going to be mayor of Temptation someday. You know how those people are."

"Leo." Rachel felt tears come to her eyes, which was ridiculous because she hadn't even realized she wanted to be married. But she did. Her mother would be so happy.

Leo's face softened. "I'll take care of you, Rachel. You'll never be sorry."

Rachel nodded through her tears. "And I'll take care of you, too. You think you don't need it, but you do."

"I'm sure I do," Leo said, patting her hand.

"No, really." Rachel put the smoothie down and went into the house for her bag. When she came back out she said, "I was going to use this to convince you I should have that production job, but now it can be a wedding present. Although I still want that production job."

"You've got it, you've got it." Leo peered in the bag. "What have you got?"

Rachel pulled out a videotape and handed it to him and watched his face go slack with surprise.

"Don't tell me—"

"Yep." She patted his arm. "It's *Cherished*, the last version. I found it in Daddy's car, along with all the other tapes when I threw my bag in the trunk. I called Wes and told him where we left the car so he can find the others, but I knew you'd want this one."

Leo looked at her with wonder. "You're amazing."

Rachel nodded and crawled onto the chaise with him. "I'm beginning to see that. And that's just in Temptation. Imagine what I can do now that we're in L.A."

"Imagine," Leo said, putting his arm around her.

Rachel looked out over the lemon tree and the palm fronds and the hibiscus and thought, *This is all mine. I'm going to be Rachel Kingsley. A movie producer.* Then she narrowed her eyes at the hibiscus.

"Leo, who weeds this place?" Rachel said.

"The gardener," Leo said.

"Fabulous," Rachel said, and relaxed into her new life.

At roughly the same time, Davy watched Clea come out of SuisseInvest Limited of the Bahamas, cross the street, and slump down onto one of the brightly painted benches that lined the edge of the beach. It had taken her long enough to get the bad news. If he'd thought he had a couple million in a bank somewhere, he wouldn't have dawdled.

She wasn't dawdling now, she was in shock. He was sympathetic. So were any number of men who slowed as they went by her. Time to get a move on. He crossed the street and sat down beside her. "Hey, Clea," he said. "Heard you're broke."

She jerked her head up and then her eyes narrowed. "What are you doing here?"

"Saving your life, which is more than you deserve," Davy said. "In fact, if you didn't have something my sister wants, I'd probably let you rot. You're a fairly miserable human being, you know."

"What are you doing here?" Clea said again.

"That's good. Focus." He put his hands in his pockets and stretched his legs out. "Let's see. You just went into that bank and found out that the bank book you took off Zane's body is for an empty account."

Clea looked around to see if anyone was listening. "I don't know what you're talking about."

"When Zane was fibrillating on the dock," Davy said slowly and distinctly, "you went through his pockets and found the bank book. And then you sat there and watched him die. And I stood on the back porch and watched you do it because I thought the poor son of a bitch was drunk." He felt his anger rise again, that he'd been that stupid, that she'd been that callous. "You can go to jail for that, Clea. It's called 'depraved indifference,' and you could go away for a nice chunk of time."

"You can't prove it," Clea said.

"I can do you a lot of damage," Davy said. "Temptation is the one place on earth where the mayor and the police chief will listen to me." She looked at him with unadulterated loathing and he shrugged. "Do what I tell you to and neither one of us will have to go back there."

Clea flopped back against the bench. "Great. Now I have to sleep with you."

"I wouldn't have you," Davy said, and Clea glared at him. "Okay, it's probably because I already have had you, but I like to think it's also because you're such a cold, conniving, murderous bitch. Pay attention. You're going to sign over the deed to that farmhouse to Sophie."

"No, I'm not," Clea said. "I'm selling it to Frank for three-quarters of a million."

"Sure," Davy said. "Go back to Temptation, explain why you let Zane die, deal with the police and the lawyers, and when you're done, how much of that three-quarters will there be left?"

"More than I'd have if I just give the damn thing to Sophie," Clea said.

"No, you'll have three-quarters of a million if you give it to Sophie," Davy said. "That's how much I'll transfer into an account for you once you send off the deed."

"And where would you get—" Clea began and then she turned on him. "You've got my money!"

"*My* money," Davy said. "It's been mine since the night Zane died and I copied the number and password out of the book in your bedroom while you were talking to the police. One wire transfer, and it was mine."

"How could you do that?" Clea said. "I had the bank book."

"It's not a passbook account, dummy," Davy said. "It's a pass*word* account. All you need is the account number and the password."

Clea looked at him with such venom, he almost moved back. "You son of a bitch."

"This is pretty easy, Clea," Davy said. "You give Sophie the farm, I give you seven hundred and fifty thousand dollars, you use it to find your next rich guy, and everybody lives happily ever after. Hell, you'll probably inherit more from Zane."

"There was a lot more than that in that account," Clea said.

"Sure was."

"I could have had all of that *and* the three-quarters from the farm," she said, and her voice had a vicious edge.

"The key words being 'could have had,'" Davy said. "That was then, this is now, and I'm bored with this conversation. You have one hour to bring me that deed transfer and the number of an account where I can transfer your money. After that, the price drops."

Clea's face smoothed out and became lovely again. "You know . . ." she said, leaning closer.

"Nope," Davy said warily. "I told you. I'm not interested."

"If you really thought I was a murderer, you wouldn't let me go," Clea said, sliding closer to him, and this time Davy did move back. "I know you. I know what you did to Chet in Iowa."

"Chad."

"You'd want me punished," Clea said silkily as she leaned closer. "Want to punish me, Davy?"

"I already did," Davy said flatly. "I took your money." He checked his watch. "Fifty-nine minutes."

"We could have it all," Clea said, putting her hand on his arm. "You and me." She was breathtaking in the sunlight, like human whipped cream.

"No, we couldn't," Davy said, trying to ignore his body's interest. "Sophie wants that farmhouse."

"Sophie?" Clea laughed low. "Sophie's just your sister. I—"

"You'll never get it, will you?" Davy said.

Clea drew back. "What?"

"Family," Davy said. "Strongest force in the world. Even trumps lust. Go get the deed."

Clea looked at him with undisguised malevolence. "This is not over, you bastard."

"Oh, yes it is," Davy said. "Because I'm sure as hell finished with it. Go get the deed."

Clea drew a deep breath and shoved herself off the bench, and Davy watched her stride back to the hotel, magnificent in her fury.

"Actually it doesn't trump lust," Davy said, when she was too far away to hear him. "It just trumps you."

"You're sure I can't talk you out of this?" Sophie said, as Amy threw her suitcase in the backseat with the rest of the camera equipment.

"Positive." Amy came back to the porch steps where Sophie stood. "I really need to just go. And maybe after a couple of months, I'll want to come back. This place has some good stuff in it."

Sophie tried to sound skeptical. "You think the good stuff is just going to sit around and wait until you come back?"

"If he's the good stuff, he will," Amy said. "But I'm not counting on it. He never even made a pass. Three weeks, and he never made a move on me."

"You didn't give him any openings."

"I didn't want to." Amy stepped back. "But he could have made one anyway. And he didn't talk to me today before the council meeting, he just took off to go to the airport for something."

"I'm sure it was important," Sophie said. "Things are a little hectic in Temptation these days."

Amy sighed. "Yeah, but he knows I'm leaving and he went to the airport anyway." She straightened her shoulders. "And I really do want to see L.A. Even if Davy says I'll hate it, I want to see it." She gave Sophie a weak smile. "I'll come back for Thanksgiving. You'll have me and Davy, just like always."

"Good enough," Sophie said, trying not to cry. She hugged

Amy good-bye, holding on tight for a minute, and then Amy pulled away to walk to the car without looking back.

"Be *careful*," Sophie called after her, and Amy waved without turning and got in the car, and Sophie realized from the way she bent over the steering wheel that she was crying. "It's okay," she called out to Amy, "you're doing the right thing. Stay out of bat country. Everything will be fine. Nothing but good times."

Amy nodded. She backed up the convertible and made her U-turn to get out of Temptation, and then she was gone.

This is good, Sophie told herself. *We needed our own lives. This is good.*

She sighed once and then walked through the house and out the back door, letting Lassie out with her this time. "So it's just us," Sophie said, as they walked down the hill. "A girl and her dog." Lassie barked and ran down to the dock, and Sophie followed her and kicked off her shoes to sit on the edge and dangle her feet in the water. The river was still high from the rain, and fast, and it flowed cool and sweet past her ankles.

"So here's the thing, dog," Sophie said. "We're out of a job, living in a house we're going to be evicted from at any minute, deserted by our siblings, discarded by our uptight lover, and with nothing to show for it because a creep of a politician stole all our work." Lassie lay down beside her, evidently overcome by the enormity of it all. "I'm looking for a bright side here, Lassie, I'm looking for a rainbow, but I am not seeing one." Lassie pricked up her ears. "Okay, forget the rainbow. What we need is a plan."

Lassie barked and bounded off the dock, and when Sophie turned around, she saw Dillie on the porch, crouched down to meet the dog, and Phin walking down the slope toward her, looking as perma-pressed as ever in his white shirt and khakis. "Hello," she said, and turned back to the river to get a grip. *Don't throw yourself at him*, she told herself, scrambling for a plan. *At least not for the first five seconds.*

Phin sat down behind her on the dock, and Sophie hugged herself to keep from reaching out and grabbing him. She could smell the sun on his shirt and feel the heat from his arm where it almost touched her.

"I'd have been here sooner, but we were waiting for Amy," Phin said. "Wes caught a ride with her to L.A."

Sophie forgot playing it cool and turned to look at him. "With Amy?"

Phin nodded, staring out over the river. "He's got so much vacation time, he can take it anytime he wants. So I suggested he take six weeks to go with her. He thought it was a good idea, and she didn't seem to mind." He stared out over the river. "It looked like the beginning of a beautiful friendship."

His sleeve brushed her bare arm, and she stifled her sigh and told herself, *Easy.* "Although six weeks is a long time," she said to make conversation, and then she frowned as she thought about it. "That's a really long time. Can Duane handle it that long?"

"No," Phin said. "Wes got somebody else to cover for him." He met her eyes, and his weren't as cool as they should have been. "Can we stop talking about Wes now?"

Sophie swallowed hard and gave up on cool. "Listen, I am really, really, really sorry about the premiere and the election, because we did make porn even though that wasn't our movie—"

"I know," Phin said. "You also helped Rachel elope with Leo, you didn't tell us Davy and Clea skipped, and you did something really vicious to Virginia Garvey. I'd love to know what that was."

He didn't seem angry as he went down her list of sins,

and he was sitting awfully close to her just to give her a hard time. Maybe she didn't need a plan after all. "Right. So sue me."

"For what?" Phin said. "You don't have any money." Sophie stuck her chin in the air. "I'm going to own this farm pretty soon."

"Really." Phin seemed interested. "And how are you going to do that?"

Sophie let her chin drop. "I don't know, exactly. Davy's going to fix it."

"Sure he is."

"Davy's never promised me anything he hasn't delivered," Sophie said. "I believe in Davy."

"As he does in you." Phin shook his head. "But he doesn't have the—" He stopped and she stole a look at him as she felt him straighten. He looked stunned. "Son of a bitch. He's got Zane's money."

Sophie blinked. "I don't think so. He didn't say anything about it."

Phin shook his head. "He's got it."

Sophie thought about it and decided he was right. It would be like Davy to find money and separate it from those who didn't deserve it. "Well, if he has it, I'm glad. At least somebody gets a happy ending out of this mess. Although, I'd be happier if the film we slaved over for a month still existed." *And if you were doing more than just sitting here.* "I still can't believe that lousy Stephen stole the tapes. And now they're gone and he's going to be mayor."

"Oh, you never know," Phin said. "Those tapes could be stashed somewhere, just waiting to be found. Anything can happen."

Sophie looked at him, exasperated. "You know, just once I'd like to see you sweat over something."

Phin scowled at her. "In the past three weeks, you've seen me sweat more than anybody else on the planet, woman."

Sophie waved her hand. "I meant—"

"I even yelled at you last night." Phin eased up. "For which I apologize."

"It was kind of nice," Sophie said. "At least you knew I was there."

"Oh, hell, Sophie, I always know you're there." Phin rolled toward her on one hip, and Sophie felt a flare of hope, but he was just digging something out of his back pocket. "Here." He held out an emerald-cut diamond ring the size of her head. "Marry me, Julie Ann. Ruin the rest of my life."

"Hello." Sophie gaped at the ring. "Jeez, that thing is huge. Where did you get it?"

"My mother gave it to me," Phin said, sounding bemused.

Then the other shoe dropped. "Marry you?" Sophie said, and the sun came out and the birds began to sing and the river sent up a cheer. Marriage was probably out—Liz as a mother-in-law was too terrifying to contemplate, and Phin would never get elected again if he was married to a pornographer—but suddenly everything else was looking pretty good.

Phin was still talking. "After the council meeting, she said, 'If you're going to marry that woman—'"

"'That woman'?" Sophie said. "Oh, gee, the holidays would have been swell."

"—'do it right,' and she took this off her finger, and handed it to me." Phin shook his head. "Surprised the hell out of me. She didn't seem upset about it at all."

"I thought you were never going to speak to me again," Sophie said.

"Then you haven't been paying attention," Phin said. "And the holidays are going to be fine. If I have to put up with

Davy, you can put up with my mother. I already told her we'd be using 'I Only Want to Be with You' instead of 'The Wedding March,' and she took that pretty well, too. Concentrate. You want this ring or not?"

It was so gorgeous. Against her better instincts, Sophie took it to hold it up to the sunlight. Amy could have lit the entire house with it. "I don't think I can live up to this ring."

"You don't have any choice," Phin said. "All the Tucker brides get it. I thought I was going to have to ice-pick Mom to get it to you, but she came through after all. There's a question on the table here. Are you going to marry me?"

Sophie looked at the ring again and sighed. "No," she said and handed it back. "But I'll love you forever and you can come sleep with me whenever you want." She stretched to kiss him, so happy that she felt like bouncing.

Phin leaned away from her. "Why not?"

"Because I ruined your reputation," Sophie said. "And because I don't want to live in that damn big house on the Hill, I want to live here. And because we've only know each other three weeks and that's too soon. But I like everything else about you, so I don't see a problem here." She leaned toward him again. "Kiss me, you fool."

Phin shook his head. "My reputation will recover, we can live here, and three weeks is plenty of time when they're like the last ones. I doubt we'll have to survive this much stress again for the rest of our lives."

"You're missing some good stuff here," Sophie said, annoyed that she wasn't getting kissed.

Phin shook his head again. "You don't get me unless you marry me. I have standards. I'm the mayor."

"Only for another six weeks." Sophie pulled back, frowning at him.

"If I'm going to win the election," Phin said patiently, "I can't be cohabitating with a known pornographer. Weddings are popular. A big plus on the election trail."

"What trail?" Sophie gestured to the yard. "We're in Temptation. You barely have an election bike path. And if you're really going to try to beat Stephen—"

"I'm not going to *try* to beat Stephen," Phin said, "I'm going to annihilate Stephen." He handed her the ring back. "Put that on and stop playing hard-to-get. God knows, you never have before."

"Hey," Sophie said, but the ring glinted like an arc light, so she held it up again just to see it sparkle.

"You'll like being the mayor's wife," Phin said. "You get to wear the ring all the time. And you can run for city council and torture Stephen."

"Mmmm." Sophie tilted the ring in the sun and watched it glow. It was huge. And politics might be fun. "Stephen's probably not going to be running for council—Stephen's going to be mayor, remember?" Sophie brought the ring into the shadow of their bodies and still it sparkled.

"Wes made Stephen acting police chief while he's gone."

Sophie tore her eyes from the ring. "What? Is he insane? Stephen with unlimited power will drive everybody in town craz—"

She stopped as the beauty of it hit her.

"Dear God. I've underestimated Wes."

"Many do," Phin said. "Will you please say yes, so I can have my last term as mayor *and* unlimited, headbanging sex? I don't think this is too much to ask. I've apologized for being a prick the other night, and I'm giving you a great ring."

"I haven't heard the *L* word, so I'm assuming this is really a political move," Sophie said, and Phin said, "Oh, for crying out loud," and kissed her, and he felt so good against her, his mouth hot against hers, that she kissed him back hard, gripping his shirt for dear life, as Dillie yelled, "Yes!" from the porch.

Phin pulled back and frowned at her. "Are you going to put that ring on? You have to now. Dillie thinks she's getting a mother."

Sophie caught her breath. "You really want to spend the rest of your life with the daughter of a thousand felons?"

"No," Phin said. "I just don't want to spend the rest of my life without you. I'll deal with the felons later. Put the ring on."

"Wait a minute," Sophie said. "Do you love me?"

Phin met her eyes and took her breath away. "More than you'll ever know."

"*Say* it," she said, and he said, "I love you. I'll always love you. Forever. It's a life sentence. Now put the damn ring on."

Sophie leaned against him and closed her eyes because he felt so good. *Don't ever let me go,* she thought, and then she opened her eyes and looked at the ring again. "Excellent." She put it on her finger, working it a little bit because it was tighter than her mother's rings had been and Phin said, "We'll have it resized to fit you."

The ring made her hand look important—heavier, adult. "This is a good ring."

"Try not to lose it," Phin said, his cheek against her hair. "That's pretty much the family fortune right there. That and four thousand *Tucker for Mayor: More of the Same* posters, which are going to be useless. I told my mother I'm finished with being mayor after this election. I have you to thank for that, too." He bent to kiss her again, and Sophie leaned toward him, thinking idly of what they could do with all those posters now that there were no Tuckers left to run—like paper their bedroom with them. *Tucker: More of the Same,* over and over again.

Or . . .

She straightened and bumped Phin's nose with her forehead. "What?" he said.

Four thousand *Tucker for Mayor: More of the Same* posters.

And Phin only had two more years of mayor before he retired in relief to concentrate on the bookstore and pool, which meant Stephen would be mayor then, unless somebody named Tucker stepped into the breach.

Hello.

"What?" Phin said.

She'd have two years to get to know everybody in town. That was only about two thousand people; she could do that. And she could make a difference, she was good at making people do what she wanted. She was born to make people do what she wanted.

"My God," she said, as the full meaning of her family's legacy for lying, cheating, and scheming hit her.

She was born to be a politician.

"Sophie?"

She leaned back against Phin. "I think I'll take your name," she said, smiling up at him sweetly. "Sophie Dempsey Tucker. It sounds . . ." She looked at the ring again. ". . . powerful."

"Why do I have a bad feeling about this?" Phin said, and she said, "Because your life just changed, but it's okay. You can trust me."

She pulled him close, and over his shoulder, she saw Dillie on the edge of the porch, holding the stick of her Dove Bar for Lassie to lick. Behind them, maple trees waved cheerfully in the breeze, cotton clouds bounced across the blue, blue sky, and the early-September sun glowed on everything in sight.

"Nothing but good times ahead," Sophie said, and kissed him.

Turn the page for a sneak peek at
Jennifer Crusie's new novel

Maybe This Time

Available Fall 2010

The human heart dares not stay away too long from that which hurt it most. There is a return journey to anguish that few of us are released from making.

— *Lillian Smith*

This book takes place in 1992.
Because.

Chapter One

Andie Miller sat in the reception room of the North-Archer Legal Group, holding on to ten years of uncashed alimony checks and the unresolved rage that had swamped her as soon as she'd walked back into the old Victorian where her ex-husband lived and worked. *This is why I never came back here. Nothing wrong with repressed anger as long as it stays repressed.*

"Miss Miller?"

Andie jerked her head up and a lock of her hair fell out of her chignon. She stuffed it back into the clip on the back of her head as North's secretary smiled at her. If that secretary had a chignon, nothing would escape from it. The secretary was discreetly dressed and probably efficient and undoubtedly in control of her emotions. North was probably crazy about her.

"Mr. Archer will see you now," the secretary said.

"Well, good for him." Andie stood up, yanked on the hem of the only suit jacket she owned, and then wondered if she'd sounded too hostile.

"He's really very nice," the secretary said.

"No, he isn't." Andie walked to the door of North's office, opened it before the secretary could get in ahead of her, and then stopped, taken aback in spite of herself.

North sat behind his massive desk, his cropped blond hair almost white in the sunlight from the large, mullioned window behind him. His wire rim glasses had slid too far down his nose again, and his shirt sleeves were rolled up over his forearms—*Still playing raquetball*, Andie thought—and his shoulders were as straight as ever as he studied the papers spread out across his massive desk. He looked exactly the way he had ten years ago when she'd bumped her suitcase on the door frame on her way out of town—

"Miss Miller is here," his secretary said from behind her, and he looked up at her over his glasses, and the years fell away, and she was right back where she'd begun, staring into those blue-gray eyes, her heart pounding.

He stood up. "Andromeda. Thank you for coming."

She crossed the thick rug, smiled tightly at him, decided that shaking his hand would be weird, and sat down. "I called you, remember? Thank you for seeing me."

He sat down and said, "Thank you, Kristin," to his secretary, who left.

"So the reason I called—" Andie began, just as he said, "How is your mother?"

Oh, we're going to be polite. "Still crazy. How's yours?"

"Lydia is fine, thank you." He straightened the papers on his desk into one stack. A lot of really heavy trees had died to make that desk. His mother had probably gnawed them down and used her nails to saw the boards. "I'll tell her you asked after her."

"She'll be thrilled." Andie opened her purse and took out the stack of alimony checks and put them on the desk. "I came to give these back to you."

North looked at the checks for a moment, the sharp planes of his face looking drawn in the dim light.

Say something, she thought, and when he didn't, she said, "They're all there, one hundred and nineteen of them. October nineteen eighty-two to last month."

His face was as expressionless as ever. "Why?"

"Because they're a link between us. We haven't talked in ten years but every month you send me a check even though you know I don't want alimony. Which means every month I get an envelope in the mail that says I used to be married to you. And every month I don't cash them, and it's like we're nodding in the street or something. We're still *communicating*."

"Not very well." North looked at the stack. "Why now?"

"I'm getting married."

She watched him go still, the pause stretching out until she said, "North?"

"Congratulations. Who's the lucky man?"

"Will Spenser," Andie said, pretty sure North wouldn't know him.

"The writer?"

"He's a great guy. He makes me laugh." *And he never forgets I exist.* "I'm ready to settle down, so I'm drawing a line under my old life." She nodded at the checks. "That's why I came to give you those back. Don't send any more. Please."

After a moment, he nodded. "Of course. Congratulations. The family will want to send a gift." He pulled his notepad toward him. "Are you registered?"

"No, I'm not registered," Andie said, exasperated. "Technically, I'm not even engaged yet. He asked me. I haven't told him yes yet. I needed to give you the checks back first." She didn't know why she'd expected him to have a reaction to the news. It wasn't as if he still cared. She wasn't sure he'd cared when she'd left.

"I see. Thank you for returning the checks."

North straightened the papers on his desk again, and then looked down at the top paper for a long moment, as if he were really reading it. He'd probably forgotten she was there again because his work was—

He looked up. "Perhaps, since you haven't said yes yet, you could postpone your new life."

"What?"

"I have a problem that you could help with. It would only take you a year, maybe less—"

"North, did you even hear what I said?"

"—and we'd pay you ten thousand dollars a month, plus expenses, room, and board."

She started to protest and then thought, *Ten thousand dollars a month?*

He straightened the folder on his desk again. "Theodore Archer, a distant cousin, died last year and made me the guardian of his two children. I went down to see them at the family home where their aunt was taking care of them and they seemed fine. Unfortunately, the aunt died in June. Since then I've hired three nannies, but none have stayed."

Ten thousand dollars was ridiculous. He had to be up to something.

But ten thousand dollars would pay off her credit card bills and her car. In one month. Ten thousand dollars would mean she could get married without debt. Not that Will cared, but it would be better to go to him free and clear—

"We wanted to bring the children here in June after their aunt's death, but the little girl had a psychotic break when the nanny tried to take her away from the family home. The boy was sent away to boarding school at the beginning of August, but he's been expelled for setting fires. I need someone to go down there and stabilize the children, bring their education up to standard for their grade level so they can go to public school, and find a way to move them up here with us."

Andie shook her head and another chunk of hair slipped out of her chignon. "North, I teach high school English," she said, as she stuffed it back. "I have no idea how to help these kids. You need—"

"I need somebody who doesn't care about the way things are supposed to be," he said, his eyes sliding to her neck. "I think that's where the nannies are going wrong. These kids are . . . different. I need somebody who will do the unconventional thing without blinking. Somebody who will get things done." He met her eyes. "Even if she doesn't stay for the long haul."

"*Hey*," Andie said.

"I would take it as a personal favor. I've never asked you for anything—"

"You asked for a divorce." As soon as she said it, she knew it was a mistake.

He looked at her over the tops of his glasses, exasperated. "I did not ask you for a divorce."

"Yes, you did," Andie said, in too far to stop now. "You told me that I seemed unhappy, and if that was true, you would understand if I divorced you."

"You were playing 'Any Day Now' every time I came up to the apartment. As hints go, it was pretty broad."

He looked annoyed, so that was something, but it didn't do

anything for her anger. "There are people who, if their spouses are unhappy, try to do something about it."

"I did. I gave you a divorce. You had one foot out the door anyway. Do we need to review that again?"

"No. The divorce is a dead subject." *And the ghost of it is sitting right here with us.* Although maybe only with her. North didn't looked haunted at all.

"I realize you're getting ready to start a new life," he went on. "But if you haven't made plans yet, there's no reason you couldn't wait four more weeks. You could use the money for the wedding."

"I don't want a wedding. I want to get married. I can do that at a courthouse." *That's what we did.* "And another thing, why are you offering me ten thousand dollars a month for babysitting? You didn't pay the nannies that. It's ridiculous. For ten thousand a month, you should not only get child care, you should get your house cleaned, your laundry done, your tires rotated, and if I were you, I'd insist on nightly blow jobs. Did you think I wouldn't notice that you're still trying to keep your thumb on me?" She shook her head, and the lock of hair fell out of her chignon again. Well, the hell with that, too.

He sat very still, and then he said, "Why have you got your hair like that?" sounding as annoyed as she was.

"Because it's *professional.*"

"Not if it keeps falling down."

"Thank you," Andie said. "Now butt out. This is a *business meeting.* It's not personal."

He closed his eyes and then said, calmly, "Andromeda, I'm asking for a favor, a big one, and I don't think the money is out of line. We didn't leave our marriage enemies, so I don't see why you're hostile now."

"I'm not hostile," Andie said, and then added fairly, "Well, okay, I am hostile. You didn't do anything to save our marriage ten years ago, but every month you send a check so I'll think of you again. It's passive aggressive. Or something. You know the strongest memory I have of you? Sitting right there, behind that desk. You'd think I'd remember you naked with all the mattress time we clocked, but no, it's you, staring at me from behind all that walnut as if you weren't quite sure who I was. You have no idea how many times I wanted to take an ax to that damn desk just to see if you'd *notice me*."

North looked down at his desk, perplexed.

"You hide behind it," Andie said, sitting back now that she wasn't repressing anything anymore. "You use it to keep from getting emotionally involved."

"I use it to write on."

"You know what I mean. It gives you distance."

"It gives me storage. Have you lost your mind?"

Andie looked at him for a moment, sitting there rigid and polite and completely inaccessible. "Yes. It was a bad idea coming back here. I should go now." She stood up.

"She said the house is haunted," North said.

"Excuse me?"

"The last nanny. She said there were ghosts in the house. I asked the local police to look into things to see if somebody was playing tricks, but they found nothing. I think it's the kids, but if I send another nanny down like the previous ones, she's going to quit, too. I need somebody different, somebody who's tough, somebody who can handle the unexpected. Somebody like you. And you're the only person like you that I know." He met her eyes, and suddenly he was the old North again, warm and real with that light in his eyes as he looked at her. "They're little kids, Andie. I can't get them out of there, and I can't leave them there, and with Mother in France, I can't leave the practice long enough to find out what's going on, and even if I could, I don't know anything about kids. I need you."

"I don't—"

"Everybody they've ever been close to has died," North said quietly. "Everybody they've ever loved has left them. They need you. Not somebody, *you*."

Bastard, Andie thought.

"I can't give you a year," she said. "That's ridiculous."

North nodded, looking calm, but she'd been married to him for a year so she knew: he was going in for the kill. "Give them a month then. You can draw your line under us, we don't need to talk, you can send reports to Kristin, hell, take your fiancé down there with you."

"I'm the least maternal person I know," Andie said, thinking *ten thousand dollars*. And more than that, two kids who'd lost everyone they loved.

"I don't think they need maternal," he said. "I think they need you."

He was pushing it too hard now. *Don't fall for this*, Andie told herself. "A psychotic little girl and a boy who's growing up to be a serial killer."

"They're growing up alone," North said, and Andie thought, *Oh, hell*.

The problem was, he sounded sincere. Well, he always did, he was good at that, but now that she really looked at him, he had changed. She could see the stress in his face, the lines that hadn't been there ten years ago, the tightening of the skin over his bones, the age in the hollows under his eyes. His brother Southie probably still looked as smooth as a boiled egg, but North was still trapped behind that damn desk, taking care of everyone in the family. And now there were two more in the family, and he was still handling it alone.

"Please," he said, those gray-blue eyes fixed on her.

"Yes, damn it," Andie said.

North drew a deep breath. "Thank you." Then he put his glasses back on, professional again. "There's a household account you can draw on for any expenses, and a credit card. The housekeeper will clean and cook for you. If you come by tomorrow, Kristin will give you a copy of this folder with everything you need in it and your first check, of course."

"My only check. I'm only staying for a month."

"Of course," North said.

Andie sat there for a moment, a little stunned that she'd said yes. She'd felt the same way after he'd proposed.

"I'd appreciate it if you could go down as soon as possible."

"Right." She shoved her hair back into the clip, picked up her purse, and stood up again. "I'll drive down tomorrow. You have a good winter terrorizing the opposing counsel."

She headed for the door, refusing to look back. This was good. She could spare a month to save two orphans. Will was in New York for the next two weeks anyway, and he'd come home to a fiancée with no debt, and then—

"Andie," North said, and she turned back in the doorway.

"Thank you," he said, standing now behind his desk, tall and lean and beautiful and looking at her the way he used to.

Get out of here. "You're welcome."

Then she turned and walked out before he could say or do anything else that made her forget she was done with him.

After Andie left, North sat for a moment wondering what the hell he'd just done. He'd had the résumés of several excellent nannies on his desk, and he'd hired his ex-wife instead because she was getting married and he didn't like it. *Fuck,* he thought, and deliberately put her out of his mind, which was difficult since she'd mentioned blow jobs. Which were irrelevant because he and Andie were over. She was right: draw a line under it. He went back to work, making notes on his current case file as the shadows grew longer and Kristin left for the night, his black capital letters spaced evenly in straight rows, as firm and as clear as his thinking—

He stopped and frowned at the page. Instead of "Indiana" he'd written "Andiana." He marked an "I" over the "A" but the word sat there on the page, misspelled and blotted, a dark spot on the clear pattern of his day.

There was a knock on the door at the same time it opened.

"North!" his brother Sullivan said as he came in, his tie loosened and his face as genial as ever under his flop of brown hair.

"Sullivan." North nodded. "You're looking well. Paris must have agreed with you."

"Everything agrees with me. You, however, look like hell." Sullivan lounged into the same chair Andie had taken and put his feet on the desk. "You can't work twenty-four-seven. It's not healthy."

"I like my work. How's Mother?"

"Now that's health. That woman was built for distance."

North pictured their elegant, white-haired mother running a marathon in her pearls, kicking any upstarts out of the way with the pointed end of her heels as she crossed the finish line.

"It's you I'm worried about," Sullivan was saying. "You're working too hard, too much on your plate, trying to run the whole practice with Mother gone—"

"My plate is fine. However, I am in the middle of—"

"No, no, it's time I helped out." Sullivan smiled at him. "I've been thinking about what I could do, but I figure you'd fall on your number two pencil before you'd let me help with the practice."

North looked down at the black pen mark that made "Andiana" such a blot. A number two pencil would be a good idea if he was going to start making mistakes.

"So I was thinking of something a little more in my area and out of yours," Sullivan said. "You know. People. You're not a people person, North. I am."

"People." North turned the top sheet on his legal pad over so he didn't have to look at the blot.

"You remember those two kids that second cousin left you awhile back?"

"Yes," North said, fairly sure that had been a rhetorical question, although with Sullivan, you never knew.

"I thought I might drop in, check on things for you, see how they're doing."

North nodded. "You want to 'drop in' to the wilds of southern Ohio to visit two children you've never met."

"Yes."

"Why?"

Sullivan grinned at him. "I want to see the house."

"The house isn't worth anything. It's in the middle of nowhere."

"It's haunted."

"Sullivan, there is no such thing as ghosts," North said, and for a moment he was twelve again and Sullivan was six, staring wide-eyed into the room where their father was laid out in his coffin. "He's not going to sit up, Southie," North had said then. "He's dead. There's no such thing as ghosts."

"I know that," Sullivan said now. "But I want to see a house that everybody thinks is haunted."

" 'Everybody' being a nanny who got bored and wanted out."

"Other people have thought so, lots of rumors. So I thought I'd go down there and talk to some of the people. See what's going on."

"And how did you find out about these rumors?"

"I did some research for a friend of mine. She's interested in hauntings, and she looked me up at a party and talked to me about the house and, you know, it *is* interesting."

"She," North said, Sullivan's motives becoming much clearer now. The combination of a shiny new hobby and a shiny new girlfriend must have been irresistible.

"Suzanne Twomey. The ghost thing is fascinating. I've talked to—"

"Suzanne Twomey?" North thought of the tiny, sharp-faced, sharp-tongued newscaster he'd avoided after one viewing. "The little blonde with the teeth on channel twelve?"

"They're very good teeth," Sullivan said, going for indignant and missing.

"They look like they were very expensive," North said and remembered Andie the first time he'd seen her, her big eyes dancing, her curly hair wild, her wide smile flashing her overlapped front teeth. She'd never had her teeth fixed.

"Well, you need good teeth for TV."

"True." That had been the first thing his mother had said about Andie. "For god's sake, North, get her teeth fixed."

"The close-ups are murder," Sullivan said.

And he'd said, "I like her teeth. I like everything about her. And now you do, too, Mother."

Sullivan was looking at him oddly. "Are you okay?"

"I'm fine," North said.

"Okay. Well, then, I'd like to take Suzie down there and look into the ghosts. I can check on the kids for you while I'm there."

"I'd prefer you didn't," North said bluntly. "I don't see Suzie Twomey being a good experience for them."

"No, no, she's not interested in reporting on kids anymore, she's on to ghosts now. She found out that the house was originally a haunted house in England and she's very excited about it. Did you know they brought the house over here in pieces and rebuilt it?" Sullivan shook his head, incredulous. "Suzie could be really grateful if I took her down there. Plus, I'd get to investigate a haunted house. I've been reading a lot about this, North, and I think there might be something in it for me."

"Investigating ghosts?" North said.

"I've talked to two highly regarded ghost experts and there's something behind this stuff. Plus I told them that there's a haunted house in the family and one of them would like to see it. Suzie would like to see it. *I'd* like to see it. We won't talk to the kids."

"The children own the house, so it's not in our immediate family," North said, picking up his pen again. "And you're not going to disrupt their lives because you think you might like to be a Ghostbuster."

"No, no, I told you, we won't bother the kids. My plan is that I take Suzie and Dennis, the expert, down there, we talk to people—not the kids, the adults around there—I see what's going on and report back to you, you get to know the kids are safe, Dennis gets more research, Suzie gets her video whatsis . . ." Sullivan shrugged. "We all win. Plus, I get away from Columbus before Mother gets back from Paris. She doesn't like Suzie. Says she's all teeth and hair."

North looked at his little brother with an exasperation he hadn't felt in years. *Southie's permanently thirteen*, Andie had said. *Thirty-four hobbies and a hard-on.* But she'd been laughing when she'd said it. . . . "Southie, when are you going to stand up to Mother?"

"Southie?"

"What?"

"You called me Southie. You haven't called me that in years."

North sighed. "Well, grow up and I'll never call you that again. You're running down there because you don't want to face Mother with your latest career plan or girlfriend. It's not much of a rebellion if you keep running away."

"I'm not rebelling. I don't have anything to rebel against. I have a great life. And to keep my life great, I'd like to avoid unpleasantness while learning about something that interests me and makes my girlfriend happy. Plus the last nanny quit last week so the kids are there alone. That's not—"

"The children are not alone."

"You hired another nanny?" Sullivan shook his head. "She won't last. Better I should go—"

"This one will last," North said. "I sent Andromeda."

"*Andie?*" Sullivan whistled and then grinned. "Ghosts versus Andie. The supernatural is going to get its ass kicked. I didn't even know she was back in town. When did you talk to her?"

"Today. She's going down there tomorrow."

Sullivan smiled. "Called me Southie, did she?"

"What?"

"That's why you called me Southie. Andie did it first."

"Yes," North said, realizing it was true. Half an hour with Andie and ten years were yesterday.

"She changed much?"

"Her hair's . . . different," North said, remembering her sitting in that chair, bundled up in an awful suit jacket, all those crazy curls yanked back, her face scowling as she argued with him. And then that one lock of hair, sliding down her neck—

"Her *hair's* different?" Southie said. "You see your ex-wife for the first time in ten years and that's all you got?"

"She looked . . ." Serious. Tense. Her old smile gone. ". . . quiet. I think she's had a bad time."

Southie's face clouded over. "Aw, hell. That's a shame." Then he smiled. "She can probably use my help."

North thought of Andie opening the door and finding Southie and his toothy, microphone-wielding girlfriend on the step with some charlatan ghost expert. "No."

"Maybe she could use your help," Southie said, grinning. "The two of you used to—"

"She's getting married again. Now if we're finished here . . ." North looked back to his notes as a hint, but when Southie didn't say anything, he looked up.

"I'm sorry," Southie said, his face kind. "I really am."

The twinge he'd felt when she'd told him stabbed at North and he put a lid on it again. "Why? We've been divorced for ten years. It's not as if I thought she was coming back."

"Yeah but it was still a shock, wasn't it? At least it is to me. Maybe I thought she was coming back."

"Well, she's not," North said, more sharply than he'd intended.

"So, who's the guy? What do we know about him?"

Southie looked serious now which was always a bad sign.

"Will Spenser. The writer."

"The true crime guy?" Southie said, raising his eyebrows.

"I think he writes mystery fiction, too."

"Probably not much difference. What did Gabe find out about him?"

North gathered his patience. "I did not put a private detective on my ex-wife's fiancé."

"Right, she was just here, you haven't had time. Want me to call him?"

"No."

Southie shook his head. "You know, she used to be family.

As far as I'm concerned she still is. We need to look out for her. This guy could have anything in his past. He's a writer, for Christ's sake."

"No," North said.

"And I should go down and check on her in that house," Southie went on as if he hadn't spoken. "I can't believe you sent her down there without backup. God knows what's down there."

"Two kids and a housekeeper. You're not going."

Southie sighed. "Suzie's not going to be happy."

"Such is life."

Southie hesitated and the silence stretched out. "All right then," he said, standing up. "You going to see Andie again?"

"No. You have a good evening." North flipped the page back to where it had been as a signal for Southie to leave and saw the "Andiana" in the middle of the page again. "Damn."

"What's wrong?" Southie said.

"I made a mistake." North flipped the pad shut, annoyed with himself.

"Sending Andie down there?"

"What?" he said, looking up.

"You think you made a mistake sending Andie down there?"

"No," North said and then thought about Andie, down in the wilds. It was probably her natural habitat. She'd been wandering around ever since they'd divorced, moving someplace new every year, teaching in some really godforsaken places. Maybe that had been his mistake, keeping her in the city. Trying to keep her at all. He shook his head. "No, it wasn't a mistake. She'll handle things."

"Yeah, she will," Southie said, his voice odd, and when North looked up, he saw Southie regarding him sympathetically. "Maybe you should go down. Get out of the office, check to make sure she's all right. Spend a night in the place so you know what it's like."

"She's fine."

Southie waited a moment and then said quietly, "You could have gone after her, you know."

North looked at him blankly. "Why would I go after her? She'll be fine down there."

"Not now. *Then*. When she left. You could have gone—"

"No."

"You ever think maybe that divorce was a mistake?"

"*No*," North said, putting as much *you-should-leave-now* in his voice as possible.

"Because I always thought it was," Southie said. "If you'd gone after her, you could have gotten her back. That's all she wanted, she was just lonely—"

"Was there anything else?" North said coldly. "Because unlike you, I have work to do."

"Right. Well, you have a good time with your work," Southie said and left, shaking his head.

Damn it. The divorce hadn't been a mistake. She'd been miserable. He'd been miserable because she was miserable. Going after her wouldn't have changed that. They were both happier now. He had work to do.

She'd looked so good, so warm, so everything he'd once wanted, rushing back in one afternoon—

And now she was getting married again. Good for her. Moving on.

He pulled his notebook back in front of him and then thought, *Maybe good for her.* Because Southie was right, he didn't know anything about this yahoo she was getting engaged to. She probably didn't either. She'd married him after twelve hours of sex, she could be lunging into another mistake. And she hadn't smiled, she'd smiled all the time when they were married. In the beginning.

He picked up the phone and called the detective agency that the firm used and ordered a background check on Will Spenser.

Then he flipped open the notebook to go back to work, saw the "Andiana" blot, and thought, *Hell.*

He ripped out the page and copied the whole thing over again. With no mistakes.

By late afternoon the next day, Andie had finished packing and tying off the loose ends of her life. There weren't many loose ends since she'd been moving around the country for ten years, which tended to limit most ends, loose or otherwise, but she did call Will in New York to tell him the good news. "Ten thousand dollars, Will. It'll pay off all my debts with some left over. I'm being practical and mature here."

"I don't care about your debts, I'll pay your debts. What I'd really like to hear is that you're going to marry me."

Of course, Andie thought, and said, "Maybe." She heard a thunking sound on the other end of the phone. "What's that?"

"That's me beating my head against my desk."

Andie grinned. "That's you beating the phone against your mouse pad."

"Same difference. Do you take this long to answer all your marriage proposals?"

It took me five seconds to say yes to North. "Yes. I ponder them, and the guys get bored and wander off. Will, I want to do this, it really is important to me to be free and clear financially before I . . . do anything."

"Okay," he said in that easy-going voice she loved. He was so Not-North. "Call me often. Tell me you love working with kids and want to have twenty."

"Twenty?" Andie said, alarmed. "I don't want any."

"Well, maybe you'll change your mind." Will hesitated and then he said, "You won't be seeing North, will you?"

Andie frowned at the phone. "Are you jealous? Because, trust me, he'd forgotten I'd existed until I showed up in his office. And no, I won't be seeing him."

"Nobody has ever forgotten you," Will said with feeling. "Just remember who you're potentially engaged to."

"How could I forget?" Andie said, and moved on to the I-love-yous before North became a permanent part of their conversation. Then she picked up the last of her suitcases and went out to deal with her mother, who was standing on the sidewalk in front of her little German Village row house in her jeans and faded Iron Maiden T-shirt, looking worried.

"I don't like this," Flo said, for the fortieth time, her long, curly graying hair bobbing as she shook her head. "I dreamed about you last night. You fell into a well."

"Thank you, Flo," Andie said as she opened the back of the car. "That's encouraging."

"It means your subconscious is calling to you. You've been repressing something. That's what the water means anyway. The falling part is probably about being out of control, or since it's you, maybe it's about running away. You know what a bolter you are."

"I am not a bolter," Andie said to her mother, not for the first time. "I go toward things, not away from them."

"I think you got the bolting thing from your father," Flo said. "You're very like him."

"I wouldn't know," Andie said coldly. "Except that I don't desert children, so no, I'm not."

"Don't go," Flo said.

"Because you had a dream? No." Andie put the larger of her suitcases in the trunk of her ancient Camry next to the sewing machine she'd already stashed there.

"There was so much negative energy in your marriage," Flo fretted.

That wasn't negative energy, that was raging lust. "I'm not revisiting my marriage. I'm taking care of two orphaned kids for a month—"

"This is a terrible time astrologically," Flo went on as if she hadn't spoken. "Your Venus is in North's Capricorn—"

Andie slammed the trunk closed. "Mother, my Venus isn't anywhere near North. If his Capricorn was in my Venus, I could see your point, but it's staying here in Columbus while I go south." She went around and opened the back door of the car and shoved the boxes of school supplies that Kristin had given her over to make room for her last suitcase while her mother obsessed about her life.

"North is a very attractive, very passionate, very powerful man, and you're still connected to him." Flo frowned. "Probably sexual memory; those Capricorns are insatiable. Well, you know, Sea Goat. And of course, you're a Fish. You'll probably end up back in bed with him."

Andie shoved the last suitcase into the back seat. "You know what I'd like for Christmas, Flo? Boundaries. You can gift me early if you'd like."

"Andie, if you keep seeing North, he's going to get you again, and you were so miserable with him—"

"I'm not seeing North. I'm with Will. I'm going to have a stable, secure relationship with a good man who loves me and won't desert me for his career. Which reminds me. I left that stupid suit jacket on the bed, so the next time you're at

Goodwill, drop it off, will you? I don't know why I kept it. I'm never going to be near anybody who'll want me to wear a suit again."

Flo folded her arms. "Will's a Gemini. Volatile. Well, he's a writer. You're not sexually compatible, you're both so scattered. You must be all over the place in bed."

"*Boundaries*, Flo." Andie closed the car door, thinking, *the sex is just fine*. Not wall-banging, earth-shattering, oh-my-god sex, but fun and energetic and damn satisfying just the same. Wall-banging, earth-shattering, oh-my-god sex was probably for people in their twenties. At least that was the last time she'd had it. "Will and I are good. And I don't believe in astrology. Or dreams." She looked sternly at Flo.

"Of course, you don't, dear. Did you get the birth signs for the children?"

"The boy is a Taurus and the girl is a Scorpio. And yes, even if it turns out that means they're going to kill me in my sleep, I'm still going."

"Well, the boy will be all right. You can always count on a Taurus. Steady as they come. Strong. The Bull." She looked thoughtful. "They like *things*, you know? Good food, comfort, they're very materialistic. If you need to win him over, that could help."

"I'd think good food and comfort would win anybody over," Andie said and Flo looked at her curiously.

"Now why would you think that? The little girl's going to be completely different. Intense. Secretive. You won't buy her with comfort. And you won't be able to bamboozle her, either. Scorpios. They'll kill you as soon as look at you. They like sparkly things, though. You might get her with sequins."

"Flo, she's a little girl."

"Although I've always liked Scorpios. They're *interesting*.

And they're survivors. Taurus, too, those are both survivor signs. Tough kids. They'll make it without you." Flo bit her lip. "Andie, don't go."

"I'm going." Andie opened the driver's side door to escape before her mother started on rising signs. "I'll be back in a month, and everything will be fine."

"No, it won't." Flo took a deep breath. "It's not just the dreams and the stars. I read your cards last night. The Emperor was crossing you. That's power and passion, so it has to be North. It was a bad, bad reading. You're going down a path that's all conflict and struggle. There's no peace there. Will can't help you, he's not strong enough for you. North's too strong."

"*Mother—*"

"Leave both of them," Flo said, serious as death. "Don't go. I'm scared for you, Andie."

"Well, stop it," Andie said and got in the car. Then she got out again and hugged Flo, who hugged her back, hard. "Sorry, Mom. I love you much. Don't worry. In a month, I'll be back and living here in town and you can run the cards for me every day if you like."

"You don't understand," Flo said. "You're not a mother. When you have a child, you can't let her go into danger, you have to be there for her—"

"Flo, I'm thirty-four. The child part is over."

"*It's never over,*" Flo said, and Andie shook her head at her obtuseness and got back in her car.

"I'll call you while I'm there," she said, and put the car in gear, and then waved at her mother in her rearview mirror as she drove away.

Sea goat, she thought, and shook her head.

A little Flo went a long way.

• • •

Andie headed south on I-71 and then turned off the interstate onto a succession of increasingly deserted back roads that became more treacherous as she got farther from civilization. The road moved in and out of heavily wooded areas that grew darker and closer together, and she began to see how a nanny could lose her grip just from the landscape. By the time she turned down the long dead-end road that the house was supposed to be on and found the narrow gap of the drive fifteen miles from the turn with its battered sign that said ARCHER HOUSE, the sun was going down, so she pulled off to the side of the road and got out to investigate in the deepening twilight.

There had been a drive there, but it seemed to have collapsed. What was left was a steep and rocky slope, not anything she'd want to drive down if she had a choice.

She got back in the car and drove slowly over the edge.

The car dipped down sharply, scraping its front fender, and then slid into the pot hole–laced lane that wound through the trees for about a quarter of a mile and came out into a meadow gone to seed with a large greenish pond in the middle of it, and beyond that an ancient three-story dark stone house flaunting two rose windows, a crumbling tower, and a moat, all its windows dark and ominous in the twilight. "Oh, god," she said and followed the drive around to the side, finding a little bridge that crossed the moat onto an untended stretch of pavement that split, the right going to the front of the house and its stone-arched entrance and the left to the back and a large flagstoned yard beside a row of garages.

She pulled the car up in front of the garages and got out, looking around the deserted yard as she slammed the door, which echoed in the gloom.

It wasn't surprising the other nannies had left; it was surprising they'd gotten out of the car when they'd arrived.

She got her suitcases out of the trunk and headed for the house, pushed the back door open, banging the cases on the frame, and then went through a small mudroom, a big, gloomy sitting room filled with uncomfortable-looking Victorian furniture including a massive green-striped couch, and another room with a long, heavy dining table surrounded by ornate chairs. Light seeped around a door in the side wall, and she opened it.

It was a kitchen, large, white, and warm compared to the other rooms she'd dragged her suitcase through, and empty except for a long wood table in the center.

A boy sat at the end, all shoulder blades and elbows in his black T-shirt, hunched over a bowl of something orange, his brown hair falling into his eyes as he looked up at her from under his thick lashes, his mouth set in a tight, hard line. Sitting close to him was a thin little girl cupping her hands around her own bowl of orange, her pale gray-blue eyes narrowed under her long, tangled, lank, white-blond hair, her T-shirt almost covered by all the stuff she had strung around her neck: an old strand of discolored plastic pearls, an ancient locket on a frayed pink ribbon, a string of tiny blue shells, a blue Walkman on a black cord, and a glittery bat on a black chain.

Oh, dear god, Andie thought, and said, "Hi."

More COMEDY.
More CRAZY.
More CRUSIE.

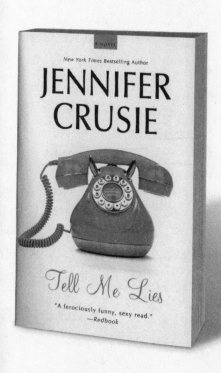

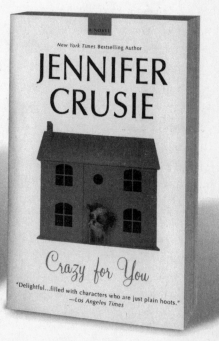

DON'T MISS A SINGLE JENNIFER CRUSIE TITLE!

Tell Me Lies	Crazy for You	Welcome to Temptation
Fast Women	Faking It	Bet Me